I0664901

Also by Alcaly Lo
Better Will Come
Shine Eye Girl

MONKEY BREAD
a novel
ALCALY LO

This novel is a work of fiction. Names, characters, places, and incidents are either the product of the author's imagination or are used fictitiously. Any resemblance to actual events, locales, or persons, living or dead, is entirely coincidental.

Copyright © 2010 by Alcaly Lo
Published by Isaiah Books
Alcalylo.com
mail@Alcalylo.com

ISBN-13: 978-0-9840798-2-7
ISBN-10: 0-9840798-2-3

For Ezekiel "Easy" Rawlins

A sunny day. Hot, of course. Hot, stifling, and muggy. Midmorning. Salimata and I driving up the Mamelles hill in the company of a man I didn't know. The car big, blue, boxy, red inside. The man not paying me any mind when we got in. Salimata and he not talking, not exchanging a single word. My first time seeing that man, my very first time in the big, blue, boxy car.

Up the narrow and winding road, my eyes on the fascinating lighthouse. Totally white, huge, gleaming, mysterious, all glass and revolving lights, unbelievably clean compared to the squalor, the anything-goes, the turpitude of Dakar. Short, way short of the top, borrowing a dirt track that opened after a sudden turn, a green tunnel digging deep into the brush, a long, skinny worm burrowing its way through the hill. Sticking my head out the window, reveling in the speed and the clash of smells--salt versus dust, sea versus earth. Gone. As abruptly as it had appeared, the tunnel gone.

After a few more minutes, full stop in front of a wooden fence. Standing on the back seat the better to see. Beyond the gate, on an open plane, a windswept compound, stretching all the way to the cliff's edge, overlooking the ocean. The playground on the forefront catching my eye. The sandbox, the slide, the swings, the kids. A whole bunch of them. Shouting, running, laughing, jumping, free.

Salimata, speaking without looking my way, her voice breaking: "Go ... go and join them. We ... I'll come back for you in a little while."

1

Me, pleading, refusing to move, knowing better, my hand on Salimata's shoulder, grabbing her sleeve and pulling, little four-year-old not so easily fooled, little boy not so easily tricked: "Come with me, Mommy. Come with me, *Yaye boye*."

Salimata turning to look at the man.

The man turning to look at me. His voice deep and loud and scary urging me on, pushing me away, chasing me out of the blue car, kicking me out of his life. "Go."

The kids' shouts filling the air, calling.

Me, unlocking the door reluctantly.

Salimata, meekly, weakly, apologetically, dejectedly, wretchedly, treacherously, still not looking at me: "*Begguena le*...."--I love you.

Me, mumbling, mad at her and angry at the man, the mean, mean man, wondering who he was, what he was to Salimata and why he had a say in my life, wanting to punch the punk and run, afraid he'd jump out and outrun and beat me--little four-year-old with short legs and an attitude: "*Begguena le*."

Clutching the small plastic horse Salimata had bought me the day before. Walking toward the fence. My Sunday stuff: a green shirt with a long, pointy collar, and pearly buttons; khaki pants; a big belt; dinosaur socks; shiny black shoes.

The car moving to turn around.

Me, stopping to take one last look.

The man busy maneuvering.

Salimata crying, her face in her hands. Above her head, glued to the windshield, a sticker: a snake, upright, ugly, grotesque, green, laughing, mocking, its tongue out.

The car disappearing in a cloud of dust.

Me, walking through tears, walking with fear, walking with a heaving, burning chest.

Like a flock of birds, colorful and graceful and disciplined, the kids converging toward me from all corners of the orphanage. Surrounding me, crowding me, overwhelming me--looking, pondering, touching, waiting, shy. First to speak and take my hand, a girl, tall and bony and smiling and intrepid.

2

Torn red sweater, plaid skirt, dusty shoes, piggy tails, jelly stains, and a big, big heart: Karine. Grabbing my hand, running, pulling me with her. The flock taking flight at once, a perfect formation, tight, fluid, beautiful, synchronized--left, right, left, then full speed ahead, all laughter and wild cheers now, carrying me, making me one with it, riding the wind.

That was the last time I saw my mother. For a long time, for days and weeks and months and years and years I waited and waited, waited for her to come back. Don't know why she left me, ditched me, pitched me, gave me up, abandoned me, forgot about me. Don't know why we couldn't stay together, why I couldn't have her near me, with me, to love and protect and teach and guide me and just be close. We didn't have such a bad life. I wasn't such a bad kid. It was just me and her, mother and son, Salimata and Christophe. She was good to me. We played. We had fun. She sang to me in Wolof. She told me *Leuk le Lièvre*--Leuk the Hare--stories. She bathed me, she clothed me, she fed me, she held me, she took me wherever she went. Everything was fine. Everything. The darkness, the evil things, the vicious things started after that fateful day. Don't know why.

I've been looking for her ever since. Never forgot what she looked like. Hung on to the memories--the precious few that I have--forever. Salimata. Salimata. Salimata. Sometimes, strangely enough, it feels like I'm the one who left.
She's in my dreams often. She's the reason I came back here, to Senegal, after spending years in America, my adoptive father's country. The reason I've always felt somewhat lost in the world. The reason, the mystery, the missing piece. Salimata. Find her, I know, and I find myself.

When a man called Ibrahim Sow shows up on my porch early one morning, my first instinct is to say no. No to the worry, the urgent plea in his request. No to the pressure-cooker, the murky waters, the stinking mud, the whirlwind of a case that I know in my gut will take me deeper inside myself than I've ever been, deeper than I've ever cared to go. Yesterday was a bad day. Another dead end while searching for Salimata. Another disappointment. Tracked a woman all the way down the coast to Mbour only to have her crush my hopes. Hacked it back home late at night and stopped by the Ngalam for a handful of neat bourbons and a Cape Verdian girl--big, brown, boozy, cheap, vulgar, trashy, robotic, sweaty, smelly, a good pretender, loud, so loud, loud down to her name: Margot. We shared a joint, killed another drink and did our business on the floor--a nasty, sloppy, messy, frenzied, uncivilized job of it. I kicked her out and slept badly, fitfully. So I wake up in a red haze, sweaty and sore from the couch. So I get an instant headache from the bell, the intrusive 6 o'clock bell, the damn bell that won't stop.

The man on my doorstep is dressed in African fashion--the long, loose-fitting tunic called *boubou*, and leather slippers. Early forties, a full head taller than me, hair cut close to the skull, nose straight as an arrow tip, lips full and arrogant in their perfection, eyes puffy and reddish. His night was worse than mine. "Chris James?"

"What do you want?"

He extends a hand. I ignore it royally, annoyed beyond words, unsteady on my feet, unhappy with the world. "Ibrahim

Sow," the man introduces himself, undeterred. "I need your help."

"I'm not open."

"It's an emergency."

"Come back at 9."

"You don't understand..."

I slam the door.

He rings again. And again.

I look for my gun without finding it. "You're trying to get killed?"

"It's a kidnapping."

"So what?"

"My ten-year-old son."

"I don't do kidnappings."

"Can I come in?"

"No."

I try to slam the door a second time. The man holds it. He holds it and won't let go. He's powerful, hardheaded, strong, used to getting what he wants--it's his way or the highway. He is Ibrahim Sow--he repeats it as if the name is supposed to tell me something, as if I should realize who he is and show due deference. "I'll make it worth your while," he says, says it as if he really means it, says it as if money is no object to him and never has been, says it because he guesses that, just like everybody and everything else, I can be bought--even at 6 in the morning, on my own porch, in my underwear, through the thick cloud of a hangover, Margot's patchouli stuck on me like an extra skin. "Just name your price."

In the couple of seconds it takes me to stop and think, the man has me and he knows it. I do have a weakness for money. And action--action's always been a friend of mine. It's the one thing that dulls the pain, the one sure thing, the thing that always works. In the thick of it, when everything is so wild and rough and unexpected, when danger's everywhere and it's kill or get killed I spring to life, I find my peace, I know myself, I feel complete, I am me.

There's definitely the promise of both money and action in Ibrahim Sow's early morning request. Something else, too. A charade, a Faustian bargain, a duplicitous game. "My son Zak was snatched yesterday on his way to the vet," he explains, still standing by the door. "I know who has him. They bribed my chauffeur, Modi, and had him deliver Zak into their hands. This isn't your average, random, money-for-ransom kidnapping. I'll need you to do two things: help me get Zak back alive; persuade my wife Marie that this is exactly what it isn't--a random, money-for-ransom kidnapping."

"Who has your son?"

"A business associate of mine named Momar."

"What does Momar want?"

"Something I took from him. Something very valuable."

"When is the exchange taking place?"

"Momar hasn't told me yet. Today at some point, I presume. We must try and get to Zak first."

"Why not just go along with whatever Momar tells you?"

"I don't trust him."

"Why must your wife be kept in the dark?"

"She'd kill me if she even thought that Zak was taken because of something I did."

The sky breaks as we're standing there. Light--fluttering, tentative, irremediable. Another day upon us. No going back to sleep. No nursing my headache. No brooding over Salimata, my lost Salimata. No drinking myself into a stupor. No Ngalam girls. I let out a sigh, half-resentful and half-relieved.

Ibrahim Sow takes an envelope stuffed with cash from deep inside his *boubou*. "$10,000 now, twice as much when Zak's home. Deal?"

I nod and shake his hand. $30,000 is more money than I've seen in a while. Almost half of what I used to make as a D.C. cop. Enough to shore me up. Enough to hold me while I make a name for myself and build a clientele in this crazy city.

A massive all-terrain takes us to Ibrahim Sow's residence. Dakar is fully awake, a good step ahead of me. Delafosse Canal, Soumbedioune Bay, the Corniche all the way to the Plateau: cars, mopeds, buses, horse carts, roadside hawkers, pedestrians, sidewalk peddlers, the sea dotted with multiple, early, tiny, precarious, rudimentary, stubborn pirogues. Ibrahim and I don't speak. The chauffeur is old, frail, cautious, uptight. We turn right in front of the twin Madeleine islands, flying down a dirt track toward a neighborhood I didn't know was there. Smooth asphalt at the bottom. Green, healthy, forever lawns. A small park with a fountain and a few benches. Mansions nestled at the foot of the ocean, all of them white. The one we want has an automatic gate, armed guards at the front and everywhere else: the lush garden, the pool, the secondary structures deep into the backyard, the razor-topped back wall.

The house is dark, quiet, lavishly and exhaustively furnished: sofas, sectionals, corner tables, rugs, plants, vases, paintings, chandeliers. It smells of coffee, rich and strong. Ibrahim leads me to his office, where he sits behind a mahogany desk. I stand by a window overlooking two huge stone sculptures beyond which the placid Atlantic beckons. Ibrahim hands me a picture. Zak is a handsome kid. Confident, friendly, smiling.

Marie Sow joins us inside the office. She's the fragile, petite, delicate, exotic, exquisite type: short, lithe, curvy, small nose, small lips, big sad eyes. Her jeans, long T-shirt, and bare feet make her look young--too young for the horror, the trauma of a kidnapping; too young for the con game her husband's about to play on her with my help. She moves silently, cautiously, rigidly, as if recovering from a formidable blow, as if the carpeted floor were littered with mines, nails, shards of glass. Her shiny, heavy braids are tied in a loose ponytail. Her skin is the color of cacao. Her face is unmade. Her stare conveys the purest, most naked hurt--innocence trampled, innocence gone, innocence lost. The look she gives me--long, appraising, vulnerable, nervous, confused, tinged with panic and a hope that dares not yet show itself, as if I've come to save the day, as if I

7

represent her family's last resort, as if the buck stops with me--the look she gives me makes me regret taking the job. That look and her beauty, her frailty. In her, instantly and for all the wrong reasons, I see Salimata.

"I want everything to go smoothly," Ibrahim Sow tells me for his wife's benefit. "All I care about is my son's safe return. Name your price."

At my prompting, he fills me in on the details. From the sofa facing the desk, Marie Sow listens intently. The tension between her and her husband is readily apparent.

"I left here at seven," Ibrahim begins. "Marie and our daughter, Yasmin, were supposed to have their hair braided. Zak played soccer with his gang until noon. I phoned from the office to check on everybody. The salon ladies had gotten here late, Yasmin and Marie were only halfway done. Problem: the vet had just called to confirm an appointment for Wolfie, Zak's puppy. Marie said cancel and reschedule. Zak said, I can go, I can do it. Marie said no. I said why not--it's his dog, let him take care of it, Modi can take him."

"Who's Modi?"

"Our chauffeur. Doubles as a gardener."

"How long has he been in your service?"

"Three months. I told Marie to give them the consultation money. Modi came back alone. Two hours later we got the phone call from strangers: one million dollars in exchange for Zak."

Both Marie and Ibrahim look at me expectantly. I admire Ibrahim's craftsmanship. He lies well, he lies fast, he lies like somebody who lies often. More than craft--an art, a second nature.

"Nothing, up to that afternoon, to make you take extra precaution?" I ask, sounding punctilious and phony to my own ears. "No reason why you couldn't allow Zak to ride with the chauffeur? Nothing at work, at home, in town?"

"Absolutely nothing. A lot of stress at work, but that's all. Stress. Work."

"Anybody else in the car?"

8

Ibrahim shakes his head.

"Who else in the house knew where Modi and Zak were going?"

"Abdi, the cook. He's the one who drove me to your house this morning. Mansour, my right-hand man--he's Modi's uncle. Anta, the maid. Mame Awa, the nanny. And the hair braiders."

"Why not have one of the security guards ride along?"

"Until yesterday I only kept them around at night. Until yesterday burglaries and home invasions were my main concern."

"Mansour?"

"With me all day. We leave together and ride home together. He lives here."

"What do you do?"

"Import-export. I took over my old man's company. A couple of them, actually. More like a holding."

"Who's the vet?"

"Old French dude. Been here for years. Runs the show with his wife, along with a couple of helpers. The office is barely four miles from here--the other side of the Corniche, a secluded spot behind the Hotel Teranga. And yes, Zak always goes. Wolfie isn't his first dog." Ibrahim sighs and lowers his head.

I look at Marie Sow. Arms crossed, she's rocking imperceptibly, absentmindedly. Too young. Fragile. Lost. "So what happened?"

"The business with Wolfie was over in ten minutes. Zak was out of the gate and walking toward Modi and the car when a silver Renault appeared from nowhere. Two men. According to Modi, the driver was the skinny type: round head, short hair, dark skin. He pointed a revolver at Modi without leaving his seat. The second man, the one who jumped out, was built like a weight lifter. He grabbed my son by the belt and threw him on the back seat of the Renault. Zak fought all the way, screaming, kicking, wriggling. They put the gun to his head and drove off.

9

Modi picked up the dog. Nobody from the vet's office saw or heard a thing."

"Did Modi try to give chase?"

"No."

"Tag number?"

Ibrahim shakes his head again.

"Where is he?"

"I sent him home yesterday after slapping him across the face a couple of times. Had he spent the night here I most certainly would have killed him."

"You should have never let him out of your sight."

"I was so enraged that I threw everybody out except for Abdi and Mansour. And I ordered all of them to keep their mouth shut. Modi's easy to find. I told him to stay put."

I try to convey a sense of urgency, following Ibrahim's script to the letter. "Does Mansour know where Modi lives?"

"Yes."

"Can he run me?"

"Yes. I'll come along. Going crazy sitting and waiting." Ibrahim pulls a wad of bills from a drawer. "Operating costs."

"Better if I stay here with you until Zak is back."

Marie Sow snaps out of her trance. "I'll go and get the guest room ready."

I put the money in my pocket. "Did the kidnappers contact you on the house phone?"

Ibrahim Sow points at the cellphone inside the *boubou*'s chest pocket.

"Who has that number?"

"More people than I can count. I use it for business."

"What did they tell you, exactly?"

"That they'll return Zak in exchange for the money. That they'll be in touch. That I'd better not call the police. Standard procedure, I suspect. It all sounded like a bad dream. Still does."

"Did you ask to speak to Zak?"

A shadow, very real, darkens Ibrahim's face. He looks away from Marie, who's now standing by the door. "No."

10

"Make sure you do, next time they call. Do you have the ransom money on hand?"

"I do. Took care of it yesterday." He says it matter-of-factly, as if a million dollars is no thing, no biggie, no problem.

Marie leaves the room. Ibrahim picks up the phone to call Mansour and have him meet us at the car.

Mansour is in his late sixties. Tall and thin of neck, shoulders, and chest. Round and soft at the waist. Walks with a limp. Gray hair, cold eyes, African garb. One of those men who always have a string of prayer beads wrapped around their fingers, either out of habit or true devotion. He takes the passenger seat.

Ibrahim drives. There's a handful of youths in front of the small park. All short and skinny, fancy hairstyles, hands busy with balls, books, sticks, sonorous gadgets: Zak's gang.

In less than a minute we're out of the neighborhood, off the trail and on Peytavin, where traffic instantly slows to a crawl. Leaving Peytavin, Ibrahim follows Ponty all the way to the giant roundabout of the Place de l'Indépendance. In front of the Clairafrique bookstore we turn right toward the port, which stretches beyond a graffiti-covered wall. Sidewalks are the usual ruckus, the circus of table vendors, open-air restaurants and barbers, invalid beggars, unfazed passersby. The masts of docked boats poke the blue sky, circled by dirty, famished, screeching seabirds.

Access to the grounds is restricted. We're cleared by port security after Ibrahim points at the sticker glued to the windshield. It makes me think of the green mocking snake on the big, blue, boxy car.

Ibrahim's company is called IEX. Sitting in a desolate corner of the port, its plane hangar of a warehouse is also protected by armed guards. Ibrahim nods toward a pair of aging cargo boats. "Mine," he says. Far in the distance is Gorée Island.

We make our way through a maze of goods sitting on pallets. Aisles are numbered, the stuff is wrapped, the floors are squeaky clean, employees wear uniforms, the only noise is that of an eighteen-wheeler getting loaded and forklifts whirring by. Ibrahim runs a big, tight operation.

Modi is just a kid. Bug-eyed, skinny, long-limbed, scared, way out of his league. Not a hair on his chest or chin. Only a few months removed from his village, Retba, where he got in trouble with a girl. Mansour, the patriarch of his family, called for him and arranged the chauffeuring/gardening job. Brought Modi to the big city. Took him under his wing. Tried to groom him for bigger and better things on Ibrahim's payroll. But Modi made one mistake, one big stinking mistake, and now he sits naked in a remote storage room, out of sight, out of earshot of the main warehouse floor. The blinds are pulled shut, the AC is on full blast, a radio is turned all the way up. Modi's arms and feet are tied to a metal chair. His face is a pummeled, bruised, bloody mass. Two men, Boris and Becaye, took turns beating him since yesterday afternoon--"tenderizing" him, as Ibrahim put it. Modi hasn't slept. He hasn't eaten. He's almost ready to talk.

"Uncle!" he shouts as Mansour enters the room.

Mansour, more contemptuous than sad, shakes his head. "What have you done?" he asks before retreating to the back, signaling his neutrality, his powerlessness.

Ibrahim and I approach his prisoner. "All yours," Ibrahim says, handing me a box of latex gloves.

Modi, blue with cold, looks at me apprehensively. I make a show of pulling two gloves out of the box, checking them, stretching them, snapping them on my fingers as if I were getting ready to go to work, as if things were about to get really messy. Boris gags Modi with a towel. Then, while the other men look on, I start hitting Modi methodically, giving it everything I have, using everything around--a stapler, a hole puncher, a binder, a trash can, my fists, reams of paper. Modi, still bound to the chair, flies across the room, lands on his side, slides a little.

13

Becaye sits him upright. I send him flying again. In five minutes he's just about done. Looking around for inspiration, I see the end of a power drill sticking out of a metal drawer. The fog in my head clears when I get the thing going--it is the most soothing and uplifting sound. Modi's eyes fill with tears. The men in the room nod approvingly, encouragingly. Only Mansour looks down. Modi's body tenses when I get close. His breath quickens. His toes curl. Piss trickles down his thighs. I jab him in the middle of the forehead. He moves. The drill draws a long, bloody line on his face, his canvas of a face. A desperate grunt escapes his throat. I undo the rag covering his mouth and take a step back, feeling like a cigarette--the artist contemplating a just-completed piece. Modi takes a deep, greedy breath, almost choking on it. His eyes seem ready to pop. "Ask him what you need to know," I tell Ibrahim.

Ibrahim hovers over Modi, careful to avoid the pool of urine. His face shows nothing. His tone is even. "Who was it?" he asks.

"A man called Tyson," Modi says through tears, snot, blood, rattling teeth, and busted lips.

"How much did he pay you?"

"500,000 francs in advance."

"When is he giving you the rest?"

"Today, 3 o'clock."

"Where?"

"Sandaga."

All Modi has is a phone number. Tyson is an ex-wrestler. He appeared at the door of Modi's rented room one evening a week ago with a sweet deal: give up Zak for a cool million CFA. Modi didn't think twice. He took the money and made the call at the very first opportunity. Tyson is the man who took Zak, the one who jumped out of the silver Renault.

Ibrahim doesn't bother asking Modi why he did it. He seems to understand men and the things that motivate them. His focus is on the task ahead, what needs to be done. "I'm not interested in you," he tells Modi. "Lead me to those men and you'll be free to go." And to Mansour: "Look into that number."

14

Mansour appears paralyzed by shame and disgust. Not once does he address his nephew or look his way.

It's 1:30. Boris and Becaye wipe Modi's wounds, dress him, and escort him out of the warehouse. They're going to sit in his room until it's time for the meeting with Tyson. Ibrahim returns home to stay with Marie, who, out of pure fear or nervous anticipation, keeps calling his cellphone. Mansour stays behind. I catch a cab to my Point-E villa.

After a shower, coffee, and a cold sandwich, I throw a fresh set of clothes and my gun in a bag. There's a message from Karine on the answering machine. "Are we still on for tonight?" she asks when I call her at work, the small Guediawaye clinic that she runs on behalf of an American NGO.

"Just took a case," I tell her. "Might keep me busy for a couple of days. Rain check?"

"Rain check," she says readily.

"You sound relieved," I tease her.

Karine laughs a little. I'm just getting to know her. Her laugh doesn't start from deep inside. It never goes further than her lips. Her eyes, her soul, her heart are barely into it, rarely into it. She's never 100% in the moment. A part of her always kicks back and watches, analyzes. "Guarded" would be a good way to describe her. The whole time I've been back I haven't seen her relax, open up, let herself go. I looked for her before I even started searching for my mother--I missed Karine, I remembered her acutely, I knew she'd be much easier to find than Salimata. Karine the little girl was as close to me as I ever got to another human being. The woman I've found is a mystery, an enigma, a wall I'm determined to pierce, topple, vanquish, reduce to rubble. "You're like my little brother or something, Chris. I'm not sure how to approach this."

"You're my first love," I remind her. "Stole my heart that morning at the Foyer. I never forgot you. What'd you expect?"

She sighs. "It just feels weird. That was such a long time ago. We were babies."

15

"Just give it a try."

A voice intrudes upon our conversation. Karine's office is very tiny. She's always overworked, understaffed, overwhelmed. So much to do. So many people to help. There's never enough time, enough money, enough supplies. Merciless work, but she appears to enjoy it. "Talk to you later?"

"You bet."

I look up Ibrahim Sow on the Internet. He's all over the local tabloids and gossip rags: playboy, gambler, enfant chéri, big shot. His houses, his cars, his farm by Retba Lake, his horses, his polo matches, his shot at the Paris-Dakar Race. IEX is one of the country's oldest and biggest firms, going as far back as the era of colonial counters. Marie's own background is spotless: prominent family, Catholic school, Sorbonne, charity work. She's not all looks, but her looks are what matter to me at the moment. I print her picture, stare at it for what seems like an eternity, and put it inside a desk drawer.

I wrap Ibrahim's envelope in plastic and bury it under the guava tree in my garden.

Corniche to Soumbedioune to the Route de Ouakam. I turn left, drive for about fifteen minutes, look for the Jean Mermoz stele--big, yellow, ugly fenced-in thing, a single bench at its foot. I turn right and stay on the main road. Second street on the right, I go down a slope. First alley opening on the left, a one-story house with a half-wall covered with bougainvillea. White iron door.

Mame Awa is more than a nanny: she's been with the Sows long enough to be considered family. I've come to see her at Ibrahim's suggestion--so Marie thinks I'm working, interviewing people, chasing leads, turning the town upside down, earning the money that Ibrahim is paying me to find Zak.

A diminutive figure, Mame Awa wears a two-piece tailored outfit called *taille-basse*, with a matching scarf partially covering her gray hair. Her flat face is dried and ancient, wrinkled around eyes that sparkle with energy. There seems to be no flesh on her fingers, only paper-thin skin, bones that are hard and strong.

"Chris James," I introduce myself.

"I know who you are. Marie just called to tell me you were coming."

I follow her into a paved yard. Mango, lemon, and papaya trees provide shade, along with others bearing unfamiliar fruits. Seven boys are assembled on a decorated straw mat. They're gathered around a large bowl filled to the rim with steaming *lakh*. "*Talibes*," explains Mame Awa. "From the Koranic school by the bakery around the corner. I provide them with lunch whenever I can. Today is special: When they're finished eating they're going to stay with me and pray."

The boys seem to relish the mixture of raisin-sprinkled gruel and fresh milk. *Talibes* are, for the most part, children whose parents can't or won't provide for. Left in the care of self-styled instructors called *marabouts*, they live a life full of privations, suffering, exploitation, servitude. In exchange for a roof and a basic Islamic education, they're sent out in the streets to beg day after day. They're everywhere around the city, so prevalent and ubiquitous as to become invisible. They remind me of the orphanage children. The ragged, disowned bunch that we were.

Mame Awa and I sit on each side of a table carrying a basket of fruits and a pitcher of lemonade. She leans back and folds her tiny arms, one of those souls too old to be fooled by much about much any more. I feel like she's seeing through me, right down to my rotten core. "Where are you from?"

"I was born here. My father--the American diplomat who adopted me--took me to his country when I was seven. That's where I was raised."

"How long have you been back?"

"Less than a year."

"Too soon to call this your home. What do you consider yourself: American? Senegalese?"

"A black man."

17

The *talibes* finish eating. The prayer for Zak begins. One voice sings a Koranic verse in its entirety, which is then repeated by the group.

"Now," Mame Awa says as she regains her seat after putting the bowl and spoons away, "you must tell me what you want to know."

I ask her very perfunctory questions about the Sow household. She answers just as perfunctorily, until Modi's subject comes along. "He's no good," the old woman affirms.

"What do you mean?"

"Modi resents Ibrahim--his fortune, his good luck, his standing in life. Just like he despises Mansour for being who he is and calls him a *dunguru* behind his back."

"What's a *dunguru*?"

"Somebody who attaches themselves to powerful men and caters to their every desire, doing all their dirty work."

"Is Mansour that kind of man?"

"No, by all means. He's like the male version of me. Worked for Ibra's father before looking after the son. A very decent man. Nicer than he cares to let on."

"What about the other helpers, Abdi and Anta?"

"Good people. Abdi is devoted and loyal. Anta is a serious woman who only worries about the three daughters she left back in her Saloum village for her co-wives to raise. She's saving all her money for the day she'll be able to bring them to Dakar."

One of the *talibes* leaves the group to go drink water from the yard faucet. He smiles shyly when he notices us looking at him. Scars run all over his skinny legs. Somebody whipped him or he just falls down and hurts himself a lot. Beside the mat, next to dirty and torn sandals and plastic shoes called *tic-tacs*, is a pile of empty tin cans.

"It's hard to believe how fast this country is changing," Mame Awa says as I take my leave. "I worry for the future."

2:25. Peytavin is made dark by the antediluvian, gigantic *fromager* trees lining its sides. I reach the outskirts of Sandaga market, Dakar's biggest. Two blocks from the heart of downtown, it shimmers with light, noise, and movement. Like a poor soul lost at sea, a police officer mans the next intersection from a steel pedestal. His arms are stretched far and wide as he blows his whistle, turning around to direct the flow one corner at a time.

Modi's rented room is by the main depot of a fleet of minibuses called *cars rapides*, next to the neighborhood gendarmerie outpost. The *cars rapides* climb the steep Avenue Blaise Diagne on tired diesels, drop their last passengers off and turn into the open-air terminal for a short stop before reloading for the next cross-town run.

Two boys detach themselves from a pitiable group loitering by a *tangana* beverage stand and approach assuredly, laying claim to my vehicle. Brothers. Barefoot, hair unkempt, filthy fingernails, crust at the corner of their shrewd, knowing, hungry eyes. "We'll guard it," the older boy bluntly declares in Wolof.

I start to sweat as soon as I take a few steps on Blaise Diagne. People are moving in all directions, the confused mass that is midday Dakar, everybody caught up in their lives, the places they need to be, the things they have to do in order to survive.

Colors. The disheartening off-black or spotted orange of the *borom xesal*'s bleached skins. The dark blue of every *car*

19

rapide, a daredevil signal man/coaxer/money man hanging from its flapping backdoor. The yellow of the merciless sun. The green of the fruits hawked by *boy poulos*, the Guinean migrants who peddle the harvest stockpiled by Lebanese merchants in the huge hangars of the nearby produce district. The pink of the well-assimilated French, mixed with the embarrassed and confused red of tourists trying to shake the begging cluster attached to their sleeves.

I follow a *car rapide* as it rolls into the depot, which is nothing more than another pothole-filled road. The rooming house is next to a *boutiku Naar,* a little shop run by a turbaned Moor officiating behind a counter topped with wire netting. The sooty wall leads me down a couple of steps into a yard where three rooms sit opposite a low-slung structure with a verandah. I join Boris, Becaye, and Modi inside a small and windowless hole. They're sharing Modi's thin sponge mattress, their legs stretched on the naked floor, shawarma wrappers at their feet. The only piece of furniture in the room is a dingy cabinet holding a solitary man's effects: a deodorant spray, a bush pick, matches, a full ashtray, empty packs of cigarettes, a Safieddine Studio portrait of a woman and a baby. The woman is pretty in a natural kind of way. Modi's Retba girl, holding their son.

Modi still hasn't gotten a hold of himself. Seeing me, he twitches. Boris appeases him with one hand on his shoulder. "Easy, Retba Boy."

Boris is a sinister, none too friendly dude. Six-two, one-eighty, blond mohawk, pierced ears, shades. He's sucking on a lollipop. We each recognize in the other a mirror image of ourselves: It takes a killer to know one. Becaye is pure muscle, not too bright, fussy about his appearance.

"Time to go," I tell them.

I tag Modi on foot. Boris gets in the S.U.V. Becaye takes my car. The cop manning the intersection whistles away in short and shrilly Satchmo outbursts. Modi is dressed in a bright blue Hawaiian shirt, baggy jeans, and white sneakers. His swollen face sports a long Band-Aid. His arms bear cuts and

20

scratches. He walks unhurriedly, hesitantly, like a man completely out of his groove, a man off to the gallows, a condemned man weighing his last options--he's realized by now that Ibrahim's promise to let him go is an empty one. Modi looks back and sees me right on his trail. I point at the gun under my shirt. Modi looks away and sees Boris and Becaye following from the road.

After a few hundred yards Modi enters one of the small trails penetrating deep into Sandaga. It's immediately darker. The numbered booths pressed against the path of compacted earth are tin-roofed cubicles made of metal sheets or brick walls that sit slightly higher than the ground. The path rings the dried-up skeleton of a baobab tree before unexpectedly taking us in front of an edifice painted a faded yellow. The enormous construction shelters row upon row of wooden tables garnished with spices, fruit, produce, clothing, and artifacts. It's the old Sandaga, the first Sandaga, from which the ever-widening circles of booths grew.

The crowd makes it hard to walk. Modi speeds up. At the bottom of the enclosed market, he enters a small lavatory. I wait in front of a stand, picking up a pair of profiled sunglasses. "*Bi nek?*"--What's up with this one?

The merchant, a Rasta teen, is engaging. "*Essaye-ko,*" he proposes, holding a mirror up--Try it.

I put the glasses on. Tilting the rectangular mirror, I change position until the entrance to the lavatory is in sight. A man is going in. Tall, sandals, shabbily dressed in an under-*boubou*.

"They fit perfect, boss." The glasses-and-watches man wants to know if he has a sale.

"How much?"

He holds two fingers up.

I peel a red bill from Ibrahim Sow's roll. The teenager apologizes before he runs to look for change. In the mirror, the lavatory's short doors slowly stop swinging on their rusted hinges. My seller comes back. He counts the change and tries to snap a watch on my wrist, distracting me. The next time I look up, the doors are moving again.

I enter the tiled washroom. Copper faucets line a wall, at the bottom of which rises a low ceramic bench. The room doubles as a place to perform ritual ablutions. Urinals and stalls are contained behind a panel. The two dilapidated ceiling fans are insufficient to chase the smell. Of the four stalls, three are free. The tips of Modi's white sneakers show under the one closed door.

It's not locked, and moves a little before being stopped by Modi's leg. "Modi?" My voice bounces off the wall and disintegrates into the market's cacophony. I look across my shoulder before pushing on the wood. The door gives a little, leaving enough space for me to slip my head inside the stall. Modi sits on the toilet with the fear of a few minutes ago forever stamped on his face. Cut from side to side, his throat reveals a wound from which blood gushes in dark-red spurts, spraying the wall, coloring the air with a fine mist, soaking his shirt and his lap. I pull the door shut.

Outside the lavatory, I look intently about. The same people are occupying the same spots. Nothing seems out of place. Avoiding the crowded inner aisles, I follow the wall all the way to the main exit. Before I reach it, a man comes out of the aisle directly on my right and makes for the flood of light. He's taller than the surrounding shoppers and hangers-on. He has a shaved, sweaty head. His polo shirt is open at the collar. Strong shoulders, large back, thick neck, big nose, beefy cheeks, quick steps, all business. He disappears into the light.

I run freely, stepping on toes and knocking down a handful of small statues standing too close to a display's edge. Shouts erupt behind me. I push for the exit, running into a slow-walking, time-taking, double-chinned and foul-mouthed matron before I can jump out of the edifice. I walk around the dried-up baobab and get slapped by the heat. There are lots of shoppers around the canteens or walking on the narrow trail. The tall and muscular man is easy to spot. I call Boris. "Got Tyson in my sight," I tell him. "Start driving."

22

Tyson leads me along small trails until we emerge from the market's garment district and its dozens of Singer-operating seamstresses. The Louis Armstrong cop is executing his lonely choreography far up the road.

I stand back while Tyson claims a silver Renault from a kid. Boris is laboring down the hill, stuck in traffic, Becaye on his bumper. Tyson pulls away a good two minutes before Boris picks me up. "He's not going anywhere," he claims, gesturing toward the overpopulated roadways. I'm antsy, but we catch up with the Renault at the first crossroads.

"Where's Modi?" Boris asks.

"Dead," I inform him.

"Good," he says.

Camberene faces us as we exit the short Autoroute. We turn right into the narrow and badly maintained road to Dalifort, a so-so suburb south of the city. There isn't much to see on the right. Palm trees border commercial gardens that spread for a short distance before yielding to the dunes flanking the highway. Every so often there's the circular and bamboo-like enclosure of a charcoal retailer. The action is on the other side, with low houses intermittently raising shabby walls from the sand. Tyson parks under a *filao* tree.

Two *boutiks* and a sole bread kiosk are stationed at the beginning of a lane that reaches deep inside Dalifort. I train my nose on the overpowering smells: dung from the horse carts making the connection between Camberene and the Old Route de Rufisque; sap from the hovering trees; charcoal from the traditional furnaces; hay; uncollected trash; open sewers. I check my gun before following Tyson on the sandy path into Dalifort. He advances between brick outer walls exuding a killer heat. Most houses are built in the familiar compound fashion, with a large central yard surrounded by individual rooms that carry a temporary look with their wooden walls and corrugated zinc roofing. The enclosures have no front door, allowing one to see deep into the clay yards.

23

Tyson greets a group of men sitting on a mat before he goes down a few steps into one such compound. I keep on walking, passing the men who look me up and down. Five of them. Young, wiry, idle, a lifetime of the tea ritual called *ataya*, conversation, and cigarettes. They appear none too happy to see a stranger on their turf, but they stay put. The walls open to reveal four separate shacks thrown at weird angles around a gnarly tree. A young woman sits in the tree's shade, sorting rice in a big calabash. Next to her, an elderly man sleeps on a low chair. Tyson is walking inside the room that is farthest to the left. Its front is cemented at the bottom to form a short and uneven prop. Its single window is obscured by dusty shutters.

"Zak could be in that shack," I inform Ibrahim from the car. "Say the word and we go in."

"We have to be sure," Ibrahim says. "If Zak's not there, then what?"

"We take Tyson and make him talk. He leads us to Zak."

Ibrahim takes a few seconds to think. I wonder if Marie is close by, hanging on to his every word. "How many men sitting in front of the house?"

"Five. We can take them, easy: Boris holds them; Becaye covers me; I go in."

"Give it an hour," Ibrahim says. "I'll bring more firepower."

"Make it quick," I tell him. "Any word on that phone number?"

"Prepaid," Ibrahim says.

It's 4:15.

Of course, Ibrahim gets caught in the rush hour traffic. It takes everything I have not to go against his wish. I was never one to wait. Never knew how. So I kill time talking with Jiby, the bread-kiosk man, standing aside as he plies his trade, smoking cigarette after impatient cigarette, keeping an eye on Tyson's house. One of the tea drinkers occasionally goes in--to use the open-air bathroom, presumably. Tyson doesn't come out.

24

Dalifort's rhythm is no different than that of the countless impoverished neighborhoods flanking Dakar. Boys play soccer in the middle of unpaved streets, pushing colorful plastic balls that easily become airborne, dribbling around human or inanimate obstacles, fleeing to the side when cars rush through. Girls jump rope and play-act. Aimless youths walk around aimlessly, trying hard to look cool, sporting the latest stuff or their idea of it. Women keep busy, always the ones hustling, bearing the brunt: selling something, anything, to make a buck, balancing provisions or water buckets on top of their heads, washing laundry with their bare hands, cleaning, cooking, grinding grain inside clustered yards, singing for courage and for strength, clapping each time the pestle goes up. I look for Salimata in their faces--I look without really looking. Salimata was not dirt-poor. She was no rough-edged maid or tenement yard prowler. She was no Margot. Of that I'm sure.

Ibrahim shows up in a fleet of all-terrain a little before 6. With him are sixteen men on loan from the same security/protection outfit that guards his residence. No mere Borises and Becayes: military garb, boots, gloves, guns galore, blades, ski masks, no tags on the cars. "They cost a lot, these men," Ibrahim tells me. "But it doesn't get any better. Wish I'd had them with me all along. Zak would still be home."

We go in discreetly. Ibrahim, who traded his *boubou* for jeans and a black Kevlar shirt straight out of Mexico City, takes the lead. Divided in two groups, we descend toward our target from side lanes. By the time the *ataya* men see us we're on them, weapons drawn. The blitz is efficient, if not very quiet. The men are made to sit in a huddle, hands on their heads. A search reveals no guns, only a couple of long knives.

Ibrahim, Boris, and I rush into the yard. The young woman and the old man are nowhere to be seen. Tyson is peering out of his room, up from a nap, naked from the waist up. He tries to shut the door. Boris and I both grab it. Ibrahim hits Tyson across the face with his Magnum, a Dirty Harry thing with the longest cannon I've ever seen. Tyson fights back. With the three of us on top of him, he's quickly overpowered. He might be an ex-wrestler but we're hungry, we're wired, we're quick, we're on a mission, we jab and kick and punch where it hurts.

Tyson is in our hands. We turn his room, and the whole sorry compound, upside down without finding Zak. Not a trace, not a single clue. Only the quivering old man, the stone-faced young woman, junk, dirty furniture, three cellphones, the shabbiest clothes, a few chickens, a famished dog, a parakeet, a baby goat, dinged cookware, a 50-pound bag of the cheapest Malaysian rice. Ibrahim makes a brave face. Deep down inside, I know, he is crushed.

The prisoners are rounded up in the yard. Tyson is kept inside his room. Two of our men keep guard on the street. The whole Dalifort is at the door. This is the only country in the world where people run toward trouble involving firearms, not away from it. Children, grandmothers, passersby--everybody. We tell them we're B.G.--Brigade Criminelle, the country's foremost law enforcement agency. There's a gendarmerie outpost at the Cité Fayçal a mere mile and a half down the road. The gendarmes never move very fast, but how long before they come and spoil our party?

Our quarry is hauled away in full sight of the gawkers. The five men on the mat, Tyson's father, and Tyson's wife are thrown in two of the S.U.V.'s. "Take them to the farm," Ibrahim instructs Becaye. "Tie them up, cover their eyes and their mouths, never lose sight of them."

Even handcuffed, Tyson drags his feet a little, encouraged, perhaps, by the amassed crowd--neighbors, friends, acquaintances. We keep our weapons out and aimed chest-high. "Snap a picture, take a video with your phone and you're gonna get it!" Ibrahim snarls. Nobody intervenes. Nobody attempts anything. The population is used to displays of force by the army or elite troops. Despite claims of laissez-faire and a democratic credo, the state is all-powerful--some call it

26

autocratic. Rights can be trampled, freedoms can be curtailed. Police brutality is neither new nor rare.

We end up knocking Tyson out and pushing him across the floor of one of the trucks when he refuses to get inside. Ibrahim drives. Boris and I keep our feet flat on Tyson's back. When he comes to, we pound his head repeatedly. "Going to IEX?" I ask.

"No," Ibrahim says through clenched teeth.

We take Tyson to a scrap yard in Bel Air, a mix of fisheries and industrial interests a mere fifteen minutes from Dalifort. Ibrahim knows Diop, the owner, a rotund, jocund, affable, bearded man dressed in greasy blues--who doesn't Ibrahim know, who doesn't know him? Diop's workers are all gone by the time we get there. After he locks his three guard dogs away we have the run of the place, settling for a tool shed concealed amid sheets of metal and racks of engine parts. Diop obligingly gets one of his big saws going for noise cover before shutting himself in his office to catch up on paperwork.

Tyson is no Modi. It takes more than threats and cuts and blows and a power drill. It takes pliers, a hammer, and a blowtorch. Ibrahim, Boris, and I all get our hands dirty. The pliers are for Tyson's nails and teeth. The hammer is for his head. The blowtorch for his eyes, his hair, his genitals. Every man has a threshold, a pain level beyond which all bets are off. Tyson's is higher than most. He huffs, puffs, grunts, sweats, yells, wails, spits, hisses, cusses, cringes, cries, resists. His tolerance for the treatment we inflict upon him is almost superhuman. "Can you believe this shit?" Boris shouts, frustrated. Even I get tired and decide to take a break, savoring a well-earned smoke at dusk. Only Ibrahim keeps his cool, going at it nonstop, ignoring poor Marie's anxious phone calls, swinging the hammer, breaking bone after bone.

In the end the softer approach works best: I call Becaye at the farm and get him to put Tyson's wife on speakerphone--Fatou is her name. Following my instructions,

Becaye has two of the farm hands strip Fatou naked. They proceed to rape her in front of the other prisoners. She plays tough at first, defiant and unbowed and full of hate just like her man. But there's no mistaking her sobs and nos and cries of disgust and shame when the boys start having their little fun, pinning her to the ground, slapping her around for good measure. "She's not getting out of there alive," Ibrahim informs Tyson. "Neither is your father. But I can promise you a quick, dignified ending for them if you cooperate."

So Tyson talks all right. The only problem is that it took us too long to break him. By the time we know what we want to know two precious hours have gone by. "Zak's on the big Madeleine island," he reveals. "That's where Momar took him last night. That's where the exchange is supposed to take place."

"Where on the island?" Ibrahim asks.

"There's a bunker all the way at the top..."

"When?"

"Midnight."

"How do I know you're telling the truth?"

"Momar will call you at 11."

"He's holding back," I tell Ibrahim.

"Of course he is," Ibrahim says, not taking his eyes off Tyson. "Momar is already on the island?"

"Yes."

"How many men with him?"

"Eight."

"How were you gonna get there?"

"Soumbedioune. A fisherman is--was--taking me. I only stayed behind to take care of Modi."

"11 o'clock?"

"11 o'clock," Tyson repeats. "You'll know then that I'm telling the truth. God is my witness."

Ibrahim takes the Magnum and puts it against Tyson's skull. "Funny that you, of all people, would invoke God," he tells Tyson before pulling the trigger.

29

Ibrahim persuades Diop to put the big saw to use. "Guess my dogs are eating steak tonight," Diop deadpans, provoking a much-welcome volley of hilarity.

We help him roll Tyson's body onto a forklift. "I can take it from here," he tells us.

Ibrahim, happy about the breakthrough, gives me a high-five before we jump back in the truck. "That Fatou thing? Pure genius, man."

Boris acquiesces grudgingly.

My car, dropped off by one of Ibrahim's people, looks incongruous among the monsters on the mansion's carport. It's an old Peugeot 404, a throwback from the '70s, the workhorse of its day--Piccoli drove one in "*Max et les Ferrailleurs.*" I was scouring car lots around the city for the big blue boxy car when I found it and fell in love with it. I still don't know much about the big blue boxy car. Nothing French from or around 1975--the year Salimata left me at the orphanage house--looks quite like it.

The house still smells like coffee--probably all that everybody's been drinking for over 24 hours straight. I make Yasmin's acquaintance when she and Marie show me to my room. They call the little girl Yaz. She's seven, no bigger than this, the most precious little thing, braids thick and lustrous just like mommy's, dimples, limpid, limpid eyes, voice full of music. She's ebullient, talkative, everywhere at once--no way she knows about Zak. So Marie and Ibrahim--he says to call him Ibra--Marie and Ibra are doing a great job shielding her.

I shower and change clothes. My room is on the second floor, across the hall from Zak's. His black laptop computer has a game controller attached to it. Textbooks are left to collect dust on a corner, next to a bookbag that seems to be still bulging from the last day of school. Zak's report card reveals perfect scores and teachers' ravings, unlike the ones I used to bring home to Vernon, my father. I sit on the bed. A world Atlas taped to the wall shows three cities marked with red dots: Dakar, Nice, Palm Beach. Pictures surround the map: a black and white portrait of a younger, pensive Marie; Yasmin wearing costumes, making faces, blowing kisses, jumping in a pool; Zak and Ibrahim leaning against a silver sports car on a crowded American street.

It's in Zak's room that the case becomes personal. I know what it's like for a kid to feel violated, terrorized, traumatized, defenseless. I know. I see Zak going through unimaginable, ignoble, indescribable things at the hands of his captors. I feel his pain, his fear, his powerlessness.

It's in Zak's room that I vow to bring him home.

I join the couple inside the office. Marie is showing a touch, just a touch of relief. On our way back Ibra wondered aloud if he should tell her what we'd found out. In the end he decided for it. "We're still giving them what they want," he informs Marie, nodding toward the duffel bag at the foot of his desk--one million dollars in cash, magic powder for Marie's eyes. "We're just going to the meeting place early. By the time they call I'll be on the big Madeleine. We'll surprise the hell out of them. We'll force them to play fair." He lays his feet on the desk, still pumped from the afternoon, the Dalifort excursion, Tyson, Diop, the saw, the steaks.

"Don't forget to ask for Zak," I remind him dutifully.

"I can't believe that he's this close," Marie says, getting up to take a look out the window. The twin islands are there, bumps on the smooth water, dark masses under the moonless sky. They're uninhabited. Nothing grows on them. From afar their rocky shores appear completely unapproachable. Ibrahim, who is an experienced sailor, says there's a way.

Marie lets out a deep sigh before walking away from the window.

"Kidnapping 101," Ibrahim tells her. "They call me at 11. I have one hour to make it out there. No preparation, no time to do anything rash. Their terrain, their advantage."

"Don't take any chances," Marie warns him.

"You know me better than that."

She hands Ibrahim a backpack containing Zak's favorite sweatshirt, a bottle of juice, a couple of candy bars. She and

31

Ibrahim are doing better, I can tell. Pulling along. Working together. This is how a family under duress works.

I lap it all up as if it were my favorite bourbon.

It's 8:30. Marie and Ibrahim hug for a long time before we leave. She holds him tight, buries her head in his shoulder. He whispers reassuring words. She cries. He steels himself.

It takes two men to carry the duffel bag full of money. We take it straight to IEX, speeding through the emptying downtown streets. Once at the warehouse, the duffel bag is put under lock and key by Mansour and switched for the real ransom: two large canisters weighing approximately 10 pounds each. "Diamonds," Ibrahim reveals as we leave the port, heading across town toward Ngor Beach's marina.

"Momar's?"

"Yes and no. We were partners in a mining venture in Sierra Leone--cliché, I know, but it was all the rage a couple of years back, everybody wanted in. Lebanese businessmen were making a killing, coming back from Freetown with loads of uncut stones and all kinds of wild stories. Momar did the prospective work and sought out local contacts. I fronted the money and equipment through IEX. Members of Sierra Leone's armed forces were in on the project. Local troops guarded the mine. Rebel soldiers who had surrendered to the government after the country's civil war did the digging. The excavation lasted a whole year--the terms of our concession. Momar shipped the harvest back to Dakar on one of my boats. He was already in talks with buyers, extremists from Sudan, don't ask me how he hooked up with them--they're hungry for diamonds now that their assets are being frozen all over the world thanks to the U.S. government. When I got my hands on the shipment I decided to keep it all."

Ibrahim smiles, driving with a sure hand and a heavy foot. It's the longest I've heard him speak. "I got a little too greedy, I guess. Zak is how I'm paying for it. Momar's move caught me completely off guard. Known him for years. Kind of grew up together. Always beat him at everything. Never showed much heart, not the ballsy kind at all. Thought I had him under control. Thought I'd take the diamonds, sell them, throw Momar a few crumbs. The money must have gotten to his head. What I get for underestimating people."

I wonder why Ibrahim is telling me all this, and if I'm beginning to learn a little too much. Intimate knowledge of powerful men's dealings can be outright deadly.

Ngor Beach is Dakar's finest. A long stretch of golden sand, palm trees, volleyball nets, empty fishermen's pirogues, towering hotels, deep waters. The marina, encumbered with pleasure vessels and speedboats, is a little too illuminated for my taste. We meet Boris by the launching pad at the end of the boardwalk. Four Zodiacs await, each containing four men--that makes it nineteen of us against Momar's nine.

Ibrahim, talking softly, lays out the plan. "We land, we spread out in an arc, we storm them, we kill Momar, we bring both Zak and the ransom back. We only negotiate if Zak's life is directly threatened."

We check our weapons. Ibrahim and I get in the same boat. We sit at the rear, canisters at our feet. He grabs the throttle. The men with us were all part of the Dalifort crew. They look rested, ready.

We start our engines, navigating painstakingly around the boats at anchor until we get to the open sea, Ibrahim leading the way. Then, following the coast, we zoom toward Soumbedioune and the Madeleine islands, passing the Mamelles lighthouse midcourse. The sea is ours and ours alone. Dotted lights make the city look tempting and beautiful. The speed makes my heart beat fast, gives me a rush.

Ibrahim's done his homework. "The bunker goes back to World War II," he informs me, shouting because of the wind.

"Who built it?"

"French soldiers. Vichy dug up tunnels and erected all kinds of fortifications along the shore."

"Is the bunker underground?"

"Part of it."

The twin islands, empty and savage, are in our sight in a few minutes. We slow down, gliding across the bay before turning the engines off and switching to paddles. As we get near, reefs and a strong current make our approach treacherous. The mist from the crashing waves fills the air. The noise is forbidding, the water rough. We follow an oblique path to the big Madeleine, maneuvering around obstacles barely outlined. The other boats mimic our every move. Powerful backward surges delay us. Rocks shine under the stars, close enough to touch, sharp, deadly, forming a line that opens unexpectedly to allow us in. Between the islands is a small enclosure, quiet as a lake. The wind falls, the current dies, the boats no longer struggle for balance. We pull the paddles up, waiting to see if anything, anyone awaits. The big Madeleine, dark and forbidding, engulfs us, dwarfs us, pulls us. Up close it is not naked at all: patches of grass intermittently carpet its flanks, small trees garnish its sugar-loaf mound. Nor is it completely dark: a light flickers among the trees, so tiny and frail it could be an illusion.

We beach the Zodiacs next to two small pirogues. A trail starts where the sand ends, sinuating all the way to the top. It's covered with footprints. Small, translucent crabs come out of tiny holes or emerge from the foamy edge of the waves.

Ibrahim's phone vibrates. It's 11 on the dot. "Yes?" His voice is calm, low, measured. "I have the stuff," he says after listening to Momar's instructions. "And I'm coming by myself. Let me talk to Zak."

The line goes dead. Ibrahim puts the phone back in his pocket. Frustration, rage, anger, apprehension--something gets a hold of him. He shakes it and gives the signal.

We deploy in a long line across the trail, sweeping the terrain as we advance. Ibrahim has one of the canisters. I carry the other, and it quickly gets heavy in my hand. We make our first mistake by not leaving men to guard the beach.

Up is the only way to go. The ground is hard, uneven, difficult. There's trash everywhere--empty beer cans, cigarette packs, plastic bags caught in the shrubs. The light glanced from the sea disappears--could be a fire that just got put out. The wind comes back with a vengeance as we get higher, deafening us, chilling our sweat, gluing our wet clothes to our skins.

Boris takes the lead. Silhouetted against the sky, guns at the ready, we climb toward the tree cover. We're halfway there when a man appears out of nowhere, stopping us dead in our tracks. He's dark-skinned, extremely tall, with square shoulders and a small head topped by a baseball cap. I crouch behind a rock. "Momar!" Ibrahim growls.

Still holding his phone, Momar sees us, freezes, turns around and runs away, leaps, bolts, dashes, disappears. We make our second mistake by not taking him out right then and there.

The last yards are the hardest. We give pursuit, following Momar into a small clearing bathed in milky light. Shouts erupt. Momar's men jump to their feet and scramble for their weapons, running this way and that. The first shots are fired, more confusion ensues, all hell breaks loose. The plan, Ibrahim's beautiful plan goes out the window. It's hard to see anything, to understand what's going on, to fathom who's who, to grasp who's doing what. Some men go and hide behind trees, the terrain, one another; some run openly; some stand in the middle of the clearing and try to take aim before unloading. I see the bunker, a smooth slab of concrete sticking out of the ground. One of the abductors is standing on top of it, a few feet above the fray, legs apart, screaming as he fires a rifle, going gung ho. I shoot him in the chest. Momar's party, it seems, is way over nine heads--Tyson's posthumous surprise, his little gift, his big parting lie. I look for Ibrahim, only finding him when I hear him shout for his son--"Zak!" "Zak!" "Zak!"

"In the bunker," I tell him.

We run toward it together.

I get there first and walk down a few steps, canister in one hand and gun in the other. My soles pin a soft object to the cement floor. I stand still, waiting until my eyes get accustomed to the darkness. The air in the bunker is stuffy, charged, oppressive, foul. Ibrahim comes in behind me, breathing loudly, heavily. I start to see my way through the thick obscurity. Crabs are everywhere inside the room. Dozens and dozens of them, small and large, their otherworldly glow contrasted by the lifeless tubes of their eyes. They move in a succession of multi-legged jumps, shells touching and claws snapping. They leave the base of the bunker's angled walls to converge toward the covered shape occupying its center. Kicking furiously into the advancing pack, Ibrahim and I prevent the crabs from approaching their prey, sending them flying against the walls or simply crushing them under our heels. We kill them one by one, shouts of refusal resonating in our ears. The crabs vanish from sight, running through invisible cracks or reduced to busted, oozing shells. Only then do we get on our knees to hover over the lifeless body of Zaccaria Sow.

The *pagne* he has been enveloped in from head to toe is covered with holes. Ibrahim runs both his palms on the elongated shape, feeling multiple layers of cloth. He moves trembling fingers upon his son's face, following the outline of the nose, eyebrows, and forehead. Something moves under his fingertips. He presses his palms all over the makeshift shroud, searching for an open end to tuck his fingers in and start unfolding it. His hands slip against the heavy fabric without success. The walls give out the illusion that they're moving, closing in on us. I start feeling the itch of allergy. Ibrahim lifts Zak off the ground. "Hold tight, baby boy," he says through tears.

We lay Zak on the bunker's roof, oblivious to the gunfire, the shouts, the movement around us. Threads fly in the wind when Ibrahim and I start unwrapping the blanket. A crab jumps from under the folds, dazed by the open air. Zak's face is exposed, gazing at the moon and stars behind closed lids. He's the spitting image of his father. There's a dark ring around his throat. His arms rest peacefully at his sides. Scratches cover his skin where the crabs have nibbled at his flesh.

An anguished cry shakes Ibrahim. He tries massaging Zak's heart to no effect. He presses his palms on Zak's cheeks and puts his lips against his, holding Zak's stiff mouth open to try and breathe life into him. I stand guard, watching over the two of them.

The battle shifts, moving down the hill toward the beach. Momar's exit is impeccable: five of his people provide cover while the other group launches the pirogues, starting the engines as soon as they're afloat. Once inside the pirogues, those men protect the ones on the beach until they join them. They don't stop firing until they pass the line of reefs.

The gunfire dwindles before dying altogether. Our boys take control of the now empty beach.

It seems that a long time passes before Ibrahim gives up. The wind doesn't ease up. It's loud as ever, it's relentless, it's making us shiver. I sit by Zak's head, lassitude and swirling thoughts finally getting the best of me. Marie Sow's face is all I see.

Seven of the abductors are dead. We lost four men, whose bodies are dropped at the bottom of the Zodiacs.

The return trip is grim. Ibrahim clutches Zak as if he were merely consoling him, comforting him, keeping watch as Zak sleeps. Halfway between the Madeleines and Ngor, Ibrahim does the right thing and angrily throws both of the canisters in the water. I feel many things: sorrow for Zak; pain for Marie; sympathy for Ibrahim, of course--sympathy, the tug of friendship, an abject sense of failure, the crushing weight of loss. There's nothing on earth more precious than a child. No superior blessing.

It happens all at once. The front door opens and they both run out. Marie is first, her bare feet slipping on the driveway's sharp pebbles. Yasmin follows. The truck's rear doors swing open. Marie jumps in, covering Zak's body with hers while a scream rises from her chest. It is bone-chilling, that scream. Bone-chilling. Primal. Raw. It rises and rises. It rises and covers everything. It makes everything stop. It never ends. Marie holds, kisses, caresses Zak's small and inert face. Ibrahim scoops Yasmin and presses her against him, shielding her from the scene, the horror, the tragedy. I stand nearby, unsure about what to do with myself. The guards remain at their posts, backs rigid with tension, ears burning, faces turned away from the car, weapons clutched tight. Ibrahim speaks comforting words to Marie, words that, her body trembling, her lips quivering, her eyes blind with tears, she refuses to hear. "Zaaaaaak!"

It's just the longest night. The police are called in, along with a doctor named Sanchez, and Ketus, Ibrahim's lawyer. The cop who shows up is Diack, a smallish man with round glasses, gentle eyes, and mild manners. Ibrahim refuses to let him take the body away. He won't even let the man take a look. "Zak belongs to us," Ibrahim tells Diack, towering over him, all anger, balled fists, a mourner's righteousness and above-the-law outrage and fierceness. "It's no. No morgue, no autopsy, nothing." I've helped Ibrahim transport Zak inside, to his room, where Marie is already cleaning him, washing him with the assistance of Mame Awa. There's talk of the funeral taking place as early as later this morning. The death certificate stamped by Sanchez lists strangulation as the cause of death.

Ketus is a wolf in a gray linen suit and pointy, fashionable shoes. He got Ibrahim's call while at a nightclub and jumped on the ball. He takes the plainclothes cop aside and talks a hole in his ear--big words, condescending smile, barely veiled threats, as if Diack were a flunky already in way over his head. "My client's the victim here, Detective. How about a little understanding, huh? A little room? His son was murdered even though the abductors' instructions were followed to the letter. Mr. Sow and myself will come by your office tomorrow--no, make that Thursday--to give his full deposition. How's that?" Diack stands his ground, hints at an escalation--more cops called for backup, due process, taking Zak by force. Mansour joins the conversation. He casually drops the name of the interior minister and several high-level officials, including Diack's boss and his boss's boss.

The cop leaves reluctantly. He gives me a long, inquisitive look on his way out.

I catch Sanchez as he gets into his car. He's a high-flying family doctor who owns a thriving practice by the sea--caters to Dakar's best and brightest, not too good for house calls, not too hung up on rules and regulations. As I approach he clutches his leather bag, ready to defend it at the cost of his life, as if a small fortune were in it--I'm sure Ibrahim made the favor worth his while. "How long has Zak been dead?" I ask him.

Sanchez puts his guard down. He throws the bag on the front seat and takes a deep breath. "Twenty-four hours, give or take two."

Nobody sleeps. I hang out with Mansour in a bungalow situated at the bottom of the Sow compound, past the pool, the laundry room and the maids' quarters. Modi's parents have yet to be told of his death, Mansour tells me. After Zak's taken care of he'll go and claim the body from the morgue and take it to Retba. Two burials, back-to-back.

Mansour spends the rest of the night in prayer. Crazy as his world has turned he has God, he has Islam. Just like Mame Awa and her *talibes*. I crash on the couch.

Zak's death is announced over the air by all the major radio stations starting at 5 am. Mansour wakes me up. He has a white *grand-boubou* ready for me when I get out of the shower. "Pray with me," he asks when I join him in the living room.

"I don't know how."

"It doesn't matter."

We go out on the verandah before dawn. Two aluminum containers are waiting. They look like tea kettles, only much bigger, with long, curved beaks and less polish. "Take one of the *satalas*. Repeat my words phonetically. Replicate my gestures."

Mansour sits at the edge of the verandah. He slips his feet out of his shoes before resting them on top of the soft

40

leather. "*Bismillahi*," he starts. We cleanse our wrists, mouth, nose, face, forearms, skull, ears, and feet before returning inside. Mansour positions himself on the right side of the rug, leaving enough space for me to stand behind. He starts leading me into prayer.

Several men come join us at the first hint of light, bringing their own rugs as well as larger mats. All strangers to me, young and old and similarly stone-faced. Rich, pious, sonorous voices soon take over the session with a succession of *surats*--Koranic verses--that are each repeated a fixed number of times. The circle that started with Mansour and me widens, gaining outer rings until it fills the little bungalow with turbaned presences and rasp voices. The walls resonate with supplications. I am lost in the middle of it all, one among the multitude.

After we stop chanting we meet outside to form a line that climbs the elongated garden. We watch our reflection in the pool. We walk on stones and then gravel. We circle the sculptures. We exit the house and gather out front, our backs to the sea in order to face Mecca, all but blocking the roadway under the rapidly coloring sky.

Zak's body emerges from the porch a few minutes later, covered in white cloth and carried on a stretcher by Ibrahim and three elderly men. They transport him outside and hold off in front of the wall. Once the stretcher is deposited on the ground the imam stands directly behind it to lead us through the *Fatiya*, the Koran's first *surat*.

Two chartered buses arrive, immediately turning around to face the road leading to the Corniche, smoke coming out of their hole-strewn exhausts. The oldest and most prominent of the mourners fill Ibrahim's cars while the rest of us climb inside the buses. I catch a glimpse of Abdi as he keeps watch over the stretcher, a befitting kaftan and simple hat replacing his kitchen uniform. We start the short trip toward Soumbedioune. The men riding with me never stop whispering prayers.

The congregation gathers briefly at the cemetery gates. The paved and wide entranceway makes a long buckle from the

41

heavily traveled Corniche, giving the cemetery adequate distance from the everyday comings and goings of mortals. More men come out of approaching cars, joining the procession without acknowledging one another. Zak's body is lifted from the all-terrain by his father, Mansour, Abdi, and another helper. We follow them first to the outside enclosure of the small mosque built within the cemetery, where the body is once again laid on the ground and another prayer is performed standing up. Then we make our way to the actual burial grounds, walking on narrow lanes through crowded plots.

The place is planted with elongated trees and seems to belong to the sky and the sea more than the earth carrying us. Most tombs are bare, marked with a simple engraved stone or piece of rock. We gather under a solitary tree, next to a freshly dug grave. After one final prayer the shrouded body is lowered. We shout "*Allahu akbar!*" several times. Zak is made to sit, facing east, his side resting against the crumbly earth. The tomb is closed amid more declamations, Ibrahim alone looking over it with his head bowed.

Tradition doesn't allow for Marie to attend the ritual. Women and children say goodbye to their loved ones in the family home or at the morgue attached to most mosques, where a body is most likely to be taken in order to be washed and prepared for the grave. And then mothers will rarely, if ever, visit the tomb. Fathers may occasionally come on Fridays to pray for the dead. Once a year, a complete recitation of the Koran dedicated to Zak's memory will be performed by an imam and a group of relatives.

The buses drop us off. Some of the mourners go straight to their cars after shaking hands with Ibrahim, but most return to the house where more rectangular mats have been installed in the shade at different spots around the garden and the backyard. Doors and gates are left open. The guards position themselves to ward off the journalists, who, unsurprisingly, show up with microphones and cameras and hungry questions. People come and go incessantly, joining one of the groups assembled on the mats or leaving shortly after offering their condolences. I catch a glimpse of Mame Awa directing the movements of a crew of caterers. Refreshments and traditional specialties reserved for the occasion are served. Marie and Yasmin remain out of sight. Mansour is sitting with the imam and other old and important-looking men on his verandah. All appear scholarly, the whiteness of their kaftans contrasting with their skins and the lawn's deep green. I walk around with my hands clasped behind my back. More women are starting to appear, dressed traditionally and modestly. They either remain inside the house or congregate on aligned rented chairs. Zak's friends, subdued, hurt, scared, on their best behavior, show up with their parents.

The sun shines with less ardor than usual. The mourners don't seem sad or exceptionally emphatic, their sheer amount a buffer against pain. A lunch of red rice and fish is served into large decorated bowls. Men and women sit separately. The food is tasty and abundant. We eat rapidly and without talking. The number of people starts decreasing after the second prayer of the day, which everybody attends by the pool, the imam again leading the way.

I join Ibrahim in his office when he calls for me. "*Sigil digale*," I tell him, offering the dedicated expression of sympathy as I shake his hand.

"*Sigil sa wale*," he answers. He's the shell, the shadow of himself. The *mucho* macho exuberance and can-do bravado of Dalifort are gone. It's only been a day but I feel like I've know him forever.

"How are Marie and Yasmin holding up?"

"Barely."

He takes an envelope from a drawer and slides it across the desk--the remaining $20,000. For the first time in my life the touch, feel, and weight of a large sum of money don't sit quite right. I look Ibrahim in the eye. "Just say the word," I tell him. "Senegal won't be big enough for Momar to hide in. I'll find him and bring him to you."

But there seems to be no fight left in Ibrahim. He frets, he fidgets, he sits in his fantastic commander-in-chief chair, his top-CEO chair, as if it has become too big for him, uncomfortable, ill-fitting or something. The battle he's just lost might have been too costly, too painful, hard to swallow, impossible to forget.

So Ibrahim doesn't answer me. It's too soon. He's feeling too much pain. There are too many ifs and what-ifs. Ibrahim can't gather his thoughts. He can't find the words.

I close the door softly behind me.

There's this group of kids by the park. Kicking up dust, standing around as I'm leaving. Zak's gang, still paying their respects. I stop the 404 as I get near. Only one of them approaches, the shortest one. His name is Ouzin. He says he was Zak's best friend. He reminds me of me: proud, quick, wary, full of attitude, not really keeping it together but pretending, acting like he is, always. "You're the detective, right?"

"Right."

Ouzin nods toward the islands. "So what happened over there, man?"

"We put up a good fight. Just got there a little too late."

"This the second time one of us gets killed. You know that, right?"

"Who was the first?"

"Samba. Zak's play cousin. Two, three weeks ago."

"What happened?"

"They claim it was meningitis. But we know better."

"Was Samba from the neighborhood?"

"No. But he was always here. He'd come see Zak and we'd all hook up and do our thing."

I shake Ouzin's hand. "Hang in there, man."

The rest of the money goes under the guava tree. Always liked to keep some cash hidden in secret places. One of those things about myself I could never explain. One more mystery about me that I can thank my childhood for. I just never feel safe

44

or prepared enough. Always waiting for something bad to happen. Don't know when or what it'll be. Just that sooner or later I'll run into some kind of big, big trouble. My adoptive father, Vernon, knew it. I know it, too. I can see it clear as day. It's coming. My day of reckoning. It's gonna be brutal, sudden, fast, total. For that reason, I'm a man never at ease. Never at ease. I tread carefully, cautiously. I don't trust. I don't love. I don't allow anyone in. I've never completely relaxed in the company of a woman. Never gave my all.

But I feel like Karine could be the one.

"Why?" she asks frankly, looking at me across a beautifully decorated table. I've slept a little, I've jogged on the Corniche, I've showered, I've shaved, I've picked up Karine from her place, we're at the Lagon II eating shrimp on a pier, the waves crashing below us, the breeze playing in her hair, the candlelight muting the green in her eyes. I'm ready to forget about Zak, the Sows, the case that left a bad taste in my mouth. Karine is surprised by my words. She wants to know what I'm about, what I want from her, what I'm getting at.

"You know me," I tell her. "You were there at the beginning."

"We spent a few years together in an orphanage," she says. "You were four when you came and seven when you left. How much do I know you? How much do you know me?"

"Those years meant everything," I tell her. "You were there for me. You were the only one. I wouldn't have made it without you."

Karine stops picking at her food. She looks at me. She, too, doesn't trust. It's not so easy. She, too, has layers on top of her layers. She's definitely not the little girl I used to know. When I joined the Foyer, when Salimata and that man dropped me off at the gate, the place had just been opened by American missionaries. Nothing foretold the horrors, the evil things that would be committed there over time. We kids had lost our families but we had one another, we had a new home, we had the good fathers, all four of them, before they turned into *bukis*--hyenas. And we had Karine. Karine was the oldest. The Foyer was her second home after a place run by nuns in Uganda--she has no memory of being anywhere else, ever. She was happy in Uganda. She has no idea why the nuns made her leave. Once at the Foyer she just naturally fell into the role of surrogate mom. We looked up to her. We listened to her. We did everything she told us to do. "I had the biggest crush on you," I confess, not for the first time.

"You were my favorite," she admits. "Always getting in trouble."

She's as beautiful now as she was then. Tonight she's made a special effort for me, I can tell: crayon, lipstick, nail polish, brush, heels, a dress that bares her shoulders. Her hair, usually in a ponytail, dances around her face. She pushes it back, sticks it behind her ears. She's unbelievable. The green eyes don't laugh--they never laugh. They're quick to flash irony and cautious restraint and a touch of cynicism. But the lines around the mouth are soft. It's Karine's skin that I can't get my eyes off. The color of honey, rich and mellow and sweet.

I'm a little nervous. I down glass after glass of a vinho verde she barely touches, watching me get buzzed with a hint, just a hint of rebuke in her body language. She's guarded, of course--woudn't be Karine if she weren't--but not confrontational, not defensive, not adamant, not against anything. She just doesn't jump. Not her type. She doesn't rush. Already one mistake in her past life, one bad turn, one divorce. It's been two years. She still doesn't feel ready. So things might happen. They just might. Who knows?

I drop Karine off without getting so much as a goodnight kiss and shoot straight for the Ngalam, sordid appetites overcoming all my good intentions. Margot sees me walking in and immediately knows what time it is. It's Wednesday night, nothing going on, Fela is making it a little better from his resting bed, making that horn blare and rant and accuse and light a fire under corrupt governments' asses everywhere around the world. Girls grind on one another on the dance floor. The blue light is making their eyes shine. It's making them look like feral, lethal cats.

"Party Boy!" Margot calls, ready to grab her cheap purse and roll. I get a glass of Pappy Van Winkle 15 from Sam the barman, Sam, my man--don't know how he gets the stuff but he gets it and I'm not asking any questions.

Margot orders a Flag.

"How many of y'all?" I prod her.

"Five," she says in her man's voice.

"Let's go," I tell her.

Sam's got *yamba*--Senegal's sticky, potent cannabis--right under the counter. He talks me into a few pills of X when he sees what I'm up to. "Let me get that bottle of Pappy 15," I tell him, laying a serious pile of cash in his palm before I and the girls file out.

It's party time all right. We hit the *yamba*, we pop the pills, we sip on some Pappy. Five naked girls in my living room. Black, white, mixed, local, foreign, tall, short, skinny, fat, fun, juicy, dry, cornrows, weaves, wigs, plaits, loose, up, ready. Margot, Tatyana, Isabelle, Vivianne, Jacqueline--where they get these names from I don't know. They put the empty bourbon bottle to use. They do me, I do them, they do one another while I watch. Always liked to watch. Big breasts, big bottoms, nipples that harden, hands that grope, lips that suck, tongues that lick, teeth that bite, slick flesh, wet pussies, hot breath, sweaty hair, raw voices, fingers that fuck, nails that scratch, thighs that throb, toes that curl and pop, the throes, the groans, the moans, the moves--it does something to me. I crave it, I have to have it, it's hard to stay away, it quiets something in me, it soothes my soul, it satisfies an hunger, it dulls an urge. Party Boy? More like Superfreak. I know where it comes from. I know why I'm that way. It's hard to stop. Sometimes I even convince myself that it's not wrong. I just got to have it. I don't mind paying for it. I don't mind paying to get it exactly right.

Tonight, in the thick of it, when usually it's all good and I'm all rapt and inching close to the zone, that coveted spot in my head, I experience a disconnect, I see myself, I'm out of my skin. The girls, the booze, the drugs---it's all too sordid, too seedy juxtaposed with the lovely evening with Karine, the stuff I'm trying to make happen with Karine. How will I look at her, pursue her, persuade her knowing what I know, doing what I do? Maybe it's just the Pappy hitting me, the *yamba* working its mojo. Long before the girls are done playing, long before the clock runs out I jump up, I bug out, I make them stop.

"Get your shit and get out," I tell them, feeling like kicking them as they lie there, feeling like putting my foot in the tangle of arms and legs and bushes and moans.

"Where's our money?" Margot asks before she even puts her skirt back on. "It's 50,000 CFA francs each."

"Out," I tell her.

They all go for their bag--guns, blades, Mace, phones? Margot, Tatyana, Isabelle, Viviane, Jacqueline. I'm faster on the draw, whipping my piece from under the phone book, pushing the girls out the door, throwing their clothes at them, a herder corralling unruly cattle. My ears burn from all the threats and insults. A heel flies and crashes into one of the living room windows, shattering it. My neighbors--well-to-do professionals with families and bourgeois aspirations and airs--will leave me another note on the 404's windshield tomorrow asking me to keep it down.

The knocks on the door make it all feel like deja vu. I'm on the couch, passed out. But it's 10 a.m., not 6. And it's not Ibrahim behind the door: it's Marie.

I'm completely paralyzed when I see her. I'm dirty, I stink, the house is a mess. Marie's dressed in all black, of course. Slacks, blouse, pumps, sunglasses. The braids are gone, a scarf covers her hair. I can't see her eyes but I know that finding me this way--seeing the empty bottle of Pappy, looking at the shoe and the shards of glass, smelling the lingering *yamba* vapors--will change her perception of me irremediably. But by the time I realize all that Marie's standing in the middle of the carpet, looking for a place to drop her purse and sit.

"You should go freshen up," she says in her little girl's voice. "I need to talk to you."

She's all business. Got a check sitting on my desk by the time I walk back into the room. A blue one, with birds and a blue sky and the sea, from her own checkbook. "5 million CFA," she says, answering the question in my eyes. "Yours if you tell me everything you know."

I sit next to her so she won't be able to read my eyes. "Not sure I understand."

"I've lived with my husband long enough to know when he's lying to me," Marie declares. "I don't believe his story. Didn't believe it then, don't believe it now. Had no choice but to go along--it all took place so fast, I had to trust that he'd take care of it. I know that things couldn't have happened the way he claims they did. I have no proof--just a gut feeling."

She pivots to face me. Her wraparound shades give out nothing. They can't hide the toughness of her ordeal. Marie's lost, now more than ever before in her life. She doesn't know what to do, where to begin, who to turn to. I thought after we put

49

Zak in the ground that she'd stay out of sight, disappear, take a trip, get away from it all, focus on Yaz, try and forget. But here she is. Marie, beautiful Marie. Too beautiful for this couch, this house, my dirty, messed-up life. Here she is ready to put up a fight. She wants to know, she says. She wants to know everything. "It's really not about you, Mr. James. It'll stop right here for you. Tell me the truth, take the money and you're done. You'll never hear from me again."

She's so close it's making me dizzy--I have to hold myself. It's clear to me that I won't take her money and look the other way. I want it to be about me. I want Marie to tell me she needs my help. I know exactly where she's coming from. So many unanswered questions. So much to unearth. Zak, her Zak is dead and she has no idea why. Danger might still lurk. Momar might be out to get Ibrahim, threaten the Sow family again. I want it to be about me.

But Marie's all business. She's sitting right next to me but she's unattainable, out of reach, out of my league. I want it to be about me. I want her to put her trust in me, to confide, to get close, to give me an inch so I can take a yard. At the same time, I'm afraid of myself. For I see far, way too far into the future. I see a Ripley scheme, I see taking Ibrahim for everything he's got--the money that flows so freely around him, the mansion, IEX, the incredible cars. I see taking Marie and Yasmin, making them mine, laying claim to everything Ibrahim owns. I see far across the chessboard, clear as day, clear as I've ever seen anything. I see far, so far ahead. Karine? Marie will be the one. Good family, Catholic school, the Sorbonne, charity work. And Yaz, Yaz, a little girl so precious, so wonderfully pure--Yaz could be my daughter, my own. I see it, oh, how I see it: manipulate, steal, kill, play God, use, lie, reap, harvest, get on top. The sweet hustle, the getaway, the clean break, the big one. I see it and it scares me. That stuff in my head, the stuff I can be capable of dreaming up sometimes.

Marie brings me back to earth. "So?"

"I don't know what to tell you."

"Don't worry about Ibrahim coming after you. He'll never know I was here."

"I'm not scared of Ibrahim."

"Then why won't you talk to me?"

"I just want to stay out of it," I confess, not lying for a second, or lying all the way, I'm too shaken and confused to understand which. "Don't want to get caught up in nobody's mess. I came here to start a new life. Not to get in trouble."

Marie's voice turns contemptuous. "You got paid. That's all you worry about, isn't it? That's all that matters."

I get up, relieved that she's providing me a way out until I can gather my thoughts. "It's just better that way, Marie. You don't want me to get involved any more that I've already been. Believe me."

It's the first time I say her name. That--and my tone-- makes her stop and look my way. It makes her wonder who I really am and what I'm really after. If only she would take off her glasses, those damn glasses, and let me look at her.

"It's Mrs. Sow to you."

Marie snatches her check from the desk and heads for the door. It takes everything I have not to call her back, not to run and follow her out of that door and into the sun, across the chessboard and into the Ripley scheme, my new life, my fantasy life, into everything that could be.

After Marie leaves I call in for glass repair and clean up the house from top to bottom. Nothing out of the ordinary here. For a while I'll be a good little boy. Then the urge will get its hold on me again. If nothing stronger counters it I'll go back to my old ways. Back to kinky sex, back to Margot and them, back to alcohol, back to the occasional joint. I'll surrender to the darkness, I'll shake hands with the Devil, I'll pay for one more dance and get my money's worth, I'll travel a few more stop-and-go miles on the road to total and complete self-destruction.

Sam shows up around four. My man Sam, not so friendly any more now that I've gone and rumpled his chicks' feathers. He's not your typical pimp, Sam. Young, a little too educated and savvy to be from the streets. Probably one of those thousands of Cheikh Anta Diop University graduates who have to find informal lines of work in these lean times--a *maitrisard*. "You're my best customer," Sam tells me as he tries to size me up on the porch, this being the first time he sees me out of his dive and in broad daylight, the first time we're not talking across a bar. "I'd hate to go and mess that relationship up." He smiles, cocks his head to the side, taps the holster in his armpit, draws me in--good student of the best genre films, a toothpick for extra nonchalance would have made the pitch perfect. "On the other hand, I have to try and keep my girls happy..."

"200,000 CFA minus 57,000 for the window," I propose, cutting through the chase.

We shake on it.

"Don't be a stranger," Sam says after pocketing the money.

I spend the next two days working on Salimata, going back to the drawing board, deconstructing her case from top to bottom, breaking it down to pieces, looking at it from different angles. The effort keeps me busy, it keeps me going, it reinforces the illusion that I'm working on myself, that I'm finding myself, that everything will be all right, that I can just tuck the past couple of days neatly away in one of the folds of my memory. I want to succeed, to lay eyes on Salimata again. Once I know who she is I'll know who I am. Maybe then I can make a change, that much-needed change. Maybe then I can get it together, slow down, stop running, find peace, live a normal life.

What's killing me is that nothing can explain what Salimata did. We were happy, we were good, we were fine before the day that man showed up for the ride up the Mamelles hill. The more I think about it, the more I'm convinced that he's not my dad, my true dad, my real dad. If the man who fathered me didn't want me around he wouldn't have waited four years to get rid of me. I felt no connection to the man in the blue car. He looked nothing like me. He hated me, he wanted me gone, he wanted Salimata for himself. The act was theirs--they were together in it, they did it in concert, they were both physically present--but the decision was his. How that man had enough sway over Salimata to make her give me up, I don't know. They weren't married, they weren't living together. Salimata had her own place. She came and went freely. She worked. She had work clothes and house clothes. She did her lips, her nails and toes. She sprayed on perfume. She put yellow ribbons in her hair. She was a single mom, she was making it, she was doing okay. What could have happened?

We used to live by a stadium. Assane Diop, Demba Diop or Abasse Ndao, near Tilene Market? I haven't been able to figure out which. Just remember looking at the towering banks of lights with awe, the awe of a little boy for all things mechanical and tall and complicated and bright. So I'm a Dakar kid. Like Zak, Ouzin, all the *talibes*. I know that much about me. I can feel the city deep inside, deep in my bones. *Ndakarou Ndiaye*. I can breathe it. It's mine. I belong in it. It's crazy, it's fast, it's dangerous, it grows too quickly for its own good but I love it, I revel in it, I know its rhythms, its people, its lingo. I've been all over it and the surrounding suburbs--by bus, car, taxicab, foot. I've been to the Archives, City Hall, the schools, the hospitals and private clinics armed with only two names--Salimata and Christophe Diouf--and my year of birth: 1971. Diouf is, of course, one of Senegal's most common surnames. There are thousands of Salimata Diouf. It took me ten months to find the four who had sons called Christophe. Everything involving the bureaucracy in this country of mine is slow and disorganized, everything takes patience and money and faith. Four matches, four birth certificates, four Salimatas, four wild goose chases, the last of which led me to the closed door in Mbour. I must assume that Diouf wasn't Salimata's last name. Maybe it was just my father's, handed down to me. Then the matches--Salimata X + Christophe Diouf--jump into the hundreds.

What is it I haven't done? Where is it I haven't looked? All the town's used-car dealers are on the lookout for a big, blue, boxy car from the late sixties or early seventies. The Foyer was shut down long ago. A developer bought it, and it's slated for demolition. I was there only once since I came back, getting goose bumps, feeling sick to my stomach, not caring for one second to go past the fence. Of the four American missionaries who founded it and ran it, only one remains alive: the headmaster, the *buki*-in-chief--Pops is what everybody used to call him. Pops isn't around any more. Hasn't been for a while. He's in New Orleans, finishing his days in a nursing home. I went to see him once after Vernon died. I drove all the way from D.C. to confront Pops. He claimed to know nothing about Salimata. "You were dropped at the gate," he told me.

"That can't be the whole story," I insisted.

Pops just shrugged me off. It was hard to be there, to look at him, to be in the same room as the man who used to treat me like his pet, his human toy. His hands, his smell--it was all coming back to me in the cramped space, the crucifix on the wall like an insult, a bloody joke. "I remember you very well, you know? You were tough. Always fighting back. You and that little girl, Karine. You guys were my favorites."

Pops was looking at me with his pales eyes, breathing slowly, his mummy flesh loose around his neck, his lips one thin orange line, hair sprouting from his ears, his long fingernails shining in the light, the hint of a smile in his raised eyebrows. Taunting me. Extracting shreds of pleasure from my disarray. Having his way with me one last time. Too close to death now to fear anything and anyone. The *bukis* never got caught for what they did to us. They never paid a dime or a single drop of blood for their crimes.

"You'd better pray I don't come back," I told Pops.

I found Pops. I found Karine. I helped Ibrahim find Zak, even if it was too late. So I know I'm good at what I do. Yet when it comes to Salimata I can't seem to get anywhere.

54

The cop Diack is at my door bright and early. "Have a moment?" he asks, eyes blinking, voice soft and low, looking just as lost and out of his element as he did a few mornings ago at the Sows'.

I allow him in. He sits, takes his teacher glasses off, rubs his eyes. "Just wanted to get your version of the events."

"Didn't Mr. Sow come in for his deposition?"

"He did." Diack puts his glasses back on. He can't seem to stop blinking. "But I'm not completely satisfied, Mr. James. There are eight bodies to account for, including that of a child. There may be killers on the loose. So do you mind?"

I tell him the story Ibrahim and I agreed upon, the same stuff Ibrahim dished out to Marie--the script, the magic powder: "The abductors called. Ibrahim and I went to the island. A small army was waiting for us on the beach. They held us at gunpoint, took the money, and started fighting among themselves. Ibrahim and I ran for cover. Men started dropping left and right. The survivors took the loot and got back on their boats. We looked for Zak and found him dead inside the bunker."

"How many men total?"

"A lot. I didn't count."

"How many boats?"

"Two pirogues."

"Why did you hand out the money?"

"It's not like we had a choice."

Diack sighs. "If what you're saying is true those men would have killed you and Mr. Sow along with Zak. They would

55

have shot you as soon as you set foot on the sand. Why leave witnesses?"

"After the dust settled they did look for us briefly. Guess they got nervous."

"Where were you and Mr. Sow during the shootout?"

"Hiding in rocks just above the beach. Waiting in the dark."

"You stayed together the whole time?"

"Yes."

Diack chuckles. "Mr. Sow claims that you went your way and he went his."

I shrug. "We hid in the same general area. It's not like we shared a rock and held hands throughout. What difference does it make?"

Diack grunts. He doesn't like me. He doesn't like my attitude. He's just fishing around, really. Grasping, throwing blind lines, beating the bushes to see what comes out. He knows from instinct that something ain't kosher. He can smell a rat long before he sees it, he's been on the job long enough to know when stuff doesn't add up. The meeting with Ibrahim and Ketus, the lawyer, must have frustrated him to no end. He probably got pushed around a little. Maybe pressure's already being applied from above for Diack to give Ibrahim a wide berth even as he looks closely into the Zak business. Ibrahim is no peon. He is a *borom dole*, a strong man among strong men, all but untouchable behind his money and connections. There's no confronting him directly. There's no squeezing him, there's no making him feel the heat. For Diack it's a fine dance, a balancing act. Eight bodies in one night is a lot, even for Dakar. The papers are having a field day, the public is clamoring for answers. Diack must heed his bosses' wish and still come up with results at the end of the day. It's a fine dance and I'm a much smaller fish, I'm a softer target, I'm all Diack's got. "Why are you here, Detective?"

"Those bodies," Diack says.

"They're not mine. I didn't kill anybody."

"Do you own a firearm?"

"I lost it. It dropped in the water during all the hoopla."

"Was Mr. Sow carrying a weapon?"

"No."

Diack nods, as if he had anticipated my answers. "I did a background check on you," he reveals after a while. "You were a police officer in Washington, D.C. once."

"I was."

He looks me in the eye. "There were a couple of allegations against you: excessive use of force; missing evidence money. Is that why you left America?"

It hits me in the stomach. It bothers me that I could be exposed so quickly, that so much information about me is out there, for the whole world and a smalltime cop like Diack to see. I wanted a new beginning when I left the force and decided to move to Senegal. I wanted to leave a bunch of dirty stuff behind. Stuff I'd rather forget about. How deep has Diack been digging? How hard would it be for him to get a hold of my old boss, Lieutenant Reyes, or Mazakis, my old partner--people at Internal Affairs, even? "All the cases against me were dismissed. '*Nolle prosequi.*' They could never prove a thing. Couldn't even gather enough steam to prosecute. I left because I felt it was time. My father had just passed away. I needed a break."

Diack gets up. "I don't believe anything you've been telling me," he says bluntly, shedding his meekness and vulnerability as one takes off a coat. "You want to know what I believe? I believe that something rather serious went down on the big Madeleine and you were a part of it. I believe there's more to this than a mere kidnapping."

I get up in turn. Though not much taller than Diack, I'm wider and thicker, and I try my best to tower over him in true Ketus fashion, to press the detective out, to intimidate him physically, man to man, to make him understand that I'm no punk, no flunky, no weakling, no *dunguru*, that it's not gonna go down like that, that if I'm going down I'm ready to go down swinging. "It's not what you believe," I tell him, stealing a line often heard from my own perps on my own beat back in the day. "It's what you can prove."

"I'm not going away," the detective assures me. "I'll get to the bottom of this. You can count on that."

"See you around," I say before slamming the door shut.

After Diack leaves I make the hole under the guava tree much deeper and drop my gun and ammo box in it. Not the safest hiding spot but it'll have to do for now. At least one of Diack's cadavers has a bullet of mine in it. I should have thrown the damn thing in the ocean when Ibrahim got rid of the diamonds.

Feeling naked without a piece, I go get me a new one from a downtown dealer named Yasser, the "Fils" in Hachem & Fils. My eyes are on the rearview mirror the whole time. Maybe Diack is already tagging along. Maybe he's put a couple of men on my trail to shadow my every move, try and catch me in the wrong.

Yasser is by himself, singing along a cheesy Julio Iglesias ballad playing on the radio, stretching the last words--

> *Où est passée ma bohèèèème?*
> *Où sont passés mes beaux jouuurs?*

He recognizes me.

"Hook me up," I ask after shaking his hand.

"What happened to the beauty I sold you a year ago?" he wants to know.

"Lost it."

Yasser shakes his head. He's short and portly, with curly hair, a mustache, a greasy spot on his undershirt. His nails are dirty, he sweats a lot. The look in his eyes is a little crazed, a little too intense. But the man knows pistols and handles pistols as if they were precious jewels. "Glock 9?"

"Nothing else will do."

He winks, takes a key, unlocks his big velvety display case, hands me a black handgun over the counter oh-so delicately. The weight, the shape, the feel, the fit are so natural and comforting they warm my heart. I tried one of these babies at the Police Academy over a decade ago and never looked back. It was love at first sight. It was like Luke Skywalker and the laser saber.

Yasser pulls a drawer open. "Did you lose the bullets, too?"

"I did."

He snaps his fingers. "They do get misplaced easily. How about two boxes?"

"Two it is. How's business?"

"Booming. You watch the news lately?"

He cashes me out. Before I hit the steamy sidewalk he's at it again:

C'était le temps des romaaances
C'était le temps des discouuurs

Back at the house, I get a request for a quote over the phone. A man named Seydou--"They call me Big Sey, I own a mattress factory"--is convinced that his wife, Bebe, is cuckolding him with one of her coworkers. "I know it for a fact, man. God is my witness. On my mother's grave. On my children's heads. Bebe threw our wedding vows to the wind, Mr. James. She's running around with the computer guy, Michel, a punk with dreadlocks and tight jeans--I saw them with my own eyes." He pauses, as if the memory is too much, much too much. "Bebe broke my heart, Mr. James. I wanted to kill myself, that day. But God is powerful, yes he is! He told me to stand on my two feet. He told me to fight like a man, to go on living and caring for my children, to refuse to go under. So I'm fighting, Mr. James. I'm trying to build a case against Bebe before hitting her with the divorce papers. I need time-stamped pictures, videos, audio recordings--you name it. I'm gonna take everything: the house, the car she drives, her clothes, her shoes, her gold, her diamonds, her platinum, the kids.... She's not gonna know what hit her. She'll never see it coming."

Big Sey's got just the right blend of anger, outrage, self-importance, and hurt in his voice. I imagine him sitting at a

59

loud desk, wiping his forehead with a white handkerchief, portraits of himself with public figures on the wall. "You should come in," I tell him soothingly. "So we can discuss this face to face. I'll cut you a deal. Sounds like you could use a break."

"The stuff she's taking me through...." he commiserates. "I'm not eating, I can't sleep at night, I've started to lose my hair in the middle.... What's your address?"

Seydou takes it down, gives me his information, asks for a price, says money won't be an issue, gets cold feet as he realizes that his wife's best friend, Nafi, lives two streets down from me. "She's a nosy one, man. Ooh she nosy. I have a big Mercedes, pretty silver, chrome wheels, vanity plates, nothing like it from Dakar to Johannesburg. It'd be just my luck if Nafi saw me. Can't we meet someplace else?"

I'm starting to like the guy. He's funny, he's personable, the case sounds just like what I need at the moment: something easy, something routine, something quick.

"How about the Lido?" Big Sey proposes. "Tonight around 11. Bebe's on a trip. A 'business' trip." Big Sey pauses again, as if he needs to compose himself. I have a hard time keeping a straight face at the other end. "I'll put the kids to bed and meet you out front. It's nice and discreet over there. We can take care of everything."

"Agreed."

He catches me before I hang up. "One last thing, please, Mr. James?"

"Shoot."

"It'd make me immensely happy if you could rough that asshole Michel up a little bit. Teach him some manners. Break his teeth or something, you know?--a leg, a knee.... I wouldn't mind paying extra. Wouldn't mind at all."

"I'll see what I can do," I tell him, laughing openly.

Karine comes over after work. Dinner's on me. Never thought she'd be able to steal away but she appears at seven as promised, traffic and all, smelling lovely, looking great in blue jeans, a pink button-up shirt and flat shoes, a fruit tart for two in her hands, her hair in the trademark ponytail. The irony in her eyes is muted. It's getting duller, softer, more forgiving each time we meet.

I go for a hug.

She kisses my cheek. "How was your day?"

"Too long."

It's Karine's first time at the Point-E house. I get almost emotional watching her walk around, go inside room after room, stroll in and out of the garden. She does it naturally, without asking--just gets up and goes explore. It feels like she belongs here, right here, with me.

The house is big, too big for a single man. I bought it with an eye on the future, an eye on a wife and a family. I bought it to plant my roots solidly into the African soil. Nothing fancy: a big cube at the end of a leafy cul-de-sac, shells on the wall, flowers on beds street side, a copper plaque by the entrance door, two stories, four bedrooms, a decent backyard. It's the first thing in my life that I feel I truly own. I have plans for it: a gazebo for the back, higher walls for the front, a pool table for the living room, a bigger kitchen, an automatic door for the garage. And it is a little too dark for my taste. I'll punch in a few more windows, knock some of the walls down, give it all the light in the world and that wide-open feel, that welcoming feel.

"You're not doing too back for yourself," Karine says.

"Thank you."

"What are you making?"

"Grilled chicken and a salad."

"Sounds good."

"You hungry?"

"I am."

"Something to drink?"

"Juice."

I make myself a stiff one and light a cigarette before I get the grill going on the small verandah flanking the kitchen. Overlooking the garden, it's furnished with a couple of straw chairs and a table. Karine busies herself with the salad, cutting tomatoes, shaving corn, slicing avocados, dicing carrots, mixing a vinaigrette. She's done way before me. Half of the chicken is seasoned with nothing but salt, pepper, and mustard. The other half gets the jerk treatment, a fiery Vernon specialty that I'm trying to recreate on my own for the first time as an homage to the old man. "Need help with that?" Karine asks.

"I got it. You just relax."

She kicks her shoes off and folds her legs under her. She's so natural, so together it makes me shake my head with wonder. Karine, the first person on earth whom I feel I know, truly know. The first woman I could give my all to without any misapprehension, any regret, holding nothing back.

It's nice and quiet. Seven is when the city starts slowing down, really. "It's when the *djinns* come out," Salimata used to tell me. "When all the little boys make sure to rush home and be quiet and extra-good."

I get misty-eyed from the thought and blame it on the smoke. Darkness chases the sunlight away. Karine looks at me. I look at her. Her lashes are long, luscious, perfect. She flashes those crazy green eyes at me and smiles. She knows now that I'm not just passing through. That whatever brought me back to Senegal will keep me around. I can feel her opening up even as she sits without speaking. Something in the air. A connection, a vibe, a gentle pull. It's our moment zero. Our beginning. We're getting somewhere. I can tell.

"I have a ceremony to attend," Karine announces as soon as we're finished eating. "You're coming?"

We take my car. The ceremony is a *n'deup*, an exorcism of sorts. It's taking place on a very small beach along the Route de Ouakam, between the Mamelles and Ngor. "Nabou is her name. She's been coming to the clinic for a very long time. AIDS. Heroin. The cutest two-year-old, Isaac, born with the virus--my godson. Nabou lives in Guediawaye, not far from the clinic. If you can call what she does living. They're all fishermen in her family. Lebous. Go out to sea every morning to fight it off bravely with all the big foreign fishing vessels."

We leave the road and go down an unlighted track. A minaret rises from the bottom, meeting us halfway through our descent, to very striking effect. The village itself is minuscule: clusters of brick homes, raggedy and bare, crisscrossed by sandy lanes; a central place with a gas pump and empty stands; pirogues drying on logs. The moon is full, bright, wonderful. The water is quiet and inviting. The smell of smoked fish is overpowering. The air is thick with the sound of drums.

We park the car and walk toward the circle at the end of the beach. Several men and women are gathered at the foot of the cliff. The four drummers, their *jembes* heavy and tall, are standing together. The men in attendance watch without moving. The women, all dressed in short *boubous* or *tailles-basses* over their *pagnes*, take a few steps inside the circle to join a lone dancer before coming back into the fold.

Karine takes my hand. "Nabou is the one in the middle. They've covered her with animal blood and milk. Sacrifices--a chicken, a red goat, a white sheep--have been made to appease

63

the spirit possessing her. The drums are working her into a trance. She'll dance until she drops, until the realm she's been inhabiting for the past few years gives way to the real world, the true world. Until the spirit that's making her do all these evil things--selling her body, getting high, stealing, getting in trouble with the police, neglecting her son--leaves her be." Karine gets closer, shouting in my ear, her breath hot, her hand not letting go. "That woman with the heavy makeup? A priestess. The heavyset *diongama*--matron--on your right? Nabou's mother, Soxna. All Nabou's siblings are here. Only her dad, Doudou, wrote her off. The rest of the family is claiming her back. Nothing else worked. They know they can't cure AIDS. It's her addiction they're going after. Her mental illness. Her depression."

The beat builds into a crescendo. Nabou leaps high in the air. She throws her arms up, she raises sand with her soles, she starts coming out of her clothes. The priestess rushes to shield her body from prying eyes. Nabou works herself into a frenzy, until, exhausted, she drops. The priestess is immediately at Nabou's side, transfixed, holding Nabou's head, spitting rapid-fire incantations.

"It's cathartic all around," Karine says as we walk back to the car. "Nabou is made to feel that her actions are not solely of her own doing--the spirit that possesses her is more than partially responsible; by attending the *n'deup*, her relatives, and the whole village, show their support, their embrace, their will to see Nabou through. Nabou will emerge from the *n'deup* clean and fresh and new and ready for a different life--hopefully."

Tonight I get a goodnight kiss. In front of my house, by Karine's car. A small kiss, gone before it truly lands, gone too quick. I take a deep breath and hold it in, surprised, shocked by the powerful emotions that the little peck unleashes. When Karine asks, "What do you remember?" I realize we've been thinking about the same thing.

"I remember being in a room," I tell her, unable to look at her. "I remember standing in front of you. Undressing. Touching you. Kissing you on the lips. And..."

Karine comes closer. She buries her head in my shoulder. She holds me. She squeezes me.

I go on speaking with my eyes shut, my heart heavy, my voice full of regret and sorrow, sweet sorrow. Sorrow for me, for Karine, for the disgusting things people are capable of doing. "I remember the noises: the voices, the clicks. I remember the flashes. I remember feeling scared. Feeling ashamed. Feeling weird."

"Me, too," Karine says, crying.

The dirt track opens on my right and disappears as it dives below the paved road. Shrubs and dark-green cacti delimit it. I slow down in front of a tall wall, continuing until I find the entrance. Dead bush, ruins, the sea. The Lido is an abandoned spa complex only a few paces from the Palais de Justice. A mere eyesore during the day, the place is a ghost town at night. Heat and the smell of excrement hit me in the face when I pull the window down. No Mercedes, no shiny Benz with "Big Sey" plates. It's a little before 11.

I push the Glock into my belt after getting out of the 404. Parts of the Lido's enclosure have been demolished. Holes gape atop piles of rubble. Under a sheet of dust, the arched entrance bears a faded inscription in blue ceramic. The complex is strewn with detritus and wild vegetation. Half-columns and paved trails sticking out of the earth for a few yards at a time are the sole remnants of gardens. Two swimming pools rot below a short flight of stairs.

I get back behind the wheel. Before I get a chance to turn the engine on two sets of lights leave the main road and speed down the track, coming straight toward me. Only then do I realize how big of a trouble I'm in.

I get out of the car and whip the Glock out of my belt. I look for a place to hide, crossing the decrepit garden and running all the way inside the *bains* through a heavy iron door

65

stuck open. My feet scatter balls of dust, sheets of plaster, pebbles, larger debris that fell off the high and vaulted ceiling. Every step, every move, every noise has an echo. The only light comes from an intact stained-glass window shaped like a half-sun. Moon rays beam through the heavy air before losing themselves on the walls and the floor.

I hear shouts, commands, feet that come after me, running men--how many of them? A timeworn counter is backed against the center of the wall, too small to provide shelter. On the left side of it another opening gapes, sucking me in. Sweat starts pouring down my forehead.

It's the actual *bains*: a large, rectangular pool surrounded by cement benches and rotten lockers. Because of the busted glass dome it's not as dark, the air not as stale. I jump into the empty pool feet first and turn to face the door, taking position, holding the Glock with both hands, elbows on a cracked tile.

The steps get closer and closer. "In here!"

I shoot at everything that comes through that door. Taking my time. Counting my bullets. My head is clear, my hands are steady, my aim is straight. Three men drop one after the other, on top of one another, almost too easily. They never make it past the antechamber. There's something familiar about them--their boots, T-shirts, fatigues; the way they move. It just doesn't come together right then. I'm too busy aiming, shooting, counting, feeling as close to death as I've ever been--this just might be it. How many, Lord? How many of them?

"Go!" a voice barks on the other side. "Go!" "Go!" But the three felled bodies block the entrance. Anybody coming behind them will have to jump, leap high or dive in, and here I am waiting with my head clear, my aim steady, my arms strong, my hands one with the pistol, a sharpshooting extension of me, my heart calm and peaceful, my blood hot and hungry for more blood. Here I am waiting and ready for anything. Here I am ready to die.

An arm appears through the opening, holding a snub-nosed machine gun, proving at once a very elusive target.

The burst of firepower it releases is deafening, erratic, high, low, sideways, way above my head, then getting dangerously close. Another arm, another machine gun stick through and start spraying. Hot nozzles spew red-orange flames. Clouds of nefarious bees rush toward me, surround me. Bullets poke the walls, shatter ever more pieces from the glass dome, chip the faience wall and engravings.

I keep my eyes on the targets even as I get stung in the scalp, cheek, forehead, right shoulder, right arm--by fallen debris, ricocheting projectiles? The Glock barks. Two more bullets, two misses. I now have the answer to the "how many" question: too damn many.

The weapons dropped by those three men lying a few feet from me look more appealing by the second. They offer a glimpse of hope, the only promise of escape. I'm waiting for the killers to ease up on their triggers, I'm ready to climb out of the pool and crawl across the littered floor of the *bains*, I'm ready to fight for my life when the fire suddenly stops. The arms disappear. The machine guns go quiet. The steps retreat. Silence replaces the voices.

I know they haven't given up. I know they won't leave until I'm dead. They came to kill, finish, terminate, exterminate, neutralize, lay waste. I know they've gone back outside to find another approach, devise another plan, wait for me out in the open. Maybe they'll set the building on fire. Maybe they'll smoke me out like a rat. Maybe they'll blow me to pieces with a grenade.

Might as well jump, the voice inside my head tells me. Might as well jump. You're no punk. You're no pussy. You don't sit around and wait for shit to happen.

Jump I do, forgetting everything I was taught at the Academy, getting out of the pool fast, sticking the Glock in my belt, grabbing not one machine gun--Uzis, up close they definitely look like Uzis--but two, bursting through the door, jumping out, going, going, going, opening fire indiscriminately, covering all sides, not slowing down even once through the antechamber, the small corridor, the heavy iron door, not stopping to look at shadows or sniff around corners until I'm out, out where it's cool and I can breathe again, out where I finally see the men for who they are--they're Ibrahim's men, of course, who else, Ibrahim's men here to cut all loose ends, true *dungurus* if there ever were ones: Boris, Becaye, and them.

They're waiting. Behind the monstrous, ever-present trucks. Behind fallen pieces of the Lido's enclosure. Behind palm trees and heaps of trash.

I take cover, letting out short bursts lest they creep up on me, the *dungurus*, the assholes, Boris, Becaye, and them. And so the game begins again, the lethal, lethal game. Under the moon, the sea behind me, absurdly, drenched in sweat, a stupid, stupid game. A game to which there won't be any winners, no, not now, not tonight.

Rising above the ruckus, sirens pierce the air, faintly at first but coming close, coming fast. I hear them from behind the iron door. Ibrahim's boys hear them, too. They hear them and they pause. They pause and they look. Then, taking a page from Momar's book, they rush the trucks, scrambling to get inside, shooting my way, running backwards, the cowards, the dumbasses, the sons of bitches--*domu xatj*--shooting even after they're inside the trucks.

I come from behind the door--might as well jump--and follow them on the track, letting loose all my rage and anger, giving free rein to the savage in me under the black sky and the silver stars, firing freely, not counting bullets any more, not stingy with them now that it's over. I let it all fly without any visible result.

Ibrahim chose well. The trucks are monstrous, yes, and they are fast. They outrun the police cars, and, on slow terrain, almost face to face on the bouncy track, they outmaneuver the police cars the same way the killers overpower the cops with their heavy artillery, forcing the flimsy cherry tops out of the way, shattering their windshields, riddling their side panels with holes. Once the trucks are on the asphalt it's over.

All shot up, the 404 is in no shape to be driven. I take my shirt off and wipe the two Uzis I've been using. I run toward the end of the garden and, standing at the edge of the cliff, I throw the Glock as far into the ocean as I can. Then I turn the 404's headlights on and go stand in front of the hood with my arms high in the air, showing my empty palms.

By the time the cops get to me they're shaken, edgy, scared, pumped, ready to mess someone up. Nearly crashing into me, they leap out, yell superfluous orders, take me down, pat me, rough me up, handcuff me, throw me in the back of one the cars.

Victor Hugo is only 15 minutes away. The Brigade Criminelle headquarters occupy the old Ministère de la Santé, a stucco building dating from the colonial era. I'm booked unceremoniously. I'm pushed, still shirtless, into a full holding cell. I'm dirty, I smell like gunpowder, I have cuts and scrapes all over but nothing is broken, nothing is missing, I'm alive, I'm breathing, all is not lost.

The perps eye me for a while. They try clumsy attempts at conversation and decide--wisely-- to leave me alone.

Diack comes for me around 2 a.m.--was he out chasing crime or did they rouse him from his sleep with the news of a big catch? He pulls me out of the dispiriting cell and hands me a white T-shirt. "Rough night, huh?"

My voice fails me. I can only grunt in answer. We go up a flight of stairs toward a corridor flanked with dozens of doors, all hermetically closed, passing several before Diack picks one. He pushes me toward the room's only furnishings, a small wooden desk flanked by two office chairs. "Coffee?"

"Please."

He leaves, comes back with two paper cups. The coffee is nice and sweet. Karine, the evening, the dinner in my garden seem like a lifetime ago. I push her out of my mind and steel myself for what's coming.

"So?"

"I was out at the Lido to meet a potential client. Two trucks full of armed men popped out of nowhere and started giving chase. I hid in the bushes until you guys showed up."

Diack sighs so deeply you'd think I just broke his heart. He palms his chin, he rubs his cheek, he considers his coffee as if he's looking for inspiration, as if the truth is floating in the dark liquid. "I've got three more bodies on my hands," he says finally. "I'm not up for more games, Mr. James."

"I want a lawyer," I declare.

Diack shakes his head, looking almost sorry for me. "Where do you think you are?"

I gulp down the last of my coffee.

Diack leaves again. In his place three dudes join me in the room. Big, black, mean, ready, uniform pants, wife-beaters, batons, rubber hoses, gloves. It's tenderizing time. I put up a good fight, but once they have my hands pinned behind my back there's only so much I can do. My lips are the first to get busted. Then my nose, facial bones, a rib or two. I clench my teeth and try to anticipate the punches.

It goes on for a good hour. Then Diack comes back in and asks a few questions. If he doesn't like the answers, which happens quite consistently, his buddies are called in again. I take refuge somewhere in my head, somewhere out of reach, summoning all I've got, all the determination I can muster, excluding all other emotions, focusing only on the will to survive, the primal need to remain unbowed, my pride, my dignity as a man. I'm safe in the knowledge that this still is the police, that there are places they won't go. Beat me down, yes. Pliers, hammers, blowtorches, saws, steaks for dogs, no. Diack is a cerebral cop. He's a thinker. He knows that what's he putting me through will only take him so far, yield him so much result. From where I'm sitting, it's just a matter of going the distance.

Diack busies himself all through the morning. He's at the Lido crime scene, at the Intérieur for a warrant, at my Point-E villa for a top-to-bottom search--a search from which he comes back all but empty-handed and profoundly unhappy. The guava tree hasn't let my down yet.

It's well into the next day that Diack decides to ship me to Rebeus, Dakar's only penitentiary. "You leave me no choice," he says.

"I'm an American citizen," I remind him, speaking around the cuts in my lips. "You can't just go and throw me in jail."

Diack's laugh is short and joyless. He seems to have gained stature, my little blinking detective. "Try me," he says.

The manually operated gate opens onto a paved courtyard flanked by offices. The high walls topped by barbed wire induce a premature darkness. Pushed into the first building, I go through expedited admission formalities with something of an intellectual detachment. The guards and the clerks all wear fatigues and combat boots. Most speak Diola among themselves. "Welcome to Cent Mètres," says Coly, the guard who's leading me to my cell. A second gate separates the administrative area from rows of two-story cellblocks pushed against the outer ring of a yard. Prisoners are out, walking alone or huddled in loose groups under the watchful eye of guards and a lone sentry inside a mirador. No trees, benches, or equipment of any kind. No soccer field or basketball court. We enter the third building on the right, which up close resembles a military barrack with a front door leading directly to a row of cells after a surveillance post equipped with a desk and telephone. Number 66 is small, narrow, damp. Bunk beds on each side, sink and toilet in the middle. I drop my blanket and bar of soap on one of the thin mattresses.

71

Out in the yard several men approach me one after the other. They all want something: a handshake, a talk, a cigarette. They all leave empty handed. Dinner is a watery lentil soup poured into a scratched plastic bowl. At nightfall inmates line up for a count in front of each cellblock. Once inside a single guard pushes all the gates locked, starting with the last one.

I'm shacking with three other prisoners. We all eye one another warily. A man called Ino is the first to break the ice. He looks like a teenager: all skin and bones, the color of copper, curly hair, long face and deep-set eyes, peculiar eyes, eyes burning with intelligence and mischief. "I'm Jacques Mesrine and Papillon rolled in one," he boasts in guise of introduction. "I'm the boss around here." The other two convicts, Laye and Iba, agree to Ino's bombast with a nod. *Dungurus* are everywhere. They follow me wherever I go. They've infiltrated every stratum and nook of Senegalese society. There's no escaping them.

Too tired to chitchat, I hit the sack.

The next morning, Ino is easy to find. He's standing in the shade, holding court, Iba and Laye at his side. People come to him with a problem and leave happy. Ino is a fixer. He wheels and deals. He's found a way to turn his time into money.

The way he smiles and shakes my hand reminds me of Sam. "Chris. My man."

"So you're the boss, huh?"

"I'm the boss."

"Can you get me a cellphone?"

"Cellphones are half a mil a piece. Minutes not included."

"Not ready to buy."

Ino smiles again. His teeth are small and sharp. He's a fantastic businessman. "I can let you use mine. First call is free--that's for you to make payment arrangements, mostly."

He produces the thing from his pocket when we're back inside 66. I call Karine at the clinic, disrupting her closing-time routine, choosing my words carefully. She panics nonetheless.

She's scared. She's horrified. "I need you to go to my house," I tell her. "The key taped to the bottom of the mailbox opens all the locks on all the doors. Go in my bedroom. Lift the tile under the left foot of my bed, headboard side. Open the safe. Take my passport and all the cash. Keep everything with you until I find a way to get out of here." I give her the combination and start making small talk.

Diack asks for me later that day. We meet in a closed room in a separate building, the A building, as in "administration." He has one of the guards remove the handcuffs. The detective looks fresh, alert, ready for his overnight shift. "I can hold you here forever," he tells me.
"You have nothing on me."
"It's just a matter of time."
"You don't have time," I remind him. "Crack your case now or watch it disappear right in front of your eyes."
"Think you know everything about police work, don't you?"
"I know enough. I was a cop once."
"A corrupt one. A dirty one."
"Don't believe everything you hear."
"No fire without smoke."
Diack takes his glasses off and rubs his eyes. He's getting frustrated with me once again. Wishes his muscle men could come and give me a run for my money. Tries a different approach. "How about we ship you back to where you came from, Mr. James? Revoke your work permit, cancel your private investigator license, make you persona non grata. Send you off with nothing but the shirt on your back. House, money, business--all gone. Bar you from reentering the country. Whatever brought you here slipping out of reach. Forever."
I shrug.
Diack gets up to leave. More than contempt, disgust shows on his face--disgust, irritation, anger, the repulsion an honest, hardworking, straight-and-narrow man feels toward bad apples, petty criminals, lowlives, losers. Diack must really think

73

I'm a scumbag. I'm surprised to find out that I care, that I'd like nothing better than to prove him wrong. "Last chance," he goes.

"I'm not what you think," I say.

Diack walks away.

Karine is not too thrilled. She tells me as much on Friday, which is visitation day. In a cavernous room that looks like Sandaga Market at noon, row upon row of benches, fans on the ceiling, the air thick and heavy, children running around, *boubous* and scarves, laughter and tears, hugs and entwined fingers, furtive kisses, prayers, curse words, joy and despair, boredom and excitement, guards on the wall and inside the aisles. "You don't belong here," Karine says above the brouhaha. I look a little rough, I know. My body still aches, my face is still swollen and bruised from the Brigade Criminelle beatdown. Karine and I don't know what to say to each other at first. One step forward, two steps back.

Karine is jumpy. She keeps throwing quick glances around. This is all new to her, it's her first time inside Rebeus. The whole country knows about Cent Métres. It's hard to miss, sitting at the bottom of the hill leading to the Plateau as it is. Every time you go or leave downtown by way of the Corniche you see the high stone wall, the mirador with the lone guard, the barbed wire. Cent Métres is where all the bad people go: criminals of all ilk, political prisoners, captured rebels from the Casamance separatist movement.

"What exactly did you do?"

"It's not what I did, Karine. It's what I know."

She crosses her arms and gives me a probing look. A good minute and a half, it lasts. The green eyes look deep inside me, searching for a reason to believe, a reason to be here, a reason to care. For a moment there it seems as though Karine is about to get up and leave, forget about the whole thing, go back to her clinic and divorcee life, back to what she knows. It would have been a good time for me to get on my knees and start begging. A smart man would have come up with plenty of

74

smooth and sticky and sugary things to say. I'm not that type of man. I'm not in the mood. I just can't find the words.

The moment passes. Karine stays. Maybe it's that evening together, our breakthrough, our little kiss by the car. Maybe it's the memory of our very first day, that morning at the Foyer when she took my hand and ran, when the flock surrounded us, made us one with it, went this way and that, riding the wind. "You're gonna have to trust me if you want me to help you, Chris."

I'm hunched over, resting on my elbows, looking down, staring at the dirty floor, far, far away from the humidity, the benches, the noises, the colors. Karine slides an arm around my shoulders. The gesture is both comforting and reassuring. Karine's big heart. A woman's infinite strength. A backbone.

I'm alone in this country of mine. Nobody to turn to but Karine. It's against everything I know and everything I am to be straightforward, to be forthcoming, to be open, to be honest, to conceal nothing. I'm a liar, a thief, a crook, a manipulator, a hypocrite. That's who I am. That's what I do. There's not a good bone in my body. But I'm also beginning to understand that there's something wrong with the way I think, the way I live, how I look at the world. I'm beginning to realize that I can't keep hiding in plain sight, under the bright sunshine. I don't want to end up alone. I don't want to lose Karine, destroy the little we've managed to accomplish. I don't want to build on sand. I have to get it right from beginning to end.

It's hard to open up. It's something I've never done before. Not with Vernon. Not with any male or female friend. Not with any peer, mentor, colleague, superior, authority figure, father figure, surrogate mom. Not with any other human being. But I try my best to do it. I look at Karine straight in the eye and I tell her as much as I can. Right there, in the middle of that nasty hall, on a long and hard bench, among dozens of other prisoners and their visitors. I do it. I let go. I become a new man. And it's scary at first.

Karine listens. She focuses both on content and delivery. Not just the events, the highs and lows, the twists and turns of the past days, but my voice, my eyes, my posture, all the little nonverbal clues--she would have made a good cop, a much better cop than me. Paranoia and shame hold me back a little: I say nothing of the man--or men--killed on the Madeleine, the stash under the guava tree, the "Fatou thing," Tyson's ugly end. That's as honest as I can be for now. That's how much of me I can bear to show. Karine is no fool. She knows what line of work I'm in. She can read between the lines. She can figure out for herself that my hands will get dirty every once in a while, that a man doing what I do has got to go the distance. I spare her the details. I want her to understand me, to know what happened. I don't need her to loathe me, to be afraid.

When I'm done, Karine has one thing to say: "Just tell me what you need me to do."

A few uneventful days follow. I stick to myself, mostly. Rebeus is a sorry jail gone global. Chinese, Lebanese, Palestinians, Syrians, Liberians, French, Cape Verdians, Nigerians.... Adventurers of all breed sweat it out together in the crucible. Cards, chessboards drawn on the dirt, workout fiends lifting one another, improvised soccer games, fights, cliques along racial lines. Life is rough, empty, sad, boring. It's not so much a matter of violence or gangs or drugs or brutality. It's more a problem of poverty, of lack of resources, of crumbling infrastructure, of overpopulation--leaks, mold, dust, floods, malnourishment, aimlessness, flare-ups, hopelessness, indigence. Inmates with mental illnesses roam freely. Homosexuality, largely frowned upon on the outside, is practiced a little more openly. Diseases are everywhere: TB, hepatitis, HIV, malaria. The rations are nasty. The water is bad. Both prisoners and their holders have nothing. That's where the Inos of the world swoop in and sweep up. Ino is a utility knife of a man, providing all kinds of useful goods and services: better food, medicine, *yamba*, palm wine, radios, jobs, clothes, shoes, and, of course, precious phone calls. Cash is worthless inside Rebeus. Ino, the dirty guards, all the *dungurus* get paid through an elaborate remittance system involving Western Union and money orders made out to trusted relatives by the inmates' people. Ino is profiting more from his jailhouse activities than from the armed robberies that got him inside Rebeus. The men involved in his ring will be millionaires by the time they get out. The guards who take his bribes and facilitate his trade more than make up for their risible salaries.

Diack, true to his word, doesn't come back. But I can feel his hand behind Warden Cabral's decision to throw me in the Hole after my first ten days at Rebeus. "For what?" I ask.

"Shut up," Coly tells me.

So down in the Hole I go. And it is, from the start, everything it's made out to be: small, suffocating, dispiriting, dangerous, confusing, confining. I lose track of time. I talk to myself. I bang my head against the walls. I experience anxiety attacks, panic attacks, asthma attacks. I steal companionship from the guards who come to hose me down, dump my shit bucket, throw my food across the floor. I live mostly in my mind, inventing millions of ways to kill Ibrahim Sow, relishing scenarios of rampage, murder, and mayhem. "You don't belong here," I hear Karine telling me over and over. "You don't belong here."

With nothing to do but think, I travel inside my mind. Back in time, all the way back to my childhood. Everything I am, everything I've done, everything that happened to me can be traced back to Salimata's betrayal. That ride in the blue car was the one defining moment of my existence. Salimata gave me away to a pack of man-eating hyenas. The hyenas violated my body and destroyed my spirit. Vernon came and saved me, but much damage had been done. I bear very powerful, deep, resilient scars. I relish loneliness. I walk alone. I set myself apart. I embrace all things dark, dangerous, forbidden, taboo. I have no love for my brother. I have no moral compass. I have no use for religion. I am a lost soul trying to make sense of itself and the world even as it roams it. I am a soul that doesn't like itself very much.

"You don't belong here." In many ways I wish I could have gotten a chance. Can't help thinking that this isn't the real me, that I'm better than this, that I should aspire to more, to bigger, to deeper, to higher, to more profound. I shouldn't let what my mother and the Foyer priests did to me affect my worldview, infect my every decision, inform my every action. I've become a person who uses, kills, abuses, hates, steals, schemes, and lies only because those were the things that were taught to me, those were what stuck, those got to me before anything, those are the ingrained values, those were the first lessons to etch themselves on the template, those form the core. They're old habits, dear friends, familiar things, beaten paths. They're what worked for me.

How much longer, I wonder, will they work for me? Can I keep a woman this way? Can I hold on to a friend? Can I raise a child? Can I progress in the world?

Down, deep down, way down in the Hole, I have an epiphany of sorts. Something happens. Something that started with the decision to trust Karine. Something new. Not peace, not yet, but a definite change. A move toward more self-knowledge, more understanding. Maybe even a little acceptance. There may be hope for me. There may exist a different road to travel.

It's not an easy thing, that epiphany. It only sets the ground for a battle between the person I am and the one I should have become, the one I would have become had I had been left alone, had Salimata not abandoned me, had the hyenas not had their way with me. The epiphany only opens the door to a world of confusion. It shines a light on my inner dichotomy, my torment, my contradictions. I'm no longer at ease. I'm not sure of anything any more. How to be from now on? Scrub the template clean? What to keep? What to throw? The epiphany is no easy thing.

And the Hole, the Hole is no joke. You either come out of it stronger or utterly defeated. I'm no more ready to confess to Diack when I get out of solitary confinement than when I went in.

On my thirty-fifth day the work crews come back from the outside with the worst rumor ever, starting a buzz that jumps from group to group, becoming more unlikely and polymorph with each minute that passes. Something happened and it's big and ugly and scary, a lot of people have died and it didn't take place at the other end of the earth. This time it happened here. We're all puzzled and a little scared, trying to tune our ears to the outside noises, searching the guards' faces for a glimpse of the truth. We debate, speculate, talk about what we know or might have heard. The polemic has no end. It goes hand in hand with a subtle sense of relief because we're pulled from our contingency. Lockdown comes and goes without anybody making a move toward the cellblocks. The inmates act like they haven't heard the siren after finishing their lentils and exiting the refectory. They remain scattered around the yard and even close to the A building, unfazed by the possibility of punishment. They can't put all of us inside the Hole, the reasoning goes, and we might just riot and resist and demonstrate until somebody speaks to us and tells us what exactly is going on outside these walls.

Finally, from radio news flashes and cellphone conversations, a narrative emerges. The *Joola*, a ferry linking Dakar with Ziguinchor, the biggest city in the south, capsized this morning around 11. Over a thousand people are feared dead, almost everybody on board. It's the first national catastrophe of this magnitude.

A collective moan comes out of our chests. Some people drop to the dirt to cover themselves with dust in a gesture of premature, feminine, cinematic mourning. My immediate neighbor hides his face in his hands. His sister always takes the ferry, he says. It's fast and safer than the rebel-infested road leaving Casamance. "Who's responsible?" someone shouts angrily.

Sleepless night, agonizing night for many. More details in the morning. The ferry was state-owned and run by the military. It was German-made and meant for the calmer waters of lakes, never for the open sea. It was overcrowded. Safety and lifesaving measures were grossly overlooked. The load distribution inside the hold and on the decks was logic-defying. There were no lifejackets or functioning lifeboats.

No crew is allowed outside the jail. The day has been declared an official day of mourning. Conversations in the yard dissect the president's speech and the rescue efforts. Everybody agrees on how things will play out: The government will be dismissed because of the *Joola* catastrophe; heads will roll and roll but nothing, absolutely nothing will change. The country still won't work and the people still won't be able to trust their leaders. They will resume living with the fear that something is going to crash or sink or break or be replaced in a putsch, their lives as mindless and worthless as those of ants being washed away in a flood. The *Joola* is truly like the country, an unfortunate symbol. We're floating on our backs, trapped inside *sunu gal*--our boat--half-dead and half-alive, our own destiny and that of our children, loved ones, and fellow countrymen out of our hands.

Phones are passed around freely, hot with use, slick from the sweat of anxious palms. Minutes and money don't matter today. Our marginality is excessively felt and resented, our physical dissociation from the larger, grieving group almost impossible to bear. There's a longing to be with families, neighbors, countrymen. The frustration is hard to stomach.

Warden Cabral orders a prison-wide search. Radio and cellphones are confiscated, adding fuel to the fire. The guards get on their game. Luckily, incredibly, unbelievably, they do not confine us to our cells.

A little after 3, Ino, who's been hanging out with me all morning, looks at the tower from the corner of his eyes. "Something's going on," he whispers, nostrils flaring like those of a thoroughbred.

"What?"

"The people...." he says, almost too low for me to hear. "They're marching on the Presidential Palace."

"How do you know?"

He puts his palm on my shoulder. "Get ready."

The air is electric. Everybody starts moving at once, as if this had been talked about, agreed upon, discussed, planned, coordinated, rehearsed. The yard is one big wave of unrest, contest, dissension, opportunism. Fists, shouts, slogans, fury, a swelling mob looking for an outlet--sticks, stones, improvised projectiles, anything. By the time Warden Cabral appears on the steps of the A Building with his microphone it's too late, way too late. "Back to your cellblocks! Report to your units immediately!" Things have a momentum of their own already. Things have gotten out of hand.

The guards form a line. The prisoners do, too. Our little group finds itself magically hidden from view.

Ino is the first inmate inside the no man's land. Soon he's at the mirador's foot. He attacks the spiraling stairs. Laye and Iba are close behind, with more men following. Cabral gets apoplectic. "All guards assume position! All guards assume position!" Somebody picks up a rock and throws it at the hanging loudspeaker, making it go quiet with a last crackle amid cheers and laughs, an explosion of joy and defiance that greets the shouts of the angry crowd outside, meets it loud and clear. Louder still are the volley of shots fired by the guards, the clamor of the prisoners trapped in the middle of the open yard, the thump-thump of feet suddenly scrambling for cover, the screams of pain, the thud of dropping bodies. There's shock, disbelief in everybody's eyes.

The tower's steps are steep, cool, narrow. I'm at the top before I know it, before I know how. The fatigue-clad sentry is sprawled on the ground, broken rifle at his side. The sky is welcoming, bright, majestic, tempting, inviting, close at hand, exciting, uplifting, intoxicating, too much. The wind sings in my face. Rebeus's stench vanishes, replaced by the pure, fresh, invigorating marine air. Here are the Corniche and the sun and the sea and the Madeleines. Here is freedom. People are amassed at the gates, facing a handful of guards in riot gear. They're fired up, the people. They're fed up, they're ready. WADE = ASSASSIN! reads a crude sign. SENEGAL = DYSTOPIA rages another. The demonstrators cheer once they see Ino and his band standing on the parapet. They inch closer to the penitentiary's enclosure. The guards move to block them. Did Ino call someone and foment this little trouble from the inside?

Ino takes the frightening leap first. "*Puss-len!*" the marchers yell, trying to give him room as he drops like a mango in rainy season. The *dungurus*, faithful to their credo, follow. Then four prisoners one after the other. Then, suddenly, my turn.

I'm on the ledge. Small bits of cement slide under my soles. Ino and his boys have been absorbed by the colorful crowd. More shots are fired, echoing the ones inside the jail. Sirens blare. Tear gas adds to the confusion. My vision is split between the two theaters, the two sides of the penitentiary's wall. A woman in a bright orange *boubou* clutches her stomach. A stone hits a guard right under his helmet. Rifles cough. Batons fly. Eyes sting. Skin tears. Bones shatter. Blood drips and gushes. Legs give out. The marchers are disbanding, running left, running right, running everywhere, running for their lives. Reinforcements are filing out of the Dial Diop barracks, a mere two miles away. Trucks, troops, attack dogs. "What are you waitin' for?" a panicked voice asks behind me.

I'm on top of the world. I see it all, I take it all in. The heartbreaking spectacle, the debacle, the massacre, the trumping of our freedoms--we have them, they're spelled out beautifully in our Constitution, we just should never ever try to use them, or else....

The air shouts in my face and ears. My battle cry fills my chest, lifts my spirit, gives me wings: Might as well jump, man. Might as well jump. It's fitting, it's symbolic that I should let myself fall into the melee, join the fight. These are my people. These are my brothers. Might as well jump.

I drop fast and straight. It's over before it starts.

I hit the ground running, blind to everything except openings in the crowd and olive-green shirts--the color of the enemy--deaf to everything that's not whizzing bullets or my own labored respiration. People are running away from the Corniche, spilling into the neighborhood that takes its name from the penitentiary. Small streets fly by: busted roads, naked sidewalks, corner public fountains, alleys of sand and pebbles, stagnating water, *boutiku Naars*, tin roofs, shacks of cardboard, plywood and zinc amid sturdier contraptions. I don't know where I'm going. I'm just running, running, ducking, feinting, dribbling, jumping over obstacles, reconnecting with my football days, my DeMatha Catholic School days, running for that touchdown, that perfect touchdown, wincing every time something hurts or stings, thinking, That's it, I've been hit, waiting for the bullet that's going to stop me in my tracks. But the pigs never give chase. They're content to aim their rifles from afar and shoot us in the back. I hear the pop-pop-pop, I hear the screams, I think I see a young man in shorts and sandals freeze on impact and fall behind, fall to the ground, fall dead, I know I should stop and check on him but my legs won't let me, they have a mind of their own, they don't stop until Tilene is in sight, Tilene, yes, the market sprawled smack in the middle of Avenue Blaise Diagne, Tilene, safe Tilene, busy Tilene with all its stands and booths and tables and shoppers and insane traffic--haven't people heard, don't they know what's going on, have they no clue that a mere five minutes away there's murder taking place?

My chest is on fire. My feet weigh a ton. I'm catching my breath, swearing off booze and cigarettes and trying to think about my next move all at the same time. Karine is the first person, the only person who comes to my mind. I can't go back to my house. I can't run all the way to America. I can't show up at the embassy's door. Karine is all I have.

Two of the Dial Diop trucks come out of a side street and start roaming Blaise Diagne. One goes north, one goes south. They stop at opposite crossroads, blocking the avenue. GMI jump out. They're a leaner, meaner version of the regular army. They have rifles, grenades, submachine guns, knives, gas canisters, helmets, shields. They have a license to check, bother, assault, arrest, jail, kill anybody they chose. GMI don't play.

I hide deep inside Tilene, hurrying among the merchants and customers, walking east, away from the avenue. Ten minutes among carcasses on hooks, vegetables, fruits, nuts, bales of T-shirts, tailored outfits, starched *boubous*, shoes on ropes, dried and smoked fish, fresh milk in calabashes--ten minutes and then Tilene is no more.

Convincing a cab to take me to Guediawaye is no small affair even after I'm sitting in the front seat ready to go. Matar is the man's name, caution is his game. He's old, he's been around the block a few times, he senses that something is wrong. Guediawaye is far from here. It's a long, arduous trip involving a few congested bridges and the nightmarish highway--*autoroute bi*. Traffic is going to be crazy. And Matar thinks I'll jump out and run without paying the fare once I get where I'm going. "Let me hold your ID," he proposes.

"I don't have one."

"You talk funny," he says, detecting the accent that most people overlook.

"I'm American," I say.

"Say something in English," he asks.

"My name is Chris," I say.

"That's too easy," Matar goes. "Say something else."

"I don't have time to keep fucking with you," I tell Matar, in plain English, with my sweetest smile. "You're pissing me off, you piece of shit, you old rag, you weasel, you stubborn monkey."

84

Matar smiles in turn. He likes the sound of that. It sounds authentic enough to him. I have him call Karine from his cellphone to ascertain that he'll see his money. He nods and grunts a few times before passing me the phone.

Karine is full of disbelief and conflict. "Chris? Are you all right? Did they free you? How in the world..."

Exhilaration kicks in. The run, Karine's voice, the comfort and safety of Matar's old cab as we get started on our trip, east all the way baby, small streets as long and as far as we can afford it. "Freed? No. Not really."

It's not just Rebeus: The whole country is on fire. My brothers. My people. They're out in the streets. They're venting, marching, shouting, stoning, kicking, burning, fighting, dying. Bene Tali, Niari Tali, Liberté, Dieuppeul, Medina, Ouagouniayes, Castor, HLM, H.A.M.O., Parcelles Assainies, Fass, Medina-Gounass, Diacksao, Camberene, good-old Dalifort--all the populous enclaves, the workman strongholds, the blue-collar lairs. Students shut down Cheikh Anta Diop University and all the public schools. They, as always, take the lead. They congregate, they lock arms, they wield sticks, they chant, they shout, they accuse, they insult, they draw signs, they hold placards. Everywhere Matar and I go, every corner we turn, the fire is getting hot, the fire is boiling, the fire is spreading, the frustration becomes verb, the verb becomes action. SOPI OU-SOPI QUAND?--Change where-change when? They were President Wade's most formidable ally, these students, these youths, these demonstrators, these rebels. They carried him to power in the auspicious year 2000, exasperated with the old regime, the Diouf regime, and 30 years of Socialist Party rule. They were ready for *sopi*--change--the platform, the rallying cry of Wade's PDS. It's been five years since. Five long years of waiting for the promised change. To the students, to a whole lot of people, to the unions and unemployed workers and drought-stricken farmers it's starting to look like more of the same: same marasm; same mediocrity; same empty promises; same incompetence; same graft and corruption; same bait-and-switch. The *Joola* is just a focal point. Senegal's anger has been bubbling for a long time. Now it's finally out in the open, for the whole world to see.

Karine introduces me to her crew and hides me in her medicine locker. The clinic is not so busy today. People are forgetting about their ailments. They're out where it matters: outside, where everybody gathers, where any voice that joins the multitude is welcome. The troops also are out. Not just the GMI but the regular army, the police, the gendarmes--law enforcement in its entirety is all hands on deck. The news channels aren't saying much, for once. The radio stations, public and private, switch to all music-all the time. Stuff is happening faster than they can report. And they know that they'd better be careful what they report. Freedom of the press is etched in our beautiful Constitution but you have to mind what you say--the beautiful Constitution is mostly for show. On paper, we're a fantastic democracy: humanism, universalism, freedom of this, freedom of that, brotherly love, all the gleaming ideals inherited from our ex-colonial masters, those enlightened souls, the French. Yet every time people try to exert, assert, use those guaranteed rights, those birthright rights, the curtain falls, the whip whooshes and slashes, the baton chokes, the tear gas blinds, the jails fill up. SOPI OU-SOPI QUAND?

Karine takes me to her house after closing the clinic. No injuries or fatalities showed up at the gate, though we're certain they're out there. I've seen them with my own eyes, I almost became one, I know they exist. The downtown hospitals must have absorbed them quietly, taken them all in.

Tanks are out, ready to quell any further sign of unrest. The army is focusing mostly on hot neighborhoods and the few roads leading into the city. The Palace is safe. The ministers' homes are safe. The Public Radio and the airport are safe. Everything that matters is safe. Wade declared a State of Emergency and a 10 o'clock curfew. The streets have emptied, the roads are clear. It all sounds and feels and looks like deja vu.

There are a few roadblocks, random searches. We go through the wide net without any problem.

It's my first time inside Karine's place, her cool place, her dream of a place. Yoff Beach, facing the tiny Yoff Island. A brown villa on a small mound, almost totally hidden from sight by an impassable jungle of bougainvillea. One level, a big central living space with all-around windows, bedrooms and a huge kitchen at the periphery. "A French architect built it for himself in the '70s. Kant bought it for his mother when he got his record deal. His mother hated it, bless her soul. We gave her our Almadies house, which was way too grand for me, and took over this one. I got it as part of the settlement. All I wanted, really."

Besides being Karine's ex-husband, Kant is a famous singer. Came from nothing, became a world-class artist, never forgot his roots. One of the country's success stories. Dakar's kids all wear Kant's trademark dreadlocks, his long Rasta hats, his huge sunglasses. Kant. It's hard not to think about him as I come into his house, use his shower, put on his old clothes. "He was supposed to pick these up a long time ago," Karine says. "Of course, he never did. Men...."

I walk around while she fixes us something. Tons of books, films, and music. Plants, candles, local furniture, local art on the shelves and the walls, the ubiquitous portrait of Cheikh Amadou Bamba standing in his white robe, holding prayer beads, staring into the distance. Sembene, of course. The only poster of Kant is that of his first album cover. It's like I'm only now discovering Karine, only now getting inside her mind. Senegal, Senegal, Senegal. She loves it dearly. Loves it with a passion. "You're not doing too bad for yourself, either," I tell her.

Dinner is a quick pasta dish. Anticipating a long night, Karine wants to drink *ataya* and I look, fascinated, as she prepares the bitter beverage. "Vernon taught me a lot about my culture," I say from my seat right inside the kitchen door--Karine is so cool she has a massive fauteuil in her kitchen. "Everything he could. Everything that was readily available. We read, we went to concerts, we watched movies, he spoke Wolof with me. *Ataya* was way past his field of expertise."

"Just watch," Karine says.

The ritual takes a small kettle, ridged glasses, Chinese "gunpowder" tea, sugar cubes, and water. Slow-going charcoal fire is best, but the stove will do. Karine pours a little over half a cup of dried tea leaves into the boiling water. After letting the infusion sit for a few minutes she fills one of the glasses almost to the top before transferring the liquid between the two of them as many times as necessary for thick foam to lace both. Then she pours the tea back into the kettle and lets it sit some more. Sugar is going in next. Then more brewing. The first serving won't be ready for another ten to fifteen minutes.

Karine turns to look at me. She crosses her arms. She leans against the sink. "So what's the plan?"

"I'd like to stay here for a few days. Think about what I'm going to do next."

"How long?"

"One week at the most."

She nods. I understand everything she doesn't tell me just then: she's got as much to lose in this as I do--her house, the clinic, her whole life. All I can do is promise myself not to bury her under my troubles, not to allow harm to come her way--ever. She is precious to me. I hope she knows it without me having to say it. I hope she understands without me being able to profess it. She is very precious to me.

We talk and talk. I take one more step away from my old self. I make good on the Rebeus resolution. I open up, I shed the facade, I drop the mask a little more. "I need to get back at Ibrahim Sow. He's responsible for everything that happened to me. Everything that happened with Zak. I need to make Detective Diack see that."

"Maybe running away was a mistake," Karine suggests. "Maybe you should have told Diack everything from the start."

Again, cadavers float before my eyes. Tyson. The man--men?--I shot on the Madeleine. "It would have just incriminated me more. There's no other way out for me: I go after Ibrahim; I bring back solid evidence that he and that guy Momar were involved in some sort of war for the control of diamonds; I give Diack everything I've gathered in exchange for my freedom."

Karine fills the two glasses with tea. I try mine with cautious lips. The stuff is incredibly strong. "They don't call it 'gunpowder' for nothing."

Karine downs hers in one go. "Where do you begin?"

"Mansour. He's the *dunguru*-in-chief. The wing man. He knows everything." I say it with a straight face, even as I see Marie the way I last saw her, Marie, my Marie, tragic Marie, leaving my house, desperate, disgusted with me, all alone in her pain, her terrible pain. "I can get Mansour to talk any day. He's not going to be any problem. None at all."

Karine raises her eyebrows at that last comment. "There's something in you that scares me a little," she confesses.

"My life hasn't been easy," I reveal in turn. "We didn't have a good beginning, Karine. We weren't dealt the best of hands, you, me, the other Foyer kids. You know that. You were right there with me as it happened. Don't know about you, but I have a dark side."

She returns her attention to the tea. "I turned my back to the Foyer a long time ago, Chris. I just never looked back. It wouldn't have been any good. I have things to show for all that we endured, of course. Things that I'll always carry with me. So don't think I haven't been affected."

I get up and come close. I need to be near, to look into her eyes, to touch her.

"It's a conscious choice," Karine continues. "You don't want your anger to cripple you. You don't want it to run your life, to decide everything you do. You don't want to put it back into the world. You don't want it to do more damage, to wreck more lives."

"It's hard to let go," I say, getting furious even as I say it. "Anger is all I have. I don't know that there's anything else in me. That's what carried me through. Through the years, through time, through everything. That's what made me survive. That's what got me where I am. That's what brought me here, right here, back to you."

There's so much sincerity in my words, so much passion, so much truth, my truth, that Karine doesn't stop me, can't stop me when I take her in my arms and press her against me, a drowning man holding on to a buoy, a lost man looking for the way. It's everything at once: her skin, her warmth, her scent, her hair, her eyes, her lips, her breasts, her beating heart, Rebeus, the escape, this house, the bullets, the dance with death. I want to lose myself into Karine. I want to become one. I want to cross into the future, our future, get started, get there already, get it going, make it happen. I want everything.

But there's no ardor in Karine's kiss. No thrill, no heat, no fire, no passion. It goes no further than her lips, that kiss. Her hands, her fingers, her breath aren't in it. She's a wall of a woman and I'm alone. Alone in what I feel. Alone in what I want. So close. So close.

I'm the first to walk away.

Karine rinses fresh mint leaves. They go into the mixture after it's been sweetened again and flavored with *sucre vanille*. The second serving is lighter than the first, and well worth the wait.

We talk a little more. The kiss, instead of joining us, pushed us a little apart. One step forward, two steps back. Karine tells me how she escaped the Foyer. At 13, with nothing but the clothes on her back, "with the help of Giselle, the Foyer's cook--remember her, no? In the middle of the night, while all the *bukis* were asleep. I got up, I walked out of the dorm, I crossed the playground, I climbed the fence, I cut through the bushes, I got on the road and followed it until I found the spot where Giselle and her husband, Felix, were waiting, the lighthouse guiding me all the way. They took me home. Giselle had been telling her neighbors about me--the little niece from Praia. She got papers mailed out from over there, not just a birth certificate but a passport in my own name, school records, a health sheet, everything--it cost her a fortune, all her savings, money she didn't have. I wanted to call the police, to tell people what the *bukis* were doing in that place. Giselle had promised me that we would take all the children away--it was never about me alone, that's how she got me to agree to the plan. But of course it didn't happen. Giselle was an immigrant, a poor woman, a simple woman. She wasn't about to go to the authorities. I'm the only one she saved. She warned me that if I told anybody who I was and where I came from I'd be taken away and sent back. I felt so bad I had nightmares for months and months afterward. I felt like I had abandoned everybody. I could hear the other children calling me, looking for me. One day, luckily, the nightmares stopped. I took that guilt and turned it into strength. I had found a home, a mother, a father. *Koumba*

Amoul N'deye--the Motherless Koumba of fairy tales--no more. I tried to be the best daughter I could be. Giselle only asked of me that I study hard, that I excel. That's what I did. I hit the books. I made her proud."

We sleep in separate rooms. I stay awake a long while. Because of the caffeine, because of the adrenaline, because of the kiss, because of what Karine just told me. She's a much better person than I am. Always was, always will be. So much I can learn from her. When Vernon came for me in 1978 the only other person I wanted to take with us was Karine. It's like the other kids didn't even exist. But Vernon, a widowed diplomat on the last leg of his West African tour, had no use for a little girl. He wouldn't have known the first thing about taking care of one. Part of me wanted to stay, to remain at the Foyer despite everything. I thought Vernon was just like the *bukis*. I thought he, too, would want to touch me, have fun with me, make me do all the things I didn't like, all the bad things. I was scared to go. But Vernon proved to be the best thing that happened to me.

Karine wakes up around 6. I wait until she leaves to get up. There's a note in the kitchen, bearing her neat little handwriting and smelling like her perfume. "Make yourself at home," it says. Next to it are a set of keys. I feel luckier than I've been in a while.

I've got the money rescued from my house. I've got my passport. Matar, the cab driver whose number was saved in Karine's phone, picks me up and takes me everywhere I need to go. "I've got two wives and five children," he tells me. "Daily expenses run up to about 23,000 francs. Give me that, plus gas, plus 10,000 francs for my pain and we're good."

"Why two wives?" I ask him.

"Why not?" he retorts.

The town is still tense. Pockets of real trouble are few and far between, however. The tanks are still out, probably will be for a few more days. No school. 43 people lost their lives during the protests. Over a hundred were injured. Add that to the thousand or so *Joola* fatalities and you wonder how the country is still in one piece, how it avoided becoming a heap of smoldering ruins.

Yasser is at again when I walk into his shop. This time he's singing along Joe Dassin. He's got a tear in his eye, he allows himself to get carried away by the romance, the soft words, the smooth come-on, the nostalgia of a bygone era.

> *On ira*
> *Où tu voudras*
> *Quand tu voudras*

"You're losing them faster than I can stock them, playboy," he tells me, a note of regret in his voice. "All those beautiful works of art. What are you doing, man?"

"Just being careless, I guess."

He shakes his head and goes in the display case. "Same thing?"

"Of course."

He pulls a Glock off the velvety lining. "Here you go. Ammo?"

"Double me up. Got binoculars?"

"Better than that: an ultra-small, mountable, zoomable scope."

"Sounds good."

Matar finds the perfect spot: Boulevard Roosevelt, the edge of the Sporting Tennis Club, a parking lot overlooking the ocean and the white houses nestled at its foot. I survey Ibrahim's mansion without seeing much activity. It's been what--over a month and a half? The guards are still there, as numerous, alert, and disciplined as ever. No sighting of Ibrahim, Marie, Yasmin, or Mansour. No children playing in the little park. I have Matar call and ask for Marie. "Not available," a man answers.

We drive by the Point-E villa. There's nobody parked out front, but I know better than to stop. I wonder if, like my car, it's lost forever.

Next stop is Mame Awa in Mermoz. The old woman, who's learned a lesson or two from the still very fresh events, speaks to me from behind her locked iron door. Or, I should say, she doesn't speak to me from behind her iron door. Claims to have retired, to have lost contact, to not know anything about the Sows anymore--"not what they do, not where they are, Mr. James. I took my leave and I'm minding my own business. I suggest you do the same."

"To the nearest Internet cafe," I tell Matar.

I hole up for an hour and a half, free-associating, researching Ibrahim Sow, digging deeper and deeper, finding a few interesting things here and there. Little nuggets, snippets of information, loose threads. Only two major security companies operate in Dakar, Top Surveillance and Lion Services, possible employers of the guards used as foot soldiers by Momar and Ibrahim. Ibrahim's farm is in Retba, the same village where Mansour and Modi are from. The map in Zak's room had three red tacks on it, one each for Dakar, Palm Beach, and Nice, in the south of France, which makes me check title and phone records for the last two cities. The U.S. search yields a street address. On the French side, no property title but eight phone numbers registered to Ibrahim Sows in the Nice area. A 411 query gives me a phone number for Palm Beach. I try it first. It rings and rings and rings. The voice on the answering machine is a young boy's, or a very young man's with an accent--Zak's? Of the numbers on the French side, none seems to be any good.

"Those long-distance phone calls?" Matar wants to know.

"Yes, old man."

"You're eating up all my minutes," he protests.

"I'll pay you extra," I say. "Promise."

"You better," he grouses.

I buy Matar lunch at a *dibi* counter, leaving him in front of a plate of braised ribs and onions to resume my forays in cyberspace. There's no Momar to be found in association with Ibrahim Sow. I add IEX's name to the string, look for cache pages, and strike gold. Momar was no random business partner of Ibrahim's: he worked directly under him at Ibrahim's firm. His photo is that of the man I saw on the Madeleine: dark-skinned, oblong head, big nose, big lips. His last name is Sy. Lives in Fann Residence, right off the Route de Ouakam. Married to a Roxaya Sy. They have a son, Samba--had, because Samba's obituary pops up a few links down the page. Samba Sy, 1995-2005, a vicious case of meningitis.

Momar's residence is a few notches below Ibrahim's. He, too, has guards keeping an eye on the front and the back. The beef is still on, it seems. Could be that Ibrahim and Momar are not done. Maybe nothing has changed since the Madeleine. Maybe I haven't missed a thing. The little war isn't over.

After Matar drops me off at Yoff I buy fresh *rougets* from a returning pirogue right on the beach and take them to Karine's house. I clean the fish inside and out, slice them, season them, stick them in the fridge. Any other day, now would have been the time for a drink. I find no alcohol, not even beer, in the most obvious places. Juices of all kinds, yes: tamarind, guava, passion fruit, apple, orange, cranberry, ginger, sorrel, mango, lemon. Pappy Van Winkle, no. Karine doesn't smoke either, and I forgot to buy cigarettes while I was out shopping for a few things. There're plenty of *boutiks* in Yoff proper, inside the small village that sits between the end of the road and the edge of the beach. I take the drought in stride and decide to swear off both evils at the same time, the soreness, the burn in my lungs after the Rebeus escape still very present in my memory. Chasing after the Ibrahims and Momars of this world, I'm going to need to be as fit as I can be.

It's a little strange to watch the sun go down without a drink and a Marlboro in my hand. It's been my time to unwind since I've been in Dakar, the beginning of festivities after a day at work, the first step on the road to the Ngalam and its playthings. Sitting in Karine's house, watching the fiery disk dip into the water, I don't know what to do with myself. In my devil days I would have started going into my host's stuff, I would have searched the house from top to bottom, I would have pried it open, I would have picked it clean, I would have made it give up its most intimate secrets. There's so much more I need to know about Karine. So much I stand to find about her past, her marriage, the true nature of her relationship with Kant, if only I decided to start looking, if only I took that first step, if only I crossed that line. I've never been one to respect people's privacy, their intimacy. I've never stopped at what acquaintances wanted me to learn. I've always treated everybody as a potential threat, the enemy of tomorrow--even Vernon, poor Vernon. In my head, it was only a matter of time before people would start to disappoint me, turn against me, hurt me, turn their back on me. I was just getting ahead, being preemptive, preparing, being prudent, anticipating, being myself. Nothing wrong with a little caution, right? I was only protecting myself, right? I had good reasons not to trust anyone ever again after what Salimata did, right? So I went into all my girlfriends' purses. Did background checks on everybody who crossed my path. Read journals, opened letters, picked up discarded receipts, rummaged inside drawers, searched garbage bins, looked into all the closets and hiding places. Chris the sneaky one, the data gatherer, the numbers cruncher, the clues collector. The information lying around was never too trivial, never too mundane. I had no respect, I knew no boundaries, I took no one at face value. Some of my friends, some of those girlfriends, and Vernon, found me out eventually. They felt violated, and rightly so. I'll never forget the hurt, the disgust in their eyes.

I dare not go there with Karine. I know better. The devil days are gone. This is a new me. A better me. I cannot break Karine's trust. Ever. What I don't know won't hurt me. What I don't know, she'll tell me when the time comes.

Karine walks in with a funny face around 8. "What's wrong?" I ask.

"Nabou," she says. "She disappeared. Nobody can find her."

"Where's Isaac?"

"Just dropped him off at his grandparents'. Nabou had left him with one of her roomates to go meet someone. That was around 10 last night."

Karine lets herself fall on the sofa and slips out of her shoes.

"Worried?"

"Yes. The *n'deup* never worked--surprise, surprise. Nabou went back to her old ways two weeks after. Now this."

"Called the police?"

"First thing."

"Want me to try and find her?"

"It's probably nothing. She might just be out getting high. Or a john took her on a trip down the coast. She'll show up tomorrow with that look on her face, that goofy look I know so well. The only thing about it is she would never leave Isaac behind without a proper arrangement--instructions, his medication, money--for his care. The girl's not all bad. If there's one thing she cares about in this world it's her baby."

"Where's the kid's father?"

"Who knows? I've never met him. Nabou doesn't talk about him."

Karine closes her eyes. I leave her to start grilling the fish. She joins me on the patio and kisses me on the cheek. "Thanks for cooking. How was your day?"

"Not bad. Learned a few interesting things."

She's showered, she's put on a gray sweat suit. The top is zipped shut, the hood covers her wet hair, her hands are inside the front pocket. She's adorable--adorable. But tonight I'm not making any moves. Tonight I'm keeping myself in check. Karine knows where I stand. It's up to her to meet me halfway. It's totally up to her.

We watch the news while we eat. President Wade is all over the place. Cajoling, ranting threatening, commiserating, sympathizing. More bodies have been pulled from the *Joola*. The recovery effort is expected to go on for a few more days. Cameras show the dead on display inside a warehouse in Dakar's port, where the passengers' relatives are invited to come and identify their lost ones. The spectacle is sickening, exploitative: bodies rolled inside shrouds, lined up on a blue piece of tarp laid directly against the cement. Soldiers standing at attention, as if keeping watch over the dead. Civilians in tears as they walk between the rows, looking for familiar faces.

"Depressing, isn't it?"

"It is."

We switch to music. Oumar Pene, Awadi, Xuman, Xalam; the protest songs of Ouza et Ses Ouzettes; the wordplays of Souleymane Faye; the craftsmanship of Ismael Lo; the soul of Super Diamano; the funk of Baobab and Rail Band.

The light is soft, the carpet comfortable. Karine shows me pictures. My favorite is the one Felix took shortly after he and Giselle gave her refuge. It's a faded Polaroid, all yellow light and muted colors. Karine stands in front of the Place de l'Indépendence obelisk. She's in a dress. Her hair is short. The look on her face is indecipherable. It's a look turned within, the look of a young girl living very much inside herself, in her own world. When Karine shows me a photograph of Giselle, a veil lifts. Giselle is a portly woman, a no-nonsense woman, a hardworking woman, a solid woman. Not very pretty, the color of rust, pitch-black hair, penetrating eyes. "She ran the kitchen. She was always good to us. Her food was delicious."

"Still is."

"Where is she now?"

"Dieuppeul. She and Felix are retired. I see them every Sunday. We go to church and have lunch together."

"You go to church?"

"I do."

"How can you?"

"What do you mean?"

"I cringe every time I see a white robe. Can't help it."

"I believe in God," Karine says. "What Pops and the others did to us ... that has nothing to do with religion. They were just using the habit as a prop. That whole overseas missionary work thing was most likely only a pretext to get close to children and prey on them in a country where laws were lax and people wouldn't be looking closely."

I shake my head. "I don't see myself ever setting foot inside a church. Or a mosque, for that matter."

99

Karine appeases me with a look. "I understand."

"Do you ever see kids from the Foyer? Have you ever bumped into one randomly?"

"No. And I wonder how I would act if it happened. Sometimes you see a face, you hear a name that just takes you back, you know? Among the crowd, in traffic, in the paper, in a conversation."

"Maybe we should try to find them. See how they've fared. Start some kind of association. A support group or something."

Karine's not thrilled by the idea. "I'm not so sure," she says, yawning.

We call it a night.

We go run on the beach a little before dawn. Yellow-clad fishermen are already at it, hauling folded nets, rolling pirogues off the logs and into the water, going out for the day. The sand is shifty--hard in places, soft and crumbly in others. Karine has grace, she has pace, she has style, she has wind. We go south, following the coast for a couple of miles, passing the Layenne shrine and a few new constructions along the way.

Breakfast is black coffee, a fresh baguette, butter, strawberry jelly. Karine leaves at seven to try to beat the traffic. Matar shows up at 7:30.

It's back to the observation post on Roosevelt. I catch a glimpse of Ibrahim leaving his house. Boris's blond mohawk shines from afar. Becaye's pinstripe suit is unmistakable. No Mansour. Three trucks in the convoy, a dozen men total.

Matar and I catch up with them in front of Clairafrique. We tag along all the way to the port. Ibrahim's going to work. Because of the *Joola*, security is beefed up. No way Matar is going in behind the S.U.V.'s. "I need one of those stickers," he says.

"Can you buy one?"

"Everything is for sale. Just gotta know where to ask."

I give Matar the money. He leaves me on Roosevelt. After finding the sticker, he'll go and keep an eye on Momar's house. I walk through the tennis club's parking lot and go deep into the bushes separating it from the edge of the cliff. There, hidden from the avenue, I find a tree overlooking the Sows' enclave. I spend half the day spread out on an overhanging branch, watching, looking, waiting, thinking. The place, shielded from the sun by heavy foliage, has an eerie peace, a surreal tranquillity.

The neighborhood below me goes through its rhythms. Maids, cooks, cleaning crews, and children own it during the day. Zak's friends go from house to house. They're constantly in motion, riding bikes, tossing a ball around, running in and out of the park. Abdi's is the only familiar face inside the Sow compound. Yasmin, if she is there, doesn't come out in the garden even once. There's no trace of Wolf, Zak's dog. Marie also seems MIA.

Matar comes back for me around 4. Nothing happening at Momar's place. Nobody went in. Nobody came out. It doesn't look like Momar lives there any more. His people might just be guarding an empty house. "Got the sticker," Matar beams.

"Let me see."

It's clear and rectangular, with the Port Autonome de Dakar anchor logo at the bottom. The windshield of the big blue boxy car flashes before my eyes. "What official sticker's got a green snake on it?"

Matar doesn't skip a beat as he hands me the most precious piece of trivia I've uncovered in a long while: "The color changes, but they all serve the same purpose: Give you access to public hospitals."

"Anybody in the medical profession can get them? Nurses, technicians, assistants?"

"No. Doctors only." Matar smiles again. "Want one?"

"Maybe."

We go down the Corniche and follow the red track. Mansions, white walls, forever lawns. A guard appears before I

101

get a chance to ring the bell. I ask to see Marie. "Mrs. Sow isn't here," he says none too nicely.

"When do you expect her?"

"Who are you?"

"An old friend."

The guard looks me up and down. He's young, antsy, a little green. I can take him easily. The other twenty or so men patrolling the grounds are another story. "Got a card?" he asks.

"Not on me."

"Got a name?"

I shrug and get back in the cab. The guard gets on his two-way. More men join him by the gate. They watch us climb the hill toward the Corniche.

Abdi picks up when I try the house phone. I imagine him in his slacks and apron and polished shoes, dignified and quiet and efficient, cooking meals that nobody cares to eat. "It's Mr. James," I tell him. "The private investigator hired to find Zak."

"I remember you," Abdi says softly.

"I need to speak with Mrs. Sow, Abdi. It's very important."

"She's on a trip," Abdi reveals obligingly.

"Where did she go?"

"I'm afraid I'm not at liberty to say."

The sticker gets us inside the port. The hangar where the *Joola* people await identification is like a circus tent. Government officials, news crews, firemen, mourners, soldiers, medical personnel, the dead themselves--it's all a busy spectacle, a big sad show under the sun. IEX's corner of the port is under vigilant watch from Ibrahim's men. Sitting in cars, patrolling on foot, standing in twos and threes, they cover all angles and points of approach, even, crazily enough, the Atlantic. So there's no storming Ibrahim's office, taking him by surprise, giving him a taste of his own medicine. There's no exacting precious revenge. Today is clearly not the day.

Karine catches me on my way back to Yoff. "They just found Nabou," she shouts, hysterical. "Can you come?"

Matar immediately busts a U. We cover the distance in a little over an hour. The congestion is out of this world.

Guediawaye is a shantytown by the sea. For decades it served as the de facto stopping point for migrants on their way to Dakar, *N'dakarou Ndiaye*, the fabled El Dorado, the modern city built by the *toubab*--white people. Not quite the anticipated big time for those migrants, but close enough. Before becoming a major player in the country's exodus woes, Guediawaye used to be a fishermen's settlement. Nobody fishes much around Guediawaye any more. The fish are all gone, the water is polluted.

It's proving to be a big problem, the water: Short and stingy as the wet season is, the rain eats up the low-lying land as it makes its way into the neighborhood from the sky, from the side, from the front, from behind, from the bottom. It goes below surface and reappears in random spots under houses, drowning foundations, seeping from bedroom floors. It takes over dirt paths and central places and dusty corners, it turns holes into pools and small lakes that are a breeding ground for mosquitoes and a constant danger for residents, children especially. It's been going on for quite some time. Everybody knows about it. Minister after minister has toured the streets--briefly, cautiously. The promised aid--containment, drainage, evacuation, relocation--has yet to materialize. Only neighborhood associations and NGOs, foreign or local, try to take on the task. The only sensible thing for the people of Guediawaye to do would be to get up and leave. But they have nowhere to go. They have no choice but to live with the water, to cohabit with the water, to fight the water, to strike a balance, to adapt, to find an equilibrium, to make do--*se débrouiller*. With wits and sweat and clenched teeth and a survivor's instinct. With sand and mounds of trash brought in by horse carts and pickup trucks, to the tune of a few hundred francs per load. The sand, the trash are dumped wherever the water appears until it is completely sponged off, until it is absorbed, until it stops seeping through,

103

until next time. If the flooding happens inside a house, then a new floor is built upon this makeshift filler, walls and roof are extended, the house is raised a few inches, maybe even a yard or so. So the people of Guediawaye, in order to fight the water, now live on top of trash carted away from Dakar's landfills.

It's the water that took Nabou. "A new spot. Right after that turn over there. It looks benign, completely normal. Like you can walk over it as you would on solid ground. But under the litter, under the garbage is nothing but water, see? It was night. Nabou was rushing, running, even. She fell through. It was deep. She panicked. She never made it back to the surface. Kids playing soccer found her the next morning after one of them almost tumbled into the soup chasing the ball."

The gendarme's tidy explanation doesn't satisfy Karine. "Nabou was a Lebou. Her people settled this peninsula. She was born in the water. A small hole wouldn't have taken her under."

"Think she killed herself?"

"No."

"How can you be so sure?"

"Isaac."

"Did she have a pimp?"

Karine shakes her head. "She wasn't a pro. Just a little lost. Fell through the cracks a long time ago. Loved her *precsion*--her high: pills, weed, liquor, H. A lot of pain inside. Something having to do with her family. Her dad, most certainly. He did something to her. I never got to the bottom of it."

Karine wipes a tear with her sleeve. I feel like holding her but there's a crowd, huge, curious, loud, obnoxious, filling the small street from wall to wall, chattering, pushing, laughing, gawking at the killing pool. It used to be that death, any death, was a big deal. Guediawaye is over it. Guediawaye has seen too much of it to be bothered. It's not just the water: It's malaria, cholera, dysentery, yellow fever, TB, hepatitis, STDs, food poisoning, raw sewage, accidental fires; it's aggressors waiting in the shadow of enclosures and around dark bends with machetes night after night.

It's not the fire-spitting mob of a few days ago, this crowd. It has nothing to do with the white-hot wave marching on the Palace, overturning cars, breaking windows, setting tires on fire, fighting the GMI and the pigs in green. That was then. This is now. There's a dichotomy, a clear disconnect. Guediawaye is unable to make the Nabou drama fit into the bigger picture. It's an anecdote, the result of an unfortunate series of events, not the indirect consequence of the government's inaptitude. Therein lies the problem: no real, sustained, organized protest; no will to challenge the status quo; no way toward a clear-headed struggle; no sweeping uprising. Passivity, fatalism are the norm.

Karine's sorrow stands out in more than one way: There never was much all-around sympathy for Nabou in Guediawaye. She was a *xaga*--a whore.

We stay until Nabou's body is hauled away by EMS technicians on foot. No ambulance can penetrate this deep into the ghetto.

Once Nabou gone, people turn their attention to Karine. Everybody knows her. They call her by her first name. She is liked, loved, respected. Three little girls in Guediawaye are named after her. Her clinic provides lifesaving services to this distressed community: first-aid, emergency treatment, child vaccination, prenatal care, counseling, family planning, mental health screening. Karine is not an MD. She holds a Ph.D. in social sciences. Her focus is women. She talks to them, she mentors them, she rescues them, she gives them shelter, she energizes them, she organizes them, she's a godmother to their children.

That day, I can't help but seeing our differences, our glaring differences. Karine tries to save people like Nabou. I use Nabous to populate my bacchanals and satiate my appetites. Karine exhausts herself trying to bring relief to an abandoned corner of the city. I can't remember ever doing something for another human being that didn't serve my own interests. Observing Karine, seeing her at work, witnessing Guediawaye's adulation for her makes me appreciate her even more. She's accessible, generous, caring, principled, strong. She's the real deal. She's worth emulating. She's a template, a different approach, another way to be in the world.

It amazes me. It puzzles me more than a little. Karine and I went through the same thing as children, more or less. We were run through the same sieve, we were cast in the same mold, we were roughed up by the same waters. Yet she ends up being so different, she turns out the complete opposite of me. I'm all darkness, demons, dissipation, conflict, insecurities, indulgence, venality. Karine is purpose, vision, work, certainty, clarity, dedication, discipline, goodwill, generosity.

"How big is Retba?" I ask Matar.

"Not big," he says.

"How far?"

"Not far."

"Can you take me?"

"Let's go."

We leave an hour before dawn. Yoff, Patte d'Oie, Camberene, Pikine. The going, for once, is good. The landscape changes near Mbao, a minor fishing village that boasts the country's only oil refinery. Poultry farms stretch their long roofs under the moon. Nature takes over immediately after the road, making villages all but invisible behind a barrier of trees or the shifting curves of dunes. Bugs get squashed on the windshield, leaving a splatter that Matar disperses with a flick of the wipers. Exiting Mbao, a much smaller road on the left takes us to Malika. At times the shrub forest disappears without warning, revealing a vast swath where tall, sparse grass rules. Solitary farms whiz by, their fenced land unencumbered with buildings--or trees, crops, and cattle for that matter. They're owned by fat cats from the city, speculators sitting and waiting for the next real estate boom, Dakar's inevitable expansion. At one major intersection the roads coming from all four corners are undisturbed if not for the intermittent electric poles that seem to lead to the confines of the earth.

We arrive before the sun, stopping by the *grand-place* to get a cup of Nescafe and a *pain-beurre* from a little shop. Retba is a hamlet cut in half by the road leading to the lake of the same name, itself one of Senegal's natural wonders--it is pink and saturated with salt.

I get directions to Mansour's house. We wait in the car as Retba slowly comes to life. Children come out to gather bread, sugar, *kinkeliba* tea leaves, and single servings of instant coffee. They look at the taxi with curious eyes. Salt trucks pass us on their way to the lake. The houses are all small. A good number of them are well built and well maintained. Mansour's got shells embedded in its wall, a garage, a slate roof, a satellite dish. Retba is a place where, at long last, *dungurus* can have their day in the sun.

I push the wrought-iron door to enter a paved and planted courtyard. A young woman is sweeping, ridding the ground of fallen leaves. Mansour is sitting on a wooden stool at the edge of the porch, rubbing palmfuls of water on his arms as he performs his morning ablutions with a gray aluminum kettle. His back is turned to me.

"*Assalamu aleikum.*"

Startled, Mansour drops the kettle. It loses its top and starts emptying. I pick it up obligingly, put the cover back in place, and hand it to him. Mansour takes it with shaking hands. I pull the bottom of my shirt to let him see the Glock. His eyes grow even bigger. "I'll wait until you're done," I say with my most accommodating smile. He gets up, gets on a rug and gets started, his voice catching a little, his tongue tripping, his throat knocking words around. I watch him from a garden chair. The woman coughs, making me look her way. I recognize her from the Safieddine Studio portrait in Modi's room--Modi's girl.

Mansour's prayer gets more fervent as it ends. Sitting cross-legged, he puts his heart and his open palms into it. Is he wondering whether this might just be his last? Is he wondering whether I've come to kill?

Finally, Mansour gets up and takes a step toward the house. I shake my head. "Let's go for a walk."

The streets are a little more animated now that the sun is out. Sheep are being led by bands of sullen children to surrounding grazing fields. A salt truck bounces up and down the white track. Mansour leads me around the village, arms behind his back. His prayer beads dangle form his fingers. He seems more composed, more like his old cocky, imperious, arrogant self. The prayer must have worked wonders.

"How's retirement?" I ask.

"Lovely. What can I do for you?"

"I'm going to ask you a few questions. Everything else depends on your answers."

We enter a clearing with a baobab tree in its middle. Heavy, oblong fruits called monkey bread hang from its branches. The tree's trunk is wide, ossified, hollow. Its gray, knotty and polished wood feels cool under my palm. One of the fruits fell overnight. Its cracked shell reveals rows of seeds on a fiber bed. The seeds are covered in flesh that is powdery, succulent, bittersweet, easily dissolved. Monkey bread. It's a child's treat, really. Salimata used to bring me some back from the market. My favorite snack. Never could get enough of it. I marvel at the shell's velvety feel, its shape, its smell, the hardness of its wood. Mansour sighs impatiently.

"Why did Zak have to die?" I ask him. "If you can tell me that I'll leave you alone. Everything else I've pretty much figured out already."

"Why should I tell you anything?"

I hit him across the face with the fruit. The shell cracks some more, but it doesn't shatter. A puff of powder whitens Mansour's face. Dislodged seeds fly away, landing on the sand. Mansour takes a step back, regains his balance. He drops the prayer beads but makes no attempt to fight back, or even protect himself. Pearls of blood adorn his smashed lips. He runs a finger on them and takes a look, his eyes full of disbelief. I hit him again. And again. Until his nose, too, starts bleeding. Until he cries "Stop!" Until the piece of monkey bread left in my hand becomes too small. I feel calm, in control, better than I've felt in a long while. This is what I've missed. This is me. This is what feels right. This is what feels good. No second-guessing, no hesitation, no touchy-feely stuff. I go for the Glock.

"No!" Mansour shouts, raising his arms at last, scared out of his wits now that the gun is in my hands. "No!"

Children are approaching the clearing. I slip the Glock back into my belt. *"Asalamu aleikum."*

"Aleikum salam."

They step far from the tree, giving us room once they recognize one of Retba's patriarchs.

"Why?" I ask again.

Mansour lowers his head. Maybe he's thinking about Modi, the power drill, that long-ago day at the IEX warehouse when he saw me ply my trade. Maybe he's tired. Maybe the beating whipped some sense into him. "It was all Boris's fault," he says. "Zak died ... Zak died because Samba died."

I encourage him with a nod.

"Momar was on a boat to Dakar when Ibra decided to renege on their deal and appropriate the merchandise. He sent Boris and Becaye to take Momar's wife and son hostage. When Boris and Becaye forced their way into the house they found Momar's wife at the boy's bedside. Samba had caught something early that day and his state was rapidly deteriorating. Boris ignored the woman's plea to call an ambulance. He put her through to Momar on the boat. She cried and begged Momar to give us what we wanted. Momar relented. The merchandise changed hands. By the time the ship's captain checked it and called with the confirmation, Samba was beyond help. It was meningitis that killed him."

"That boat--was it one of Ibrahim's?"

"Yes."

"Wasn't Boris in contact with Ibrahim and yourself during the home invasion?"

"Yes."

"Whose decision was it not to get help for Samba?"

Mansour doesn't have it in him to look me in the eye. "Ibra's. Based on information relayed by Boris--essentially, that Samba didn't appear to be in mortal danger."

My palms are itching. From the urge to hurt the pathetic old man standing in front of me? From the monkey bread's allergenic shell? "Why didn't Ibrahim just have Momar killed in Freetown to secure the diamonds?" I ask.

Puzzlement makes Mansour raise his head. Either he doesn't understand the question or he has no clue what I'm getting at. For a second there the old shrewdness makes a comeback. I grab him by the collar and pull his face close to mine. "Tell the truth."

He winces. "Logistics. This was Momar's operation from beginning to end. Ibra had to wait until Momar got on the ship to make a move."

Mansour struggles to free himself. I tighten my grip on the *boubou*. Our faces are only inches apart. I'm cool, calm, strong. He's sweaty, smelly, weak, old. It's almost too easy.

"What else, Mansour? What is it you're not telling me?"

"Momar is Ibra's brother. The goal was to pressure him, not get rid of him. Ibra didn't wish for Samba's death. It was a powerplay gone wrong."

"What did you just say?"

"They're brothers. Momar is the fruit of a meaningless union that occurred during Xadim's--Ibrahim's father--marriage. The pregnancy was kept hidden. The woman married quickly and got her husband to publicly claim Momar as his. Xadim compensated her financially."

Mansour stops. Sun rays are coming through the baobab's sparse cluster of leaves. It's getting hot. Retba is now full of noise, of movement. The more people around, the less room for me to maneuver. "How long have Momar and Ibrahim known each other?" I press on.

"Forever. Xadim wanted them to be best friends. Momar was always around."

"When did they learn that they were brothers?"

"Xadim told them on his deathbed. Ibra refused to accept the truth. Momar reacted the opposite way. He's always looked up to Ibra."

"Does Marie know?"

111

"Nobody knows. They kept it a secret so as not to tarnish people's opinion of Xadim. He was a very important man."

"Did Xadim care about Momar?"

"He did right by him. He expressly asked Ibra to take Momar under his wing. He wanted the two brothers to work side by side and expand the empire he had spent a lifetime building."

"That never happened, of course."

Mansour shakes his head. "Ibra wouldn't hear of it. But I kept on insisting, until a place was progressively made for Momar within IEX. Momar is no Ibrahim. He always felt like he never got his due. He wanted to prove himself. Which he why he took on the venture."

I take a few seconds to absorb Mansour's words. It's almost too much. Brothers killing each other's son. Brothers at war. "Momar was on his way back with the loot. Why not just wait and split the proceeds? Would a couple million dollars really make such a difference to Ibrahim's bottom line?"

Mansour sighs. "Ibra loves to compete. He always beat Momar at everything. Always. It was more about ego, I think."

"Why leave himself open to Momar's move, then? Why leave Zak so vulnerable?"

"Ibra thought he had won. He thought he could convince Momar that Samba's death was an accident. He thought he could shut him up with money. But Momar had changed in a way that Ibra couldn't grasp, couldn't foresee. The trip had helped him become his own man, at last. He must also have started to deeply hate Ibrahim after losing his son. He kidnapped Zak ten days after burying Samba."

"What's your role in all this?"

Mansour shrugs, *dunguru* till the end. Sweat is now falling down his cheeks. The prayer beads lie half-buried in the sand, forgotten. "I was Xadim's right-hand man before becoming Ibra's. Xadim was from my generation: No matter how successful he wanted to become there were places he didn't go, there were lines he didn't cross. Momar was Xadim's one big mistake. Ibra? Ibra is all ambition. Pure ambition. He stops at nothing. I try my best to advise him in all matters, personal and financial. I try to slow him down, to make him take caution. But he is very much his own man. He doesn't tell me everything. He doesn't always listen."

More people are walking through the clearing. Young men on their way to harvest salt from the lake. Farmers going to work their plots. Women carrying buckets of water on their heads. Mansour wipes his face and picks up the beads. He knows now that he's safe. I have the nagging feeling that there's much he isn't telling me. Much more. "I saw Ibrahim throw the diamonds away with my own eyes. So why are he and Momar still at it? When does it stop?"

Mansour walks away, hiding his face from view as he answers. "I don't know. I left after we put Zak into the ground. I'm done with that part of my life. And if I were you, I'd leave it all alone and mind my own. Ibra is going to kill you."

"You can tell him I'm coming," I say to Mansour's back. "You can tell him I'll take him for everything he's got: his wife, his little girl, his company, his cars ... everything. You hear me? Tell him."

Mansour shakes his head. I think--I'm not sure at all--I think I can hear him laugh.

I take a seat inside the stifling cab. Village elders have taken possession of the four benches under the biggest *grand-place* tree, settling in for a day of idleness interspersed with meals, prayers, and salty comments.

We leave Retba in a cloud of dust, Matar grinding the gears of the old taxi.

I get home to Yoff with one thing on my mind: To hold Karine tight, to hold her tight and never let her go. My sweet lady, my friend, my woman. It's been that kind of day for her, too. We turn the radio up, we turn the radio down, we dim the lights, we dance on the carpet, we float, we sway, we rock, we hum old tunes, la la la la la la la, we let go of everything wrong with us and with the rest of the world, we make a little space where nothing else exists but what we share, this thing, this bond, this connection, this circle of two, this story, we daren't yet call it destiny but it is starting to look that way, isn't it?--has been since the Foyer, the devil years, Karine, sweet Karine and Christophe. Tonight nothing is complicated, difficult, cruel, scary, out of reach, out of bounds. Tonight there's no burden, no burn, no clouds, no shadows, no drizzle, no rain in the forecast. Tonight we dance, we sing, we whisper, we feel, we cherish, we want, we're revealed, soul to soul, gaze to gaze, Karine and Christophe. Tonight we're meant to be, loneliness out the window, ice broken, ice shattered, desire overwhelming, tacit understanding, full meaning, misapprehensions overcome, barriers vanquished, distance bridged, triumph close at hand, la la la la la la la, a night to last our whole life through, the first minute, the very first second of our eternal summer. It's fine, it's fun, it's tender, it's growing, it's inside, it's switched on, it's us, it's overdue, it radiates, a light, the prize, warmth, happiness, ease, longing no more, hunger acknowledged, need satiated, all the things glanced beforehand, the things hoped for, the treasures, the bounty, the coveted reward. Karine and Christophe, meant to be, together, finally, la la la la la la la, laughter, eyes, hearts, hearts, hearts. Karine and Christophe, yes, better than we ever thought it would be, better than anything and anyone we've known, soaring, searing, Christmas in the Sahel, new horizon, rapture, magic spell, born again today, born anew, godly sanction, blessing, wouldn't dream of letting this go, wouldn't want to pass each other by. A high. The high of love. Karine and Christophe.

"Chris?"

"Yes."

"Where do we go from here? What do we do?"

"We build. We build something beautiful and grand. We go and go. We never look back."

"Is it ever that simple?"

"It can be."

"You know nothing about me."

"I know enough. The rest will come in time."

She kisses me. Karine kisses me. Karine. The green eyes, up close, are full of sparkles. They fill my world. They're all I see. Karine. The dream. The end of the road. The answer. It's her. Always been. *Suma jigen*--my woman. *Suma xarit*--my friend. *Suma waye*--my buddy. *Suma nit*--my people. All I need. All I have. "Don't leave me, K. Don't go and change your mind. It's my biggest fear, you know? To be abandoned. To be left behind. Since forever. Since Salimata."

"I'm not leaving you, Chris. You got me."

"Promise?"

"Promise. The same goes for you."

"What?"

"Don't go and let me down."

"Never."

"Even indirectly."

"I promise."

"Chris?"

"Yes."

"This case. This whole thing. Can you just let it go?"

"No."

"Why not?"

"Ibrahim took everything I have. Everything. My whole life. I'm a fugitive. I can't go back to my own house. I can't move freely around my own city. I have to get it all back. Everything I lost. Everything he took."

"Then what?"

"Then I can slow down."

"Then we're free to do whatever?"

"Completely free. Whatever."

"I understand."

"Karine?"

"Yes."

"I've always loved you, you know? You were always here. Always."

"I know."

"Karine?"

"Chris?"

"I have issues. Lots of them."

"We all do."

"So you'll have to work with me."

"Don't worry."

Eyes full of sparkles. Honey in her kiss. Cinnamon in her skin. The world in her touch. Karine.

I should listen to Karine. I should call Diack and spill the beans. He can take what little I know and build a case around it. Diack is a cerebral kind of cop. There's more to him than meets the eye. He's after the truth big time. Doesn't care what his bosses tell him. Crime dog going for the juiciest bone of his career. Cream of the cops. Dakar in flames. A dozen deaths still unexplained, including that of a child. Diack would know what to do with the information I've gathered. Diack would know what buttons to push, what doors to tear down, what walls to scale. Diack would know.

But I've never been too keen on trusting people, especially not with my freedom. Always been hardheaded. Always think I can get myself out of anything and everything. I lie. I steal. I cheat. I do what it takes. I'm nimble on my feet. I stay one step ahead. I'm Chris motherfucking James.

So I keep watching Ibrahim come and go between his palace by the sea and IEX's warehouse. I dispatch Matar to Fann Residence every day to see if Momar is showing his face. I turn the case around and around in my head to devise my next move. Short of summoning my own little army and storming Ibrahim's lair, there seem to be very few options available. Ibrahim learned from his mistakes. Boris, Becaye, and them are everywhere. When Ibrahim moves, they move. Three shifts a day every day, clockwork rotations, impeccable uniforms, shiny boots--the men are always fresh, always ready, wouldn't look out of place among the Presidential Guard. Ibrahim goes from car to building, from building to car. Momar, at long last, is being taken seriously.

So Marie's the only card I have left to play. Finding her isn't such a big hassle after all. I have one Florida phone number and eight Nice phone numbers. I call all of them at least once a day, until seven out of the eight Nice numbers are struck out of my list. Then I start calling the one Florida number and the one Nice number I have left, letting them ring forever, letting them ring, ring, ring. Until the answering machines pick up. Until, one fateful afternoon, frustrated out of my mind, I start leaving a message on the Florida number. And in the middle of it, after I've stated my name and hesitated and begun to explain why exactly I'm trying--I've been trying--to get in touch with her, well, in the middle of it all she picks up the phone, as luck would have it. Marie herself. Marie Sow. "Yes?" As if it were the most natural thing.

"It's Chris."

"I know."

"I ... I wanted to talk to you."

"I'm listening." She's calm, Marie. She's poised. She breathes evenly. No outward curiosity, no overblown interest. Not just an ocean between us but a barrier, a big barrier. The barrier of class, the social barrier, the conventions that keep people like her far away on their own cloud and people like me where they belong, down on the ground.

"Not on the phone."

"I'm in Florida," she says matter-of-factly.

I fumble a little. "I see ... I mean, I know."

She gets impatient. "So?"

"I have something you want."

"What?"

"The truth."

She remains silent so long that I think she's gone.

"Hello?"

"I'm here. How much?"

"That's not... I'm not after money."

"Then what?" The way she says it.... As if money is all that makes me get up in the morning. As if it runs me, makes me tick. As if I aspire to nothing else than hitting people in the wallet. Some kind of lowlife, your common hustler.

"I'm no *dunguru*. I'm not that cheap."

"Congratulations."

I'm losing her. I'm losing her sure as day. The tone, the attitude, the distance, the barrier ... the pain. Sweet Marie lost her son and embraced her darker side. She's been down in the Hole, she's seen the Devil, she's tasted the fire and the fury, she knows now that life isn't a bunch of roses and the Sorbonne and charity work and mansions by the sea. She knows now that the sucker can knock the wind out of you, steal the salt from your taste, send you flying high and smash you against the pavement when you come back down. She knows. Marie knows.

"When are you coming back?" I ask.

"I don't know. Not now. Maybe never."

"I'll come to you," I announce without thinking.

"Really? Call me when you get here, Chris. Maybe I can pick you up from the bus station or something."

"This isn't a joke."

"I'm supposed to care?"

I'm losing her big time. And so I go and give it all I've got: "You were right: Ibrahim did this to you."

She stops breathing. I imagine her at the other end, sitting pretty, sitting in the lap of luxury, silk and gold and precious stones, ornate ceiling, hand-carved trimmings, paintings and vases and fine linens, fresh-cut flowers, deep carpets, Persian rugs, furniture everywhere, swimming pool behind a sliding door, curtains blowing in the Florida breeze, a shiny thing or two in the pristine garage, all that money just like a cocoon choking her, mothballing her youth, her vitality, her individuality, her personality--tragic, tragic Marie. The memories, still fresh, too fresh, like a flood. Her voice, small again, more like the one I know, like a little girl's--Marie is afraid to hear the answer even as she asks, "Ibra did what?"

119

"Everything that happened with Zak. Everything you suspect, and more."

"What do you mean?"

"It was never about money. He paraded that million dollars before your eyes so you'd never find out what was going on. He hired me as much to help find Zak as to keep you in the dark."

Marie Sow tries to fight it. She tries to hold on to the wobbly bastion, the last remnant of her once-perfect union. "Why are you willing to talk, suddenly? What changed?"

"Your husband tried to kill me. He's cleaning house. I'm in hiding. You're my last chance."

Silence, once again. Marie's adding what I've just revealed to the clues collected here and there, her own misgivings, her deductions, her intuition, her gut feeling. "You have to tell me more. Why should I trust you? Why even listen to you?"

"Does the name Momar Sy ring a bell?"

"It does," she says immediately, in a whisper almost, in a strange way, a loaded way, a way that's hard to read, a layered way, a double entendre. She too, knows more than she lets on. She, too, is now wondering what, and exactly how much, I've found out.

"See you in Palm Beach," I tell her before hanging up. "I'll make sure to call from the bus station."

Karine won't have it. There's this thing we've just started. It's big, it's beautiful, it's a feast, it's summer. We're, as the saying goes, living off *amour et eau fraîche*--love and cold water. Every day. Every night. We can't get enough. Like wanting something all your life, getting it, discovering it's even better than anything you imagined, ten times more exciting. Infinite possibilities. A new sky opening up. The high. The high of love. We've found it, what we were looking for. We've found it, we've found it, we've found each other, we've got the missing piece. Karine and Christophe.

120

"Stay," she says over and over and over again. "Stay."
She's afraid for me, my Karine. She knows where I'm going, she
knows how I'm going, she sees there might be a huge price to
pay--she sees it clear as day. In her mind Marie is trouble,
Marie's formidable, Marie's fearsome, Marie's the enemy.
"Stay," Karine says, and the more she says it, the more I know
I've got to go. The high of love, the spring we drink from every
day, all the things we do, *l'amour* and *l'eau fraîche*--they're
putting me to sleep, they're smothering me, they're dousing the
rage, I can't hate clearly any more. The more I stay, the more I
stall. The more I stall, the more I risk to lose.

"Stay."

"I'll be back soon. It won't take long. One week. Two,
at the most. Loose ends to tighten."

"I need your help."

"What can I do for you?"

"Isaac. I'm trying to adopt him."

"Seriously?"

"Yes. I'm his godmother, remember?"

I smile despite myself. A child of our own. A little baby
boy. "Let's do it."

"I need your help," she repeats.

"What do I have to do?"

"Nabou's dad, Doudou. He's the only one against it."

"I'll go and talk to him. Consider it done. More reasons
for me to straighten this stuff out. So I can live in the open. So
we can rescue all the needy kids out there. The *talibes*. All
Senegal's orphans."

"And Chris?"

"Yes?"

"Something about me you need to know."

"What is it? You're scaring me."

"I can't have children."

"What do you mean?"

"I can't. We tried, with Kant. We tried and tried. I'm all
messed up inside." Karine starts to cry. "It's because ... it's
because...."

I hold her face between my palms. Her tears fall freely. They roll, they race down her cheeks. "He raped me," Karine says, sobbing so hard I have a hard time understanding her. "Pops. Before I left. Time and again."

All I can do right then and there is hold her, smooth her hair, shush her, kiss her tears, talk to her softly, lie beside her, give her comfort, give her warmth. I feel guilty, once again, for not saving her back then, for not protecting her, for abandoning her to her fate, even though I was but a helpless, defenseless child myself. I feel immensely guilty. My baby, my beautiful little girl. In many ways we never left the Foyer and we never will. Karine and I didn't go through the same things after all. We weren't cast in the same mold. We weren't run through the same sieve. She paid a much bigger price than I did. She paid in blood.

That evening is when I set out on a journey, a one-way trip, the furthest into myself I've ever gone. Further than the depths where Ibrahim took me. Further than when I was locked up under Rebeus. Karine's revelation sets something loose in me. Something evil. Something famished. Something lusty. Something uncontrollable. Something murderous.

It's pouring when we leave. It's pouring and it won't let up. Yoff, Patte d'Oie, Camberene, Pikine, Mbao, Rufisque. The rain is like a blanket. We need it, want it, can't get enough of it. The earth is hurting, the seeds are drying, the farmers are despairing, sand is filling all the wells, the Sahara is steadily gaining, desertification is shutting down entire villages faster than rural exodus ever could. I drive Karine's car with one hand and hold her with the other, pressing her against me so our heads touch. It's hard to tell when night becomes day because the rain falls and falls, everything is seen through a veil, dark clouds hang low and thick, thunder claps, lightening zaps, the roadside is empty, the palm and coconut trees shake, leaves and branches fall, debris are scattered around, the color is dark-gray to black, neither day nor night, apocalyptic. Leaving Dakar is like entering a different realm, going from a semblance of modernity--a botched, haphazard attempt at modernity--to archaic Africa, the Africa of savanna grass and huts, baobabs and lions and gazelles and smiling villagers, the Africa of the Fortier postcards Vernon used to collect, the mythic Ndofane of Salimata's *Leuk le Lièvre* stories. It's always a little like that. Dakar, unruly and anarchic as it is, is so much more developed than the rest of the country, so far ahead.

Karine is not asleep, after all. "Chris?"

"Yes?"

"What will you do when you find Salimata?"

"*If* I find her."

"You will. I have no doubt that you will."

"It depends on how I wake up that day. I'm two-minded and two-hearted when it comes to my mother: Either full of love or detesting her with a passion. So I can't call it at all. Don't know what I'll do. Go all crazy, probably. Take my anger out on her. She lied to me. She left me behind."

Karine yawns and stretches. Her hand comes to rub my neck. "You should try to forgive. That's what I did. Made my peace with it. Tried not to think about it. I never drive up the Mamelles road. I never go back to even take a look. I'll be glad when they raze the place altogether."

"I'm not as strong as you, Karine. And I'm definitely not as kind."

In the middle of our trip, under the driving rain, we stop. A beach, small, virginal, catches our eye coming down a hill. We drive over small dunes until a bend hides us from the road. We park, we undress, we run, we frolic, we dive, we swim, we lock lips and hold hands underwater, we come out greeted by more water and a little thunder, we go under a few more times. Don't know if there're sharks, barracudas, current, jellyfish, people, danger, a rip tide. The sea is like an undulating sheet with a million little perforations. Walking out of the waves, we fall on the sand. There never was a thing more intense than the love we make on that beach, lying on that sand, wind howling, rain falling, waves crashing, nature all around us, protecting us,

123

harboring us in its midst. There never will be. It's unmatched, it's tender, it's fulgurant. It leaves us shaking, gasping for air, holding on to each other like two lovers lost at sea. It leaves us full, too full for words.

There are two gallons of drinking water in the trunk, purchased just in case. I wash the salt and the sand off Karine with one. She washes me with the other. Her body, plump, voluptuous, glorious, is a reddish gold under the stormy sky. Her hips, the hips that might never bear fruit, are moon crescents. Her hair, tangled by our dip, is parsed with hazel. Her nipples are two flattened orchids. And then there's those eyes. She is a *métisse*--a mulatto. I'm either Sérère or Diola, the most Christianized of Senegal's dozen or so ethnic groups. Sérère, most likely, because of my features: gray-black skin, small nose, small lips, medium height, medium build, hair that curls and never seems to grow long.

Saint-Louis reminds me of New Orleans--the little that I saw of it when I paid Pops a visit at his nursing home. The water that surrounds it and runs through it--not just the Atlantic but the Senegal River, *dekh-gui*, as it is affectionately called; the narrow cobblestone streets; the hanging balconies; the ochre walls; the wooden shutters; the ancient doors. Everywhere, traces of the French, testimonies of their passage and the city's colonial past.

Karine checks me into a waterfront hotel called *La Chaumière*. On the bed, in the tub, our bodies can't seem to get enough. It's hard to say goodbye.

"Two weeks?"

"Two weeks."

"You're gonna call?"

"Every day."

"You be safe, Chris."

It's funny how close, how attached we've become in the span of a few days, how easily everything came. As if it had been here all along, waiting for us to mind it, tend it, give it life, make it grow.

It's still raining as Karine drives away. Still pouring. The blessing is turning into a curse. Seeds will be washed away, plants will be uprooted, stalks will rot. From not enough water to too much in a matter of hours. We can't win. We truly can't win.

They call them *begguedem*--the want-to-go. They are young men, mostly. Those who couldn't find work at the Ngalam or within the ranks of one of those security companies. Those who despair to ever stumble upon a semblance of opportunity in their native country. Those for whom even mythic Dakar is another dead end, an El Dorado way past its prime, the overrated Senegalese dream, a promise never fulfilled. They tried and tried. They went to school, they graduated, they looked and looked, they applied for jobs, they waited and waited, they applied again, they grew restless, they voted Wade and PDS all the way back in 2000, they hoped and hoped, they waited some more, they marched, they saw no change--*Sopi* où-*Sopi* quand? In 2005 they have their backs against the wall. They're disillusioned, impatient, tired, broke, desperate, at wits' end. Senegal has no middle class: You're either at the top or at the bottom. And it sure is no meritocracy: You don't beat the odds, you don't pull yourself by your bootstraps, you don't go from rags to riches, you don't make something out of nothing, you don't turn 50 centimes into a franc. There's no ladder to climb, no upward mobility, no sky to reach for. You live, you die pretty much where you were born. And so the *begguedem* have decided to try someplace else, to leave en masse, to go and seek in a foreign land, if not fortune, then at least a better life, a more dignified life. By boat, by pirogue, by foot; stowed away in the landing gear or cargo hold of intercontinental planes. Without any fear, by any means necessary. Anyplace but here.

It's our country's great shame, this new phenomenon, especially after the international press makes such fuss of all the migrants who die in their dogged pursuit, victims of the travails, the dangers of the diverse routes. Lost at sea, drowned, dumped in the Sahara by the Moroccan authorities after they get caught trying to reach Spain through Gibraltar.

Here at home the *begguedem* are never far from the collective consciousness. They expose their rotten condition, they hold it up for the whole world to see, they embody the malaise gripping our society. They'd rather risk death than stay. Should they care to acknowledge them, the *beggeudem*'s vicissitudes would cause a terrible blow to our dear leaders, our incredibly incompetent *dirigeants*, the fat cats, Wade and them. It would make them reevaluate themselves and their ruinous policies, it would make them rethink their approach, it would give them the heart to try and cater to the needs of Senegal's most precious resource--its youth. But who has time to hope? Who has time to wait?

Early one morning, onboard a puttering fishing trawler that leaves the northernmost point of Saint-Louis to venture out into the high sea, I'm one of the *begguedem*. Over one hundred and fifty souls packed anywhere there's room: the deck, the hull, the hold, the cabin's roof. Leg to leg, arm to arm, body to body. Of all the vessels traveling to the Canary Islands in the next 24 hours, this, the Koumba Castel, is the one I deemed the most seaworthy. It is also the one that costs the most: $2,000, the luxury cruise of the Atlantic's smuggling expeditions, whereas spots on a pirogue bench go for as little as $1,100. In an overcrowded canoe you're open to anything, out for the waves to toss, the sun to bake, the rain to drench, the storms to drown, the current to lose, the Spanish Coast Guard to block, intercept, and tow back. The Koumba Castel, low in the water as it treads, gives me the best chance to sneak out of the country unnoticed and make it to my destination alive.

It goes smoothly, mostly. Weuss, our skinny and hirsute captain, makes a living taking such cross-Atlantic trips. Aided by a handheld GPS device, he pilots the boat himself, taking only a handful of breaks through the three days and three nights that the crossing lasts, an aide bringing him cup after cup of caffeine-laden *ataya* and relieving him of his duties when he must surrender to sleep or the call of nature. My traveling companions are not all Senegalese. They came to Saint-Louis from Liberia, Nigeria, Ghana, Ivory Coast, Mali, Guinea Bissau. Our group includes women, a few children, even. Feverish, anxious, sullen, sad, excited, restless, free--each and every one of us is feeling something. Some, unused to being on the water, get sick right away. The smell of vomit is so pervasive as to become undetectable. We weren't allowed to bring anything that didn't fit in our pockets. Cellphones, Spanish phrasebooks, and small Korans are the most popular items. Money for the fare changed hands before we left Saint-Louis. To Weuss's credit, food and water are abundant.

Despite cloudy skies we have good weather, the ocean is kind, luck smiles all the way to Gran Canaria. A few nautical miles from the coast, Weuss switches off all the signals and starts approaching his favorite disembarking spot even as a fine mist envelops us. Pandemonium breaks when powerful lamps illuminate the beach. We're not too far to swim and it is what most people do without waiting, without wasting a single minute, without having to be told: Jump overboard and make a go at it. The Koumba Castel empties of its load. Two Spanish Coast Guard vessels leave their promontory and immediately pick up speed, shooting straight for us. I choose an empty spot and let myself fall into the water.

It's every man for himself. The water is cold, crowded, loud, rougher than it appeared from the boat's deck. Only when a swell lifts us can we see the shore, correct our position. Some *begguedem* start struggling right away, splashing around like trapped birds, their shouts, their pleas for help largely ignored. A panicked man grabs my arm as I swim past. I push him, punch him and shake myself loose, keeping my eyes on the tiny lights in the distance. Every man for himself.

The Coast Guard slow down as they get close. Their bullhorns, sirens, and powerful engines drown out our shouts. Circles of light dance on the water, adding to the confusion. The Koumba Castel having long ago retreated, the Spanish don't bother giving chase. Rather, they maneuver toward the biggest clusters of immigrants and start hauling them aboard one at a time, saving some from a certain death.

Stroke after hungry stroke, stingy with my breath, I find my groove. Fast as I'm going, some of the *beggeudem* beat me to the punch. Quicker than I thought it would, the beach appears. It is crowded with uniformed men and exhausted, freezing swimmers. Rocks festoon it. Its sand is dark, much darker than in Africa, and firm under my feet. The air is not as heavy, not as fragrant. We're indeed in a different part of the world.

Hands pull me from the crashing waves. A Red Cross blanket is thrown around my shoulders. I am made to sit with the others. The reception committee is well-organized. Lamps; fence at the beach's edges; smoking-hot coffee in foam cups; German shepherds; vans to carry us to a detention facility right as the sun breaks. We the *beguedem* look at one another without exhilaration or jubilation, realizing how close we came to lose it all, conscious of the fact that we offer a wretched spectacle, worrying about what's coming next. Over a hundred and fifty souls boarded the Koumba Castel. On Gran Canaria our number doesn't top ninety, and it doesn't include any of the women and children seen on the deck. It is safe to assume that the Atlantic claimed them.

In the Spanish men's eyes, various things: scorn, fatigue, disillusion, pity. A few hands rough us up. A few unkind words fly: *africanos*; *cabrones*; *negritos*; *gente de patera*--boat people.

Triage begins as soon as we're herded inside an enclosed yard. The facility is some sort of military base or camp. Barbed wire, electrified double fence, signs painted directly on the ground, numbered barracks. We're searched and made to file in front of an officer sitting at a desk. Questions are asked in plain French. There seems to be no doubt in our holders' minds about the Castel's port of origin, but *beguedem* cannot be sent back as long as they refuse to state their nationalities. The man frisking me finds the Ziplock bag containing my passport. His eyes open wide. He stares at me, and then at the sitting officer, in disbelief. "*Un americano?*"

It takes three days before they let me go. I tell them I'm a freelance journalist working on a story about the *begguedem*, my poor African brothers who travel to distant lands in search of a better life. I tell them I wanted to live it as they live it, see it with my own eyes, feel it with my own bones. Immediately, I'm pulled from the rest of the group. The U.S. embassy is called in Madrid. I don't have press credentials, of course, but my identity is checked through all the proper channels. In the end, the Spanish authorities have no choice but to set me free. My passport is duly stamped before it is returned with a tap on the wrist and a warning: "You have one week to leave Spain, Mr. James."

Leave Spain I do, right after I collect $5,000 wired to myself through Western Union in several installments before Karine and I drove to Saint-Louis. From Gran Canaria I catch a plane to Madrid, where a pre-booked flight takes me straight to Dulles Airport, landing on a bright Sunday morning. After a shuttle bus to downtown D.C., I set up camp in a rundown Motel 6.

Much as I hate to admit it to myself, the city feels more like home than Dakar. This is where I grew up, went to school, worked, became a man. This is what I gave up, not because someone or something ran me out, but because I was ready for a change. The Internal Affairs investigation, though it ended on a positive note for me, had been long and stressful. My work buddies, even the ones I knew to be just as dirty as I was, were steering clear of me as if I radiated an unbearable heat. With Vernon recently deceased, my support system was nil. I was tired. I was lonely. I was lost. The time was ripe for a move. So I resigned from the force, left the house bequeathed by Vernon in the care of a property management company, took all the cash I had squirreled away--all the stolen money Internal Affairs was so doggedly looking for--went to Senegal, set up shop, and went about giving myself a new start, a fresh start, the right kind of start, beginning with the effort to find Salimata and my roots.

I feel much like the same person now as I was then. Maybe because I have yet to find my mother. The big chunk is still missing, the hole is still gaping, my origins are still a daunting, limiting, unnerving mystery. And old habits are close enough to the surface to break free from their tabernacle and make a full comeback--that much is obvious when the cab driving me around passes a few of my old haunts: the Skylark, on New York Avenue; Macondo Lounge and the Penthouse, uptown; the Camelot, on M Street. The itch, the urge are still here: Go in; get a table; get a bottle; get a couple of thick-bodied, long-haired, caramel-skinned, lace-clad girls; get a party started. The itch and the urge are still here. Despite Karine, despite everything that happened, despite the Rebeus stint. The itch and the urge are still here. Whatever is wrong with me is inside me. I take it wherever I go. It won't disappear because I switch cities. What, I wonder, will rid me of my flaws?

"Dre."
"Chris."
We lock palms and share a half-hug. Dre is as laid-back as I remembered. Goatee, skull cap, dressed in all black, long fingers that pluck the meanest sounds out of a bass, daytime job at the MCI Center, side hustle renting cars for extended periods of time from a Florida Avenue secondhand lot. Clean cars, reliable cars, understated and properly registered cars, convenient cars for people unable to put stuff in their own name or people who, like me, need a ride that won't attract attention. "How's that green Toyota?"
"Solid. How long you want it?"
"A few days. Same rate as before?"
"Depends on how it comes back."
I slip five hundred-dollar bills in Dre's palm. "I'll baby it."

131

Dre counts the money before sticking it in his pocket. "That's wassup."

"Still got that connect at the MVA?"

Dre nods. "Price went up, though."

I slip him another five bills. "I'm in a hurry."

"Come out back."

He takes my picture with a digital camera. The next day, I have a valid Maryland driver's license.

The hardest part of my road trip down south is not to fall asleep at the wheel. The Toyota runs almost too smoothly. I stop for coffee wherever I see a sign, I munch on little nothings. Any other time I would have enjoyed myself. America is the most beautiful country in the world. Vernon and I used to crisscross it incessantly--we went north, south, east, west, everywhere. He had purchased a camper just for that purpose, so we could go on long trips, go for any reason, just get up and go. I try not to think too much about him, not to let the memories strike too deep a chord. What would he say if he saw the way I live? What would he think? Vernon was no fool. He knew just what type of person I was, knew it before I knew it, knew it better than me. I suspect that he also knew just what had made me become the type of person I was, though through all our time together I wasn't able to reveal to him exactly what had happened at the Foyer. Vernon was no fool. As I was growing up, he neither put me in a box nor glossed over my mistakes. He just pointed out what I was doing wrong, he told me why it was wrong, he showed me a way to correct it, he urged me to keep working on myself. Vernon was the man. He was a good dad. Can't say I didn't have a decent role model. Can't say I didn't get my share of blessings.

Vernon is far from my mind by the time I cross the Florida line and make my way to Palm Beach. My mind is full of Marie. She and Ibrahim must be Lebou. They love the sea. Wherever they go, the sea follows.

Their house is a waterfront property on Ocean Boulevard. High walls, trees sticking out, tall windows. No guards, no sign of life until I see the garage door open and a young woman drive away with Yasmin in the back seat. I call from the Toyota. Once again Marie lets it ring, ring, ring. Once again she picks up at the last possible moment, right when I begin leaving a message. "Chris?"

"I'm here."

She's everything I remembered, and more. Petite. Exquisite. Perfect oval of a face. Enchanting, enchanting eyes going for the temples. Bare feet. The slightest touch of makeup. Her cheeks, her neck. The hair is all gone--a lingering sign of mourning? No braids, no ponytail. A short cut that reveals, exposes, offers her face to the world. The lines around her mouth are harder, more defined. Her hand is minute, cold. It shakes a little. Is this the first time we touch? It is. I'm dazzled. I'm rattled. I'm dizzy.

The living room is white, all white. Less furniture than I thought, less than in Dakar. The little there is, of course, is sumptuous.

We don't know what to say, at first. I have to prod myself, I have to remind myself of my purpose--this is no reunion, we're not friends, there's work to do, Marie doesn't know me from jack, she doesn't know the first thing about me, she doesn't care. She's all apprehension, all worry, much like when I met her for the first time. She waits for me to open my mouth, tell her everything, let her know what I need from her. She waits for me to crush her, to blow her world to smithereens, to turn everything to ash. "So?"

"I owe you an apology. When your husband came to hire me that morning, all I saw was the money. Ibrahim wanted to conceal the fact that Zak had been taken in retribution for a business deal gone wrong. He said you'd kill him if you ever found out. I regretted participating in the subterfuge as soon as I met you. But by then it was already too late."

"What kind of business deal?"

"Ibrahim bankrolled a diamonds venture in Sierra Leone. When his partner, Momar Sy, was on his way back with the load, Ibrahim pressured him into giving it all up by taking Momar's wife and his son, Samba, hostage. Something went

133

wrong, and Samba died a little after Momar relented. Ibrahim got what he wanted. But Momar quickly regrouped. He bribed Modi into delivering Zak into his hands. Turned the table on Ibrahim. Asked for the diamonds in exchange for Zak. I have a feeling that Ibrahim knew Zak was doomed. We did our best to beat the clock. We turned Dakar upside down, we spared no effort, we stopped at nothing. Momar killed Zak long before he lured Ibrahim to the Madeleine. He was planning to kill Ibrahim after he got the diamonds back. Now it seems that they're still at it. It won't end until one of them dies."

Marie's beautiful eyes are full of shock, horror, disbelief. "Momar? Momar killed Zak?"

"He did. He had no intention of ever returning Zak alive."

Marie buries her head in her hands. Getting close, touching her, pulling her to me is easier than I thought. She's tiny in my arms. So tiny. Her sobs mirror my own sorrow. Her tears wet my shirt. Marie. Shadowboxer, woman in a man's world, Salimata.

She gets up and leaves the living room. I sit and wait, afraid to move, surrounded by white walls, white chairs, white rugs, a white piano. The pool, the garden, the toys glanced through a French door are welcome splashes of color.

Marie comes back. I search her face without finding traces of unraveling or despair. Wounded, yes. Crushed, blown to pieces, torn apart, no. She's pulled through after leaving Dakar. Here, alone with Yasmin, in the lap of luxury. I thought she'd go plain crazy after losing Zak. I thought she'd crawl somewhere and waste away, let herself die. It seems she has survived the blow, it seems she hasn't allowed the pain to take her under. So I misjudged her from the jump. So I underestimated her. So Marie is stronger than I thought. That much, as she sits across from me, is obvious. "How long have you known Momar?" I ask.

"Forever. He's the one who introduced me to Ibrahim. Momar and I ... we had started dating. But once Ibrahim and I set eyes on each other, that was it."

"They're brothers. Half brothers. Ibrahim and Momar."

"No way."

I tell her Xadim's story. I recount my conversation with Mansour: the baobab tree, the monkey bread. It only brings more layers to Marie's incredulity. The truth is hard to swallow, hard to imagine and comprehend, too big--brothers doing brothers like dogs. It just adds more fuel to the fire, begets more questions, spawns more mysteries. "Ibra never told me. In a weird way, what you've just revealed makes sense. Momar was always around. Always. Even after I chose Ibra over him. He worked at IEX. I could never understand the bond between them. It wasn't friendship. It wasn't mere acquaintanceship. There definitely was something there. Something hard to grasp. Something too fleeting to define. They competed at everything. A love/hate relationship. And this is the way it played out, eventually."

"When was the last time you saw Momar?"

"Months ago. Ibra didn't want us to go to Samba's funeral. Momar and Roxaya--his wife--didn't come to Zak's. I was wondering what was going on between them. Ibra wouldn't say a thing. Now I can see why. It was all his fault. He bears responsibility for all this."

The lines around Marie's mouth get deeper. The eyes, the voice get tough. Ibrahim wasn't joking when he told me he feared Marie's reaction. Behind the doll facade is a lion heart. There's no telling what she will do now that she knows.

"It's not over," I say, afraid for her. "Momar is still out there. He might try and come after you and Yasmin. Does he know about this place?"

"We lent it to him once. He, Roxaya, and Samba spent a vacation here."

"Maybe you should go somewhere else. Somewhere he can't find you."

Marie shakes her head. "I'm not running. Ibra had hired round-the-clock security for us. I dismissed them after the first day."

"You shouldn't have."

135

"We had over a dozen guards in Dakar. What good did it do us? I'd rather count on myself."

"You have a gun?"

"In my purse."

Back from the grocery store, Yasmin runs inside the living room, trailed by her baby-sitter, a Florida Sate sophomore. The little girl is as lively, as bubbly as before. A bit taller, even more beautiful. A dress, a barrette in her combed-back hair, pink Chuck Taylors. I wonder how she absorbed the loss, how it will affect her as she grows up and goes through life. "Remember Mr. James?" Marie asks her. Yasmin nods slowly, smiles a little smile, climbs close to Marie, and presses her head against her mother's chest. "I want daddy," she says. Marie's eyes meet mine.

Why'd you think Ibra allowed Zak to venture out of the house alone with Modi, that day?"

"He relaxed a bit too early. He had the diamonds. He thought the game was over. He never saw Momar coming."

"That's the first thing that alerted me, you know? The beefed-up security. We went from two guards every night to a dozen men all day-all night. 'Are we in danger?' I asked Ibra. 'Is something going on?' He said it was just Dakar, the rise in burglaries and home invasions, poverty driving all the kids to desperate acts. I know when my husband lies. I just wish I had understood how serious the situation was."

"It's not your fault."

She shrugs. "I've been trying to tell myself that. It's not easy."

"Whatever happened to the dog?"

"Wolfie? Gave him away.... Why didn't you talk to me that morning, at your place? How heartless of you."

"Too much had happened too quickly. I didn't know what was what. And that was before your husband tried to get rid of me."

When Marie thanks me for trying so hard for Zak, when I see her face light up and open into a smile, her very first smile, I lose it. We're at the gate, I'm taking my leave, I'm almost gone. Though we weren't able to come up with a plan beyond the promise to get in touch once we both make it back to Dakar, we're now tentative allies. We're standing close to each other, physically close, too close, and that proximity is at once more than I can handle. It plays a trick on me, it takes over, it throws me into uncharted territory, it makes me act recklessly, inconsiderately, stupidly, foolishly--it makes me act without thinking at all: I take Marie in my arms and I kiss her. Marie, my Marie, shadowboxer, lion heart, grieving mother, Salimata. Gave me an inch and I'm taking a yard. Made a little progress and I'm going for it, I'm jumping out there, I'm playing my hand, I'm making my move, I'm going for it, I'm going for it: the big break, the getaway, the master play, the chessboard, the Ripley scheme, taking Ibrahim Sow for his wife, his life, his daughter, the houses, the cars, IEX--everything he's got. Karine forgotten that quick, as if nothing ever happened, as if we weren't on a beach rolling among the waves, as if I were man unattached, totally free. It all goes to my head: Marie, the Florida sun, the inch, the itch. I get high, I stop thinking, I stop seeing clearly.

Marie fights it, this kiss. She fights it with everything she's got. Had her purse been nearby she would have pulled her piece and shot me pointblank. How could she not have? We're not friends. She doesn't know me from jack. I'm the man her husband hired to help find her son. I'm the help. I'm nobody. She's just lost so much. Much too much. More than anybody should ever lose. And with the latest developments she stands to lose even more: her marriage, her fifteen-year marriage, her gilded life, the ground she stands on, and maybe--who knows if Momar isn't lurking, stalking, waiting for the perfect moment to strike again?--maybe her precious little daughter, the apple of her eye, her heart. So push me away Marie does. Deliberately, immediately, unambiguously, firmly. "Are you crazy?"

It hurts me. The way she says it, the look on her face, the disgust in her voice, how quickly she slams the gate and disappears from sight, leaving me alone on the sidewalk. I stare stupidly at the house, wondering what it is exactly I have just done. It feels awful. It feels cheap. It feels low. One step forward, two steps back. I'll never understand myself. I'll never change. I'll never know why I do what I do. I'll never have any control over my emotions, my feelings, my actions, my deeds.

I'll never know what's what. I'll never be able to behave correctly, normally. I'll never be capable of empathy, sympathy, respect, loyalty. It's not just Marie. It's Karine, whom I have now betrayed in a matter of days.

It just floors me. It stones me. It makes me want to kill myself. It makes me want to surrender to the shame. Why fight it? I see now that I won't break the run, I won't stray from the doggone line. I'm wired a certain way and that's it, there's no overriding the circuitry. I see nothing but my misguided instincts. I always play to keep. Why fight? It's vain, it's useless, it's hopeless, it's futile. I should just go ahead and kill myself. Rid society of a confused soul, a seriously disturbed bastard.

I get in the Toyota and drive all the way to New Orleans in a fit of murderous rage--rage against myself, against the world, against the forces that made me who I am, against the man who was the instrument of those forces. No radio. No music. Just me and my thoughts, the voices in my head, the pieces of my broken heart, the chill in my bones.

Mirroring my mood, the weather turns darker and more dangerous the closer I get to Louisiana. The sky is not just black, opaque, unyielding: it is dead. A hurricane, a big one, Katrina, is on the way. People are fleeing New Orleans as I'm getting close. Strong winds, torrential rains, flooding, evacuation orders, state of emergency. Not once do I pause and wonder if I should turn around. "Are you crazy?" Of course I am. Always been. Forever will be. What was I hoping? That Marie would return my kiss? That she's as mesmerized by me as I am by her? That we would make love, cut loose all moorings, sail into the future? What was I thinking? I've just let Karine down in a big, big way. I've just made a serious turn in the wrong direction. Might as well kill myself. I'm alone. Alone in my mind. Prisoner of it. Alone I'll end up. Perhaps it's just as well. I'm worthless. I know no limits. No boundaries. No decency. No kindness. No generosity.

I drive straight into the storm. I ride the winds. I taste the water as it crashes against piers and levees, breaches waterfront sandbag defenses, sweeps cars off driveways, lifts homes clean off their foundations, turns power lines into double dutch ropes, makes leaves into a carpet and matches out of trees. I welcome Katrina with open arms. We both came to claim, to break, to eliminate.

New Orleans is a mess, a big circus, a nightmare of confusion, fear, desperation. Everybody's leaving. Only those without means or without a clear head are staying behind--everybody's leaving as I enter the city. I know no names or addresses. I know nothing. I just remember how to get there: this highway, this exit, this store as a major landmark, this turn, this street, this building--rider on a storm.

The oppressing, stifling nursing home smells of death. Sanitized death, organized death, assisted death. It feels worse than the drama playing out outside the walls, the musty walls with their ugly pictures and cheesy paintings and faded signs. There's nobody at the reception desk. An old man is sitting on a bench all by himself. Hope flashes in his eyes when he sees me. Voices, noises everywhere. "I'm here to give a ride to Mr. Matthew Zepp," I tell the first nurse I see, a black man with an earring, an Afro, and stained whites.

"Mr. who?" he asks, pushing a woman tethered to an oxygen tank toward the ramp-equipped double door.

"Mr. Zepp," I repeat, dangling the Toyota's keys.

"Oh, he gone," the man says.

I move to block his way. "Where?"

"Hotel Carolina, downtown, on high ground. We moved some of our people there temporarily."

"Cool."

He's right behind me, pushing his charge. The woman in the wheelchair looks at the sky. She's a tiny, hunched, trembling, fragile thing. Her eyes fill with wonder, a wonder that quickly turns into fear. The sky, dead as it is, is moving horizon-to-horizon like an upside-down motorized walkway. It's not opaque any more. It's some kind of green. White lines cross it, electricity that zaps and reaches madly across the distance.

The nurse sees the Maryland tags on the Toyota. "What you really want with old man Zepp?" he asks as I'm getting

140

behind the wheel. Will he remember the number? I wonder. Will he be able to pick up my face out of a lineup?

"I owe him something," I tell him. "Promised him I'd be back."

The Carolina is a bitch to find. Too much going on. Power out, lights gone black, traffic jams, panic, boarded homes, shuttered businesses. Nobody with the patience, the time, the inclination to give out directions. Cars, pets, people all over. Trucks loaded to the max, trunks open, suspensions low, RPMs on red, engines hot, transmissions, too, passengers on roofs and hoods and pickup beds and running boards. Men, women, children exiting with the bare necessities, going God knows where. Others taking nothing, nothing at all, perhaps because they never had anything to begin with, empty-handed as they walk away from Katrina, hoping the rain holds for a little while longer, until they reach some type of shelter, a bridge, a clearing in the woods, an abandoned warehouse--something. A little help, finally: "The Carolina? Right here in Vieux Carré, man. You're not far at all. Pass that pub, make a left at the next light, watch your right. Green building between a disco and a bakery. Can't miss it. You wouldn't happen to have a buck or two on you, would you? I'm all messed up, man. This fuckin' hurricane."

I've got that new world in my view

There's a woman standing in front of the hotel. A nun in full habit: long white skirt, white socks, white shoes, white blouse, long gray scarf. She's holding a tambourine. She shakes it, bangs it, smashes it against her hip as she sings, nods, stomps, snaps the fingers of her free hand, bobs her head. She's not the only person on the sidewalk--just the only one you hear, the only one you see. Maybe she's here every day. Maybe people know her by now. They've heard her tirade many times before, and so they're not paying her any mind. The nun is not here for money. There's no container holding coins or a few crumpled bills at her

141

feet. She's just here. She's all about her song and her message, her weird message.

On my journey I pursue

I get out of the car. I look up. Green facade. Four floors. A blue neon sign, antiquated, switched off or plain broken. I'm ready to go in, ready to bang on each and every door, ready to tear down all the walls. He's here. He's somewhere inside the Carolina. It's the last stop for both of us. I know it. I know it as sure as if I had written it on the wall myself. I've found him again. I've found Matthew Zepp. As I stare with my head up, he appears face against a third-floor window. His crinkled and ravaged face. His old, old face. His pale eyes taking it all in--the monstrous sky, the wind that kills the trees and pushes the water past the levees in an unstoppable surge, the street, the Toyota, me. Matthew Zepp sees me. He sees me and I can tell he recognizes me, too. I'm Chris. Chris James. Chris motherfucking James. Here as I had promised, just as I had promised. Here to settle all the scores. Here to end it all. Here to put the biggest *buki* there ever was out of business.

Yes I'm running, running for the city

It's just as insane inside the Carolina as it is outside. Wheelchairs blocking the halls. IV stands, gurneys, bags, shoes, walkers, canes, clothes, metal trays, uniforms. Transplanted patients. Angry, overwhelmed, snappy, pushy caregivers. I make my way up the crowded stairs. Nobody stops me, nobody asks where I'm going, nobody cares. Third floor. I go left and start counting the doors. Third door, I stop and push on the wood.

Lord, I've got that new world in my view

The nun's voice is as clear as if she were standing in the middle of the room. Pops is sitting on his bed. By the open window. By himself. There are a few boxes scattered around.

142

His closet is open. His wheelchair is near the door. His parched hands are where I can see them. He looks just the same. Cunning eyes, bushy eyebrows, thin lips, sunken cheeks, shiny bald spot, liver stains. And he smells just the same. That Old Spice stuff. The stuff that, to this day, gives me the chills, stops me in my tracks, lets loose unsavory memories.

He nods. He has enough poise, he has the nerve to nod. "Chris."

"Pops."

It's incongruous to call him that. It hurts as I say it. But that's what he wanted us to call him back at the Foyer. It's his name.

He searches my hands. He looks into my eyes. He scans my pockets for a revealing bulge. Maybe I have nothing on me. Maybe it's tucked in my back. Maybe I'm planning on doing it with my own hands. Pops shifts on the bed. "What brings you to this neck of the woods?"

"A promise."

He sighs. There's a crucifix nailed to the wall, not far form his head. As if Pops knows God, loves God, obeys God. As if he understands the first thing about God.

> *Come on, get an army, help me run this holy righteous place*

I take a step toward the bed. Pops freezes. The arms, the hands, the fingers, the torso, the legs--everything is in decay. The breath, labored, deep, slow, smells like iron. Yet the eyes, the eyes are still full of treachery. I take a second step toward him. Surrounded by people, cocooned in loudness as we are, nothing else exits but this wretched room. It's not Pops I see. It's us, all the Foyer kids. It's the things Pops and his acolytes used to make us do. It's what he inflicted to Karine. And it's not hard summoning all my hatred. It's not hard at all, it's doesn't take long. That hatred is right here in my middle, waiting to be tapped. It's hot, it's spreading, it's growing hotter. It's in my eyes and clenched jaw and fingertips. It's in every wall that I've walked into, every challenge I've faced, every dirty deed I've committed, every lie I've told, every confused corner of my soiled mind, every beat of my self-loathing heart.

"I have something for you," Pops says.

I take a third step.

Can't you hear then, save your callin', well he's knockin' at your door today

Pops lifts a finger. "At the bottom of the closet. Inside a shoe box. I think you should take a look."

I'm almost upon him. His chest starts rising and falling rapidly. His fingers grab the spread. But the gaze, the damn gaze is still full of cunning. I'm close. Too close to stop. I ready myself for the kill. My eyes are on Pops' neck. My hands are almost upon it.

"Your birth certificate is in that box," Pops says. "Don't you want to know who you really are? Don't you want to know who your mother is?"

The tease, the taunt: like a knife slicing into my chest. "Stop talking."

"Beautiful woman," Pops continues. "Not so tall. Cocoa skin. Shapely. Gorgeous hair."

I can't do it. My hands have a will of their own. They stop in midair, midway to the tempting throat. They won't touch it. They won't squeeze it. They won't crush it. Not yet. My mind travels far, far away. Back to that day.

A sunny day. Hot, of course. Hot, stifling, and muggy. Midmorning. Salimata and I driving up the Mamelles hill in the company of a man I didn't know. The car big, blue, boxy, red inside.

"She first came by herself, you know? She's the one who made all the arrangements."

"You're lying."

Pops laughs. He laughs at my distress. He knows me so well. "She gave you up, Chris. We were expecting you. With much anticipation, I must say. Me and the boys. Touching, how

144

you kept waiting for your mother by the gate. Wouldn't eat, wouldn't sleep, wouldn't come out of your clothes. We had a good laugh about it. 'I'll be back soon....' That's what all those women used to tell their children."

I punch Pops hard across the face. The laughter stops.

Pops raises a hand. "Salimata Sene," he says in a whisper. "That's your mother's name."

Shivers run through me. I cannot make myself hit Pops again.

He catches his breath. "In the closet," he says. "The shoe box. Go look."

John, talkin' 'bout a new world

I walk backwards. The sly smile comes back on the old man's lips. Somebody runs in the hallway, runs from one end to the other. I freeze. The steps disappear down the flight of stairs. My back touches the closet. I lower myself. I rummage around. The box is red and white. It smells new. Inside, a throve of documents.

Said I saw a new heaven and a new earth

Pictures. They're all I see. I'm transported back in time. Again. In a flash. A trip both discomforting and disheartening. I am six, going on seven. Right before Vernon appears to take me away. Karine must be about nine or ten. It is night. The *bukis* place us in front of each other in a brightly illuminated room. They make us shed our clothes. They make us caress each other. They make us kiss. Pops snaps pictures while the others watch and touch themselves. They make Karine lie down.

So let us humble ourselves, dear one, get ready for the new world

We start crying when they push to take it further. We try to get off each other, we try to get out of that room. The *bukis*

145

hold us. They are not done. They prod. They cajole. They threaten. They shake. They slap. They lift Karine up. They pin Karine down. They force her legs open. They hold my head against her crotch. They lay me on top of her. I am mortified. Karine can't breathe. Her face is wet, wet with tears.

I can still remember how they felt against my skin, those tears. Here it is before my eyes: Karine; me; naked; that night. How little we look. How skinny. How scared. How terrified. How powerless. No father. No mother. Motherless Koumbas, both Karine and Christophe. Left for a band of hyenas to devour.

Prepare yourself to live in that holy city

In the box, more things. Birth certificates, yes. Names--full names. Dates, places, logs. The missing details. The holes. The links. Pops knew who all of us were. He had always known. When he left Senegal he took it all with him--our history, our genealogy, our souls. He condemned us twice: abused children; disaffected orphans.

Lining the bottom of the box, one more thing: a green piece of clothing whose texture and pattern immediately unlock another set of memories, another smattering of sensations, another round of unease. I take it out and unfold it. It is my old green shirt, my shirt of twenty-some, almost thirty years ago. My Sunday shirt. The one with the long collar and the pearly buttons. The one I had on when I went through the fence and walked into the Foyer.

"Thought that might be of interest," Pops says from the bed.

When I look up to meet his gaze, he has a gun in his hand.

That same city, that same kingdom that Jesus was talking to his disciples about

Pops shoots as I launch myself at him. The bullet grazes my shoulder. I land on top of his frail body and smack the gun

146

out of his hand. His smell--metallic, foul--fills my nostrils. The smell of evil, of sickness, of disease. "Don't!" he yells.

I straddle him. I hit him across the face with my elbow. His teeth tear through my skin. He screams for help. I look for something, anything, to shut him up.

When he left them and gone back to his father

The pillow. It fell from under Pops. I grab it and push it against Pops' head. He tries to slide from under me. He's still got a little vigor left, Pops. He's not ready to go. Not without a fight. He kicks. He cries. He moans. He throws wild punches. My arm is strong, my breath is measured, I'm calmer than I've been in a while, it has never felt so right. The pillow is in place, perfectly in place, sucking the air out Pops' putrid lungs.

Don't forget it, amen, let not your heart be troubled

It's done. Pops stares at the ceiling with big, bulging, unseeing eyes. His mouth, blood-red, useless, gapes open. His arms are sprawled across the bed.

I stay a while by the door, listening, nursing my shoulder. I wait for somebody to come in and inquire about the fuss, the shouts, the struggle, the shot. It's hard to believe my luck when nobody comes.

Believe in God, believe in me also!

I gather the pictures, the documents, the shirt, Pops' gun. I put them all inside the box. I do my best to wipe everything I've touched. New Orleans is going down. Maybe even high-ground Vieux Carré won't make it. Maybe the Carolina will fill with water and become an aquarium. By the time Katrina's done with this town, who knows what'll happen? I might just get away with murder.

147

I've got that new world in my view
On the journey I pursue

The sky opens. The rain starts falling as I step out of the Carolina. A cruiser pulls up before I hit the pavement, lights flashing. I hold my breath. My hand goes inside the box. My fingers clutch the gun. The cop--black, beefy, exhausted--only half-raises himself from his seat. "Come on, Sister Gertrude, you should go seek shelter now. Don't stay out here in the middle of the storm. It's about to get bad."

Yes I'm runnin'

The nun doesn't miss a beat. She stomps, she nods, she shakes her tambourine. The cop looks at me. I have one hand under the box and the other hidden inside. I have a hole in my T-shirt where the bullet narrowly missed the thick of flesh. I have a bloodstain that the rain has yet to wash away. The cop shakes his head and disappears inside the cruiser. I finish crossing. I drop the box on the front seat.

Running for the city
Lord, I've got that new world in my view

The nun is still singing her crazy song, her nonsense song. I know for a fact that after, long after, well after today, each and every line of it will stay embedded in my memory.

Once out of New Orleans, by the side of a quiet stretch of highway, I burn all the pictures, the shirt, and the box itself. The *buki*s weren't just after Karine and me. There were more than a dozen children in the box. Unknown faces. Unfamiliar places. Ignoble acts. I burn the pictures. I burn them all. It's poignant to watch the flames go up and struggle to stay up in the rain. It's sad and poignant.

I scatter the ashes. I throw Pops' gun in the middle of a sprawling wheat field. A door has been shut, finally. Another one has just opened. My body's worn. My nerves are shot. Yet my spirit soars. I'm sure I'll feel different about it tomorrow, in a month, a year. Right now it's untainted, shiny, open. A new beginning. An exorcism--a *n'deup*. A new world in my view.

　　With trembling fingers, sitting inside the car that smells like wet seats and smoke, my breath fogging up the glass, I flip through the stack of papers. Index cards, official documents, paperwork from the Foyer. Karine is from Abidjan, Ivory Coast. Her last name is Dietleng. Both her parents are listed on her birth certificate. Mine is flimsy, yellow with age, weighed by two red 3,000-franc stamps that show monkey bread dangling from a baobab tree. My full name is Christophe Robert Diouf. I was born August 1st, 1971. Two names are scribbled in expansive letters under my own: Salimata Sene; Maurice Diouf.

"Forgive me," I tell Vernon. "I did not mean to hurt you in any way. You took me in. You gave me love. You raised me. You taught me how to be a man. Through it all, I couldn't bring myself to open up to you. I didn't know how. I could not trust you enough to confide, to meet you halfway, to disclose what I had been through. More than once, I came close. But it was too hard. I didn't have it in me. Worse, you never got a truthful word from me. You never got straight A's and two trouble-free days in a row. The teenage years were hell--how did you survive them? I stole from your wallet. I smoked cigarettes. I drank. I used drugs. I drove your car without permission. I hung out late. I dropped out of DeMatha. I did all the things bad kids do. I tested you. You were always patient, Vernon. Never weak. You knew me better than I knew myself. You were the best dad anyone can hope for."

It's peaceful by Vernon's grave. It's shady. There's barely anyone around. The wall bordering Bladensburg Road is far enough that the sleep of the dead stays undisturbed. I've brought flowers in a vase. I've pulled the weeds encroaching on the headstone. I've told my adoptive father how much I love him. I've said words I could never bring myself to pronounce while he was alive. I've apologized. An easy, carefree, innocent, talkative, happy-go-lucky child I was not.

I swing by the house I grew up in, the one Vernon left me. My one rental property, netting me above of $12,000 a year after maintenance, property taxes, insurance, and management fees. The money is delivered in monthly installments into an escrow account. It's my nest egg, my cushion, my retirement plan, a little something I've been setting aside in case I have to make a quick exit from Africa.

The house is on 16th, at the edge of Rock Creek Park, in the part of D.C. nicknamed Gold Coast. A quiet, more than solid middle-class and upper-middle-class neighborhood. The house itself dates back to the 1920s. Two stories, vinyl siding, slated roof, chimney, a small driveway, a porch, a walled backyard. The rooms are very small. All the first-floor partitions were knocked down to create an open floor plan, much like I'm proposing to do in Point-E. Light, space, and warmth greet you as you come in. From the front door you can see across the whole house, all the way to the garden. Dark wood, African art, books everywhere. It's the one true home I've known, and I miss it. I miss its order, its peace, its comfort. I miss Vernon's jerk chicken and football talk. I miss seeing him read at his desk.

"Damn!" Dre shouts after taking a look at the Toyota's odometer. "What, you went cross-country on a motherfucker or something?"

I shut him up with a G. "Just ran a coupla errands."

He takes a drag from his Newport and counts the money. "That's wassup," he says after he's done, a smile softening his dark face.

With time to kill before I board my plane I call Mazakis, my old partner in the force. He's been on leave for the past two months, nursing a bike injury. "Fell off the damn thing and broke my arm," he says as he meets me at the Florida Avenue Grill for a drink. Mazakis is, even by police standards, a big man. Third generation Greek American, high school education, a badass whose dad beat way into his teens to toughen him. Pitch-black eyes, bad teeth, boxer ears, boxer nose, a weird mop of strawberry hair falling over his forehead, likes his beer and Sunday football, Dallas fan in a Redskins town. The bike is a getback from Reyes, our boss. Mazakis got snagged in the same

Internal Affair investigation that nearly took me under. We were both suspected of shaking drug boys for their money and their goods, of keeping much of the cash netted during a drug house raid, of covering our tracks by intimidating witnesses and tampering with evidence. The inquiry dragged on and on. Mazakis and I were put under a microscope. We were trailed, our homes were searched, we were submitted to a polygraph test, which I passed and Mazakis failed. Eventually, all the charges were dropped.

"I'm still watching over my shoulder," he reveals. "How's Africa treating you?"

"Fair."

"You sure?"

"Positive."

"Somebody called Reyes not so long ago. Some detective from Senegal. Said you ran afoul of the law over there. Wanted to get some background on you. Reyes was all tickled: 'Your boy can't seem to keep his hot ass out of trouble, now can he?' I had to shut her up."

"Good-old Reyes. She still a pain?"

"*Is* she. Got me on bullshit details for the past few months. Constantly bustin' my balls. I'm thinking 'bout quitting. That's probably what she's hoping for."

We walk around Columbia Heights, which used to be part of our beat. The old hangouts are gone. New buildings have gone up, more are coming. 14th and Clifton, once a drug-infested corner, is starting to look like Dupont Circle. Mazakis shakes his head. "Gentrification is a bitch, ain't it?"

We clicked from day one, Mazakis and I. Two messed-up souls locked together in a patrol car. We relished the action, the power, the license to let loose our vilest instincts. The way we looked at it, things were going to hell no matter what we did. So we took care of ourselves and we took our kicks where we found them. We talked to people any way we wanted. We frisked civilians for no reason. We roughed them up. We weren't shy about using our guns, batons, Tasers, Mace, and handcuffs. We got drunk. We got high. We passed girls around. We "protected" businesses for perks and cash.

Mazakis and I, we were kindred spirits. We were brothers in arms. I'm not as bitter as he's become. My money stretches a little further than his. I have Senegal. I have a couple of houses. I have a business. All Mazakis can look forward to are the 12 years left before he can retire and enjoy his pension.

I shake his hand before going into the subway tunnel. "You be easy now."

"You, too."

The return trip to Dakar is convoluted. Washington to London. London to Banjul, Gambia. Gambia is an aberration: a sliver of land jutting west to east from Senegal's midsection, effectively cutting it in two. Same people; same customs; different languages; separate nationalities. During the late-19th century Scramble for Africa the French claimed Senegal while the British clung tenaciously to Gambia, surrounded though they were. Banjul, the capital, survives off two things: tourism and duty-free commerce. It is a sleepy and dusty trading outpost constantly crisscrossed by army trucks. The army and its mighty ruler, President Jammeh, are always busy, always at war: against homosexuality and depravation; against potential putschists; against witches; against political opponents, unions, journalists, critics, and dissidents; against Gambia's own bewildered population. It's hard to believe newspaper accounts of the president declaring that there are no gays in Gambia--"zero!"--and of villagers being rounded up by troops and made to drink a fetid concoction believed to cure AIDS and expose evildoers and charm throwers on the spot. Banjul, with its gleaming beachside hotels, encroached downtown shanties, sprawling military barracks, and slapdash markets, is a mini-Twilight Zone, a creepy, scary place.

I make my way to Karang, the desolate border town with Senegal, in less than an hour. There, I hang around bars and shady dives for a couple of days, dropping a few careful words in handpicked ears. My hotel receptionist connects me with a mule, a weed mover who bypasses the border by way of the sea. His name is Vieux. He is young, quiet, tough, capable. His motorboat is red, powerful, a little too loud, spanking new.

We leave Karang in broad daylight, following the coast. The boat swallows wave after wave, leaving a long, white trail, raising a double wall of mist. There's barely enough place to sit. Aside from four jerrycans of gasoline and a drum of water, the floor is crowded with parcels that do not look or smell the least bit like *yamba*. I'm guessing cocaine, whose arrival into these parts has also made the news of late. Narcotraffickers are testing new routes, going cross-Atlantic directly from South and Central America to Guinea, Gambia, or Senegal, and from there by air to Europe. Vieux's boat and the high-power rifle he keeps close at hand point that way. I'm happy to pay him the $200 he asked for and let him take me where I'm going.

The trip lasts less than an hour. Vieux drops me off a little before we reach Saly Portudal, the bustling Senegalese resort town dubbed Sin City. I jump in the water, wade to the beach and make my way through short bushes until the main road called Nationale Une, giving Saly a wide berth. For a mere $10 a truck driver hauling a precariously fastened mountain of charcoal agrees to give me a ride to Rufisque. "Take me all the way to Guediawaye and I'll double the price," I propose.

"Deal. But I won't go in. Wouldn't fit."

"No problem."

His smile is bright and earnest. He extends a hand across the cab. "My name is Camara."

"I'm Chris."

It's been raining a lot. Guediawaye is full of stagnant water. It's at every corner. It pools in the middle of lanes. It bubbles under mounds of trash. It seeps through the sand. It overruns foundations. It leaves, at its highest level, lines on walls that are as tall as a small child. How many more Nabous? I wonder. How many drowning deaths since? How many to come?

What saves me from Karine's fury is the group of patients crowding her waiting room. Karine can hardly believe it's me at first. She doesn't know if she wants to be angry or glad, happy or sad, mad or relieved. The green eyes go from surprise to affection to reproach. Had it been just us, had it been just the two of us I would have undoubtedly felt her wrath.

"I waited and waited," she says once we retreat into her cramped office. "You never called."

"I brought you something," I tell her, opening my backpack.

She sees the big commando knife purchased in Banjul. She sees my passport in a Ziplock bag. She sees the cash I've traveled with. She sees the waterproof box containing the documents. "What is it?"

Her birth certificate is at the top. I pull it delicately from under the rubber band holding the pile together. I hand it to her without a word. Karine takes it. She reads it silently, urgently. She reads it over and over. Her left hand comes to cover her mouth. The fingers holding the piece of paper start to shake. She looks at me, tears falling from her face. She tries to speak, but she can't. Her heart is too big, suddenly. Her tongue is too dry. Words escape her.

I pull her to me and kiss her forehead. She clings to me and cries with abandon. Then, once she feels a little better, once she knows what she wants to do, she pushes herself from me, she takes the birth certificate, she tears it into tiny pieces, she lets the pieces float to the floor. I wince, I almost shout in an attempt to stop her. But she does it fast, she does it quickly--she rips that little rectangle of paper, that memento from another world, another time, another life into illegible, unrecoverable bits. Then she looks at me. "Thank you, Chris. Thank you, but no thank you."

My *métisse*. My sweet pea. My scared little girl. I pull her to me once more. She pushes back. She wants to be left alone. I refuse to let her go. "Pops is gone, Karine. He's gone. He'll never hurt anybody ever again. I made sure of that."

She needn't know the details. She doesn't want to. Later, at the Yoff house, in bed, Karine tells me how happy she

155

is for me. Happier, in fact, than she is for herself. "Ivory Coast? Abidjan? I thought I was Ugandan. I remember Kampala distinctly. So it must have been the second stop, for me. It was a much better place than the Foyer for sure. Nuns ran it. They were stern, but they were fair. We weren't beaten. We had clothes. We had toys. We did things like cultivating a small garden and feeding chickens. We took trips. We were as carefree as you can be living in an orphanage. Why did they ever make me leave? How long was I there? Why wasn't I kept in my country of birth?"

Karine shakes her head. She's sitting in the lotus position in the middle of the mattress. My head is resting on one of her thighs. She's cried, I've cried, we've cried together. There are 73 files in the box, including ours. All those lives. All those destinies. Those interlocked lines.

The light is off. The windows are open. The muslin curtains are pulled. The moon, invited in, lets loose its gorgeous and generous palette. Karine's eyes glow. Her curls, lustrous, shiny, full, roll down her back. Her body is a milky, dreamy landscape. "It'd be easy to find out who I am. You told me as much several times. As easy as a phone call, maybe. I'm just not ready, Chris. I'm not sure I ever will be. I might never go down that road. I'll take what I know. I'll take Giselle and Felix and work with it."

I kiss her knee. She raises her head toward the ceiling and lets out a deep sigh. Her breasts, her throat, the outline of her jaw.... She's out of this world, intoxicating, much too desirable. I pull her down. Her cheeks, her lips taste of tears. We kiss, we rest, we tune our ears to the movements of the sea. "But you should go for it, Chris. Definitely. You've been trying hard enough. It should get much easier from here."

"It should. I'm like you: overwhelmed and a little scared. Now I'm almost worried about what I'll find, how I'll react, how I'll be received. But I can't turn back. My thing is, what if the people we're looking for are also looking for us?"

Both Karine and I decide to let the matter rest for now. Much work remains to be done. We need a clear head. We need focus. Karine's precocious bid to adopt Isaac is hitting a roadblock--Nabou's father, Doudou, is vehemently against it. "My mistake was to start the procedure so soon. I didn't give the family enough time to process things, to work everything out. All I saw was the kid and his well-being: 'Is he eating right?' 'Is he getting his medicine?' 'Does he have everything he needs?' Nabou never got along with Doudou. At times she seemed downright scared of him. I felt that Isaac would be better off with me. He knows me more than he knows them. And I'm attached to him, you know? I am. I want him to have a good life."

"I'll go and have a talk with Doudou," I tell Karine.

My tone makes Karine look up. "You're not gonna hurt him?" she asks. "Are you?"

I silence her fears with a peck on the forehead. It's my new favorite spot. "No."

That's Karine.

On my side of things there's this unfinished battle, the little trouble, the duel with Ibrahim Sow. Finding Salimata won't help me if I remain a marked man, a fugitive in my own country, a man barred from entering his own house, a man on the brink of losing everything. So my priorities are clear. So my work is cut out for me.

Marie calls my cellphone from Mame Awa's as soon as she makes it to Mermoz. Part of me never believed she'd come back. Part of me never thought she'd call. Not after that maladroit, misinformed, unfortunate attempt at a kiss. I thought she might choose to stay away from me and my problems, my issues, my baggage, my psychoses. I thought she might choose to stay in Palm Beach, pretty and nice and cool and quiet and safe in that all-white oceanfront property, the lap of luxury. But here she is, Marie, talking to me as if nothing ever happened, as if we're really really all good. Marie, who always takes me by

157

surprise. Marie, who's something of a wonder in her own right. "What do we do, Chris? What's next?"

"It depends. How's things with Ibrahim? Where do you stand?"

"We're talking. I want a separation. I want Yasmin. I want to move on. I'm not returning to the house--ever." She says it defiantly, with enough conviction to make me an instant believer.

"What's his take on it?"

"The usual stuff: 'Let's think about it,' 'It's too soon,' 'You're upset,' 'You're still mourning Zak,' 'This isn't the time to do anything drastic'.... The usual stuff."

"Did you confront him about Momar?"

"I did. He denies everything. Calls it a lie."

"Do you believe him?"

Marie hesitates a little. Did I expect her to take me at face value? "I don't know what to believe," she says. "And there's one more thing: He knows I've been talking to you. He knows you managed to find me. So you'd better watch your step."

I do the only sensible thing: I take Marie straight to the source, to a person whose word she can trust. I take her straight to Retba in old Matar's taxicab, Yasmin riding along.

Mermoz, Patte d'Oie, Camberene, Mbao, Malika. We ride, we talk, we plot. Marie opens up a little. Yasmin is withdrawn, sullen. Could be me. Could be Matar. Could be Ibrahim. Could be the uncomfortable back seat. Maybe this is the way she'll be from now on. Kind of like I was as a child: not too prone to trust adults, to laugh out loud, to jump around, to get excited. A child without an inner light, without shine, without gloss. A child without magic. "She misses our old life," Marie says after Yasmin falls asleep. "She misses her brother. And then school is about to start. I'm not sure yet where she's going to go. I don't even know where we're going to live."

Mansour isn't home. "Try his plot," Modi's girlfriend tells us obligingly. I wonder why she's always there. Has she become Mansour's maid? Did he take her in in a gesture of retroactive magnanimity? Is he dutifully watching over her and her baby now that Modi's gone? Or does he have a darker motive in mind? *Dungurus* need love, too. The girl is young, she's strong, her hips fill her *pagne* fully, she's not ugly, she might just be willing. And as *dungurus* go, Mansour has made out okay. His plot isn't by the lake like Ibrahim's, it's not a super-operation but it is of decent size, it is walled, it is equipped, it is populated with fruit trees and vegetable beds and irrigation trenches, it holds a few dozen heads of cattle, it is worked by a handful of villagers, it lacks not the amenity of a single-story bungalow, a bungalow in front of which Mansour is sitting on a long chair as we drive through the open gate and follow a driveway, raising dust and chasing butterflies from their nectar-filled spots amid slender flowers.

Yasmin, knocked out by the heat, doesn't rouse from her sleep. The old man gets up as Marie and I get out. The omnipresent beads are in his right hand. Workers give us a passing glance before turning their attention to their duties.

"Mansour."

"Marie."

They don't shake hands. Never was much love between them. They resent each other, Marie just told me. They both had access to different parts of Ibrahim. Parts that were mutually exclusive, partitioned, neatly defined. Parts too wide apart to accommodate much of a relationship, let alone a friendship, between the two counsels.

"To what do I owe the pleasure?" Mansour asks Marie.

"Tell her what you told me," I instruct the *dunguru*. "Tell her everything."

He turns defiant, the *dunguru*. I'm on his turf. He thinks about it for a moment. He's got his men. He's standing on his own land, bought with his own sweat, enjoying the fruit of his labor after all these years of taking orders, cleaning up messes, fixing things, catching mistakes. Mansour thinks about it. The monkey bread whipping is far from his memory. Or maybe it is too close, still close. Maybe it stings, tugs at his pride. Maybe he wishes he could make up for his humiliation.

Mansour looks at me with all the hatred he can muster. I give him my most earnest smile. I tap my belt, where the Glock patiently rests. Mansour looks at me. He looks at his men. One is tending a maize crop. One is fiddling with a water pump. One is just trying to look busy. They're young, they're devoted, they probably know their way around knives and machetes. Mansour looks and thinks. He think and looks. Marie brings him back to the matter at hand. "Tell me everything," she says. "Now!"

How ferociously she says it. How imperiously. Mansour simply has no way to go. Hurt me? Hurt Marie? Refuse to speak? If only.

I watch from the car as they circle the property, walking in the shade of the wall. It's not a dialogue, a conversation, a heart-to-heart. Mansour does most of the talking. Marie asks questions. She requests details. She interrogates. She weighs. She examines. Not once does she takes her eyes off Mansour. I almost pity Mr. *Dunguru*. He can't bring himself to hold himself upright, to walk a straight path, to look Marie in the eye, to stop sweating. I pity the man. Maybe one day he'll find peace. Maybe one day he'll be released.

The return trip to Mermoz is very quiet.

"I know where to find Momar," Marie tells me the next day.

"It was about two years ago," Marie explains. "I told you how I knew Momar before I met Ibrahim? How nothing ever happened between Momar and me--that once Ibrahim came into the picture, that was it? Well, Momar never stopped trying with me. Even after Ibra and I got married. Even after Momar himself got married to Roxaya. Never stopped. I never gave him the time of day. But I never told Ibrahim, either. It was more like an annoyance, you know? No use making a big fuss about it. So every once in a while Momar would pop the question, like clockwork. And, like clockwork, I would turn him down. Until this one day, this one time when Ibrahim really hurt me. Went out and cheated on me openly. I thought, What better manner to get back at Ibrahim? The way they're always trying to outdo each other, their game of one-upmanship. The way Ibrahim despises Momar. So I called Momar. He jumped on it, of course. Asked me to meet him on Gorée Island. He owns a house there. Something nobody--not even Roxaya--knows about."

After Marie describes that house to me, after she tells me where and how to find it on the crowded island, I have one last question for her, my blood boiling, my head spinning, my heart clutching my ribcage as if I were a concerned party in the triangle, the intimate drama involving her, her husband, and her husband's half brother. As if I had every reason to be furious, every right to ask. "Did you do it?"

Marie snaps back. Instantly, angrily, jolted by the words. "Say what?"

"Did you go along with it? Did you sleep with Momar?"

I don't know what comes over me right then. Jealousy, I think. It must be jealousy. And disgust. I'm losing my mind a little more each day. I'm losing it.

Marie holds my gaze. I have no way of knowing what she sees in my eyes. "None of your business," she answers.

Gorée is one of those places that are hard for a black man to visit. Full of history, tragedy, madness, sadness, wistfulness, hurt. During the slave trade the island served as a holding place for captives en route to the Americas or the Caribbean. One can see artifacts from that wretched time--chains, metal chokers, handcuffs, hooks, pistols--on display at the House of Slaves. One can visit the dungeon. One can stand at the threshold of the Door of No Return, the opening overlooking deep, dark-green waters, through which enslaved Africans left the continent for the last time.

Gorée is also a much sought-after beach, a resting spot. After the ferry docks, I make my way among tourists and *dakarois* out for a day in the sun. Local kids rush the passive ferry attendants and run across the deck, only to climb on the rail and dive from on high. Then, back at the surface, laughing, slicing through the water like dark dolphins, they fight over the coins thrown at them. The island was long ago declared a Unesco World Heritage site. People the world over come to see with their own eyes the remnants of a harrowing, violent past. Black men and women from the Diaspora make the trip to pay tribute to their ancestors. But Gorée is not much different from the rest of Senegal. It is extremely poor. It could use more infrastructure, a revitalization, better education, decent public services, utilities that work, a lift into modern times for its 1,000 or so permanent residents. Here, too, people survive on nothing. Here, too, they smile and welcome visitors even as their bellies contract with hunger.

Momar's house is near the island's highest point, only a few paces from the Church of St. Charles. It's a steep climb. The streets are narrow and shady, some earthen, some cobbled. Habitations are in various stages of disrepair. I walk in front of Momar's dwelling without stopping. The small door is topped by an elaborate arch. The high brick wall gives out nothing. I turn around. Tourists going into the historic church are the only

162

other people on the street. I stop. I turn the door handle. Locked. I push. The door doesn't move an inch. I knock. I knock again. I knock louder. Nothing. Where is Momar? Where are his bodyguards? I swear in frustration. I kick the door two, three times.

As I turn to start my descent toward the beach and the next ferry, I almost bump into Momar. He's walking past the church, impossibly tall, blacker than black, a loaf of bread under his arm. Baseball cap, sunglasses, coat-hanger shoulders, jeans, espadrilles, a polo shirt, a nonchalant cigarette. He sees me, freezes a little, sees the video camera around my neck, relaxes, breathes better, approaches without any misgiving. "Looking for the church?"

I take a quick step to fill the gap between us. I pull the Glock and stick it deep into his stomach. "Looking for you," I whisper. "No fuss. No sudden moves."

"I ... I don't have any money," Momar stammers.

"I'm only here to talk. Open the door."

I must not be very convincing. Momar drops his bread. He drops his keys. It takes him three attempts to find the right one.

We enter a sandy courtyard. I push a massive latch to secure the door behind us. A silver lizard jumps from under a pile of leaves.

Momar's love nest is a very small house fronted by an overflowing, citrus-scented garden. Somebody took great care restoring its windows, its trimmings, its floors. It's cozy, if a little dark. Built-in seating lines the wall. The kitchen is spare, too tiny for serious cooking. The bedroom, in an alcove, is almost an afterthought. The feeling, the impression is that of a cabin. Momar, tall as he is, barely fits inside the living room.

I make him pull a wooden chair and sit on it. I make him tie his feet with a piece of string. I make him join his arms behind his back. I hit him strong enough with the Glock's butt to make him pass out. I tie his wrists together. I tie his arms to the back of the chair. I pull the camera from around my neck and set it up in a nook between the walls, where the angle is just right. I

163

check for clarity and sound. I capture an image of Momar's ID card. I search the doll house from top to bottom. Momar has a little over 1.2 million CFA in 10,000-franc notes, 15,000 euros, a Magnum much like Ibrahim's, an AK-47, and not much else. He's been hiding alone. Eating noodles, salami, camembert, and peanuts in the shell. Drinking water by the gallon and Flag beer. Watching Jean Gabin and Lino Ventura movies. Reading Le Soleil, Le Monde, Kessel, Saint-Exupery, and Simenon.

Momar comes to right as I'm placing a chair for myself in front of him. He blinks. He licks his big lips. He turns his neck. He tries to move. "I'm about to ask you a few questions," I say, going through my little routine. "Answer truthfully and we're straight. Answer less than truthfully and accept anything that comes your way. Deal?"

He swallows hard. Just doesn't seem that tough up close, Momar Sy. Just doesn't look like he's got the fiber. Something soft in his eyes. Something a little lost. It's easy to see how Ibrahim would beat him at everything. Easy to understand why Ibrahim would underestimate him. They are worlds apart. Ibrahim had Xadim living under the same roof. He was next in line for IEX. He had Marie. He had the looks and the money. No pretty girls for Momar. No high-society wife. No Paris-Dakar Race. No silver spoon. Yet this is the man who went to Sierra Leone and brought back a diamond harvest. The man who hired Modi and had him killed. The man who murdered Zak.

I hit the "record" button and take my place in the chair facing Momar. "State your name."

Momar tries his best to look fierce and uncooperative. He's Jean Gabin. He's Lino Ventura. He's a tough dude caught in a bad jam. "Who the hell are *you*?"

Sighing with frustration, I get up and stop the recording. I get close to Momar. I whip out the Glock. I hit him across the mouth with it. The steel cracks Momar's lips. It smashes two of his teeth. It caves them in. Momar screams.

I wait until he's a little calmer to get the recording going again. I get back in my seat. "Name?"

Momar tries to speak. Blood gets in the way. It streaks his teeth, it bubbles, it drips from the corner of his lips. Sighing again, I stop the recording. I wipe Momar's mouth and his cheeks with a towel. I hit the "record" button once more. I sit back down. "Name?"

"Momar Sy," Momar goes.

"How do you know Ibrahim Sow?"

Momar swallows. "He's my brother. Half brother."

"You and Ibrahim Sow work together, yes?"

"Yes. We ... we used to. At IEX, the company that my--our father left us."

"Why did you kill Ibrahim Sow's son, Zak?"

Momar swallows again. I'm waiting for him to run out of saliva any minute now. He looks at me. He looks at the video camera that misses nothing from its resting point. He lowers his head. All I have to do is sigh loudly, clutch the Glock and act like I'm about to get up for Momar to wince. "Ibrahim killed my son, Samba," Momar says loud and clear. "I went crazy. I lost it. I wanted to pay him back for what he had done. I wanted revenge."

"How did you do it?"

Momar hesitates. I sigh. He rushes to beat me to the punch. "I had someone else kill Zak. I couldn't bring myself to do it." Momar's voice breaks. His eyes well up. "Zak was like my own son. I loved that kid."

"So who did it?"

"Man named Tyson."

"Where is he?" I ask for the camera's benefit.

"I don't know."

I get up. "It's the truth!" Momar shouts. "Tyson disappeared a while back. His whole family is gone. They left everything behind. He must have gotten scared or something."

"Why were you and Ibrahim fighting in the first place?"

"We had made a deal. I had come to him with a business proposition. He agreed to back me. I went and did all the work. I completed my task. I accomplished everything I had set out to do. But Ibrahim tried to stiff me out of my share. Took my wife

165

and son hostage to make me give up the goods. Allowed the bout of meningitis that afflicted my little boy to go untreated. Effectively condemned him to death."

"Why are the two of you still at it? When does it end?"

Momar regains a semblance of confidence, of bravado. He's Jean Gabin. He's Lino Ventura. "When one of us is dead. That's when."

"The diamonds are gone," I remind him. "You both lost a loved one. Why not call it a day? Why not just drop everything, forget, rebuild? Why not call a truce?"

It's as if everything I've just said went over Momar's head. He stopped listening a long time ago. He stopped at the very first word. "Diamonds? What diamonds?"

"The diamonds you got from Sierra Leone," I tell him, not bothering to get up. "Don't act like you don't know. Ibrahim told me himself what this was all about. Those diamonds are gone, by the way. Ibrahim threw them into the sea right in front of me. Don't think that you'll get your hands on them. It's over. Might as well give up, count your losses, stop everything."

Momar laughs. He laughs so hard it hurts him. "Diamonds? It was never about diamonds!"

I get up. I grab the Glock. Momar can't stop laughing, he won't stop laughing. I sigh. I stop the tape. I come to stand in front of my prisoner. "You don't have to hit me," Momar interjects. "I'll tell you everything I know."

It was never about diamonds--Ibrahim working his mojo on me, spreading a little puff of the magic powder in front of my credulous eyes. The canisters he took to the Madeleine, his noble gesture on the pirogue as we were bringing Zak's body back to Dakar? All for show. Momar, tied up as he is, is having the time of his life. He gets agitated, he can't get the story of his one good move fast enough. Recognition is what he's after. A little sympathy. A nod to his creativity, his toughness, his skills. Nobody's ever taken him seriously. Besides, I'm the only audience he's had in a while. "Diamonds? Sierra Leone? Please. That's so '90s. I had something much better than that, man! I

166

had some serious shit in my hands. Some serious, serious shit. Better than diamonds. Better than gold. It's uranium I was after, man. U-ra-ni-um."

"What?"

"I'm tellin' you. Went all the way to Congo to make it happen. Out there in the jungle, man. For five months and sixteen days. Dealing with all kinds of complications: animals, rebels, malaria, the official army, Rwandans, refugees.... It was do or die, man. Do or die. It took everything I had to pull it off."

"Uranium?"

"Uranium. On Samba's grave. Can I get a cigarette?"

I light one up and stick it between his busted lips. Momar sucks on it greedily. His mind wanders a little. Maybe he's thinking about his son. Maybe he's back in Congo.

I take a few steps in the garden. I walk around in circles. I come back in.

"So who are you, man? You're not gonna tell me?"

"I'm Chris James. I'm a private detective. Ibrahim hired me to help him find Zak. I was on the Madeleine Island, that night."

"You were? Sorry for shooting at you. Nothing personal."

"No worries."

Momar's head hangs low. "So Ibrahim sent you, huh? I guess that's the end for me, then. This is where it stops."

"No," I tell him. "Ibrahim didn't send me. I'm here for myself."

"How did you find me?" he asks, showing more presence of mind than I would have thought him capable of.

"One of your old girlfriends. They tell me you're quite the heartthrob around town."

"Aw please, man."

Momar is tickled by the joke, mistaking it for a compliment. As he sees my mood turning somber, more serious, his eyes cautiously search mine. I came ready for anything. I came ready to avenge Zak, kill Momar and take his head back to Marie. I have no animosity in me left. It's all gone for the day. I have only sadness, a creeping fatigue. Momar is like a child himself. He's also a little like me--the perennial underdog, the eternal also-ran. At least I had the luck of knowing what to expect from life early on. People like us don't win. We don't have the looks, we don't have the smarts, we don't have the start. We spend all our lives playing catch-up. Momar worked hard at what he understood to be his one big break, his time to shine, his "*Touchez Pas Au Grisbi*" heist. He gave it his all and still came up short. Would I have done anything differently?

For a moment there I'm tempted to walk away. Go, disappear somewhere, turn my back on it all. Just for a tiny, fleeting moment. Ahead or not, you never quit. Those were Vernon's own words.

Momar's look and his voice are almost commiserating. "He played you, too, didn't he? Ibra took you to town, huh? Just like he did me."

I take my seat. I press my fingers on my face. I rub my eyes. Why am I feeling so tired, all of a sudden?

"You all right, man?"

"Tell me about Congo. Tell me more about the uranium."

"What do you want to know?"

"Where is it from?"

"Goma. That's where you find everything in Congo."

"You extracted it yourself?"

"Hell no! That stuff's dangerous, man. You gotta be pretty desperate or seriously crazy to dig around for it. The closest I got was the edge of the big hole, at the mine."

"What does it look like?"

Momar shrugs. He's not Gabin any more. He's Indiana Jones. He's seen it all. It's all old news. "Metal rods. Don't look like much."

"How does it keep?"

"Canisters with an embedded Geiger counter. The same kind Ibrahim had with him that night. I thought he had my stuff in it. He had me fooled, too."

"You had the uranium. Then what?"

"I had the product and the market; I had people lined up to buy."

"Who?"

"A bunch of dudes from Sudan. Extremists. They were staying at my hotel. Next door to me, matter of fact. Kept me up all night with their prayers. Very serious dudes. Big beards. Skullcaps. Never laugh, never look at women, never set foot in a bar. Allah this, Allah that, the sharia, jihad, the caliphate. Can't get them to talk about anything else. They might not have been there for any particular purpose. I guess word about me got around. They approached me about buying. They offered three million dollars cash. I told them to meet me in Dakar."

"Why didn't you just go for it? You had the uranium; they had the money."

Momar looks away. He won't admit that he was out of his league, that setting up an exchange with a group of hardened operatives in a foreign land was more than he could handle. "I'm still beating myself up over it, man. My one big mistake. It cost me everything. Ibrahim was expecting me to bring the uranium back. The boat that would take me home was already on the way. That's what we had agreed upon. It was a matter of loyalty, brother to brother. Call me stupid."

"Did the Sudanese ever make it to Dakar?"

"They did. They were ready, too. Didn't even balk when I jacked the price on them."

"What's the new going rate?"

"Five million dollars."

"They're still biting?"

"Like crazy. Waiting for me to say the word. I just happen not to have the merchandise in my possession any more."

"Where is it?"

"In Ibrahim's hands. Where else? He hasn't thrown it into the sea, I can guarantee you that."

"How do you know he hasn't sold it?"

"No way. Ibrahim doesn't have those kinds of connections. He likes to keep his hands clean. That's why he still needs me."

"What do you mean?"

"He called me yesterday to propose a truce--took him long enough. He brings the stuff, I bring the Sudanese. We bury the hatchet, we complete the sale, we split the money."

I stand up, rejuvenated, refreshed. "What did you tell him?"

Momar sneers. "I told him no. I'm broke, I'm tired of fighting and holing up, my only child is dead, my wife won't speak to me for nothing.... But damn if I ever get caught trusting my dear brother again."

I start untying Momar. He frets a little, mistaking my intention. "Easy," I tell him. "Relax. We're on the same side."

He stretches. He smiles. He rubs his wrists. "I need to pee."

I nod. "Go. Leave the door open."

He gets up. His legs give out. He falls. He gets up again. He goes pee. "So what do you want me to do?" he asks from the bathroom.

"You're gonna call Ibrahim. You're gonna tell him you've changed your mind."

Like a good boy, Momar washes his hands. He washes his face. He rinses his mouth.

"What's in it for me?"

I tell him the first thing that comes to my mind. "We put Ibrahim out of circulation. We share the dough. You take over IEX. I get the cops off my back."

"Momar looks at himself in the mirror. His eyes get big, too big for his long face. "Brilliant!" he shouts. "Brilliant!"

I grab the camera. I play a bit of the recording for Momar's sake. "There's enough on this to put you away for a long time," I point out. "So no crazy moves. No double cross."

Momar nods. He sits on the built-in bench. He places the call to Ibrahim in front of me.

I go and wait for Doudou on the sand. Ouakam is many things by day: a surfing spot for French kids; a market where buyers patiently await the day's fresh catch amid rows of smoked fish drying on tables; a regular, if very small beach; a *boutiku Naar* dispensing everyday necessities like cooking oil by the ladle, milk by the cup, coffee by the spoon, sugar by the cube, cigarettes by the stick; a lone fuel pump for the pirogues' engines; a tailor for the *boubous*, the *grands-boubous*, the *tailles-basses*, the dresses. Tall, thin, colorful, the minaret overlooks it all. Ouakam is one of those enclaves where time has been sitting still. One wonders how long the village will last. The place is ripe for development. It is screaming for a decent road, hotels, restaurants, smart boutiques, a rich man's villa or two. One day the city's fat cats will wake up and devise a semilegal way to appropriate the gold mine they've had their eyes on for quite some time. One day the Lebous will stand to lose all the land that's been rightfully theirs for generations.

Doudou makes it in time for the afternoon prayer. He and his men pull their boat from the water. The buyers leave the open-air market and approach leisurely. The haul is meager, as I'm sure it's been for the past few years. It's not just Ouakam. I saw it in Cayar. I saw it in Mbour. All the fishing villages are dying slowly. They can't compete with bottom-trawling industrial vessels. Fat cats sold permits to Korean, Japanese, and European interests, allowing them to pillage the Senegalese waters at will. Fat cats sold their country's own fishermen out. They condemned them to a slow death. They saw only the quick

171

infusion of foreign currency, ostentatiously sought out in order to shore up the budget. Most of the money, of course, ended up lining the fat cats' fat pockets. Fat cats are pushing hundreds of thousands of their countrymen out of the only way of life they know.

Doudou's wearing his condition on his weather-beaten face, his downcast eyes, his hard body, his short beard, his thick fingers, his busted nails, his scars, the smell that clings to his pores. We talk on the way to his house, if one can call the rundown compound that is half-buried in sand a house. "You're going to give Isaac to Karine," I tell Doudou. "You're not going to make any more trouble. You will drop the matter nice and easy."

Doudou stops walking. He comes out of his yellow waterproof jacket to free his arms, his chiseled chest. There is more toughness in that gesture than a Momar can muster in a lifetime. "The boy is mine," Doudou tells me as the muezzin starts the call to the 5 o'clock prayer. "I'll never let him go."

It's just me, probably. My galloping imagination. My paranoia. But in those words, in Doudou's claim, in Doudou's eyes, I recognize something. Something I used to see in Pops. I guess I'm some kind of expert now. I can smell *bukis* all over the world. I can sniff them out for who they are wherever they are. Doudou is one. I could bet much on it without losing any sleep. He's one. No way of knowing what he did to Nabou. No way of finding out what he really means by "mine." But he's one.

I turn to face him. "I have two things in my pocket, Doudou. You can have either: gun or bundle of cash. Which one is it gonna be?"

We're staring deep into each other's eyes. No fear in his. No fear in mine. "The boy will be cared for, Doudou. His health will be tended to. He will be loved. He'll never set foot on a pirogue if it ain't for fun. He'll have the best schools. He'll have the best mother on earth. He'll have a chance at a regular life, a normal life. Let him go."

Doudou seems eager to cede a bit of terrain. He's sharp. He knows an opportunity when he sees one. He knows Ouakam is dying. Tomorrow, next year, two years from now the fish will all be gone. Tomorrow, next year, two years from now the fat cats will come and claim the sand that is swallowing his compound the same way they took his livelihood and gave it away--the same way they sold all the fish in the sea. "How much?" he asks.

"More than you've seen in your whole life. A one-time payment. You give up Isaac for good. You stay out of his life. Only the grandmother can visit."

"How much?" Doudou asks again.

We walk into his yard. We enter his standalone room. Doudou is doing it the traditional way, the old-school way, the poor man's way: his room at the center of the courtyard--the biggest, nicest, most modern-looking, most comfortable; around it, like satellites, his wives' digs, a room each, not just for themselves but, until they outgrow the arrangement, for the children they give birth to. Doudou rarely ventures out of his quarters. His wives take turns sleeping with him. Whoever's turn it is provides the collective husband's dinner for the duration of the turn--two or three nights in a row, generally--and looks after his every need. It's all prearranged, codified, ratified, accepted. It's the old-school way, the poor man's way. Everybody on top of one another.

Doudou and I sit on his woven mat. His first wife, Soxna, Nabou's mother, whose turn it is today, deferentially brings us water. I remember her from the *n'deup*. She's got a tired, resigned look on her face. Her lips, her chin are tattooed black. Her legs are heavy. Her toes are wide apart, her heels are cracked, her soles are thick. Her scarf is cocked to the side, showing a sweep of graying hair to which an amulet is pinned.

Doudou impatiently chases Soxna away. I pull the bundle out of my pocket. I hand it over. I make Doudou sign his name on the documents I've brought after he counts his cash. He'll never have to chase disappearing fish again should he choose to. He'll never have to mend another torn net. He'll never have to risk breaking his back hauling a dugout canoe on the beach.

"Bring Isaac," Doudou tells Soxna when we're done.

Isaac hides behind his grandmother and peers at me cautiously. He's a bit short for his age. A bit small. "You're going to go with your uncle Chris," Doudou tells him, showing no emotion. "You're going to be a good little boy. Hear me?"

Isaac nods slowly. Soxna lets out a sob. Doudou silences her with a look. Isaac stares at me, his huge eyes full of curiosity. I smile my biggest, most radiant smile. He smiles in answer.

Soxna bathes him behind a partition in a corner of the yard. She dresses him in shorts and sandals. She hands me a plastic bag containing a few items of clothing, a week's worth of antiretroviral medication, and a snapshot of Nabou. Then Soxna walks us to the car, holding the child's hand. "I'm sad to see him go," she says softly. "But I'm also glad. I know *Doctoru*--Dr.--Karine will take good care of him."

She hugs and kisses Isaac before he goes and sits in Matar's cab. He holds his only toy, a car made of wire, with empty condensed milk cans for tires.

"You're welcome to come visit whenever you want," I tell the old lady.

She cries as she walks away.

"How did it go?" Karine asks as I open the door. I move aside to reveal Isaac. Karine drops her book. She kneels down. She stares at the little boy as if she can't believe her eyes. "*Tata* Karine!" Isaac shouts--Auntie Karine. He shakes his torpor, he gets animated, he starts jumping in place. Karine wraps her arms around him. "Not '*Tata*,'" she corrects him. "*Maman* Karine."

We're not ready for anything, of course. Not knowing if my plan would succeed, I just told Karine that I was on my way to try and talk Doudou out of his madness "or reluctance--whatever the hell is wrong with him." Karine didn't expect me to bring the boy back. She didn't know that today would be the day she'd become a mom--a *maman*.

174

So the first week is a scramble. We clear a room. We paint. We furnish. We fill Isaac's life with as much softness and joy and attention and tenderness as we can gather. Karine, for the first time in a long time, takes a few days off. I watch her transform. I watch her go through a metamorphosis. I watch Isaac settle into a new regimen with glee. I watch him bond and get attached not just to Karine, but to me. I watch myself take a little one under my wing. I'm amazed that it's so easy, that it feels so right, that it feels so good, that it comes so naturally. Isaac's affliction is almost an afterthought. There are rules to follow, precautions to take. Once understood and absorbed and folded into a routine, they become a second nature.

It changes our lives from the very first second, Isaac's arrival. Far from making it more difficult or fragmented, it makes it more complete. You never realize how empty even the most beautiful of houses is until a child walks in and graces it by his presence. Karine blooms. She glows. I look at her and I see the little girl who took me in at the Foyer. It's her mission. It's her one job in life: Save all the little boys in danger. Keep them out of harm's way.

We talk. We talk all the time. About the future, mostly. About raising a family. About giving Isaac everything we missed out on growing up: a home, two parents, birthdays, soccer games, road trips, Sunday dinners, Christmases, *Tabaskis*--the biggest Muslim holiday--and *Tajabones*, Senegal's Halloween. About providing all the love we never had. About doing something for many more children. Abandoned children, at-risk children, children like the *talibes*--the Koranic school students, the little beggars. So many of them are in need. Maybe we can help. Maybe we can find a way.

It's a blessed first week. A treasured and cherished hiatus.

By the following Monday it's time to turn my thoughts to the duel with Ibrahim Sow--the little trouble.

Matar drops a copy of the recording made on Gorée Island at the Brigade Criminelle headquarters. I give Diack a full

175

day before calling him. Late in the evening, at the beginning of his shift, from a prepaid phone. "That footage proves nothing," the detective tells me from the go.

I have no problem agreeing. "It's not meant to. I just wanted to throw a bone your way. So you know what the real deal is."

Diack plays it cool. He sounds hostile. Belligerent, almost. "Escaping like you did? That's not going to make your case any better. Just tack more time onto what you're already facing."

"You had me in jail for no valid motive, Detective. What was I supposed to do?"

"I didn't have a motive then. I have one now."

"What do you mean?"

"I went back to your house. You want to know why? Your passport hadn't turned up during the first search. I knew it had to be somewhere. I knew that by finding it I might stumble upon something interesting. So I went back. I looked and looked. The garden was last on my list. I got lucky. Didn't find the passport, but I dug out a lot of cash. And a weapon. A dirty one: Ballistics linked it to one of my Madeleine bodies. Throw me a bone? You got something big coming your way."

"That was self-defense."

"Save your explanations for the assizes court. My job stops at finding you and locking you up. The only thing that can help you is delivering Ibrahim Sow's head to me on a silver platter. I'm after him more than I'm after you. You're an annoyance. A mere nuisance. You're nobody."

"I'll give you Ibrahim Sow," I tell Diack. "I'll give you extremists from a foreign country operating on Senegalese soil."

Diack is still not biting. "You're only talking a good game. I need something tangible. I need something I can wrap a case around."

"Patience," I tell the detective. "Did you question Ibrahim about the information mentioned in the video?"

"And let him know that I'm on to him? Who do you think I am?"

"Good. I'll call you back in a few days. Get ready to make your move. And talk to your bosses: I want complete immunity. All charges dropped. A clean slate."

"I can't make any promises," Diack says. "The more you cooperate, the better your chances."

"I know how the system works. I was a cop once."

"A bad one. A rotten one."

"You don't like me, do you?"

"People like you give law enforcement a bad name. And I don't need you walking around Dakar like you're on home turf. This is my city."

"It's mine as well."

Diack laughs derisively. "I don't think you know where you're from, Mr. James. I don't think you know who you are."

I take a deep breath. Something has definitely gotten into my diminutive little detective. These tough times. Dakar's rising body count. Perps too powerful to touch. Where are the mild manners, the circumspection? "Ever put names on those Madeleine corpses?"

"Not a single one. The same goes for the men at the Lido. The ones you personally laid to rest. It's like they appeared out of thin air. Nobody knows them. Nobody has come forward to claim them."

"There are two big security companies in Dakar," I inform Diack. "Top Surveillance and Lion Services. They're more like mercenary outfits catering to Dakar's rich and powerful. They did the footwork for Ibrahim and Momar when those two were going at it. They provided the soldiers for their proxy war. Raid both companies' offices. Look at employee records. Match pictures, specs, and measurements to your bodies."

Diack, ungrateful as he is, hangs up without thanking me.

Marie calls. "It'll be over soon," I tell her after filling her in on the latest developments.

177

She, too, has a hard time believing me. "Uranium? That sounds crazy. Way too far-fetched."

"It is."

"I want to be there when it goes down," she announces after a short break.

"Why?"

"To see what Ibrahim is up to with my own eyes. To catch him in the wrong. To confront him face to face. To kill Momar with my own hands." She says it with much fire, Marie. Much conviction. As if she's killed before, as if she knows how it feels, as if she's really capable of murdering someone in cold blood without losing a single second of sleep.

"It's going to be dangerous. Lots of men."

"So?"

I sigh. "Do you even know how to shoot that gun of yours?"

She chuckles. "I don't do guns. Never owned one. I just said that in Palm Beach to act tough. To scare you away."

"And it worked really well, didn't it?"

I have her meet me at Yasser's. Greasy, hairy, sweaty, and unkempt as ever, he's filling out an order sheet while Henri Salvador croons.

> *Maladie d'amour*
> *Maladie de la jeunesse*
> *Si tu n'aimes que moi*
> *Reste tout près de moi*

"Again?" Yasser shouts incredulously when he lifts his head and sees me.

"I'm here for a friend," I tell him. "How's life treating you?"

"Better than ever."

I look around while waiting for Marie. There's a brand-new display case next to the one doubling as a counter. On the wall behind Yasser, rifles, shotguns, and machine guns are propped up under lock and key. Everywhere around the shop posters advertise armor-penetrating bullets, jam-free automatics, high-caliber pistols, accessories, customizing options. "You're stocking more of the heavy-duty stuff nowadays, aren't you?"

Yasser nods. "Lots of requests for big pieces. The bigger, the better. That's what I'm seeing right now. That's the trend I'm detecting."

"Ever heard of Top Surveillance and Lion Services?"

Yasser smiles. "They're my biggest customers after you."

"You provide both with weapons?"

"I provide everybody."

"Ibrahim Sow?"

Yasser doesn't even take the time to search his memory. "Absolutely. Smith & Wesson .357 Magnum. Two years ago."

"Momar Sy?"

"Wanted the same exact gun. Paid extra to get his name engraved on the handle."

I shake my head. "Do you know how much heartbreak you're facilitating? How many conflicts you're enabling? You're like the nerve of war or something."

Yasser smiles. What I've just said is like music to his ears. It makes him proud. "That's who I am. That's what I do."

Marie walks in. "Tantalizing" would be a good way to describe her. Her heels and designer jeans make her look almost leggy. The short haircut, no-frills as it is, empowers her. Her perfume goes to my head, and Yasser's. "I have just the right one for you," he tells Marie right away.

She likes the Beretta he shows her. She likes it a lot. "Try it," he encourages her. "Downstairs, in my shooting range. See how it feels."

The room in the basement is a dozen yards long. It smells like a battlefield. It is soundproof. Absorbing foam lines all the walls to prevent ricochets. The target is a life-size cutout of President Wade. After putting noise-canceling headphones on, Marie gets gun-shy. "I've never fired a weapon before."

I come near. I stand behind her. I close both her hands around the Beretta. I put my hands around hers. I show her how to place her legs, shift her weight, hold her arms, check the safety, take aim, and shoot.

The Beretta has very little recoil. Marie shouts with excitement. She shoots again and again, hitting Wade on the head, the shoulder, the neck. My chest pressed against her back, I feel every detonation, every trepidation, every beat of her quickening heart. I feel her warmth, the softness of her skin. When Marie inadvertently leans against me, our cheeks touch.

Oh, maladie d'amour
Maladie de la jeunesse

"I'll take it."

Yasser rings Marie up. He takes it him upon himself to throw in an extra box of ammo. "Hanging around this guy, you're gonna need it."

We shake hands after I grab the bag.

"See you soon?" he jokes as Marie and I step out.

Marie's car is around the corner. Blanchot is all noise and people. Everybody's out shopping. School is starting next week. "Found something for Yaz?"

"The American School in Hann. We're moving nearby. A three-bedroom in the dunes. Big backyard. Nowhere near the water, but it has a pool. She's already talking about a dog."

Marie's car is a brand-new, astonishing, bewildering Porsche. "Zak's favorite," she explains. "He was pestering me to get one. This model, this color, these wheels, this engine, this package. My son loved his cars. People are going to wonder what's gotten into me, but I don't care. I can just see Zak looking down on me, jumping with excitement. Call it a tribute. I can have my own way of mourning, can't I?"

I hold her door as she lowers herself into the seat. The car fits her totally. It fits her like a glove. She slips her shades on. "You got all the information you wanted from me," she says, looking up. "You found Momar. You don't need me any more.

So why are you keeping me in the loop? Why are you helping me?"

"None of your business," I deadpan.

She laughs a little. "I guess I deserve that." Then: "Seriously?"

I shut her door. "I have my reasons. And no, they have nothing to do with your checkbook."

Marie fires the engine and eases out of the space. I notice the monster S.U.V. parked five cars behind for the first time. A thin ribbon of smoke is escaping from its open window. Two men are sitting in the front. The driver has a hairstyle that is hard to forget: Boris's blond mohawk.

I catch up with Marie at the light. She lets me in. "Need a ride?"

"Your husband's bodyguards followed you."

She looks in her rearview mirror. Boris is two cars behind. Becaye is sitting pretty in the passenger seat. No way of knowing how many men are in the back, if any.

We leave Blanchot and drive toward the Boulevard de la République. "What should I do?" Marie asks as she steps on the gas. "Which way to go?"

After République we go Roume, circling the Place de l'Indépendance. Marie weaves in and out of traffic, gunning for openings as soon as she sees them, shifting gears like a pro, driving the car like it's meant to be driven. We need an empty expanse of road. We need open spaces, a long stretch where pure speed is going to make the difference. Such spaces, such stretches are few and far between in downtown Dakar at five in the afternoon. I pull the Glock from my waist, I lower the window, I keep my eyes on Boris.

"Ponty?"

"No. Sarrault."

We pass the Gentina bakery and Maurel & Prom, the big toy retailer. Marie is not outwardly nervous. She's focused on her driving, one hand on the steering wheel and the other on the stick. "Right at the Corniche?"

"Yes."

The two-lane road bordering the coast is winding and narrow. Traffic is more fluid. To our right, a wall of rocks and trees. To our left, a slope, abrupt in places, rolling gently toward the sea at others. We widen the gap separating us from the truck, which is slower in the turns. The Lagon restaurant, the vet's office, the bathing spot of l'Anse Bernard fly by. Marie grabs her phone, puts it on speaker, and dials Ibrahim's number. He picks up at the first ring, as if he'd been waiting. "Get your people off my back," Marie tells him.

"It's not you they're after," Ibrahim says in his poised, contained, smooth voice. He's alone at his desk, at home or at the warehouse, fielding up-to-the-minute updates from his boys, directing the show. "Stop the car. Let them take Chris away. Go on about your business."

I unbuckle my seat belt. I turn around and straddle the low seat, left leg upright, right leg jammed into the opening above the hand brake. I move the seat forward until my spine is against the dashboard and the back of my head rests on the windshield.

"Make them stop," Marie tells Ibrahim. "Now!"

"Just do as I say," Ibrahim insists.

I'm not such a good mark with my left hand. Not at 90-plus miles an hour, facing a moving target, on a road that twists and turns and goes up and down. Still, I bust off a couple of shots that raise puffs of dust as they hit the exposed side of the overhanging cliff. Becaye leans outside his window with what looks too much like an Uzi not to be one. There are no cars between us, just a hundred yards or so of smooth and empty road. I know in my heart that Becaye won't shoot, he won't dare return fire for fear of hurting Marie and incurring his boss's wrath. I know that as long as I'm with Marie I'm somewhat safe.

"Why are you after Chris?" Marie asks.

"Chris is a liability," Ibrahim declares matter-of-factly. "He has to go."

Marie makes a sharp right. I slide from my seat, almost ending on the steering wheel. Marie's not done talking. "I know everything," she says into the phone, to my utter dismay. "How much longer do you think you can get away with what you've been doing?"

I regain position and fire another shot. It hits the truck's left headlight. Boris eases off the gas. The distance between us accrues again.

Ibrahim's voice is almost detached when he asks, "What do you know?"

"Everything," Marie repeats as we start the climb toward the Palais de Justice. I shake my head, I tell Marie to shut up, but she doesn't see me, she doesn't hear. "Momar," she goes on. "Samba. The uranium. Everything."

183

Ibrahim remains silent.

"You shouldn't have," I tell Marie. But of course it's too late. Much too late.

"You have to choose," Ibrahim says after what seems like an eternity. "Stop the car now and come back to me like a dutiful wife, or accept what you have coming. Your fate is in my hands. Do you understand?"

Marie clenches her jaw. Her grip on the wheel gets tighter. She works the clutch. She switches gears decidedly, defiantly, ferociously, increasing our speed midway through the climb. Behind its gates, the Palais de Justice complex teems with people and parked vehicles, a good amount of police cars among them. "My son is dead because of you," Marie shouts into the phone. "So how can I choose you? How can I ever come back to you? How can I trust you with my life and Yasmin's? You're a criminal, Ibra. You're gonna pay. You're going down. It's only a matter of time." She's pure resolve, my Marie. Righteous anger. Fury, even. When did she come to this conclusion? When did she realize that there was no turning back, that she had passed the point of no return? What did it take?

Ibrahim sighs audibly. His next words are his final goodbye to his wife, a farewell to the mother of his children. "Remember this, Marie: I did everything I could in order to spare you."

He hangs up. We're on top of the hill, overlooking the sea, the city, speeding toward the setting sun, going fast, incredibly fast, too fast, much too fast. My heart sinks, my senses freeze as we go airborne, rocket people, eyes open wide, hearts aflame, wheels spinning, engine loud as a wounded lion.

We land with a thud. The suspension holds. Marie, incredibly, keeps us on the road: We swerve but get immediately back on track. In front of us, a straight expanse of asphalt but many more cars threatening to slow us down. I look out the window, I watch the truck lift off in turn, I see the truck land, I see the truck starting to pull closer. Becaye leans out with the Uzi. A car coming in the opposite direction blows its horn. "Give it all you've got," I urge Marie.

She steps on it as Becaye sprays us with his first volley. We can't hear the Uzi but we see the dots impacting the road, we swear we can feel the bullets whiz by. "Ibra told them to open fire!" Marie exclaims incredulously. "He told them to kill me!"

There's no outrunning the truck, as in a few seconds we'll catch up with the cars ahead and be forced to slow down.

"We have to get out of here," I tell Marie. "Turn into the first side street that opens up."

She slows down to maneuver the sharp right. Becaye's second volley flies above our heads. "Stop the car," I tell Marie as soon as we're inside the shelter of the residential neighborhood. The calm street is straight out of an opulent dream: impeccable sidewalks, sprawling lawns, rotating sprinklers, high walls, driveways, statues, fountains, majestic porches, long, polished cars, and the inevitable uniformed guards.

I jump out of the Porsche. I run toward the turn we've just cleared. I take position seconds before the nose of the truck appears. I start shooting before Boris is completely engaged into the street. I direct my fire at Becaye, the most obvious, the most immediate threat. Two bullets go through the windshield and hit him on the neck and chest, pinning him to his seat. Blood stains the glass as it cracks into a widening star.

Becaye drops the Uzi to the ground. The truck passes me in a flash, denying me the time to turn my attention to Boris or the other potential occupants. The truck goes straight for the Porsche idling by the roadside. I hold my fire. "Marie!"

She burns rubber, cutting her front wheels into the circular driveway a few yards away. Boris plows through the now-empty space and keeps going, passing a handful of bewildered guards in front of what TV reports will identify as the prime minister's mansion in this evening's breaking news.

Marie comes down the driveway and scoops me up. In an instant we're on the Corniche, headed back downtown. The truck is nowhere in sight. No police, no sirens giving chase.

We cut through small streets, reliving the past minutes, shaking a little as we come off the adrenaline high. "Where to go?" Marie asks.

"Yasmin," I tell her. "You have to go get her right now. Where is she?"

"Mame Awa's. We were going to move into our new house today. I just got the keys this morning."

"Does Ibra know about the place?"

Marie shakes her head. "I bought it with my own money. Just like this car. But if his people have been following me around...."

I complete her thought. "Neither house is safe."

We make it to Mermoz before Ibra's men. I stay by the door to keep watch and place a phone call while Marie runs inside. Mame Awa's alley is quiet and shady. Butterflies, bees, bougainvillea, orange light. I relish the break even as I keep an eye out for silver trucks. Karine is at work with Isaac, whom she does not yet want to entrust to the care of a sitter. Maybe I'm catching her at a bad moment. Maybe she's busy, or tired, or plain stressed out. Maybe she sees right through me. Either way, she's not too pleased by my request. "Why can't they go to a hotel?" she asks. "Why do I have to take them in? I knew from day one that that woman was going to be trouble."

"Ibrahim would find them anyplace else. At least they'll be safe with us in Yoff."

Karine weighs her next words carefully. I feel guilty to bring my problems to her doorstep. I feel guilty for my feelings toward Marie and Yaz. When Karine speaks next I feel a wall falling down, coming between us. "You care about them, don't you? It's not just a job any more."

I take a deep breath. "I do care," I say, like a man jumping into the unknown. A man putting on the line a hard-won love, the love of his life, the best thing to ever happen to him, a thing that shouldn't be touched.

"Chris?"

"Yes?"

186

"Are you trying to tell me something?"

The cliff, suddenly, scares me to death. I take a step back from the edge. "No, Karine. Everything is all right. We're all right. I just need you to help me out with this one. I just need your understanding."

I can almost see Karine nod slowly. Her big heart, her generosity, her self-effacement. " I guess it's okay."

The children hit it off way before the two women do. Marie and I have stopped for groceries. We've set up Yasmin and her in the bedroom next to Isaac's. We've cooked dinner. We've talked about Isaac's ailment. We've spoken with Yasmin about what to do and what not to do.

Karine frowns a little when she sees Marie in her kitchen--the territory thing. But decency, *teranga*--the sense of hospitality that is a big deal in Senegal--and the big heart kick in. The women shake hands and exchange a brief, perfunctory smile. Karine: ponytail, golden skin, tall, full-figured, almost sculpturesque, so much bigger. Marie: small, short, the unctuous, dark chocolate of her complexion, her short hair, her tiny features, her model looks and runway clothes, her perfume, the fragility that really isn't. "Thanks for putting us up," she says.

"Don't mention it."

Karine hugs Yaz and forces a rare smile out of her. Isaac hugs her, too, and the smile widens, it widens and turns into laughter. They run off to a corner of the house.

Dinner is served. The kids reappear. We sit around the table. The kids blabber away. They fill the table with easy conversation, relaxation, and, at least in my case, giddiness. I start breathing a little better. Marie is at ease, if guarded. Every once in a while her thoughts wander, her fork stops in midair, her eyes have a faraway look. I can't keep myself from watching her, checking on her. And Karine, well, Karine watches me watching Marie. Is she getting mad? Does she regret her kindness? I can't tell. Nothing she says, nothing she does is out of the ordinary.

187

The evening goes by nice and quiet. I help with the dishes. I hold the bank during Monopoly. I help putting the kids to bed. I wish Marie a good night. I call Momar while Karine showers, wondering if he's going to pick up, cursing myself for not taking his weapons, his money, his keys, for letting it all come down to him, for leaving it all in his hands--what if he bails out, what if he decides to cut his losses and run, what if he goes and sides with Ibrahim, what if he lets me down in a major way?

But it seems I have nothing to worry about. Momar is being a good boy. He's doing everything according to plan. We're partners, we're tight, I'm his new best friend, his role model, his Jean Gabin, his Lino Ventura. "Good to go," he tells me. "The Sudanese are on their way back to Dakar. They're touching down tomorrow. How they're getting five million dollars through customs, I don't know."

"Where is the exchange taking place?"

"Ibra's farm, on the banks of Retba Lake."

"When?"

"Day after tomorrow, 9 p.m."

"You proposed it?"

"Ibra did. He's in a rush, suddenly. Like the stuff's hot in his hands. You're putting some serious pressure on him, aren't you?"

"Trying my best."

"My man."

Karine is out of the shower. She's dimmed the lights. She is sitting on the bed, applying lotion over her skin. Her long fingers, her palms, the smoothness, the moisture, the gloss, the glow, the rub, the song she's humming. Any other night this would have been my job and I would have made an intricate, long-lasting, delicious foreplay of it. Not tonight. Tonight belongs to the wall, the goddamn wall, the wall between us.

Karine gets up. She walks to the closet. She lets me see everything I'll be missing from now on. The wonderland of a body. The fleshy back, the full breasts, the soft belly, the lush triangle, the thighs, the interminable legs, the bountiful, plentiful, beautiful ass. Karine shows it all off. She struts it. She works it. She eye-candies it. She gives me one good long peek before handing me a pillow and a light blanket. "The couch." And how sweetly, how gently, how nicely, how suggestively she says it: "The couch."

I take my punishment to sleep. The couch, a night alone are a fine tradeoff for the knowledge that Marie is safe, the contentment that having both women and their children under the same roof procures me. I must be a family man at heart.

Marie joins me in the living room around two. We're both wide awake. She sits on the couch's arm, she whispers a question. "Why are you sleeping here?"

"Got kicked out."

"Sorry.... It's my fault, isn't it?"

"Can't say it isn't. I'll survive."

She gets up. She, too, likes sweat suits with hoodies. She, too, looks adorable in them. "Feel like going for a walk?"

I kick the blanket off. Marie watches me. My dark-blue skin, my chest, my abs, my arms, my white boxers, the blue jeans that I slip on, the gun that I stick in my belt.

We sneak out. Yoff Beach is dark and deserted. No moon tonight. Just a very clear sky, stars that sparkle from here to eternity, a light breeze, the cool sand, Yoff Island an elongated, fogged-up mass. We walk at the edge of the waves. The village, but for a few windows, is shrouded in peaceful darkness. Marie rubs her arms as if she were cold.

"How are you holding up?" I ask.

"I don't know," she says. "I keep thinking that I could have died today. That it could have been the end. It's a lot to take in."

I nod.

Marie turns to look at me. "You were quite the action hero, this afternoon."

I return the compliment. "You handled yourself very bravely. More than bravely."

"It was a big shock, you know. Ibra ... Ibra used to be my everything. Ours wasn't a perfect marriage, of course. I stuck with him through a lot, *vaille que vaille*: other women, gambling, grandiose money schemes.... Even after understanding how much he had to do with Zak's death I had a hard time bringing myself to hate him, burn the bridges, cut off all ties. After what took place today...."

I look in Marie's eyes. A little gratitude, yes, definitely. Sadness. Uncertainty. Loneliness. Retrospective fear. Anxiety. The end of life as she knows it.

We both stop walking, as in tacit understanding. We face each other. In a movie this would certainly be it, the perfect moment for a kiss, the scene when the action hero reaps his well-earned reward and sweeps the tragic beauty off her feet for a long and tender embrace.

I'm not sure Marie's ready for it. I'm not sure I am. And it's a measure of how much I've changed--dare I say "matured"?--that I don't force it, that I show an ounce of decency, that I hold back in the name of respect, that I think of Karine first and foremost, that I take the time to appreciate the fact that Marie is at too vulnerable a passage in her life for me to take advantage of her.

At the end of the day, this is not a movie. Marie is a woman of flesh and bones. I don't have to see her wounds to know they're there. She doesn't have to yield to the whirlwind of emotions tossing her around for me to understand that she's under extreme duress.

And so it is that I learn to take my time. To listen. To be a friend. To lend a helping hand.

Karine goes off to work without Isaac, who stays behind to keep Yasmin company. Marie keeps the children occupied. She, too, is good with them. She knows all the songs, the lullabies, the alphabet games, the hot toys, the fairy tales. She knows Karine's "*Koumba Amul Ndeye*," or "Motherless Koumba"--the Foyer's score, the Senegalese Cinderella theme. Marie knows Salimata's *Leuk le Lièvre* stories, the ones especially dear to my heart. To listen to her as she tells them to Yaz and Isaac, to watch her get animated as she recounts them, to see the children rapt with attention is to relive my past, to brush up on the memory of precious moments spent with Salimata. The quintessential stay-at-home mom, Marie does everything effortlessly: minding the children, picking up behind them, feeding them, taking them through different routines at different times of the day. Maids didn't spoiled Marie. Money didn't prevent her from learning the basics of housekeeping or taking up the challenges of child-rearing--it gave her more tools to be good at them. "Before I married into wealth I was born into wealth. My father was Alassane Ba, an industrialist who served as minister of finance for over a decade under both Senghor and Abdou Diouf. My mother died early. My sister Yacine and I had no choice but to take over her responsibilities, to adapt, to learn quickly. My dad was all about public service. He raised us right. We weren't your typical little princesses."

Because she asks, I tell her as much as I can stand to reveal about the Foyer, Vernon, Karine, my life as a cop, my decision to move to Africa, my search for Salimata. Marie, too, proves to be a good listener. "So much pain," she muses even without having heard the first thing about the *bukis* from my mouth.

"If only you knew," I tell her.

I learn without much surprise that the townspeople steered away from the place. "There was this cloud hanging above the Foyer, this stigma. Tucked away from sight though it was, you never forgot it was there. Rumors abounded. Of out-of-wedlock babies being dumped there; of mothers leaving their newborns at the doorstep never to look back; of white American priests having power of life or death over black African toddlers and youths. You know how important children are in our culture? How sacred family is supposed to be? To abandon your child is to break the biggest taboo. People felt sorry for those mothers, those children. The Foyer was a safety valve for Dakar's high society: It helped a lot of politicians, businessmen, and people of 'noble' stock save face. It provided a quick solution to a big, messy, and very public mistake. It pulled a convenient cover over young women's shame. The Foyer was a monument to our collective hypocrisy, a shrine to our double standards. Nobody was sad to see it go."

I have to hide the turmoil raging inside me as Marie speaks. I have to quiet the burning fire, the painful tug in my heart. I have to look away. Toward the window, the sea, the sky. Toward the things that were. Toward everything that could have been.

It makes time go by. It takes our minds off the coming confrontation, the looming tussle, the little trouble. It makes us all move a little more freely around one another when Karine gets home.

We spend a good evening, all in all. The women seem to bond a little. When time comes for dinner they throw something together, they throw me out of the kitchen. "Cool house," Marie says.

"My husband Kant bought it," Karine crows.

"Kant is your husband?" Marie asks. "*The* Kant?"

"*The* Kant," Karine hammers, looking my way.

"*Ex*-husband," I point out, shaking my head, a little jealous, just a little, wishing I could find the punk Kant and grab him and smack him, wondering who he is and what he still is to Karine, wondering how I'll react if she ever talks about reuniting with him and rekindling the flame, anticipating how I'll take Kant's guitar and break it over his head--*the* Kant, the little punk.

Needless to say, the couch it is for the second night in a row.

I call Diack early the next day. "What do you have for me, Detective?"

"A verbal promise of immunity from my direct supervisor."

"That's all?"

"Take it or leave it. That's more than I was willing to give."

"My house?"

"You get it back."

"My detective license? My gun permit?"

"Sure." Diack takes a deep breath before switching gears. "Any progress?"

"It's going down tonight. Ibrahim Sow's farm, by Retba Lake. 9 p.m."

"And you're just telling me now?"

"Just found out," I say, lying through my teeth. "Bring plenty men. Bulletproof vests. Heavy artillery. Ibrahim Sow has people galore. They come equipped. They're not afraid to shoot."

"Not any more. Top Surveillance and Lion Services have been shut down while we're investigating their operations. They should be out of business for a while."

"Good timing."

"Stay out of the way and let us handle it. Am I making myself clear?"

"Clearer than clear, Detective."

"Good."

Marie draws me a map of the farm. It's located between the lake and the village that Mansour calls home. "Xadim started small. Bought a plot from an old Peul. There was nothing in Retba back then. Just that pink lake and its huge deposits of salt. Xadim saw the place's touristic potential before anyone else, even before the Paris-Dakar Race made it its final stop. Xadim wanted to buy his way all the way down to the lake's banks. He died before his wish became reality. Ibra completed the task for him. Unlike his father, he had no interest in crops or tourists or nature reserves. He walled the property and turned it into a horse farm. Ifra, Mansour's oldest son, oversees it. Fruit trees are the most they ever planted. The children and I never spent much time there. Ibra used to go every weekend. It was his secret garden, his little toy, his project, his *garçonnière*. I suspect him of taking many of his mistresses there."

I look at the map. The farm is buffered from the outside world by a eucalyptus forest. A single path connects it to the lake. Inside the walls, a driveway loops around a well to end in front of a medium sized country house. The stables, long and low-roofed, are to the right of it. Then, in quick succession, the overseer's quarters, a barn, a shed big enough to hold a tractor, and a workshop. Central to the property is a corral--oval, sanded, bare. The fruit trees are at the periphery. "How many entrances?"

"Only one. A double gate."

"How high are the walls?"

"High enough."

"Barbed wire?"

"No. Security was never a big issue. Not like in Dakar."

I try to dissuade Marie from coming. "Let the cops do their job. Let justice follow its course."

Marie, of course, won't hear it. She won't have it. "I have to be there, Chris. For Zak. For everything those two men did to me. They have to pay. I have to see it for myself that they pay. I have to make sure. I want to watch as Ibra and Momar are being put away. I want them to look into my eyes. I want to be the face, the embodiment of their guilt. The voice of their victims. So the toll can be tallied. So the damage, the wreckage they've caused becomes real."

"It's going to be crazy. You're talking dozens of men with all kinds of guns. Some of them with nothing to lose. In an enclosed space. In the dark. What are the chances of getting out of there alive?"

"I have to be there," Marie says obstinately. "I just have to."

"What about Yasmin? Suppose something happens to you?"

"Nothing will happen to me."

"How are you so sure?"

Marie kills the talk, she shuts me up, she clinches my acquiescence with a smile and a little sugar. "You'll look after me, Chris. Won't you? I'll be safe as long as I'm close to you."

We put the kids to bed early. We dress in all black. We check our guns. We load up on bullets. There's something of a locker room ambiance in the Yoff living room--the camaraderie, the lure of the unknown, the anticipation, the ritualistic preparation, the pep talk before the battle. When we're done Marie sneaks into her bedroom and holds a sleeping Yasmin for a long, long time. When she comes out of that room, I know she's ready.

Karine walks us to the door. "Come back in one piece," she says as she hugs me. "Both of you." She puts a little feeling in her kiss. A little warmth. A little honey. A little spice. Enough to give me hope. Maybe upon our return the couch and I can bid each other farewell and go our separate ways. Maybe I can carry a victorious outcome and hero's welcome all the way to Karine's bed. Karine's lips graze my neck, setting it on fire. "Rain check," she whispers as Marie looks on.

Marie and I are off to Retba in the Porsche. Yoff, Patte d'Oie, Camberene, Pikine, Mbao, Malika. We don't speak. I wonder how far Marie will go. I wonder if her wish to see her husband pay for his sins entails doing the dirty job herself, dipping her fingers in his blood. I wonder, not for the first time, if she has it in her to kill a man, any man, let alone a man she once loved and may well still love despite all her claims to the contrary, a man whose children she bore. Was I right to allow Marie her wish?

Arcs have to follow their courses, I tell myself. Destinies must get fulfilled.

I try to focus on the task ahead. I do the mental work. I pump myself up. Back in D.C., once outside the police station, driving into a potentially life-threatening situation, Mazakis and I used to blast dirty rap or heavy metal. We did our best to let go of our humane side, what little kindness or niceness or compassion for our fellow human beings we had. We tried hard to unleash our inner beast, we strove to achieve a complete transformation into clearheaded killing machines.

One by one, I rid myself of all feelings, all emotions, all ties, all restraint. The well of hatred, the ball of rage simmering deep inside me is here, always here, ready for the tapping. It's a friend, an ally, an asset, a familiar face, a comfortable place. I can always rely on it. It always has my back. It has never let me down. Never. The well of hatred, the ball of rage is me.

We make it to Retba in less than twenty minutes. Instead of turning left into the village Marie borrows a sandy track one mile down the road. She cuts the headlights off. We find ourselves engulfed in a cloud of dust. Marie drives without hesitation, drawing a circle into the bush that brings us close to the farm's rear.

We stop at the edge of the trees. We start sprinting between the skinny trunks, arms glued to our sides and head inside our shoulders. The clatter of our feet stomping dead leaves makes it impossible to distinguish any other noise. Shadows take otherworldly shapes that dissolve into the salty air. The farm's enclosure is gray, smooth, thick, about seven feet tall.

Making a step of my palms, I help Marie propel herself up one of the trunks hugging the wall before passing her the Beretta. Perched on the wall, she relieves me of the Glock while I climb in turn. Dust falling from the leaves tickles my nose. Once on top, still under vegetal cover, we kneel to survey the scene playing out inside the farm.

The house's verandah and windows are illuminated. A powerful light shines from the roof. Near the well, two canisters identical to the ones Ibrahim threw in the water at Soumbedioune Bay sit on an upturned wooden crate under the surveillance of two armed men. These are not the people Ibrahim used in the past. They look a little too rough, unpolished, jumpy. These are farm hands lampooning as security guards. Two of them are standing by the gate, along with a diminutive figure that Marie identifies as Ifra, Mansour's son. The training oval is empty, and so appear the shed, the barn, and the overseer's home. The stables, in front of which Ibrahim's all-terrain is parked, are in the dark.

I help Marie slip off the wall. I watch her go hide among the fruit trees, disappearing in their embrace. After crawling to a spot protected by small branches, I let myself fall to the ground.

This part of the garden is crisscrossed by paved lanes. Under the trees, it's almost completely dark. Mango sap as well as a whiff of citrus fill the air. Marie's nowhere to be found. I can sense her presence without seeing her. I dare not call her name. Around the well, the guards appear on the alert. Catching the light, their automatic rifles glimmer with the promise of death.

The gate starts moving, pulled by Ifra and the two men at his side. A pickup rolls in at low speed. The gate quickly closes behind it.

Mansour, Ibrahim, and Momar file out of the house. They come down the verandah stairs, they cover the short distance separating them from the canisters, they stand and wait. They don't speak, they don't address one another. Ibra and Momar are both carrying their long-barreled Magnums in their waist. Mansour has his prayer beads.

197

The pickup comes to a halt. The three men getting off are young and dressed casually in jeans, sneakers, and T-shirts. Beards, of course, but not overly long or thick--not out of place at all. They come stand in front of the line formed by Ibrahim, Mansour, and Momar. The men in the two groups barely exchange greetings. One of Ibrahim's men climbs on the pickup's bed. He seizes the dark tarpaulin covering it and pulls it back, exposing four jute bags. He pokes into all four with a knife, culling handfuls of green bills from each.

The Sudanese start moving toward the canisters. Momar walks with them, talking with his hands and appearing more than a little nervous from my viewpoint. His head turns left and right, going from the pile of cash to the canisters. The Sudanese, by contrast, seem calm to the point of dullness. One pulls a small device from his pocket and kneels in front of the canisters. The second bends over and unlatches them one after the other. The third keeps watch. Momar, Ibrahim, and Mansour all take a couple of steps back. The Sudanese peer into the canisters. The device, probably a Geiger counter, starts ticking audibly. The Sudanese exchange a nod.

Momar shakes his head. He points at his watch. He takes a step toward the buyers. The one closer to him pulls an odd-looking revolver from his belt and aims it at his head. Momar raises his hands. He turns to look at Ibrahim, who shrugs before telling his men to start unloading the jute bags. Two of the farm hands and Ifra get on it. The other two stand at the receiving end, along with Mansour. A furtive movement on the side of the house catches my eye as the first bag is being dropped on the verandah. When I look closely, I see nothing but shadows.

Shots ring out on the other side of the wall. A burst of automatic fire is followed by a second. The sound of a powerful engine rises behind the gate. Shouts can be heard briefly before the metal caves from the push of an armored truck. Five men in fatigues jump out and deploy themselves, forming a half-circle containing the well in its center. The three Sudanese, who've all quickly drawn their weapons, are in their line of fire. So are the

guards, Momar, Ifra, and Mansour, who's still holding the end
of one of the heavy bags. Ibrahim, hiding behind his people,
starts to back away toward the house. Momar is standing
between Diack's men and the trio of Sudanese, Magnum in
hand. Intense confusion can be read on his face. His eyes go
from his foreign associates to the law enforcement troops.
Excited by the clamor, the horses start moving inside their stalls.
I see Diack advancing toward the well. He walks without
rushing, his eyes on the men standing by the open canisters with
their weapons at the ready. "Drop your guns," he commands
calmly, arms extended, the butt of his automatic resting in his
left palm. The Sudanese confer in their language. "Drop your
guns," Diack repeats as he keeps walking toward them, reducing
the distance to a mere few yards.

"*Ibra!*" Momar shouts as his brother reaches the
unguarded verandah. There's a smirk on Ibrahim's face, the
condescension of a man who wins even when he loses. "*Ibra!*"
Momar shouts again, looking for his brother behind the line of
cannons and bulletproof vests. Mansour and Ifra stand petrified.
The farm hands let go of their rifles. "Drop your weapons!"
"Raise your hands!" The enforcers yell orders as they close in
on the trio of Sudanese. The latter open fire simultaneously,
chanting "*Rabbi labeika!*" with voices in which fear seems to
hold no grip.

Momar shouts one last time before he trains his gun on
his own temple and presses the trigger. The detonation is lost
amid the concomitant exchange of heavy fire. The Sudanese's
white T-shirts get bloodied up. One of Diack's men spins before
falling to his knees. Screams, the deafening sound of the
weapons and the neighing of the horses fill the yard.

I start to run toward the verandah. Marie, who appeared
in front of the stairs, is holding the Beretta to the back of her
husband's head. "Marie," I call softly as I get close, holding my
hands up. "Don't."

"Stay where you are," she says without moving.

"I'm not trying to stop you."

"Then go away!" she shouts, shoving the cannon deeper into her husband's shaved skull.

Ibrahim winces. Fear shows in his eyes.

"I'll do it," I tell Marie. "Better me than you. I have nothing to lose."

Ibrahim lets out a deep sigh when I stick the Glock between his eyes. "You have a beautiful child to live for," I tell Marie. "Doesn't that count for anything?"

"Ibra's made it impossible for me to go on," she retorts. "Can't you see?"

"Don't do it," Ibrahim pleads.

Marie steels herself. The whole world becomes still. Everybody, everything around has disappeared. Nothing exists but the three of us. "For Zak," Marie says, her eyes crazy, her voice raw and thick as if she were about to inflict the most damaging pain not just to Ibrahim but to herself as well, her finger slowly squeezing the trigger.

It all comes back to me after I slump to the ground, my senses rebooting one by one: the people watching; the rifles aimed at the rounded-up farm hands, Ifra, and Mansour; the Sudanese men in the throes of agony in a heap on the ground; Diack telling everybody to hold their fire; the smell of cordite; the bang; the shape that suddenly appeared on the stables' roof, making me jump in front of Marie.

The earth feels hard under me. My eyes close against my will. I find myself isolated inside the dark and deep night within. It's hard to breathe. I try to get up and I can't. Sleep comes to me, a forced and brutal sleep. Pain becomes me.

"Chris!" Marie screams from far away. I struggle to open my eyes. She calls my name again. Her face is close to mine, her fingers tilt my head toward the light. Diack's men shout in their radios as they search the yard for snipers. "Hold my fingers," Marie says.

"How does it look?" I ask.

"It's not bleeding too bad. Right side, under the ribs. They've called Sangalcam. Medics are on they way."

"Who shot me?"

200

"Man with a blond mohawk," Diack says from far above. "Ibrahim had him posted on the stables' roof. We got him."

"Where's Ibrahim?"

"Gone," Marie reveals. "I dropped my gun when I saw you go down. Everybody started shooting. He ran away."

I feel myself slipping away. "Don't," Marie says, wiping the sweat off my forehead.

The ambulance makes it through the busted gate half an hour later. Marie doesn't let go of my hand.

I wake up chained to a hospital bed. My left hand, clasped in metal, also has an IV drip attached to it. Dr. Pape Toure, who patched me up, smiles in apology. He's dark-skinned, tall and lanky. Sports a hip, salt-sprinkled goatee, and a funky tie under his white coat. "Where am I?" I ask him.

"Le Dantec," he answers. "Sorry for the handcuffs. The good new is, you're out of danger."

"How long have I been here?"

"Three days."

I drift back to sleep. The next time I open my eyes, it is night. The light is soft, ambient, diffuse, atmospheric. The hospital walls are bare, stained yellow. The floor is tiled a faded blue. The smell is that of rot, of blood, of too much bleach, of death.

"How are you feeling?" Marie asks as she hovers over me in the morning. Her eyes are brighter than I've ever seen them. They shine. They shine for me. "You saved me," she says. "For the second time, you saved me."

She kisses my forehead. Her lips are firm, firmer than Karine's. Different though they feel, they convey emotion, they carry affection just the same. Weak and groggy as I am, I'm almost ecstatic.

It lingers long after Marie pulls back, that kiss. In Marie's eyes there's the promise for more, much more. I must have awakened to a dream, a new world, Sister Gertrude's sought-after new world, the new world in my view. Have we

202

really traveled this far, Marie and I? Have we accomplished this much? Have we begun?

She helps me raise the pillow and prop my back against the wall. I keep pulling on my wrist, forgetting that it is chained to the frame of the bed. The handcuffs chip away at the white paint, exposing rust. "That damn detective," Marie fumes. "I give him until tonight to come and get these off. He's been warned: I'll go all the way to the Interior Ministry if I have to."

I am not the only patient in the room. There's about half a dozen of us all together. All in various stages of recovery. All with family and friends fussing over our health, comfort, and well-being. Nurses glide in and out, their whites immaculate, their voices low, their smiles automatic, their eyes and hands full, busy, probing. The oppressive air seems to be made even more so by the lazy, antique ceiling fans. Beyond netted windows, foliage and a piece of blue sky offer the only touch of normalcy. The post-surgery room at Le Dantec epitomizes everything that is wrong with Senegal: poverty, lack of resources, underfunding, absence of adequate infrastructure. Le Dantec lays bare the ills, the holes, the deficiencies, the neglect. "I wanted you to go to Casaous, the downtown private clinic," Marie says apologetically. "Diack objected. I was in too much shock to argue with him just then. I did summon Dr. Pape Toure, who is a friend of the family. He came here and operated on you. He oversaw your care."

It's my turn to thank Marie.

She fills me in on everything I've missed. "Karine and the kids are okay--they'll come visit you in a little while. Ibra is nowhere to be found. Nobody knows how he slipped out of the farm. Mansour and Ifra are in jail. The papers made a big deal of the uranium and the Sudanese extremists, of course. That's all everybody's been talking about." Marie exhales loudly. It doesn't show on her angelic face, but the last few days must have been a crunch.

"How are you?" I ask.

203

"Hanging in there. I have to be everywhere at once: IEX, the farm, police headquarters...."

My blood turns hot. "They're bothering you?"

Marie presses a palm against my cheek. Like her lips, it is firm, it is cool. I feel every curve, every bump, every line, every crease. "I can handle it," Marie says. "It's not me they're after. They just have a lot of questions. Diack is a real pain, but he knows where to stop."

"Get you a good counsel. Don't try and go it alone."

Marie nods. "I have the best lawyer. His name is Ketus. Ket, for short. Diack is terrified of him."

I nod in turn. "I know Ketus. He's quite formidable."

Marie stays until Karine and the children show up. I get kisses, flowers, presents, hugs. I get a whole lot of love. I sense something different in Karine. A little distance. Stiffness. Reserve. The wall, the wall that came and fell between us is still here, intact. Karine is standing a little to the side. She's letting everybody else crowd me. She's at the edge of the circle. As if she isn't too sure of her place any more. As if she doesn't know where she belongs, where she and I are in the scheme of things, where we stand. As if our stars have become misaligned, as if something or somebody has come and thrown us out of whack. I can hardly blame her. Haven't I just jumped in front of bullets to save another woman? Haven't I almost given my life? "Nothing to lose," I told Marie when we both were holding Ibrahim at gunpoint. It wasn't true then, and it isn't true now. Karine means a lot to me. I have Karine to lose.

"Sorry," I tell Karine when Marie takes the kids in the hallway to give us a chance to talk alone.

She's brave, my Karine. Never puts herself first. Never thinks about herself. Her hand seeks mine. We connect through interlocked fingers, once a simple and natural gesture of endearment, today an act both tentative and bittersweet. "Don't be. You just focus on getting better. Make that your priority. I'll be here for you. I'm not going anywhere."

"I love you," I declare spontaneously.

It hits her in the heart. It makes her raise her head. It makes me feel light in the head and warm in the chest. It makes me happy that I've finally found the way, and the courage, and the words to express myself.

Karine looks at me. She searches deep inside my eyes. I let her in. Like a man who, at last, no longer seeks to hide. A man ready to come out and embrace the light.

Karine's face slowly opens into a smile. Not just her lips, her mouth, the lines around her mouth, but all the way up her cheeks, around her eyes, inside her green eyes. "I love you," she says. Slowly. Deliberately.

Diack appears shortly after my evening checkup, my round with Dr. Pape Toure and the nurses. Still as short and ungainly, my bespectacled detective, but with a spring in his step, a newfound swagger, a welcome lightness around the shoulders, a glistening fire behind the nerd glasses.

"Why are you holding me prisoner, Detective? What about our deal?"

"I'm just loath to let you completely off the hook," Diack confesses candidly, sitting at the edge of the bed. "I'd love nothing better than to teach you a lesson."

"I came one step away from death," I tell him. "Don't you think that's punishment enough?"

"That's because of your own foolishness," Diack reasons. "I had asked you to stay put."

"I was only there for Marie--Mrs. Sow."

Diack gives me a strange look. It's true, I realize: The man really hates my guts. Maybe more so now that I've broken his case for him. "How about unlocking these?" I ask, pulling on the chain.

The detective comes close and obliges with a sigh of deep regret.

"Knew you were a man of your word," I say.

"Don't tempt me," he grouses, ready to take his leave.

"Any word on Ibrahim?"

Diack shakes his head. "He's out there somewhere. I'm not closing the inquiry until I find him."

"Watch your back," I warn him.

Diack stops and throws me one last look. "*You* watch your back."

The Point-E house feels empty and alien. The garden, with holes everywhere, is a mess. The few flowers that weren't uprooted have withered. My guavas, mangoes, and *sapotis* have ripened, softened, and dropped to the ground; ants have feasted on them. My chairs are broken and overturned. My grill is lying on its side.

Inside the house, things aren't much better. The carpet in my office was pulled, the curtains were ripped. Random tiles are missing in random spots. My bedroom is one big heartbreaking scene.

The police gave the house back to me, yes. But I don't know where to begin. It's not mine any more. It's not the house I knew. It's not the house I remembered.

At least I'm not alone. That much becomes quickly obvious. It's not just Marie, Karine, Yasmin, Isaac. It's Mame Awa, Abdi, Anta. They make a field day of giving me a hand. They make a fun occasion of it.

The Point-E house bounces back. It roars back. It becomes more alive than it's ever been. It is a new birth, a true resurrection. Never will I disrespect it, and myself, again. The Ngalam, at the other end of my street, holds no sway. I am cured. Through my convalescence, not once do I feel the old impulses, not once do I acknowledge the old demons. They're as good as gone. And, gone with them, my carpe diem, my indulgences, my days--my life--of debauchery, debasement, and hedonism.

I take stock. I look around. I follow my people's moves. Marie shuts down the Corniche house and transfers Mame Awa, Abdi, and Anta to Hann, providing some kind of continuity for Yaz. She leaves Zak's room in the same state as it was the day he went to the vet--that wretched, fateful day. She empties the pool and covers it. She parks all Ibrahim's fancy cars and his trucks indefinitely. She goes through all his papers, unearthing, in the process, more secrets, more betrayals. Bank accounts, shady deals, illegal merchandise, payments to politicians, judges, policemen, and customs officers. Ibrahim had his fingers in more pies than can be accounted for, in the end. He was after everything: luxury goods, precious stones, minerals, contraband. And women, of course. Scores and scores of them. "I knew him, but I didn't know him," Marie confides. "Our world, what I understood to be our life? Nothing but a lie. I can only blame myself. Always been that way: Once I trust, I trust. I busied myself with the children and my own work. I never infringed upon his domain. There were plenty shadows, of course. I took those with the good. Rarely, very rarely, he would take something too far and I would snap. It was only a matter of time, I guess...."

"Those secret bank accounts," I tell her: "Leave some open. The biggest ones. Monitor them. Ibrahim is nothing without his money. Sooner or later he'll come back for it, he'll try and tap into his reserves."

So Marie plays detective. She play forensic accountant. She plays C.E.O. And because she's Marie, she puts lots of energy and a ferocious intelligence into it. Fragile? Exotic? Doll-like? Lost in a man's world? My mistake. A very misguided first impression. Marie is tough. She's smart. She's quick. She's steady on her feet. She's at the tidy IEX warehouse every morning handling the levers of power, controlling operations, shoring up finances, evaluating inventory, talking to suppliers, checking on the boats, docking the merchandise, storing it, putting it on semis, getting it out to her retailers. She wants to see everything and know everything. She wants to clean house before she sells the business and breaks away clean.

And she's not afraid to ask for assistance: She gets Ketus to help free Mansour and Ifra in exchange for the *dunguru*'s total collaboration and a little cash. Mansour, who's been a right-hand man to important figures most of his life, and who, perhaps, exists only through and for his role at another person's side, reenlists only too happily, prayer beads in hand, full cooperation the new word of the day. Rebeus will put the fear of jail into anybody, young or old.

So Marie works hard. She calls me. We talk every day. About any and everything. We meet. Something's definitely taking shape there. Something new. Something fresh. Something exciting. Something inevitable. More than a tug: a pull, a force, a magnetic field.

Karine feels it, that tug, that force. She, too, knows it is real, undeniable, unstoppable. Oddly enough, she doesn't fuss, she doesn't fight, she doesn't make a big deal of it. "You can only hold on to something that you already have," she tells me. "If it disappears, if it ups and flies away, if it vanishes from your sight even as you try to keep it forever, that means it was never yours. That means you were living a dream, an illusion, a mirage."

An illusion we're not. I love Karine. She loves me. When I'm not talking to Marie, when I'm not out on the town or hanging around Hann with her, I'm with Karine. The couch, the wall have disappeared from our lives. She doesn't deny me her body any more. Perhaps because of my injury, my near-death experience. Karine is mine. She's here for me. She's not going anywhere. She wants my happiness.

"Chris?"

"Yes?"

"I'll leave it in your hands. So be it, if Marie must win. Follow your heart. But before anything happens, sit me down and talk to me. Let me know. Give me my proper respect. That's all I ask of you. You don't owe me eternal love. What you do owe me is honesty. Treat me like I treat you."

So Karine and I have what we have. We created this thing, this beautiful thing out of thin air. We built it, we made it strong, we reveled in it. We're still reveling in it, it is not as strong, it is still here, it exists. Not in limbo. Just a little feeble. Just a little less vibrant. Like a fire in mid-life. Down in intensity but far from dead. Easily doused out of existence or easily revived. Our love, our relationship can go either way. Karine leaves it in my hands. "It's up to you," she says.

A big responsibility it is. Implicit in it is the power Karine entrusts me with. She wants to stay with me. She's found what she was looking for. She's willing to go where things take her. I can make her life a heaven or I can make it hell. A big, terrifying responsibility it is.

My way of dealing with those matters is to not deal with them, to let them sort themselves out. Marie is in no rush. I am in no rush. Karine is content in her wise, fatalistic, philosophical stance.

The children are a welcome point of focus. They've become inseparable. Yasmin wants to be around Isaac whenever she isn't in school. With both Marie and Karine working long hours, I end up doing much of the back and forth--the driving, the outings, the fun trips, the picking up and dropping off, the zoo, the park, the beach, the movies, the go-cart races. The pure joy of being around children. Seeing ourselves in their eyes. Wanting, pledging to protect them. Perhaps it is for them that we're not making waves, we're not fussing, we're not fighting, we're behaving ourselves in the middle of much emotional tumult and shifting dynamics. Out of respect for the children. Our children.

The tussle, the little trouble is over, yes. But there still is no trace of Ibrahim. He's like a ghostly presence in our lives, an unseen guest. "He'll reappear," Diack says when I show up at his office in response to a mailed summons. "It's just a matter of time."

He hasn't asked me in just to shoot the breeze, my little detective. He's returning my two guns and the money found in my garden. He makes a show of counting every bill, after which he makes me sign a discharge.

"Thank you for your integrity," I tell him.

"This is how honest cops behave," Diack comments sardonically, laconically.

209

I extend my hand across the desk. Diack ignores it.

"I don't want our paths to ever cross again," he declares. "I know you're after Mrs. Sow. I'll be watching. If I catch a whiff of anything improper I'll come down on you with all the weight of the law. This time I won't be as lenient."

"For the tenth time, Detective: I'm not as evil as you think."

Diack gives me one of his long, long looks. "You'll never be like us," he says. "You'll never be us. You know why? You have no *jom*."

I know what *jom* translates into. What I do not know is what Diack means by "us." Honest cops? Senegalese men in general?

The 404 is out of commission for good. I go and find me another vintage car: a 1982 Citroën CX. Silver, long, profiled, thin and narrow in the front and wide and fat in the back, with small donut tires and a hydraulic suspension. A beauty. A thing more of the future than of the past, any past.

"I quizzed a few buddies of mine about that car you're looking for," Sagna, the lot owner, tells me after we conclude our deal. "Your big, boxy car from the early '70s. Still can't figure it out."

"No worries," I say. "I have a way around it. I don't need to find that car any more."

I go after Salimata Sene first. Maurice Diouf can wait. I have no memory of a dad, of a man in my everyday. There was never anything there, therefore there isn't anything to miss. If Maurice proves to be the man in the car, I don't want anything to do with him other than make him pay. Salimata is another matter. I miss her. I miss her terribly.

So I'm going after her first.

Matar works his contacts. Le Service des Mines--the department of motor vehicles--yields fifteen driver's licenses and six car registrations. It costs me a bundle but this is it, it's now or never, money is no object, whatever it takes to open doors and grease palms and transform recalcitrant employees and underpaid officials into cooperating agents. Dollars are a beautiful thing.

Fifteen names. I was born in 1971. My age window for Salimata Sene is between 1941 and 1953--I don't believe she could have been older than 30 or younger than 18 when she had me. Eleven names get automatically scratched off my list. I go on the hunt, copies of the women's licenses in sweaty and trembling hand, my legs wobbly, my head swirling. Of the four Salimatas that remain, one runs a rooming house in Fass, one works at the Sonatel phone company, one is a retired teacher, and one owns a catering company downtown. Neither is the right one, neither proves to be my mother. It's obvious as soon as I see them. I know before we even exchange a word. My heart doesn't recognize them. Theirs doesn't jump at my sight.

Maybe Salimata doesn't drive. Maybe she never applied for a license. Maybe she did, but in another city, another province, in which case I will have to go inquire with the Mines of the other ten administrative zones that Senegal is divided into, because the nationwide system, of course, isn't centralized or even integrated. A daunting task, but not an insurmountable one.

I check the public record. Two Salimatas are listed as sole home owners in Dakar. One in Dieppeul, the other in Amitié. They were born respectively in 1980 and 1976.

L'Hotel de Ville provides me with a harvest of marriage licenses. The most promising dates back to May 1975. Salimata Sene, born April 9, 1945, in Dakar, residing at 1587 Sicap Baobab, to Pape Sar, from the Medina. The houses at both addresses have been demolished long ago. In their places stand, respectively, a five-story building and a gym. From a residential neighborhood, Sicap Baobab has morphed into a commercial hub over the decades. Demba Diop Stadium isn't far. It is the only landmark from bygone times. Its banks of lights still stand. Could be the arena of my memories. Could be the structures I imagined to be witches' homes. Could very well be. But my mother didn't drop me off at the Foyer until the summer of '75--the day was hot and muggy, July or August weather. She couldn't have gotten married in May of that same year to a man whose name was different from the one on my birth certificate. Or could she?

Next stop is L'Etat Civil, to make sure that Salimata is still alive. More grease, more dollars. The system is computerized, to my surprise, but it is broken four days out of five, but the power is out, but the database technician is sick. It takes patience. It takes nail biting. It takes nerves of steel. Hard as I try to take my mind off the thought that Salimata may not be any more, it gnaws at me: What if, what if, what if? It'd be the last stop. It'd be the end of things. It'd mean that I must remain a stranger to myself, a mystery forever.

So I wait and wait. Two whole weeks before Matar comes back with news, rather incomplete news: Nineteen Salimata Sene passed away from 1960--the first year the records were compiled, which is, perhaps not coincidentally, Senegal's year of independence from France--to the present. Only five were born in my age window. Those names are only a departure point. I must now find cross-references in order to contact their families, find pictures, glean more clues. Two ways I can do this: turn to Le Soleil, the country's state-owned newspaper, where obituaries have been a fixture since day one; visit the town's seven cemeteries and ask to see their records.

Le Soleil's Web site is in its infancy, the archives section still under construction. I go to the Centre Culturel Français, home to the country's first, biggest, and most modern library, and consult microfilms of the daily. The library is a model of efficiency, of exhaustivity. I have dates; the librarians have slides. If need be, full copies of Le Soleil can be pulled for in-house consultation.

Now it is my forehead that is sweating a river, making it hard for me to see. It is my fingers that prove unsteady, making it hard to take notes. The five deceased Salimatas all have long obituaries with names of surviving relatives, loved ones, and friends. Four of the five have pictures. It is hard to discern all the features on those black and white portraits. Besides, I have to make sure. So I request all five editions of the paper.

They're on my desk in no time. Small, yellow, smelly, dusty, in excellent shape. I peer over the pictures. Two of the four Salimatas are light-skinned. One is a light shade of brown. The last Salimata has the right complexion. She has a high forehead, slanted eyes, braids that run to the back, a gracile neck. Her smile is reserved, almost demure. Could be my Salimata. Could very well be. I make a photocopy of the page before returning the checked items.

Bel Air is where the woman was buried in 1985. The cemetery is not far from the place where we brought Tyson, the scrap metal operation run by the man Diop, the owner of the steak-eating dogs. Maybe this is why Diack hates me so much, I reckon: He can sense everything I have withheld from him; he can guess the extremes I've gone to in my heyday as a ruthless gun for hire. The bodies rotting in unmarked graves; people like Tyson; the "Fatou thing."

I push the gate. The cemetery is sandwiched between a tile company and a fish processing plant. It is crowded, but well tended to. Headstones are right on top of one another. Trees confer peace, shade, and privacy. I amble around aimlessly before bumping into the custodian, a Cape Verdian man with blue overalls, a gardener's tools and a gardener's dirt-encrusted nails. "Help you?"

"I'm here to visit the tomb of Salimata Sene."

The man drops his pruning scissors and lights a cigarette. I look at him with envy.

"Want one?" he proposes.

I shake my head.

"What year?"

"Pardon?"

He exhales a cloud of blue smoke. "What year was she admitted?"

"1985."

"What month?"

I consult the photocopy. "September."

He starts walking. I follow him along a zigzagging gravel path. We're the only people around. Birds chirp happily. Leaves and hanging branches sway in the breeze. It's a lovely early-dry season afternoon. "This place first opened back in 1924," the custodian says. "Only French citizens were laid to rest here. Of course, all that had changed by 1985."

Salimata's headstone is in granite. She was 40 years old when she died. A flower was laid on her tomb not so long ago. A white rose. It is dry, but not decomposed. "Somebody visited recently?"

The man nods. "Her daughter."

"Got a name?"

A shrewd expression crosses the gardener's gray eyes. "Maybe."

Dollars are a beautiful thing.

The custodian has a name, an address, and a phone number. "Not everybody cares about their dead," he muses. "Those who do come often. They update their contact information." He scribbles a couple of lines on a piece of paper and hands it to me. I take a look before I slip it in my pocket.

"What's it to you?" he asks as we step out of the office and into the light, into the peace, into the early-dry season afternoon.

"What do you care?" I ask in turn.

The girl Ouli Sene could be my sister. She is short, on the heavy side. Her skin is a rich, deep, unctuous, beautiful black. Her eyes, like those of the Salimata in Bel Air, are a little sad. Intrigued, unsettled by my request, she has accepted to meet me immediately. In a public place, of course. In the presence of her husband, Ali.

We sit at Patisserie Laeticia's terrace and order iced teas. Students from the Cathedrale and Jeanne d'Arc schools stroll leisurely on their way home, the girls' blue uniforms complimenting the green of the heavily planted Avenue Pompidou.

Ouli's revelations promptly clear the air. "I was born in Dakar in 1969. I grew up with both my parents in the Castor neighborhood. I can assure you that my mom didn't give birth to a boy named Christophe in 1971. But I do wish you good luck in your travails."

I thank both Ouli and Ali for their time and leave them to finish their drinks. The pity, the compassion, the earnestness in their eyes and voices prove too much.

Where else to look?

I reflect on the latest effort. I feel vanquished, beaten, worn out.

"Don't give up," Karine presses me.

"You owe it to yourself," Marie chimes. "And you've come too far."

They're right, of course. It's now or never.

I turn to the Internet. No new thread there, no new path to travel, no uncovered range, no warm scent to pick up. Only old, cold hits. So, in despair, against my own better judgment, convinced in advance that it won't yield anything good, I plug Maurice Diouf's name in the search engine. A full page of results gets displayed. Random stuff. No cross-references to boxy blue cars, laughing snakes, medical professions. It's like starting from scratch. I wearily envision, I already dread the days ahead--the trips to Les Mines and L'Etat Civil and the Centre Culturel, Le Soleil's moldy pages, the utility companies databases, the money to shell out, the mounds of information to sift through, the mountains to move.

The second page of results is shorter. It has, at the very bottom, something different, something catchy, something amusing, something interesting. Something that may not be relevant to my quest in the least, but that may provide a distraction, a welcome divertissement. Something called "*La Ballade de Maurice Diouf*"--"The Ballad of Maurice Diouf."

The link leads to an error page. The cache, where information stays long after the original content has been removed from the Internet, is another dead end.

So "The Ballad of Maurice Diouf" proves elusive from the first second. It's a tease. It's a bait. It's a mystery that I gladly pour my energy into. Because my poor brain needs stimulation of a new genre. Because I get goose bumps without knowing why. Because it is the first thing I get excited about in a while. "The Ballad of Maurice Diouf." Is it a song? Is it a story? An epic? A fairy tale? How old is it? Who wrote it? Who sang it?

I surf the Internet for hours on end. "The Ballad of Maurice Diouf" doesn't yield its secret. There is nothing. Absolutely nothing. Not a word. Not a sliver of information. Bookstores, digital or brick-and-mortar, are baffled. Music sites are mum. Message boards are helpless. Is it a book? An epic? A fairy tale? "The Ballad of Maurice Diouf." "The Ballad of Maurice Diouf."

Like all good things, things destined to happen, it comes to me by chance, when I least expect it, like a gift from up above. An instance of serendipity, a happening, a stroke of luck.

I'm downtown, waiting for Yasmin to come out of her ballet lesson. I'm walking around to get my mind off the search, not even thinking about anything. I'm looking at windows. I'm watching people. I'm counting the minutes. I'm planning the rest of the day. I'm seeing the evening unfold in my head. I'm turning into Blanchot. I'm stepping inside Yasser's boutique just to say hello. Yasser being Yasser, he's behind the counter leafing through some industry publication. He's wearing his stained wife-beater. He's looking just as disheveled. He's singing along some vintage song, some old and half-forgotten number.

"You're starting to worry me," he says when he sees me. "How many Glocks do you go through a year?"

I raise my palms. "Just popped in to say hi, Yasser."

"You sure? I got a new shipment in just for you. Buy three or more, get a discount."

"I'm sure."

Yasser grins at his own joke. He bobs his head and snaps his fingers and catches the song's chorus as it comes back.

That's when I hear myself ask, "Ever heard of something called 'The Ballad of Maurice Diouf'?"

Yasser frowns. He reaches for a knob and turns the music down. "Say what?"

His reaction makes my heart beat faster. "'The Ballad of Maurice Diouf.'"

Yasser's excitement is immediate and contagious. "How do you know about that? That was way before your time!"

I get close to the counter. "You know it?"

Yasser nods vigorously. "Of course."

"What is it?"

"It's a classic, that's what it is. A classic!"

"Yes, Yasser. But *what* is it?"

"I thought you knew?"

217

"If I knew, why would I ask you?"

"It's a song," Yasser says when he's done laughing at my expense. "A very old one."

"How old?"

"Oh, I don't know.... Thirty-some years, maybe?"

"Do you have it?"

Yasser shakes his head. There's real regret in his voice when he speaks next. "Nobody has it. It was a local thing. Extremely local. I can't even remember who sang it first. All Dakar's bands covered it. My favorite version was from Ouza et Ses Ouzettes. A homegrown hit. Strictly homegrown. But, boy, did we dance to it. I can still remember those nights: The Thiossane Nightclub every Saturday; the wide-legged pants; the hats; the big belts; the two-tone leather shoes; the girls in minis, high heels, and long, curly Brigitte Bardot and Barbarella wigs...."

"Nobody would have that record? You're sure?"

"Don't you think I've looked for it long enough? Crazy about music as I am?"

I plant my elbows on the counter. Not completely discouraged. Not yet. Just a bit frustrated. Maybe some old guitar player will know the song. Ouza dropped the Ouzettes eons ago but he is still alive, he's still singing and doing shows. Maybe I can have him unearth an old tape or something. Maybe he still remembers the lyrics. This is progress. This is hope.

I take a deep breath and start toward the door. Yasmin is almost done. I don't want her to wait even a single minute. Who knows what Ibrahim might be up to? "Thank you, Yasser."

I have a foot on the sidewalk when he calls me back in. "So you don't want to hear it?"

"Hear what?"

"The song."

"I thought you just said you didn't have it?"

"I don't have it."

Exasperation gets the best of me. "Then what are you talking about, Yasser?"

218

Yasser smiles shyly. "I can sing it for you. If you want...."

I'm dumbfounded. "You know the words?"

"Of course."

"Why didn't you tell me?"

Yasser is almost indignant: "You didn't ask!"

I close the door behind me. I approach the counter. My heart is beating fast. My fingers are shaking. My feet are just about to fail me. "Let's hear it."

Yasser takes a deep breath. He clears his throat. He puts his palm flat on his hairy chest.

Maurice, Maurice	Maurice, Maurice
Ame sans peur	Fearless soul
Maurice, Maurice	Maurice, Maurice
Homme de l'heure	Man of the hour
Ennemi public	Public enemy
Incompris	Misunderstood
Brillante promesse	Shining promise
Tôt partie	Gone soon
Maurice, Maurice	Maurice, Maurice
Espoir brisé	Broken hope
Maurice, Maurice	Maurice, Maurice
Coeur cassé	Broken heart
Là pour nous	Here for us
Avant quiconque	Before any other
Tes frères de sang	Your blood brothers
Pleurent en silence	Cry in silence

I write it all down. The song, rendered in a soft and nostalgic falsetto, brings tears to Yasser's eyes. It brings tears to mine. It give me chills.

"Maurice Diouf was our very first folk hero," Yasser says. "He was tough. He was strong. The French were all afraid of him. He ran this town."

"He was a man of flesh and blood?"

"Of course."

219

"You knew him?"

"My dad did. We had just emigrated from Beirut and opened up shop. I was too much in awe to go and shake his hand, but I sure wanted to. Maurice was in and out all the time. He was just like you: Always misplaced his guns."

"Are you serious?"

"Dead serious. He used to stand right where you stand. Loved his American-made six-shot Colts. Just could never hold on to them."

"What did he look like?"

Yasser's eyebrows join as he concentrates. "Short. Dark complexion. Broad shoulders. Round head. Close-cropped hair under his fedora. Pencil-thin mustache. Scary eyes. You favor him a little, come to think of it. Don't know why I never noticed before. You're just much bigger."

"Scary eyes? I don't have scary eyes."

"You're just used to them. But they *are* scary. Ask around."

"So Maurice was a gangster?"

"You could say that. But a classy one. Not one of those cheap bastards you see running around nowadays. Maurice had style. He was a rebel: He taught us to shake French rule. He obeyed no law but his own."

I can't bring myself to ask my next, and last, question. "Is Maurice ... is he dead?"

There's a sad note in Yasser's voice. "Yes. They caught him. They put him in jail. He got shot on the day he came out. That's why the song was so powerful. That's why it endured. The tragedy of it, you know?"

I shake Yasser's hand.

"What's it to you?" he asks as I step out.

"You wouldn't believe it if I told you," I answer, rushing to go pick up Yasmin.

If Detective Diack and I were friends I would ask him for Maurice Diouf's police record and call it a day. If elephants had wings they would fly all the way to the moon and back.

The Brigade Criminelle is the modern incarnation of the Antigang, which itself succeeded the Police Départementale as the main law enforcement agency of its day. Different eras. Different generations. Same building. Same registry of files. Diack is out of the question. And Senegal has no Freedom of Information Act. And if it did, tough luck exercising it.

"We have better than Diack or the Freedom of Information Act," Marie boasts, buoying my spirits: "We have Ketus."

The super-lawyer gets on the case. Two days and a fat fee are enough for him to produce the file. Marie, beaming, brings it to me at the Point-E villa late in the afternoon, finding me at a low moment after a long day, a real low point for me. "It's the most beautiful present I've ever received," I tell her, meaning every word. "I owe you one."

"A life for a life," she says. "You saved me twice, so you're still ahead."

Marie sounds sweet. She sounds eager. She sounds game. She is standing in front of me, waiting for me to say something. Marie. A full-fledged woman. Beauty, femininity, maturity, sophistication.

I'm more aware, suddenly. Of everything. The song of the birds in my garden. The rays of sun sneaking through the office window. The soft touch of color on Marie's lips. The empty spot on her ring finger. The place on her neck, right below her jaw, where I've been dreaming to bury my head. The yearning that starts deep inside me, like a shout growing louder and louder, more pressing. The needles that run up and down my spine, like a pain all too delicious.

"Like that power suit," I say, not knowing what to say, not saying what I really want to say, feeling awkward and goofy and corny even as I say it.

"Thank you," Marie answers, smoothing her skirt with her palm. Modesty, poise, confidence, glow.

She awaits. We're inches from each other. With her heels, she's almost taller than me. She wears glasses at work. She wears glasses and she looks damn good in them. How lovely a figure Marie cuts! It's stronger than ever, the pull. It's almost impossible to resist.

She awaits. Again, the time is ripe for a kiss. Again, I pull back and allow the moment to fly away, unseized, unused, unfulfilled. A man only has his word, and I gave mine to Karine.

Marie kisses my cheek. "Put that file to good use," she says. "I took the liberty of hiring a detective to gather everything that could be found on the subject. Thought I might give you a break. Le Soleil ran a few pieces back in the day. No recording of the ballad, but we're still looking."

"You're the best," I tell her, not believing my luck.

Marie's gaze, her sultry voice are playful as she asks, "Am I?" Her gaze, her voice tell me she knows how conflicted I am. How fickle. How unsophisticated in matters of the heart. How emotionally immature. Her gaze, her voice allow for a reprieve. They ask not that I make up my mind today. They demand not that I reveal myself. They command not that I come out of the dark and declare myself. They shout not that I state my intentions, that I disclose my vision for her, my vision for me, my vision for Karine, my vision for the pull, my vision for the feeling--the feeling that dares not yet say its name. They are content to set the stage for Decision Day, to leave it all up in the air, to leave the resolution for another time. Marie's voice,

Marie's gaze tell me that Marie understands. Marie's voice, Marie's gaze tell me that Marie already knows me very well.

It's irrefutable: I look just like Maurice Diouf. His mug shot is that of a defiant man in his thirties; a man not the least stunned or preoccupied about the chain of events that brought him in front of a police camera and flashbulb. A man eager to make the best out of whatever the future brings. A man proficient in the art of extirpating himself from every jam that life throws his way. More than the mustache, straight nose, and small lips, the eyes draw you in. They're limpid, detached, full of passion and adventure, of irreverence, of cockiness, of nonchalance, of unbridled violence. His rap sheet unfurls like a Godard movie: cars, jewelry, cash, gold ... Maurice was after it all. He hit the Banque Nationale de Paris on Avenue Roume twice. He exchanged fire with the police on four occasions. He killed five men, all known figures of the underworld. He escaped the squadron tightening its grip on his lair on more than one instance. He finally got arrested when one of his acolytes ratted on him and all but delivered him to the *poulets*--the cops--in October 1971. Maurice Diouf was a badass before "badass" was a word. He had been declared enemy public number one by the police but his exploits, and his trial, struck a sympathetic chord across all segments of the population. At the end of his assizes court argumentation, the prosecutor requested a life sentence. Maurice got six years. Reduced for good behavior, his bid expired in June 1975. A bullet ended his life two blocks from Rebeus Penitentiary on the afternoon of his release. He was shot in the back. Curiously, Le Soleil, which up to his arrest had been unfailing in its coverage of Maurice's antics, didn't run an obituary.

My next trip is to Rebeus. Warden Cabral receives me in his office. A good sport, he holds no grudge about the way we parted ways when I was a guest inside his walls. "Nice jump," he says. "Life goes on. What can I do for you?"

"Do you keep logs of visitors?" I ask.

"When we remember to do it," he answers honestly. "Why?"

"I'd like to consult old ones."

"What years?"

"1971 to 1975. Do you have them?"

"Any particular prisoner in mind?"

"Maurice Diouf."

Cabral knows his inmates, dead or alive. He knows his history. He relaxes in his chair. "I'd have to look," he says, caressing his soft chin with short, thick fingers. "It might take a while."

"It means a lot to me," I tell him, reaching for my wallet.

Cabral picks up the phone. "You'll have to read them here," he says after hanging up.

The five logs, pushed on a cart, arrive in under twenty minutes. They weigh over four pounds each. It takes me two hours to pour over them. Luckily they're neat and organized.

"Rebeus was brand-new, back then," Cabral informs me. "Senegal, too. People took care in what they did. Not like today."

"Indeed," I concur.

Maurice Diouf was a high-risk inmate. He only had four visitors the whole time he was in jail. Salimata Sene visited twice, both times with an infant in tow, both times at the very beginning of Maurice's term--September 1971 and December 1971. A man named Pape Sar, also in December 1971. A woman named Xaar Diouf, who alone came regularly--26 visits, almost one every other month, for four-plus years. Another woman, named Maty Dia, who showed up only sporadically.

The names come with extra information: addresses, dates of birth, the type of identification presented. The addresses listed for Salimata Sene and Pape Sar are the ones on the May 1975 marriage license--Sicap Baobab and Medina. I take copious notes, feeling the cut, the stab of betrayal as Maurice must have felt it.

"What's it to you?" Cabral asks when he sees me wiping my eyes with my sleeve.

"Maurice Diouf was my father," I tell him.

The warden's eyes moisten. "Isn't that something?" he says, sticking the handful of hundred-dollar notes he's just gotten from me in his shirt pocket. "Isn't that something...."

Of all the people I've been trying to find, Maty Dia is the only one who's never moved, got married, or changed her name. She lives near Tilene Market, in a populous building that is part of a complex built around a wide courtyard. Her place is dark, full of stuff, covered with heavy rugs, open to the cool November air and the sounds of Avenue Blaise Diagne. She is a big woman with ruined skin, a face that is still pretty, a voice that alcohol, tobacco, and a hard life made raw, deep, self-righteous, sarcastic, and a touch whiny. Cats seem to be her only company. "I have no regrets," she confesses. "I've lived my life to the fullest."

Maty Dia is also the only person I lie to, telling her I'm a journalist doing research. The closer I get to the truth, the more I feel like hiding my motives.

"About time someone wrote a book on Maurice," Maty rails. "Now that was a real man."

"You knew him well, didn't you?"

"*Did* I. He was my lover. Six years, I gave him. We ran together. Did everything. Went everywhere. Until that bitch Salimata stole him from me. As soon as she came in the picture Maurice dropped me, discarded me like an old sock. Didn't matter that Salimata was Pape's girl. Maurice wanted her, and so he took her. A lot of good luck, she brought him. All the luck in the world. And who was there for him, in the end? Who went to see him in Rebeus? Who wrote him letters and brought him packages religiously? Good-old Maty.... You're not taking notes?"

"I have a very good memory. Who's Pape?"

"Pape Sar. He was part of Maurice's crew. Another snake. Good for nothing. Getaway car driver. All but useless." Maty lifts her puffy eyes toward me. Her voice grows louder. "You didn't hear it from me, but word on the street is Pape Sar

225

is the one who snitched on Maurice. All it takes is a jealous man, don't you think? *Maladie d'amour!*" Sidetracked, Maty Dia starts humming Henri Salvador's song, lost inside one of the deep holes in her mind.

"What was your favorite 'Ballad of Maurice Diouf' version?"

Maty's eyes soften. "I see you've done your homework. 'The Ballad of Maurice Diouf....' Nobody's mentioned that to me in years! Rail Band did a good job of it. Lots of rhythm, fancy orchestration--like everything they did. But Ouza ... I like Ouza's version the best. The harmonica did it for me. Soul over drumbeats, anytime. Emotion over energy. Finesse over raw power." Nostalgia makes Maty shake her head. Those years were the best of her life. It's been a long time since they came and went. It's been a long and lonely road. "Want to see what Maurice looked like?"

"Of course."

She raises an arm. It is fleshy, huge. Like the rest of her body, it has been purposefully if amateurishly bleached by the repeated use of a steroid cream. It's gone from the polished ebony still visible around Maty's joints to a crass, repulsive orange. "That commode with the broken foot. Third drawer. Get the album."

Maurice had style. His suits wouldn't cause a stir if he strolled the streets in them today. He wore his shoes shiny, his shirts open at the collar, his fedora low on the eyes. He had a black 404. "That man was something else," Maty says.

She closes the album and leans back. The intricate wicker chair that resembles a throne creaks under her weight. She rubs one swollen foot with the other.

I get close enough to smell the alcohol in her breath. "Pape Sar and Salimata ... are they still around?"

Maty turns suspicious. "What was your name again?"

"Chris," I tell her. "Chris James."

"Dead," she says, looking away. "They're all dead. Maurice, Pape, Salimata.... Those are all people of the past, God bless their souls." Maty crosses herself. "Only poor Maty remains, the guardian of memories, the bearer of the flame."

"Salimata's not dead," I interject, almost shouting. "I know that for a fact."

My words give Maty a jolt. "Then you know more than me," she says.

A heavy silence settles in. I try to spark the conversation anew. "You really loved Maurice, didn't you?"

The beautiful eyes fill with tears. "He should have stayed with me," Maty asserts. "Put that in the book. Tell them Maty said so: Salimata was no good for Maurice."

She puts the album down. She takes a swig of Canadian whisky straight from the bottle. I ask a few more questions. Maty's answers get shorter and shorter. Her tongue gets thick. The whisky gets in the way. Soon, she's asleep.

I pry the bottle from her fingers and put it on the kitchen counter. A cat comes and rubs against my leg. "I'll be back," I tell the snoring matron.

I buy myself a fedora, a white shirt, and a gray suit. I wear them the way Maurice did: open collar, low brim, attitude.

"Like that suit," Marie coos.

"Taking me out?" Karine purrs.

Kaolack is the capital of the Sine Saloum province. About a hundred or so kilometers south of Dakar, on the mouth of the Saloum River, in the middle of Sérère country. Peanuts and bad water is what it is most renowned for. It's a slow, sleepy town. The sun bakes it year in, year out. Outside its center most streets are unpaved. Constructions are, just like everywhere else, a jumble of old and new. Mud walls stand next to brick facades. Sheep and goats roam freely. There's dust everywhere you look, sand everywhere you walk.

Xaar Diouf did move a long time ago. Fortunately for me, not too far. She is renting a room in the compound that she used to own. A small space away from the main house, deep inside the dirt yard, in the corner opposite the laundry lines.

227

I find her sitting on a mat, legs stretched in front of her, her back against the room's rickety wall. She's sorting black eye peas destined, perhaps, for her dinner.

She looks up and notices me as I cross the yard toward her. Her fingers come to rest on the edge of the bowl sitting on her lap. Her eyes, veiled by cataract, strain to get a better view.

I kneel in front of her. She brings her face close, very close. I see every pore of her skin. I see her wrinkled nose. I see her dry lips. I see the milky film covering her irises. I see the flock of gray hair under her headdress. Her hand comes to stroke my cheek. "Maurice...?" she asks haltingly. "Is that you?"

"I'm not Maurice," I tell my grandmother. "I'm Maurice's son. I'm Christophe."

Her shout is one of joy. She opens her arms. She flings herself into me. Xaar Diouf is tiny and frail. Her bones, her frame feel hollow. Her heart pounds-pounds-pounds. Nothing could come between us. Nothing could pull us apart. "*Alhamdoulillah!*" she exclaims--all praises to Allah. "I thought I would never see you again."

"I'm alive," I tell her. "I'm alive and well."

It's hard to describe our embrace. It is strong. It is fierce. It is almost desperate. It is acceptance. It is love. It is triumph. It is gratitude. It is a dream that finally comes to be. It is happiness, pure, singing, soaring. It is a wound that aches no longer. It is a prayer that is answered. It is a wish magnanimously granted. It is reaffirmation of a tie, enduring even as it tapered. It is blood recognizing blood. It is a testimony to the resilience of hope. It is the snapped-off limb reconnecting with the tree. It is discovering the stock from which I sprung forth. It is the reassuring knowledge that the end of my long search is in sight. It is claiming my life back from the Foyer and the *bukis*. It is pulling it back from the abyss into which Salimata's ugly act had thrown it.

Xaar's fingers dance over my face. They touch, they pinch, they rub, they caress. Her tears are warm on my skin. I wipe them gently with my thumb. "How did you find me?" she asks.

228

"I don't know. I just looked. I never gave up. I got lucky."

Elation takes her, sweeps her, carries her. Emotion gets the best of her. Xaar gets up. She claps her hands, she calls everybody. From the main house, from the surrounding rooms, from the kitchen, they come running. Tenants, the owner, the owner's wives, children, maids.... Xaar Diouf parades me before them all. "This is Christophe," she tells them. "This is Maurice's son."

It's a flurry of names and smiles and hands and compliments and well-wishes. Everybody agrees: I look just like my father. Xaar spent her whole life here. They all know her story. The tenants, the owner, the owner's wives, the children, the maids are her family. When she got too old, when her dead husband's military pension lagged far behind the cost of living, when she found out she couldn't keep up with the house any longer, she let it go.

Yaxya, the Moor who bought it for a song and the pledge to allow Xaar to live rent-free in the shack deep inside the yard, throws me quizzical looks. He wonders what my reappearance bodes for his business deal. There's a whiff of something fishy, something not quite right. But I'm not here for him. Not today. Today I'm all about Xaar--Mame Xaar is what tradition requires that I call her from now on, conferring her the title reserved for grandparents, and, by extension, all persons of old age.

She invites me into her room. It is tidy and cool, a little dark. It smells of incense. A bed, a prayer rug, prayer beads, a small armoire, a few *boubous* and *pagnes*, photographs. Mame Xaar, content with her lot in life as she appears to be, lives in destitution.

I take off my shoes. I sit on my grandmother's bed. I drink cold water, not from the faucet, but purchased from a man on a donkey cart. I munch on dried fruits.

We spend the rest of the day on a cloud. Talking, talking, talking. Covering years and years. Doing our best to make up for the lost time, the water under the bridge. From past to present, from yesterday to today, from then to now. So many questions.

The afternoon, the evening are not enough. I check into a hotel. I recount the day's events to Karine, and then Marie. My mind races, my heart overflows. I spend a sleepless night thinking about Maurice and Xaar and Salimata and Pape Sar and everything I still don't know.

I join my grandmother for a breakfast of *pain beurre* and *kinkeliba* tea. She retrieves a small bundle from inside the folds of her grandest garment. She hands it to me with a smile. "For you."

I open it. It's a silver bracelet, one like all Senegalese men, almost without fail, wear on their right hand.

"Does it fit?"

It does.

"I'm glad," Mame Xaar says. "I bought it when you were born. Every year I would purchase a small amount of silver and get a jeweler to melt it and add it to the bracelet, making it bigger, making it grow as you grew. I had to sell a lot of my stuff to make ends meet through the years. But I never parted with your talisman."

It touches me beyond words. The gesture, the patience, the thought. "I'll wear it proudly," I tell Mame Xaar.

We go walk the downtown streets before the sun gets too hot. We sit on a bench facing the Saloum. We gather condiments for a lunch of rice and fish in an old covered market. We talk. We talk. We talk.

"My husband died during the Second World War," Mame Xaar tells me. "He was a *tirailleur*--a sharpshooter. His letters from the front were full of bitter descriptions of the mistreatment his unit endured from the French--the very people fighting alongside him, the people whose homeland he was trying to save. The open racism, the contempt, the neglect.... Maurice idolized his dad. He blamed the French for his death, and everything that followed: the fact that my husband's body was hastily buried in a mass grave; the humiliation of having to travel every month to Dakar to collect the meager pension allotted to us, his survivors. It affected Maurice profoundly. Growing up, he chaffed at the mold that French institutions wanted to cast him in. He rebelled. Against authority, against oppression, against colonial rule. By the time he entered adulthood he was an accomplished criminal who'd moved to Dakar because Kaolack was too small. He lied, he stole, he cheated, he killed. The day Senegal won its independence from France was the happiest of Maurice's life. It was a day he thought he would never come to see. By then he had made a name for himself. There was no turning back. Crime was the only life he knew. He only became more violent, more daring in his feats. People both feared and revered him. I didn't agree with his choices. Not even a tiny bit. Not for one single second. But he was my son. He was my son and I loved him."

"What about my mother?"

"Maurice cared about her. As much as a man constantly on the run can care about somebody and commit to them. He used to tell me about her. There were shadows. You were born not long before Maurice got caught. Salimata brought you to Rebeus to see him. And then she disappeared. Maurice said that she had gone to another man, the same man who had given him up to the police. It weighed on him heavily. Not the fact that Salimata had left, but that she had taken you with her. He had dreams for you. He wanted you to have a good life. 'Find Christophe, *Yaye boye*'--Mommy dearest. 'You be the one raising him. Don't let anything happen to him. Hold him until I get out.' I tried to find Salimata. I tried and tried. But she had moved. I knew not where to look. I didn't even know where to begin. It drove your father crazy. Not knowing if you were okay. Being unable to ascertain if you were safe, or even alive. It ate him up. More than the bars and the walls surrounding him, the uncertainty shrouding your fate constituted his punishment."

Maurice wanted to change. For me. For Senegal. He wanted a normal life. If there ever was a line in his mind between criminality for criminality's sake and criminality as a protest against the invader's chokehold on our country, that line

231

should have all but been erased on April 4, 1960--Independence Day. Maybe Maurice was just ready for something new. Maybe he was tired of running, of living off the land. Maybe Rebeus had made him reflect upon the path he was following, much like it did me.

"Some people must have thought he was going to go after them. They must have feared his wrath. They had no way of knowing that the man who went inside the gates four years earlier wasn't the same man who was now coming out. They waited for him at the end of the street."

Mame Xaar takes me to my father's grave. Maurice was buried in a Muslim cemetery at the edge of town. A barren, windswept place with little shade, little comfort, dry grass, old newspaper pages flying around, plastic bags caught in branches.

An engraved rock marks Maurice's spot. It's hard to know what to say to him as I stand there, Mame Xaar waiting a few feet behind. My only hope is that he has found some sort of peace. My only thought is that so much of what we become, so much of who we are as people is shaped and driven by forces beyond our control. How much of a chance, how much of a start did Maurice ever have? How much did I?

As we tread back toward the town, Mame Xaar asks about my own story. I wrap my arm around her shoulders. I press my head against hers. I tell her nothing about the Foyer and the *bukis*. I tell her Salimata left me with close relatives who took me to America and gave me the best life a child can hope for. I tell her I had a marvelous time coming up. A fantastic time. A superb time. A magnificent time. A grand old time. All lilies, honey, and roses. All the time.

A sunny day. Hot, of course. Hot, stifling, and muggy. Midmorning. Salimata and I driving up the Mamelles hill in the company of a man I didn't know. The car big, blue, boxy, red inside. The man not paying me any mind when we got in. Salimata and he not talking, not exchanging a single word. My first time seeing him, my very first time in the big, blue, boxy car.

Up the narrow and winding road, my eyes on the fascinating lighthouse. Totally white, huge, gleaming, mysterious, all glass and revolving lights, unbelievably clean compared to the squalor, the anything-goes, the turpitude of Dakar. Short, way short of the top, borrowing a dirt track that opened after a sudden turn, a green tunnel digging deep into the brush, a long, skinny worm burrowing its way through the hill. Sticking my head out the window, reveling in the speed and the clash of smells--salt versus dust, sea versus earth. Gone. As abruptly as it had appeared, the tunnel gone.

After a few more minutes, full stop in front of a wooden fence. Standing on the back seat the better to see. Beyond the gate, on an open plane, a windswept compound, stretching all the way to the cliff's edge, overlooking the ocean. The playground on the forefront catching my eye. The sandbox, the slide, the swings, the kids. A whole bunch of them. Shouting, running, laughing, jumping, free.

Salimata, speaking without looking my way, her voice breaking. "Go ... go and join them. We ... I'll come back for you in a little while."

Me, pleading, refusing to move, knowing better, my hand on her shoulder, grabbing her sleeve and pulling, little four-year-old not so easily fooled, little boy not so easily tricked: "Come with me, Mommy. Come with me, Yaye boye.*"*

Salimata turning to look at the man.

The man turning to look at me. His voice deep and loud and scary, urging me on, pushing me away, chasing me out of the blue car, kicking me out of his life. "Go."

The kids' shouts filling the air, calling.

Me, unlocking the door reluctantly.

Salimata, meekly, weakly, apologetically, dejectedly, wretchedly, treacherously, still not looking at me: "Begguena le...."*--I love you.*

Me, mumbling, mad at her and angry at the man, the mean, mean man, wondering who he was, what he was to Salimata and why he had a say in my life, wanting to punch the punk and run, afraid he'd jump out and outrun and beat me--little four-year-old with short legs and an attitude: "Begguena le."

Clutching the small plastic horse Salimata had bought me the day before. Walking toward the fence. My Sunday stuff: a green shirt with a long, pointy collar, and pearly buttons; khaki pants; a big belt; dinosaur socks; shiny black shoes.

The car moving to turn around.

Me, stopping to take one last look.

The man busy maneuvering.

Salimata crying, her face in her hands. Above her head, glued to the windshield, a sticker: a snake, upright, ugly, grotesque, green, laughing, mocking, its tongue out.

The car disappearing in a cloud of dust.

Me, walking through tears, walking with fear, walking with a heaving, burning chest.

"I know that Salimata and Pape are alive," I tell Maty Dia. "So don't waste my time."

I found her slumped on her chair, just as I had left her a couple of days ago. Hadn't it been for the empty whisky bottle at her feet, I could have believed that she never even got up. The album is where I had last seen it. A few photographs have been pulled out. Maty has been doing a whole lot of reminiscing. It doesn't look like it's done her much good.

I squeeze her shoulder. I come close, so she can see in my eyes that I'm not joking, that time is up, that she needs to tell me everything I need to know, that I'm through playing and being nice. "Where are they, Maty?"

"What's it to you?" she, too, wants to know.

"Maurice Diouf was my father," I tell her, not feeling the need to conceal my identity any longer. I am who I am. The world needs to know. The world needs to understand. I am who I am. Christophe Diouf. Maurice Diouf's son. Xaar Diouf's grandson. I am who I am.

I stare deep into Maty's eyes, her beautiful eyes. She stares deep into mine. Yasser must be right: There's something in my gaze that scares other people. What Maty sees makes her look away. It makes her cheeks quiver. It makes her chin tremble. It makes her give out the information faster than she can talk. "They're around. Pape Sar owns a car repair shop in Allées Centenaire, five minutes from here."

My heart starts beating faster. Blood rushes through my veins. Standing there, I almost get lightheaded. "And Salimata?"

"She ... she stays at home most of the time. Pape never wanted her to work."

"When was the last time you saw her?"

"A couple of months ago. We bumped into each other at Tilene. It's not like we're friends."

"Where do they live?"

"Gibraltar."

Maty gives me a street name and a number for both the house and the repair shop.

"I was never here," I tell her. "You don't know who I am. You're going to forget everything about me."

The orange-skinned woman regains her composure. "After what those two did to Maurice, I don't care what you do to them. We're on the same side."

Allées Centenaire is a majestic avenue leading straight to one of the city's finest monuments, an obelisk engraved with the mosaic of Senegal's emblem: the savanna lion. A multi-lane road lined with small houses, boutiques and salons, it lost much of its luster over the years, a decline accelerated by the encroachment of dozens upon dozens of small, Chinese-owned businesses. Rumor around town is that one of the fat cats in the government sold a batch of passports to Chinese nationals looking for a country to emigrate to a few years ago. How the deal was brokered and how much the passports went for and who the fat cat in question is are facts that remain open to speculation. What is certain is that the Chinese are here and that they are here to stay. Centenaire is now a dirty, messy, busy Chinatown. It is an aberration. It is surreal.

I watch the man Pape Sar come and go for two days. His hours, his habits, his routine, his car, his trip to and from home. I park in front of his house for hours on end without seeing Salimata. But there's no room for mistake: Pape Sar is the man who drove Salimata and me to the Foyer on that summer morning. It's him all right. He's much smaller than I remembered. Much smaller. His skin is dark. His shoulders are broad, his head is shaved clean. His voice gives away his personality, his fabric, the stuff he's made of: mean, mean, mean. He talks to his employees any kind of way. He's rude and condescending to his customers. There's a glint, a hint of danger in his eyes. Pape Sar is not an easy man, a fluke of a man.

I catch him as he closes the shop. All the employees have left. Centenaire is busy, too busy for anyone to pay attention. Cars zoom by. Pedestrians haggle with Chinese merchants about their cheap wares. Centenaire is busy.

The Glock goes between Pape Sar's shoulder blades. "Don't turn around," I tell him. "Let's go back inside nice and gentle."

Overall, Pape Sar reacts the right way. He knows just what to do and what not to do. He's been held up before, or he's done much holding up himself. He knows not to make any sudden moves. He knows to keep his hands where I can see them. He knows to speak in a low, confident tone of voice, without turning his head: "You're making a mistake, punk. One, I don't keep cash around. Two, I'm not the type to be messed with."

His voice almost sends me swinging. It almost makes me puke. His voice. That voice.

The man turning to look at me. His voice deep and loud and scary, urging me on, pushing me away, chasing me out of the blue car, kicking me out of his life. "Go."

Hatred is an evil thing. It is quick, it comes from nowhere and burns and ravages. Hatred is all-powerful.

I push the Glock a little deeper into Pape Sar's flesh. "Hurry up."

We go in. I lock the door behind us. I make Pape turn all the lights back on. I motion for him to keep walking. He complies sullenly. He's a docile captive for now. He does everything I say. He doesn't even try to steal a glance at me.

We pass a small office and enter the repair floor. It is squeaky clean, crammed with cars and equipment as it is. I make Pape Sar stop in the most empty spot, a clearing amid the junk, an opening in the organized mess. It seems fitting that the getaway car driver should spend his life around more cars. Pape Sar had one love in life, he found early in life the thing in life he was good at and he stuck with it.

Pape Sar stops and looks around. Nothing to grab. Nothing to get a hold of and hurl at me. He's standing in the middle of his repair floor with not a single way of defending himself. He's standing in the middle of the floor, in full sight, in the middle of the white light, completely at my mercy. I feel like killing him right there. I feel like shooting him in the back, just like he did my father. Do him like a dog, like he did Maurice. Pape Sar. Gateway car driver. Woman thief. Snitch. Judas.

Hatred, man. Hatred runs deep. Hatred never forgets. Hatred never forgives.

"You can turn around," I tell him.

He does. He appraises me. He looks me up and down. He does the math. We're the same height. We're the same build. I have youth on my side but Pape Sar thinks he's got his chances, he likes his odds, he thinks he can take me. I can read his mind as if it were an open book. He'll wait and see which way things are going. He'll wait for the moment when I'm not fully engaged, he'll sit and watch for the window of opportunity to open. Pape Sar's been in tough situations before. Centenaire isn't that safe. Repair shop is a tough, bare-knuckles business. Repair shop owner is a dangerous occupation. And life with Maurice couldn't have been a walk in the park. Life in Maurice's gang must have had its share of near misses for the getaway driver. Bullets flying. The *poulets* giving chase. Plans going awry. The boys fighting for a bigger slice of the pie.

"Recognize me?"

"I don't have any money to give you," Pape Sar declares. "And no, I don't know who you are."

I walk into the circle of white light. "Look again."

He does. Nothing changes in his expression. He keeps his cool. It's not who I am, he tells himself. It's what I've come to do. Behind his eyes, like a crazy software running fast, all kinds of computations.

I retreat into the darkness.

"What is it you want, punk?"

"Don't want your money," I tell him. "That's for damn sure."

"So what are you here for?"

"Maurice Diouf."

Pape Sar shakes his head slowly. Snitches, Judases are never surprised when their day of reckoning comes. Snitches, Judases know they live on borrowed time. It's never a matter of if, with them. Just a matter of when and where and how. Pape Sar knows.

He asks the one question I've now come to expect from everybody's mouth, the first question that crosses everybody's lips: "What's it to you?"

"Everything."

238

Pape Sar pays a little more attention now. Maybe it's who I am after all, not what I've come to do. "Who are you?"

"Maurice Diouf's son."

Pape Sar shakes his head slowly. "Maurice Diouf had no son ... none that I know of."

"Let me refresh your memory," I tell Pape. "A big, blue, boxy car. A hot summer morning. A ride up the Mamelles hill. Maurice's girl, Salimata Sene, in the passenger seat. Maurice's son, Christophe, in the back. You, driving the car. You, stopping at the Foyer's gate. You, making the kid get out and walk through those gates. You, making Salimata give up her son. The son she had with Maurice. Remember me now?"

I'm almost shaking. The Glock, all the way at the end of my arm, can't seem to sit still. Hatred, man. Pure hatred. I'm ready to let it all fly. I can't kill this man, this motherfucker, this snake, this piece of shit fast enough. I want to see him riddled with bullets. I lust for his blood, I hunger for it like I've never hungered for anything in my life. He's my worst enemy. He's my father's worst enemy. He deserves no mercy, no pity. He deserves nothing but the most atrocious of deaths.

Hatred, man.

Under the circle of white light, Pape Sar absorbs my little speech. It gets through his snitch's skull. It sinks deep into his brain. It fires his neurons. It makes him open his eyes wide. It makes him shout in disbelief. It makes him take a step out of the circle of light, a step closer to me, a step dangerously close. A step too close.

"Christophe? You're Christophe?"

"Stay where you are!" I warn him, itching to shoot. "Keep your hands up."

"No," he says, taking another step.

"Don't move!" I warn again.

Pape Sar doesn't listen. He gives me every reason to put him down. He gives me every reason to shoot. He keeps on approaching, he doesn't heed my call, he closes the gap. I aim straight for his forehead.

Pape takes step after step. It's like I'm not talking to him. It's like he doesn't see the gun pointed at his face. "You don't understand!" he shouts.

He's on me. One hands reaches for my chest. The other goes for his back pocket.

I pull the trigger twice.

Pape Sar goes down, dead before he hits the floor.

I kick him while he lies there, arms stretched out, mouth open, blood oozing from the hole in his forehead. I kick him and I spit on his body.

I take a minute to collect myself. Behind the repair bays' metal curtains, Centenaire sounds much the same. It hasn't stopped talking and walking. It hasn't stopped haggling over prices. It still smells bad. It still speaks Chinese. It still showcases the Chinese's own brand of urban decay.

Pape Sar had nothing on him. Not a gun, not a knife, not a brass knuckle. He was reaching for his wallet. I don't bother fishing it out. I don't try to figure out what it is he was trying to show me. I know everything about the snitch Pape Sar I need to know.

The man turning to look at me. His voice deep and loud and scary, urging me on, pushing me away, chasing me out of the blue car, kicking me out of his life. "Go."

The man turning to look at me. His voice deep and loud and scary, urging me on, pushing me away, chasing me out of the blue car, kicking me out of his life. "Go."

The man turning to look at me. His voice deep and loud and scary, urging me on, pushing me away, chasing me out of the blue car, kicking me out of his life. "Go."

The man turning to look at me. His voice deep and loud and scary, urging me on, pushing me away, chasing me out of the blue car, kicking me out of his life. "Go."

The man turning to look at me. His voice deep and loud and scary, urging me on, pushing me away, chasing me out of the blue car, kicking me out of his life. "Go."

I go straight from Centenaire to Gibraltar. Ready to deal
with Salimata as soon as I'm done dispatching her lover to hell.
Ready to confront all ghosts, all demons. Ready to settle matters
once and for all. Not the right mind to go and meet the mother
you barely know. Not the ideal mood to sit and discuss things
civilly. Hatred still running me, blood calling for more blood,
Maurice singing his song, walking with me, riding in the CX
with me, cruising through the twilight with me. The ballad in my
head, that day up the Mamelles hill playing and playing before
my eyes like a horror movie. One down, one to go. Salimata's
time is up. Don't know what I'll do to her. Don't know how it'll
go.

*Salimata, speaking without looking my way, her voice
breaking. "Go ... go and join them. We ... I'll come back for you
in a little while."*

*Me, pleading, refusing to move, knowing better, my
hand on her shoulder, grabbing her sleeve and pulling, little
four-year-old not so easily fooled, little boy not so easily
tricked: "Come with me, Mommy. Come with me,* Yaye boye.*"*

Salimata turning to look at the man.

They were in it together. Why should she deserve a
better treatment? She's even guiltier than Pape Sar ever was. She
betrayed Maurice. She listened to that snake Pape Sar after
Maurice got put away. She went to him. Pape Sar hated me just
as much as he hated my father. Maybe Pape Sar thought he was
better than Maurice. Maybe he thought he'd have the run of the
crew. The girl Salimata, muscle to assist with the heists, his own

241

getaway car driver. Salimata was weak. She was scared. She was young. Pape Sar hated me. He wanted me gone. Everything in me made him think about Maurice. That's why he never came around me. The sight of me made him sick to his stomach. It reminded him of his treachery. And who knows?--I could have grown up and learned the truth, I could have grown up and grown strong and come back and killed him in revenge. Who knows? And so Salimata gave me up. She threw me to the *bukis* and looked the other way. My own mother gave me up. She wasn't woman enough to say no. She wasn't strong enough to protect the little thing that she gave birth to, her bundle of joy, her little baby boy, her Christophe. She wasn't bold enough to stand up to her lover. She gave me up. She threw our life away.

Salimata, speaking without looking my way, her voice breaking. "Go ... go and join them. We ... I'll come back for you in a little while."

Hatred, man.

She washed her hands of me. She drove off with Pape and never once visited, never called, never wondered how I was doing, never bothered to find out if I was safe, if I was being fed, if I was treated fairly, if I was happy. Salimata never looked back. She just never did. It's like I never even existed. It's like she wanted nothing else to do with me. I could have gotten killed. I could have gotten abused in the worst way. Which I did.

And for what? I now wonder, sitting in the parked CX a couple of blocks away from her house, waiting for the night to fall. Pape Sar was no Maurice Diouf. No heists, no money, no glory, no sticking it to the white man, no ballad. Whatever pipe dreams Pape Sar sold Salimata never came to fruition. Thirty-odd years later he's a small business owner, they're living in so-so Gibraltar, not by the Corniche or in Fann Residence or the Almadies, not even in Mermoz or Point-E. Gibraltar. Salimata sold her soul for Gibraltar. I hope to God that it was worth it. I hope to God that she took her kicks where she found them. I hope she had a good run. I hope she had a ball. I hope the sacrifice was worth it.

"Come with me, Mommy. Come with me, Yaye boye.*"*
Salimata turning to look at the man.

The street is busy. Two lanes full of speeding cars. No shops. Clean, empty sidewalks.

I ring the bell. It sure isn't much of a house. Pale walls, high and strong. Trees sticking out. A slate roof. Three bedrooms, if even that. The illusion that she, and Pape, are somewhat protected from all danger, that they've made it, that they are safe.

I ring the bell again. The porch light comes on. Do they have children? I wonder. Did Salimata ever give the man Pape Sar kids of his own? Did she give birth to a brood of little snakes, little snitches? Did she raise them right? Did she protect them from *bukis*? Did she keep them away from the Foyer? Did she tell them *Leuk le Lièvre* stories at night? Did she buy them little plastic horses and Sunday clothes? Did she give them special treats for their birthdays? Did she walk them to school every morning? Was she there when something hurt, when things weren't right, when they had no one to turn to? Did she come for them when shadows circled close? Did she press a cool hand on their forehead when they felt sick? Did she fight their ills with tender words and tickles and juicy, sonorous kisses? Did she fill their rooms with toys and decals and spinning suns and moons and stars and fairy tales?

"*Nidiaye*? Did you forget your keys again?"

Salimata thinks it's her beloved husband, her Pape. She calls him *Nidiaye*--Uncle--the title obedient, traditionally-raised wives use to address their all-powerful husbands. This must be the time Pape comes home from work every day. Her Pape. Her dear husband. The love of her life.

The Glock wants to jump out of my pocket. It is still warm. It is not done. It still wants some. I wrap my hand around it. I tell him to sit still. True, I don't know what I'm walking into. But how much trouble can Salimata be?

She pulls the door open. Salimata pulls the door open. She finally does. She pulls it open and she freezes. "Can I help you?"

"Hi," I say.

She's not what I remembered at all. She's not the young girl in the car driving away in a cloud of dust. Time hasn't been kind on Salimata. Short as I am, she is even shorter. Gone are her huge eyes, her dreamy eyes, her arched eyebrows, her gracile neck, her gazelle limbs, her pretty hands, the hands that used to tirelessly caress my little face. Gone are the breasts that used to keep me in their warmth. Gone is her youth. She is now a *diongama*, a *dieg,* a woman of considerable girth, a woman of a certain standing, a woman of aplomb and grace, a woman with an established place in society. Salimata Sar, spouse of Pape Sar, small business owner, residing in Gibraltar.

It's easy enough to look in her eyes when I ask, "Do you know who I am?" My voice doesn't falter. My legs don't let me down. My hands don't jerk this way and that. The Glock stays put.

Salimata starts to shake her head. She moves to shut the door.

"Look again," I prompt her, offering her my most innocent smile, using my most charming voice. I can be so enticing when I want to. I can be so treacherous, can't I? It's because I learned from the best. It's because I learned early. "Take your time."

Salimata searches my face. Shapes, lines, texture, contours. My eyes, my ears, my hair, my cheeks, my nose, my chin, my lips.... Something clicks. Something falls into place. She lets out a long sigh. She lowers her eyes a little. Mame Xaar pressed her fingers on my skin. She couldn't get close enough. Salimata takes a step away. I've smiled. I've spoken in my sweetest voice. I've held my arms up the better to embrace her. But Salimata takes a step back. She doesn't fling herself into my arms. She just takes a step back.

"I know who you are," she says evenly, as if her worst fears have come to life, as if the worst day of her life is now dawning. "You're Christophe."

The door that was closing on me slowly opens again. "Come in."

I've lived every second of my blight, wretched life thinking about this woman. Imagining how our reunion would be. I've moved mountains to find her. I've shaken the earth. I've looked everywhere under the sky. When the moment finally arrives, when we're face to face it's a weird thing, almost. There's no joy. No excitement. No happiness. Just the knowledge, the intimation that nothing will ever be the same again. We're two strangers.

My eyes dart left and right. Salimata's living room is full of solid, massive things. Leather everywhere. Everything wiped clean, everything in place. Incense to ward off the chill and an evil spirit or two. Something nice wafting from the stove in the nearby kitchen. No photographs of children on the wall. A portrait of Cheikh Ahmadou Bamba, the founder of the *Mouride* brotherhood. It'd be funny if Salimata and Pape have become devout Muslims. It'd be extremely droll. It'd amuse me to no end.

"How are you?"

"I'm good."

She smiles tentatively. She plays hostess, as if I'm some kind of visitor, somebody paying a social call, a vague acquaintance dropping by. "Something to drink?"

I shake my head. We can go on and dance around each other forever, I realize. We can never address the matter at hand. I don't want that. I certainly don't want that.

"Why did you leave me?" I ask my mother pointblank. "Why did you give me away?"

Salimata looks at the carpet. She hunches her shoulders. She clasps her hands together. She's a model of a housewife, I realize. Her *boubou* is richly decorated. Her head scarf sits at just the right angle. She's wearing rings and a gold chain.

Did I expect her to crumble? Did I hope she would drop to her knees and beg for forgiveness? Did I want to see tears? Was I wishing for an apology? Did I bet on remorse, regret?

Salimata is far from sticking to any of the scripts I've written for this day. Taken aback, yes. Needing to collect her thoughts, maybe. But annihilated? Drowning in sorrow? Destroyed? No.

"There was no other choice," Salimata says. "Pape and I had to go. We had no relatives who wanted you, who could take care of you properly."

"The Foyer was the best you could come up with? That was your idea of a safe haven? Do you know what I went through there?"

"It was the best choice," Salimata affirms. "The place was new. It seemed well run."

"Why couldn't I stay with you?"

"We were on the run. We needed to get away. We were on our way overseas. A young child.... It would have made it impossible."

"Why did you have to leave?"

"Pape ... Pape had done something bad."

I say it for her. "Pape had just killed Maurice. He had just killed Maurice and he needed a place to hide."

Shaken by my words as Salimata appears, she doesn't refute them, she doesn't deny a thing.

"Why did Maurice have to die?"

She clasps her hands tighter. She has decorated her palms with henna. Salimata, the perfect wife. Clean as a whistle. Innocent as a lamb. "It had to be done. Maurice had sworn to kill Pape."

"Why?"

She remains silent.

"Because you had gone to Pape while Maurice was in jail. Because you were keeping me away from Maurice. Because Maurice knew that Pape had given him to the cops."

Salimata stiffens. As I'm talking, I, too, am looking at her intently. Her face. The way she holds herself. It's like knowing somebody without really knowing them. Like trying to make a coherent whole, a gestalt out of bits and pieces: an inflection; a tic; a move; a gesture; a roll of the eyes.

More memories are rolling forth, ripping through, breaking fast through the fog. All of them happy. How Salimata used to whisper in my ear. How she bathed me. How she always bought me treats. How she fixed me *lakh* and made me monkey bread juice. Long-lost, beautiful memories.

But Salimata feels not the least maternal toward me tonight. "Don't speak about things you know nothing about," she scolds me.

"Tell me I'm wrong," I say. "I dare you to prove me wrong."

"You don't know what you're talking about," she says again. "Maurice ... Maurice was a very violent man. A bad man. People mythicized him. They lionized him. They sang songs about him. But living with him was living in constant fear. Given the chance, he would have killed Pape Sar without blinking. He would have killed me, too."

"That's not true," I tell Salimata. "Mame Xaar told me Maurice wanted to change. He wanted only to find me and be with me and raise me."

"Maurice told Xaar what she wanted to hear," Salimata claims. "He was far from a changed man."

"Why did you keep me away from him? Why did you stop visiting?"

"Because it wasn't right," Salimata says, looking away for the first time.

"You had Pape," I tell her. "You could have gone on with your life. You could have left me with Mame Xaar. She would have held me until Maurice got out of jail. I would have been fine."

"That's what Maurice wanted," Salimata admits.

"Then why didn't you do it?"

"Because it wouldn't have been right," Salimata repeats.

"How can being with my grandmother not be right?" I ask Salimata.

She shakes her head. "Xaar is not your grandmother," she affirms. "You're no kin to her."

I get up from my seat. "What do you mean?"

"Xaar is not your grandmother," Salimata repeats. "And Maurice is not your father."

My blood start bubbling. It boils. It burns. "You're lying!"

Salimata remains calm. She looks at me with pity. Not love, understanding, compassion, or hurt: pity. The Glock calls from deep inside my pocket. Oh, how it calls. How it calls.

"I was with Pape before I ever became Maurice's girl. Maurice took me from Pape. Snatched me from right under Pape's nose. Swept me off my feet. He was everything a young girl could dream of--at least at first. Handsome, dangerous, edgy, flashy, fun. But after a while, after he beat me once too many, I had had enough. I went back to Pape. Maurice, of course, wouldn't have any of it. He beat me again. He beat Pape badly, nearly killing him. He refused to let me go. Pape and I had no choice but to keep our relationship secret. When he learned I was pregnant, Maurice kept me close. When you were born, he went crazy with joy. He never knew that you weren't his. Nobody did. It would have been the end of me."

The Glock, in my pocket, calling. Saying, Kill her. Saying, End it all. "Lies!"

Salimata opening her palms. "I'm telling the truth."

"Did you tell Pape?"

"Of course."

"How were you so sure I wasn't Maurice's?"

"I know. A woman always knows. You are Pape's son."

Terror, seizing me. Darkness descending fast. Enveloping me. Taking me in. Taking me under. More darkness than I've ever seen. I, who've already seen so much and been through so much. It will never end. It will just never end. I was born under a blood-red cloud. There's no redeeming me. I always lose. I lose even when I win. Christophe. Christophe Robert James-Diouf-Sar.

248

"Why wouldn't Pape come around me, then? Why didn't I get to know him like I got to know you?"

Pain in Salimata's eyes, finally. Compassion, maybe. A little love, even. Cold, Mommy. Cold, *Yaye boye*. How cold I feel all of a sudden.

"Pape had to be careful. Through my pregnancy and the first months after you were born, we both had to pretend. Maurice was always watching. He was wherever you were. Crazy about you. Never left you for one moment. Never allowed you--or me--out of his sight. He's the one who bonded with you. He's the one you got attached to. He's the father you got to know."

Crying, now. Both my mother and I. Crying.

Salimata wipes her eyes. I feel sorry for her. I feel like I'm now beginning to know her, to understand a little. Young girl. Scared girl. A violent, claustrophobic world. Having to watch your every word. Having to keep a tight rein on your emotions.

"I would sneak out. I would try and steal a moment for Pape to see you and be with you. But you wouldn't let him touch you. You would cry and cry and cry. You would throw a fit, small as you were. And so Pape got frustrated. And so he began to have doubts. But I knew you were his."

Doubts in my mind, too. Seeing Pape Sar how I've left him, sprawled on the cement floor of his shop. Wishing there could be hope for me. "Why wasn't Pape around after Maurice got sent to Rebeus? What was keeping him from being with us?"

"There were two other men in the crew. They were after Pape."

"Because he had betrayed Maurice?"

Salimata nods. "He did what he had to do," she says in Pape's defense. She loved him then, she loves him now. The backstabbing snitch and his girlfriend. "Pape wanted out, and so he went and cut a deal with the police. The word got out after Maurice got arrested. Pape went to see Maurice in jail. Maurice himself told him that he wanted him dead. So Pape hit the road and went to hide in Casamance. I stopped going to see Maurice in jail. I cut all ties with his family. I moved to Sicap Baobab, not far from Demba Diop Stadium. I took care of you until we learned that Maurice was about to get released. Pape came back in town. He didn't stay with us, to play it safe. We got married in secret. After ... after he killed Maurice, he had to flee again. This time, he wanted me to come."

"What was that blue car he was driving that morning?"

"A stolen Fiat 132."

"Where did the two of you go after dropping me off?"

"To France. To Marseilles."

"Just like that? No remorse? No looking back?"

Salimata bows her head. The apology, the plea for forgiveness never comes. Maybe she's the fatalistic type. Maybe she just goes through things and doesn't stop and wonder why. Maybe she's not too prone to turn her soul inside out and surrender to worry. Maybe she's all empty in the head. Maybe she listens to the men in her life way too much. Maybe she allows them to have too much sway over her. She had Maurice, Pape Sar, and me in her life. Maurice was dead. Pape Sar didn't want me around. Salimata could have chosen me. She went with him.

So Pape Sar is the love of her life. He's the one. Even now, as we're sitting across from each other, sorting through the big bloody mess that is our life, grabbing left and right and coming up empty-handed and heartbroken, even now she worries about him, she wonders where he is, she looks at the clock on the wall and she frowns, she reaches for her phone.

It rings before she gets a chance to press a single button.

I watch. I look on as she answers it. Now is the time. If I'm going to do it, now would be the time. Before anybody knows I was ever here. Before Salimata gets it in her head to call the police or fight me or get the neighbors or stop me somehow.

It takes but a second. It takes but a second during which I cannot bring myself to lift a finger or get off my seat or pull the gun out of my pocket. I'm tired. I'm at my wits' end. I feel empty of love, of hate, of feeling. Sadness is the only emotion I seem capable of. A profound, overwhelming, exhausting, debilitating sadness.

Salimata drops the phone. Both her hands come to cover her mouth. Her chest lifts up. It rises and rises. It fills with air.

I tense up, awaiting the scream, the primal scream. I tense up, I crouch, I wait. But the scream never comes. Salimata hoists herself up. She stumbles. She falls. She gets up again. She looks at me, the slumbered heap on the couch, the body that is heavy as lead, the monster, the man who has committed the ultimate sin, the ineffable act, the man guilty of parricide.

Salimata doesn't have to ask. Salimata just looks at me and she knows. Just like she knew when Maurice and Pape didn't, just like she was certain when they weren't, just like she knew when nobody was willing to believe her. She's got strong intuition, my mother. When it comes to Pape, at least, she can read between the lines, she can see far into the future. Had she been able to read into mine, she would have known that the Foyer was an evil place, she would have picked up the *bukis'* scent long before they gathered around me and the other children, saliva dripping in anticipation of a bountiful feast. Salimata knows. When it comes to Pape, she knows.

"What have you done? What have you done?"

It is finally here, the primal scream. It is here. It is powerful. It is everywhere. In my bones, in her eyes, in her fingers, in the scarf that falls from her head, on the blank television screen, on the walls. Salimata lets it out. It escapes her throat and fills the room, the house, the street, the whole world. It escapes her throat and hits me in the face.

Her eyes crazy, her breathing labored, her footing uncertain, Salimata approaches. She takes a step, and then two. Just like Pape Sar earlier, before I shot him. Salimata takes a third step. She comes close. I do not go for the Glock. I do not make a move. I am incapable of lifting a single finger. I am paralyzed.

Salimata is not coming after me at all. She does not want to be anywhere I am. She does not want to be close. I am the enemy. I am the worst thing to ever happen to her. Trouble now,

251

trouble then. She runs past me. She runs outside. She runs away. All the way to the middle of the street, where an incoming car blows its horn and hits its brakes and screeches like hell before it plows into her.

Silence, suddenly. Devastating silence. Then shouts of horror and disbelief.

I find my legs. I get up. I get out. I exit the house. I venture out onto the street. I see the car stopped at a weird angle in the middle of the road, its headlights on, its motor running. I see the hapless driver looking down, his face ashen. I see the shoes, the beautiful *boubou* trampled and torn. I see my mother lying on her side, mortally wounded. I see Salimata breathe her last breath.

I make it as far as the front of the Point-E house. I stop the car. I turn off the lights. I call Karine. I call Marie. "She's gone!" I tell them between sobs. "Salimata is gone!"

They both come to the rescue. They get me out of the car and inside the house. They throw me under the shower. They take my clothes and they burn them in the garden. They take my two Glocks away. They put me in bed. They call Dr. Pape Toure, who shows up within the hour and sedates me.

How long do I sleep? How long do I remain dead to the world? How long do I stay walled inside my pain? Salimata and Pape Sar are no more. Had I stayed away, they would both be alive. Had I not reappeared into their lives, nothing would have happened. Salimata and Pape, found and then lost.

It hurts. It cuts like a knife. It sends me flying high before it smashes me against the ground. It fills my head with thoughts of death. I want to do something to myself. I want to waste away. I want to hit a wall head-on and split my head open. I want to bash my face against concrete. I want to get my hands on a gun and blow my brains out. I want to finish myself off.

Karine and Marie won't hear it. They won't have it. One of them is always sitting by my bedside. One of them is always keeping watch. I am never alone. There isn't anything around that I can hurt myself with. They feed me. They bathe me. They talk to me. They are kind even when I'm not. When I cry, when it's too much and I let out my own version of the primal scream, when I curl up and weep and wail like a child, when I hurl my food against the wall, when I take the bed sheets and rip them to pieces, when I try to stab myself with a knife, they are there to comfort me. Karine and Marie.

Even the most acute of pains must come to pass. One cannot hold on to distress, much as one would sometimes like to, much as one can sometimes feel inclined to. It is, like its counterpart, happiness, a fleeting state.

My recovery comes gradually. I turn my interest to different things, regular things, normal things like the time and the weather and the news and the people around me. I venture farther and farther away from the bed. I take a few steps in the garden. I allow Isaac and Yasmin to come visit. I listen to their playful, happy chatter. I play board games with them. I help with their homework.

After the thought dislodges itself from my psyche, after it becomes clear to myself that I'm not ready, willing, or even capable of committing suicide, it's just a matter of picking myself up and facing the day. I slowly take back all the charges conferred to the women in my life. I start cooking my own meals again. I clean up my own mess. I do not stay in bed after the dawn breaks.

Karine and Marie gradually relax their vigil. They trust me around kitchen knives again. They give me back my guns. I won't speak about what took place, and they're tactful and mindful enough not to ask. They offer solace in small, meaningful ways. From each, I get something. From each, something is learned.

Karine or Marie? The question looms larger and larger. Even during those days, those dogged days, those crazy days. It never leaves my mind. Soon, I know, I must make a choice and announce it. Karine or Marie? Marie or Karine?

I finally gather the steam necessary to confront the last ghost on my list. Point-E, Mermoz, Ouakam, Mamelles. I make a left and climb the winding road toward the lighthouse. It glistens, it shines, it reigns supreme over the city's highest spot and its most dangerous stretch of coastline. The hill's landscape is disconcertingly different. Way, way short of the top, where only the bush used to be, houses and all kinds of new constructions. Way, way short of the top, no chlorophyll tunnel, no worm burrowing its way through. Way, way short of the top, the dirt track has been replaced by a paved road.

I park the car at the gate and get out.

They're still there: the "Foyer" sign, the playground, the sandbox, the slide, the swings. All the kids have long gone. The *bukis*, too. The place looks small. It looks rickety. It looks old.

It takes a lot to walk through those gates again. I keep seeing a little boy with so much fear, so much confusion inside. A little boy crying his heart out every night. A little boy refusing to eat and to play. A little boy waiting and waiting for his mommy, his Salimata. A little boy wishing he knew the way home. A little boy in a green shirt and khaki pants, clutching a plastic horse.

It is night. The place is deserted. Only the wind roams it. Only the waves crashing against the cliff disturb its quiet. Only the revolving flash from the lighthouse illuminates it.

Memories. Not all bad, surprisingly. The *bukis* were shrewd enough not to crush our tender spirits all the way. They knew to parse the bad things with enough good things to keep us going. There were outings--to the zoo, to Mamelles Beach, to the Le Paris movie theater. There were picnics. There were toys and plays and soccer games. The *bukis* knew how to do their thing.

I pull a jerrycan from the CX's trunk. I douse all four buildings with gasoline. I make a liquid trail leading far away from the enclosure. I drop a match in it. I watch the trail light up on contact. I watch flames rise from the dirt. I see them race at the speed of light all the way to the first building with a big, hungry woosh! I watch the fire jump from building to building. It is a beautiful, heartwarming, overdue thing.

Violence won't let me be. It won't give me a break. It won't stay away from me. It's Kant--*the* Kant-- who decides he wants Karine back, forcing me to hold a one-on-one with him and set him straight the old-fashioned way: an empty place, just

255

the two of us, bare fists. It's Yaxya, who, I come to find out, purchased the Kaolack house from Mame Awa for less than a song, forcing me to hold another one-on-one at the end of which I give him two options: Pay a fair price for the property or allow ownership to revert to Mame Xaar. Wise man that he is, Yaxya chooses the first option.

Salimata and Pape didn't have children after me. So I have no siblings. So I have no blood relatives still alive. So I'm glad I've found Mame Xaar. I've found her and I want to hold on to her. One thing that Vernon taught me is to take my blessings where I find them. So if the old lady ever hears the truth, it won't be from me. I have neither the strength nor the desire to inform her of what took place between Maurice, Pape Sar, and Salimata Sene. I may have lost Salimata and Pape and Maurice, but I'm far from alone. I have a grandmother. I have Mame Xaar, the one person on earth except from Maurice and Vernon to love me unconditionally, then as now. So much has been lost, yes. But much has been gained. In the end, I have the family that I make for myself.

And it's growing, that family. It's growing fast and big and strong. It's a lively thing. It's a thing that fills me with more bliss, more contentment than I thought I would ever experience. It's a precious time. A very precious time.

I propose to Karine on the beach where we made love on our way to Saint-Louis. It's April. It's cool and windy. It's just us. We don't know the place's name--maybe it doesn't have one. It's not just a physical place, a longitude and a latitude. It exists in our hearts. It has special meaning. Hence the proposal on the sand, a textbook thing replete with a painstakingly put-together picnic, a checkered cloth, a basket full of victuals, a bottle of sparkling wine, two flutes, and gut-churning stage fright. It's hard to hold oneself one one's knee, I find out. Harder than I ever thought. Still, I pull it off, ring in hand.

"Karine Dietleng," I go. "Will you marry me?"

Karine laughs when she sees how precarious my stance is. She flashes her green eyes one time. "Are you sure?" she asks. "Is this what you really really want?"

"Of course," I tell her, offended that she should ask. "No doubt in my mind. None whatsoever."

The green eyes consider me. They hold me in their halo. They entertain the thought of a lifelong commitment to Christophe Robert James-Diouf-Sar.

A gust threatens to topple me. I retain my balance miraculously. The gods must be with me.

The green eyes fill with tears. They consider much. The perfect ending to a story begun when we were children. Not a storybook ending, by all means. But one of our own design. One we can definitely live with. "You were at the beginning," I tell Karine. "I want you to be at the end."

"It's yes," Karine says, giving me her hand. "Of course." She's touched, my Karine. More so than she cares to let on. She's learning, my Karine. Learning to trust. Learning to open up. Learning to give herself completely.

I slip the ring on her finger. Just then, just when it's on and on tight and all the way on, the wind succeeds in its disruptive plan and I fall to my side. Karine joins me on the sand. She lets herself fall on top of me. She kisses me.

Leaving the beach feels like passing a milestone. Nothing will be the same from now on. Nothing will be what it used to be. And that's just fine.

The civil ceremony is at the Hotel de Ville. I'm in a suit. Karine is in show-stopping white. Marie, Isaac, Yasmin, and Mame Xaar are joined by Felix, Giselle, and the Dietlengs. Karine's mother, Yvonne, and her sister, Anne Marie, have made the trip. "Wouldn't miss it for anything," is what they said when I tracked them down and filled them in. They've only been reunited with Karine for a week. So this is very fresh, this is new, this is joy piled atop more joy. That thing I said about the people we were looking for looking for us? It applied not to me but to Karine. Her folks were easy to find, just like I always thought. When Karine tore her birth certificate to pieces, the names and dates on it were already engraved in my memory. I knew where to go. The Dietlengs were in Ivory Coast, the place where Karine is from. In Abidjan's phone book. Solidly anchored in Abidjan's middle class. A family of *métisses*.

Karine's story is in many ways just as heart-wrenching as mine. "When I fell in love with a black man, my father, a white man, went crazy," Yvonne told me. "He wouldn't accept it even after I left his house and got married. He plucked Karine from the hospital a few days after she was born. He gave her up for adoption to a group of nuns who were leaving to settle in Uganda. Four years passed before my husband and I managed to track the nuns down. When we got to Kampala, it was too late. Karine had been transferred to yet another orphanage, at my father's request. The head nun, who alone knew where Karine was, stonewalled us. We threatened. We sued. My father went to jail. He, and the nun, took their secret to the grave. That's where our luck stopped."

Karine's father passed away three years ago. Yvonne and Anne Marie, who is five years younger than Karine, are my wedding present to Karine. Her wedding present to me is a *grand-boubou*. Heavily starched, majestic, embroidered in the front and in the back. A garment fit for a king.

Straight after the wedding ceremony, we fly to Paris, a city neither of us has ever seen. It is everything we expected, and more.

Back from my honeymoon with Karine, I propose to Marie. She and I have no place of special significance. No secret beach where we once made love. No street where we exchanged a kiss. No magical bridge or romantic park or sumptuous venue where we let our hearts sing and allowed our hearts to become one. Marie and I have nothing. Marie and I have never even touched. I know not what her lips taste like. I know not what holding her feels like. Yet here we are.

It's so soon, everybody tells us. Too soon. For tradition, for the town, for decency, for common sense. It hasn't been a full year since Zak died. It's been just a few months since Marie's divorce from a still-at-large Ibrahim was granted. The townspeople frowned on the Porsche. What a weird way to mourn, they said. But a marriage? A polygamous union at that? The townspeople shook their heads in disbelief.

In that, they had plenty company. "Dad wouldn't have understood," Marie's sister, Yacine Ba, intimated.

"Not right," Mame Awa said.

Marie silenced them all. "I love Chris," she told them. "He loves me. Yasmin is crazy about him. He treats her as if she were his own daughter. That's all that matters to me."

So we're getting married. This is Senegal, after all. It is all perfectly legal. It is sanctioned by the law. It is the solution I came up with. It is the choice, the choice that never was. Karine or Marie? No. Karine *and* Marie.

How did I ever pull this one off? I didn't know which woman to choose. I really didn't. And so I chose both.

The idea appeared crazy even to myself at the time I thought it up. But it grew on me. It grew on me big time. Two women. Two wives. Two houses. The modern way. Marie in Hann and Karine in Yoff. Christophe James as the traveling, itinerant husband. Half of the week here, half of the week there. Everything done in respect. All sensibilities managed. All details laid out. All arrangements spelled out. All precautions taken. All health-related concerns analyzed and discussed.

The obstacles were formidable, of course. Intimidating. Because of my vow to never do anything to hurt Karine, I had to talk to her before I broke the plan to Marie. The first time I tried, Karine got up, left the room, and didn't say a word to me for five full days. The second time, she stayed in the room but buried me under such a barrage of obscenities that *I* got up and left, my ears ringing. The third time was better, but only slightly. "You've been in Senegal too long, my friend," Karine railed. "You're just like the rest of these men out here: Letting that five to one women-to-men ratio go to your head."

259

Convincing Marie was no easier task. "Why two wives?" she immediately wanted to know.

"Why not?" I retorted, borrowing Matar's words.

"That's no kind of answer," Marie snapped, getting angry.

Neither wanted to listen seriously. Neither thought I really meant what I was saying. But I held on to my vision. I held on and never let go. I assured Karine that I had not once reneged on my promise. I explained to her the nature of my relationship with Marie. Next, I sat Marie down and I declared my feelings over *ataya* glasses. Then I told both that I couldn't live without either.

We discussed it separately. We discussed it in common. The women talked about it without me being present. I believe they both relented in the end because they truly want my happiness.

"Suppose we say yes," Karine told me at the end of a long session in Yoff's living room. "How do we know you're going to stop at two? What if you get up one day and decide to go for No. 3? I'll give you Marie: The two of you met under extraordinary circumstances. Given your past, it was inevitable that you wound up getting attached to both her and her daughter. And I know she definitely understands our bond. So, in a weird way, you have valid reasons to try and claim us both. But I'll be damned if you have me running a harem, Chris. I'm nobody's head concubine."

"It's about family," I reasoned when it was my turn to speak. "It's about surrounding myself with the people who make me happy. I don't want to lose you. I don't want to lose Marie. I want us to stay together through all our lives. I want us to become a family. It means everything to me. There will be no No. 3."

"Are you sure?"

"I'm sure."

"How sure?"

"100% sure."

"Would you put it on paper?"

"Of course. And there's one more thing: I want to protect both of you and our children. I want nothing bad to ever happen again. That's my pledge to Marie and to you: Nobody will ever hurt you again."

So Marie and I are getting married. We go see Zak together. We kneel in front of his tomb and we ask for his blessing. "You were such a good kid," Marie says, talking to him as if he could hear her. "You were my joy. You held a special place. You still do. You always will."

The Hotel de Ville, for the second time in less than a month. Me in a suit. Marie in show-stopping white. Karine, Isaac, Yasmin, and Mame Xaar joined by Yacine Ba and Marie's girlfriends. Polygamy it is. Polygamy all the way.

My wedding gift to Marie is a collage made of the poems and drawings found inside Zak's laptop. Added to that, a video testimony of his friends, the Corniche gang.

Marie's wedding gift to me is "The Ballad of Maurice Diouf" rendered by the man himself, Ouza, during a private concert at the Hann villa.

For our honeymoon, Marie and I fly not to Paris, but to Washington, D.C. The Gold Coast house is between tenants, which suits us perfectly. We take up residency in my old room. Coming here was Marie's idea. She wants to know everything about me. The place I grew up in, the schools I went to, my favorite hangouts.

She's not shy about asking questions. "Did anything really bad happen to you at the Foyer?"

"Yes."

"Did anything bad happen to Karine?"

"Yes."

Marie is sweet. She is whole. She applies herself. She wants to make everything work. Everything. Always. There's this hunger when we kiss for the first time. This passion. We've been waiting for so long. We've done it right. We were friends, we were allies before anything. We took no shortcut. We skipped no steps.

There's one last question, one nagging question lingering in the back of my head.

"Marie?"

"Yes, *Nidiaye*?"

"Momar ... did you ever?"

"What?"

"That thing you told me about. Gorée Island. Taking revenge on Ibrahim. Did you go through with it?"

Marie looks me in the eye. "No. Of course not. Angry as Ibra had made me, hurt and lost as I was, I knew better. It was bad enough that I ever entertained the idea. Ibra didn't know my worth. That didn't mean I had to go and make the same mistake."

"I know your worth," I assure her, turning playful.

It is hard to believe that Marie is mine. It is hard to believe what I've achieved without scheming or lying or stealing or cheating. The first night Marie and I make love, I dream that I'm at the Foyer's gate again. There I am standing alone, an adult, ready to go in and meet my fate. My heart is heavy. My eyes are full of tears. Out of nowhere, a flock. Karine, yes. And Marie. And Yasmin. And Isaac. And Mame Xaar. Grabbing my hand. Pulling. Running. Taking flight at once. A perfect formation. Tight, fluid, beautiful, synchronized--left, right, left, then full speed ahead. All laughter and wild cheers now, carrying me, making me one with it, riding the wind. Away from the Foyer. Above the open sea. Toward the horizon. Toward a whole new world. My flock. My family. The family I made for myself. My clan. Everybody sharing a cloud. The cloud sailing the blue skies.

Like the word *teranga*, or hospitality, *jom* more than defines the Senegalese character: it embodies it. Like *teranga*, *jom* reaches further than a mere word, attribute or trait, becoming a concept, a system of attitudes and behaviors. *Jom* is what made El Haj Omar Tall, Lat Dior Ngoné Latyr Diop, Samory Toure, Alboury Ndiaye, Cheikh Ahmadou Bamba, Maba Diakhou, and countless others, including common folks, stand up to the French invader when all the odds were against them, when they faced capture, long-term imprisonment, exile, and certain death. *Jom* is what makes the average Senegalese man and woman get up every morning and go out in the world to try and make it in the harshest conditions possible, in the toughest environment imaginable. *Jom* is, above all, pride. It is dignity. It is honor. It is noblesse of thought and noblesse of deed. It is abnegation, courage, resilience, backbone. It is awareness of one's standing in the order of things. It is understanding one's place in the grand scheme of the universe. It is moral fiber. It is choosing the sacred over the temporal.

Karine has *jom*. Marie has *jom*. Detective Diack, who once threw the word to my face, has *jom*. Momar had no *jom*. Ibra has no *jom*. Mansour has no *jom*. I'm learning to have *jom*. Hyenas, by virtue of their inherent perfidy, are incapable of *jom*. The *Leuk le Lièvre* stories of my childhood are all about lessons, exercises in *jom*. Senghor, who spearheaded the Negritude movement and who became Senegal's first president after stewarding it through the independence process, had lots of *jom*. Abdou Diouf, who succeeded him at the helm, had *jom*. I'll say it, I'll put it out there and I'll stand behind it: Today's leaders, Wade and his cronies, all the fat cats, have no *jom*. They know not the suffering and the tribulations of the Senegalese people. They feel not the crushing weight under which much of the population struggles. They fathom not the depth of the malaise gripping Senegalese youths. They offer no accountability for their mismanagement of the country's resources and strategic industries. They profess no vision for a way out of underdevelopment. They, like many people of their kind all over Africa, are experts only in the art of looking busy, of wearing expensive suits, of driving big cars, of building mansions, of funneling public funds out of the country, of devising 1,001 ways to enrich themselves at the country's expense. They are people of grandiose tastes and unlimited thirst for the good life. They are illusionists, men of smoke screens and spectacular devices. They are con artists for whom public office is a mere steppingstone in the pursuit of material fortune, a green light to myriad "business" opportunities. The notion of public service is relevant only to the extent that it allows them to position themselves better in the one race that matters: the rat race. Senegal? They care nothing about Senegal. Let it burn. Let it crash and go up in flames. But only after they get out of it everything they need.

The two formidable women I've married are all about Senegal. I, if I want to show *jom*, must try my best to embrace Senegal. It is not enough to declare one's allegiance to a culture, to feel cocooned and sheltered and nurtured in its soft and warm embrace, to enjoy its traditions, to speak Wolof and wear *boubous* and silver bracelets and eat *tiep bou diene*--rice and fish--and shop at Sandaga and watch the traditional form of wrestling called *lamb*. The embrace must go both ways. The embrace must come with acceptance, the acceptance must spawn dedication, the dedication must transform itself into concrete efforts to improve the common lot, to help the less fortunate, to work for Senegal.

264

It's in this spirit that Marie, Karine, and I launch the Zaccaria Sow Foundation, a nonprofit dedicated to the welfare of street children. Not just the *talibes*--the forlorn, ubiquitous Koranic school disciples who spend much of their formative years in the city streets begging for their pittance--but all needy children. It's many things at once, different things to each and every one of us. It's a way for Marie to honor Zak's spirit, bring her scattershot charity work under one vast umbrella, and put the Corniche house to good use. It's a way to turn the proceeds from the sale of IEX to a competing group--Ibrahim Sow's money--into good work, civic-minded work. It's a way for Karine to apply her talents and her focus to a broader base, with a bigger impact--more Isaacs to bring in from the cold, more young mothers to bring into the fold. It's a way for me to build a better Foyer, a safer Foyer, a Foyer without *bukis*.

We all roll our sleeves up and put in work, conscious all the while that far-reaching and well-meaning and sweeping though our effort is, it only represents a beginning, a drop of water in the sea. For it's not enough to protest, to denounce the conditions one is living in, to criticize those in power. The end game is really about changing those conditions, about attacking them head-on. In due time, the fight must be taken to the fat cats. The solution, ultimately, is political.

Life is also continuity, even in the midst of change. Detective work no longer holds any appeal. Diack's pursuit of the country's main security agencies creates a vacuum into which I'm all too happy to wrangle myself. My outfit, called Bouclier--shield, in French--isn't a militia. I don't provide firepower for rich businessmen. I do not offer all-inclusive services for fat cats engaged in proxy wars. The twenty or so men under my supervision are all professionals. Mazakis, whom I've reached out to as my right-arm man, helps me steer them right. My old partner is settling into Senegalese life with ease. No more lieutenant to break his balls. No more bicycle patrols. A man needs good allies, and I trust Mazakis to have my back.

I offered Yasser a 25% stake in the business and he jumped on it. I get great discounts on weapons and gear. He gets to move his inventory and diversify his investments.

Bouclier is all about protection. It's an extension, a direct product of what we've all been through. It's a state of mind. The newspapers tell us so tirelessly: Ours is becoming a more fragmented, a more violent and divisive world. I've seen it for myself: In Ibrahim Sow's relentlessness; in Momar's wishful, eager amateurism; in the narcotraffickers' recent discovery of the South Atlantic route, with Senegal as a major transit destination for cocaine; in the *coups d'état* that intermittently shake the region, making you wonder who's next, and if Senegal will escape that fate forever; in the country's climbing assault, robbery, and murder rates; in my own blood-tainted rampage; in my propensity to look at the world behind the shutters of my battered soul.

Violence is the theme of the times. Ibrahim Sow is somewhere out there ruminating his defeat and preparing for revenge. Of that I'm sure. When he comes, I'll be ready. I promised Marie and Karine that I'll defend and protect them against anything. A man only has his word.

I'm not crying over Pape Sar. He meant nothing to me. I meant nothing to him.

Salimata is another matter. For a moment there, while we were talking, I sensed possibilities, I got a good feel for what could have been. Those possibilities, of course, were crushed, they were negated before they even came to see light. By the time I came face to face with Salimata, Pape Sar was dead. I had pushed the object of my quest completely out of reach. I had set the stage for my own downfall. Had I gone to her first, the outcome would have been different.

Pape Sar and Salimata. Salimata and Pape Sar. They're buried together. Even death couldn't pull them apart. Their love survived Maurice Diouf. It survived me. It survived Pape's criminal activities and dirty deeds. Some things are just that strong.

To my own astonishment, I am able to live with myself. For someone who's been instrumental in so much desolation, I carry my burdens well. I'm sure that, toward the end of my life, my actions will catch up with me, the burdens will become heavier and stick closer to my mind. They say old age is when all the mistakes of one's youth come back to haunt and torture and torment. My only hope is to do enough good in between to redeem myself. Even the scale. Achieve some sort of balance.

Cover design: Erica Meade.
Photography: Camille Mosley-Pasley.

www.ingramcontent.com/pod-product-compliance
Lightning Source LLC
Chambersburg PA
CBHW031612240626
47153CB00002B/731